The Celebrated Letters
of
JOHN B. KEANE

KU-586-967

The

Celebrated Letters

of

JOHN B. KEANE

MERCIER PRESS

MERCIER PRESS
PO Box 5, 5 French Church Street, Cork, Ireland
and
16 Hume Street, Dublin 2, Ireland

© John B. Keane
Individual *Letters* books © 1967, 1972, 1974, 1975, 1978

The *Letters* of John B. Keane are available in paperback in
individual volumes.

ISBN 1 85635 156 4

10 9 8 7 6 5 4 3 2 1

The characters and events in this book are purely fictional and no reference is intended to any real person, living or dead.

*This book is sold subject to the condition that it shall not, by way of trade or
otherwise, be lent, resold, hired out or otherwise circulated without the publish-
er's prior consent in any form of binding or cover other than that in which it is
published and without a similar condition being imposed on the subsequent
purchaser.*

Printed in Ireland by Colour Books Ltd.

Contents

Preface

Dear Reader,

The letters that follow came about as a result of a conversation between Sean Feehan of the Mercier Press and me.

We had both long believed that the letter is the simplest and most permanent form of communication and even when tampered with or altered the recipient may engage an authority who will have no difficulty in spotting the deception. The countryside abounds in such authorities.

Letter-writing, however, is fraught with risks and men have incriminated themselves by committing their views or allegiances to a missive dependent on human hands for its safe transport. A letter can be steamed open with disastrous consequences as you shall see.

I have always found it difficult to understand why the letter has failed to assume a greater role in fiction. I would hold that creative writers through the ages have missed out on this under-used system of storytelling.

Saint Paul was the master letter-writer. He knew that the contents of his numerous epistles could not be distorted as by word of mouth. Consequently his directives ring as truly to-day as when first written. The enduring spirit of Christianity owes much to the uncompromising prescripts of the man from Tarsus.

For years I had toyed with the idea of novelizing the letter and after a few abortive beginnings I managed to produce a series of novelettes which, taken as a whole, seemed to be as effective and satisfying, if less orthodox, than the novel. I chose stock characters if you will, the priest, the politician, the farmer, the matchmaker and others. The first was entitled *Letters of a Successful T.D.* It became an overnight success and is still going strong after many editions.

I grew up in a time when there was no alternative to the letter as a means of communication except, of course, in the case of emergency when the phone in the local barracks of the Civic Guards became the extreme resort. You may say why not a telegram! A telegram is a letter, a stunted one, shorn of embellishment, a sort of Beckett of the epistolary scene and often even more confusing, open to many interpretations, its length dictated by the circumstances or by the generosity of the sender. Always less satisfactory than a letter the telegram left too much to the imagination, often with harmful results. The letter might be slower but it was safer. The letter writer could expand to his heart's content especially if he was romantically disposed towards the object of his calligraphy.

Alas and alack there are too many letters which are dictated by hate and envy rather than by the spirit of love. Who amongst us has not been in receipt of an anonymous letter or even barrages of these loathsome and poisonous dispatches! The anonymous letter is the only blighted insertion in the great patchwork quilt of communication. Its origins are malice, ignorance and mental instability but fortunately the writers of such letters are in a minority and are deserving of our pity rather than our contempt.

I will now conclude in the hope that this finds you as it leaves me, in good health and amicable disposition.

Sincerely yours,
JOHN B. KEANE

JOHN B. KEANE

Letters of a Successful T.D.

CHAPTER ONE

Tull MacAdoo, T.D., writes to his son, Mick:

Saturday.

Dear Mick,

There's no doubt that this world is full of gangsters and crooks as you'll find out all too soon. Their numbers grow and grow and it isn't easy to make an honest shilling. The thing to do is to forage between honesty and crookedness and do the best you can.

I pulled a nice one last week. I got word, from a friend working in the County Council, that work on the new road to Kilnavarna was to commence on July 1st. You probably know who the friend is. He wouldn't have his present job but for me. You'd never guess what I did! I got into my car and out with me to Kilnavarna on Monday morning. I went around to the one hundred and twenty five houses, and asked them if they would like to see the new road opened on July 1st. They were very pleased, but most of them (particularly that bloody cynic, Flannery, the school principal) doubted it.

'You're a great one for the promises, Tull!' Flannery said.

I felt like hitting him a lick in the gob. He's the rat who said I was under the bed during the Troubles. Anyway, the new road opened as promised on July 1st and they think I'm a small god now in Kilnavarna. There's eight hundred and fifty seven votes there and I could safely say that I'll get five hundred in the October elections. It was a nice move – I never did well in Kilnavarna, as you know.

You'll never guess who got the job of rate collector. By eleven votes to ten, at last week's meeting of the County Council, your uncle Tom scraped home. Your mother is delighted, Tom being the only brother she has, but of course a scallywag without wife or child.

He's doing well for himself when you consider he left the national school from the fourth class. 'Twas from studying the television programmes in the papers that he learned how to read. He has no Irish, of course, but he learned two or three great sentences from that young Irish teacher out of the Gaeltacht, and the best of it is that nobody can understand him. You must hear him rattling them off some time. You'll be flabbergasted. You'll split when you listen to him. He has the life frightened out of the Irishians here. Not one of them can understand him.

It wasn't easy getting those eleven votes. The party was sound enough but the two County Council Independents were a problem. A present of a tried greyhound bitch fixed one but the other is tougher. Cribber is his name. I think you met him once. He's the cranky, red-haired fellow, who's always on about maternity schemes.

'I'm not a doggy man!' he said when I offered him a bitch pup. It so happens that we'll be appointing a Clerk of Works for the two new Technical Schools in the County and Cribber's first cousin wants a job. The first cousin is a proper scut, too, the same as Cribber, but it's worth it to get uncle Tom the job. Q.E.D. as they say in geography.

Oh, by the way, your request for a tenner is a bit Irish. Is it booze, or women, or both? I'm enclosing a fiver. When I was your age, I worked for two and fourpence a day as a ganger in the quarries, and when I couldn't get work I cut timber and sold it by the assrail in Kilnavarna and Ballyfee. Bloody good firing it was, too!

I hope you're studying. This is your third year now and I'm getting fed up with it. If you don't come through,

you'll have to come home. I should be able to fix you up
as a Health Inspector, D.V., although 'twould be nice to
see you a doctor.

Your mother was often better. Tom's appointment
brightened her up a bit. I hope he doesn't do any fiddling
like he did the time we got him a job as paymaster. He
was lucky then. If it wasn't for me, he'd be in jail.

Your sister Kate is engaged to a fellow from Lislaw, a
farmer and cattle-jobber. He's well connected, so it should
mean more votes. I'm trying to fix it so she won't have to
give up her job in the library. The Dail reconvenes in a
fortnight, so I'll be in Dublin for a few weeks. I hate the
hotels. The food sickens me, most of all what goes for
mashed potatoes. There's no flavour off the cabbage or the
turnips. I can't stomach tinned peas or beans. There's a
good pint of stout, of course; I'll say that for it.

I don't like this caper of yours, sending wires for
money. I don't like wires. They frighten me. How do we
know but maybe 'tis dead you are, or worse. So cut it out,
will you, like a good boy, and for the love of God, do a bit
of study or you'll disgrace us all, yourself included.

Your mother is saying a novena that you'll get your
exam. If you pass it, I'll let you have a holiday in Ballybunion for a few weeks. 'Twould be a great suck-in to
that rat, Flannery, if you passed. When somebody told
him last year that Mick MacAdoo had failed his pre-med
for the second time, he got a fit of laughing. 'No trouble
to Mick!' he said. 'Where would he be got?' So get cracking or he'll turn us into a laughing-stock. He has it in for
me for years. Don't ask me why, unless 'tis plain downright jealousy. He's well in with the canon and the curates. He knows who to soft-soap. Did you hear he's
supposed to be writing a book? If there's one word about
me in it, I'll bankrupt him.

I got an I.R.A. pension for Sam Heffernan. God
knows, he deserved it. I'm not saying he was on the run
or anything, but he's voted for me constantly for thirty
years. He got the Disability, too. He said he fell off a bike
during a chase from the Black and Tans. The boys all
know 'twas off the gable-end of the house he fell while he
was thatching it but the poor fellow has arthritis all right

and he walks around with a walking-stick now, like a bank manager. He gave your mother a present of a gold charm-bracelet after I gave him the news. That was decent of him. I could name fellows I placed in cushy jobs and they'd cut my throat to-day. There's no thanks in the world these days. I often laugh to myself when I think of all the turns I did for people; people, mind you, that wouldn't give me a vote now if they were paid for it.

> For the present, God bless!
> Affectionately,
> Dad.
> Is it long since you were at confession?

★　★　★

Mick MacAdoo writes to his father:

Dear Dad,
Got your letter. I'm up to my eyes in study. I'll need ten more pounds by return of post for new text books. I'm really swotting, so I'll have to close now. Tell my ma I'll write to her to-morrow and give my love to Kate. See you all soon.

> Your loving son,
> Mick.

P.S. They don't say Q.E.D. in geography. It's in geometry they say it.

★　★　★

Tull MacAdoo writes to his son, Mick:

> Tuesday.

Dear Mick,
Kathy Diggins is four months gone, maybe five. They say it was some fellow in a blue motor-car from Tralee. What-ever colour the car was, he certainly had a good shot.

Your mother is in bed since Thursday with her nerves and Doctor John says she'll have to spend a month in the nursing home. The change will do her good. Don't ask me about it. I only know what I'm told by the doctor. I invited Dr John in myself. He's not a party man, but he doesn't give a damn about anyone, give him his due.

I got your letter and I'm glad to learn you're studying hard. About your request for ten pounds I'm not so glad. Who are you trying to cod? I sent you £10 for text books two months ago. I enclose £5 and suggest you get them second-hand. Anyway, I don't believe a word of it. And what's this story about a hacksaw? Are you cutting off people's bones already? Mind you don't cut off anything else by mistake!

I met a man here lately who tells me that he knows a lecturer in the college. Could he be got at?

Your sister Kate will be getting married in six weeks to the fellow from Lislaw (Harry Lawless). He's a Protestant but she says she'll get him to turn. She says the nicest wedding present you could give her would be to pass your exam.

The match between Kerry and Cork was a washout. Cork forwards hadn't a clue. Incidentally, I'm off to Dublin to-morrow for the first meeting of the new Dail session. We're sure of a majority for the Reclamation Bill but the Civil List business could be tricky. Never trust an Independent.

He's with you one day and fit to cut your throat the next. There should be a Civil List. I might get honoured myself if certain people died. Flannery, the schoolmaster, for one. He says he has incontrovertible proof that I never fought in the Battle of Glenalee. Incontrovertible, if you don't mind! He's always whispering that he has positive proof that there never was a Battle of Glenalee. Of all the rats in Ireland, this fellow takes the cake. How could he know what we went through? Nothing to do but sit on his behind all day, contaminating the pupils. You heard, of course, what he said when he was asked if he would vote for me in the October elections. 'There's nine candidates,' he said. 'Now, if there was twenty, I'd give Tull MacAdoo my number 20, but a number 9 is asking a bit too much!' I went to Corrigan, the solicitor, to find out if this was actionable but he said no.

I asked you in the last letter how long since you were at confession, but no answer. Don't you know that there is no luck where there isn't sanctifying grace, or do you want to be damned?

Your sister Kate is doing the Nine Fridays that you'll pass the exam. Don't disappoint her. I hope your mother's nerves will be cured for the wedding.

Sam Heffernan drew his first I.R.A. pension this morning. A number of smart Alecs around here say he doesn't deserve it. 'Twas him pulled the Union Jack from the English 'bus that brought the touring Rugby team ten years ago. Not much, I know, but he did his share before that, too, and he was never an informer like more I could mention.

The new road to Kilnavarna is well under way. Flannery tried to get jobs for some of his supporters but I shot that down quick. Every ganger on the job is a pal of mine, so what I say goes.

I hope you're not boozing and that you're glued to your books. 'Twould be a great feather in my cap if you passed the exam. I wouldn't give a hatful of crabs if you never passed another. I've no worries much about my reelection. With hard work, I'll be returned to the Dail, although it won't do my health any good. You're my major worry.

I hope to get the drainage scheme going here before October, as the Minister is anxious to put up another man with me. He's always mentioning the night you put him to bed after a certain wedding. But 'sotto voce' as they say in France.

Next week I'll be proposing that Kate be left keep her Librarian's job after her marriage to Harry Lawless. As Chairman of the Vocational Education Committee I should be able to swing it. Flannery is also a member and he's bound to start off about jobbery and nepotism.

Your mother will be writing to you to-night and enclosing some money. She wants you to buy a sportscoat and flannel pants and suede shoes. I suppose you'd better wear the suede shoes to humour her. Hobnailed boots I was wearing when I was twenty-two. I hadn't a penny to my name till I got the Post Office here. Mind your books, if you have any sense. We went out with the gun against the British to give your generation a chance. Make the most of it and don't leave us down.

The Minister was asking about you the other day in a letter. It should be no bother to fix you up with a dispensary or a hospital when the time comes. You can learn the Irish from your uncle Tom. He is boozing worse than ever since he got the rate-collector's job. Say a prayer he doesn't fiddle. I might not be able to get him out of it this time. Flannery knows too much and so do too many others. I have a lot of crosses, boy, and my stomach was never the same since the hunger-strike.

Mrs Buckley of Glenappa is in the Bon Secours in Cork with suspected cancer of the breast. It may have to come off. Call to see her the first chance you get. She was never a vote but a few calls from you with a pound of grapes or a bag of oranges or something like that and we'd have all the Buckleys voting for us. I never know how to talk to them but you might, since you're a student. These are the little things that get the number ones.

When you're answering this, write a long letter and give us a bit of news. Your mother is always worrying about you.

Affectionately,
Dad.

CHAPTER TWO

Mick MacAdoo writes to his father:

Dear Dad,
Thanks for the fiver. It will have to do, I suppose. I'm night and day at the studies now and I appreciate your offer of the holiday in Ballybunion, but I'd much prefer Bundoran. It's farther away and a lot of Scottish girls

spend their holidays there. Nothing bad intended. Just the
desire to get away from here.

Tell my mother not to worry and I hope she gets
better soon. Send me £3, will you? I need it to half-sole
two pairs of shoes and I owe for my laundry. About
pulling the professor here. Get it out of your head. These
fellows don't give a hoot about T.D.'s or anyone else. I'll
pass in spite of them. Don't forget the £3.

Your loving son,
Mick.

P.S. I was at the Cork v. Kerry game, too, and I agree
with your findings. If they had switched McGrath from
full back to mid-field they might have won. I lost £2 on
the game so if you have any conscience you'll send me
that as well. The name is at stake, if I don't pay up.

M.

★   ★   ★

Tull MacAdoo writes to his son, Mick:

Dublin.
Sunday.

Dear Mick,
As you'll see from the above address I'm back in Dublin
again for the new session which begins to-morrow. I'm
not feeling too hot at the moment. I arrived in by the 9.20
last night and met that messer, McFillen, the parliamentary secretary. I couldn't very well say no when he asked
me to have a drink. Half-past three in the morning when
we wound up. He drank two bottles of brandy and spilled
two more. He abused the night porter and insulted Mrs
MacMell. A good job he's a parliamentary secretary. If he
was an ordinary individual, he wouldn't be let out in
public with drink inside of him and, a funny thing, he's
the man who's always going on about drunken driving.

I'm enclosing the fiver – three pounds for the shoes
and laundry and £2 to cover your bet on the match. Why

the hell didn't you tell me you were going and we could have met. If you wanted money, you'd locate me quick enough.

I haven't eaten a bite so far to-day. Stomach too upset. I had two gins-and-tonics this morning to get rid of a shake in my hand. Only for them I wouldn't be able to write at all. I'll try to eat something later on. My stomach was never the same since the hunger-strike.

Your mother is out and about again. She should be in bed all the time but one of the girls working in the Post Office hightailed it for England with a carpenter from Kiltubber. I daresay he hammered a nail or two. Not even a day's notice! Looks mighty suspicious on the face of it. However, she swiped nothing. Your mother isn't able for the work now but somebody has to keep an eye on things while I'm at the Dail. She was all for bringing Kate home from the Library, but sure that would be lunacy. I advertised for a girl the day before yesterday. With the help of God there will be a few replies to-morrow or after. 'Tis very difficult to get a really honest one.

Your uncle Tom was off the bottle when I was leaving. I made him promise that he wouldn't touch it for three months – but you know Tom! He is probably hitting it hard again while my back is turned. I'll have to buy a new hat to-morrow. Some rotten whelp whipped my hat off the rack in the foyer in MacMell's and made off with it. There was a pair of gloves stolen, too, from the Minister. This place is a hive of robbers. You daren't shut your eyes or turn your back for a minute. The Minister's secretary had a typewriter whipped out of his car last week.

The elections are drawing near. I'll start my campaign in earnest when this session ends. Stay stuck to your books and, who knows, you might wind up a Minister for Health some day. 'Twould drive Flannery out of his mind. He was in the Post Office before I left for Dublin and he asked if you were studying. I didn't like the way he asked it, so I didn't answer him. He has awful bloody neck to come in at all.

'Are you going up for the new session?' he asked me.

I made him no answer to that, either. There's a catch to all his questions. I've that much off by heart about him.

'By Gor, Tull, you're a patient man,' he said. 'Twenty five years in the Dail and never a hum or a haw out of you. The opposition will all drop dead if you ever say anything!'

He was gone before I could come outside the counter.

I got a letter last week asking me if I would address the Yeats' Society in Kilnavarna. I'd swear he was behind it. He's an insulting scut, but he'll go too far one of these days.

The first session to-morrow should be lively, but we have a strong majority. Even the Independents are behind us. We should see the final stage of the Reclamation Bill before the end of the week and then there's the business of the Civil Honours List. You could be on that list some day if you study hard enough. Excuse me – but it has just come over the Tannoy that I'm wanted on the 'phone.

I've just got word from your mother that old Mayney Haggerty is dead. What a time she picked, and the Dail opening to-morrow. That means that I'll have to go down to Tourmadeedy this very evening and motor up again first thing in the morning. I wouldn't mind but I've a sick head that's ticking like a time-bomb.

There's bound to be a wake there to-night and I'll have to put in an appearance. 'Twould cost me fifty number ones if I didn't show up but, by God although I've done a lot of things in my time, I've never missed a funeral. Here's a bit of free advice for you. If you must go to a funeral, make sure you're seen at it. Go well up in front of the hearse and look as solemn as if 'twas your own mother that was being put under. Better still, put in an appearance at the wake and drink porter out of cups the same as the boys. They like that. 'God,' they'll say, 'isn't poor oul' MacAdoo the fine soul, drinking' his cup o' porter there in the corner the same as the rest of us!'

Mass cards are vitally important, too. It's the Mass cards they remember when the corpse is rotten in the grave.

There's a priest here on the Quays and he'll sign four Mass cards for a quid. That's only five bob a twist. Well worth it.

I was thinking for a second of asking you to come up from Cork to the funeral, too, but the journey's too long and it wouldn't be right at the height of your studies. 'Twould look well, of course, if the two of us were seen there together, but it's out of the question. Send a telegram, and don't forget it! I told your mother to ring Kate. Kate is as cute as a pet fox at funerals.

I'd better conclude now if I'm to get started for home. Write to your mother. She's expecting it and, for the love of God, for once in your life try to answer a letter without a demand for money. Your digs are paid and you get your two quid allowance every Monday morning. I don't see what you want more for, unless 'tis booze.

> Look after yourself and God bless.
> Affectionately,
> Dad.

       ★   ★   ★

Mick MacAdoo writes to his father:

Wednesday night.

Dear Dad,
I trust you got back safely from Mayney Haggerty's funeral. I sent the telegram, and I went to see Mrs Buckley of Glenappa. I took her a pound of grapes. The telegram cost five and three and the grapes cost five bob. I had to take a taxi to the hospital because I hadn't time to wait for the bus. The taxi was four and six, and you ask me not to write for money. Where am I to get it from unless 'tis you, or do you want me to swipe it? I badly need six quid as soon as you can send it. I need four for fees and two for meals out while the exam is on. You make me laugh when you ask if I'm boozing. Boozing – on £2 a week!

What's this you say about hunger-strike? I never knew you to be on hunger-strike. I'm writing to my mother to-night. Don't forget the 6 quid.

Your loving son,
Mick.

★ ★ ★

Tull MacAdoo writes to his son, Mick:

Dublin.
Tuesday.

Dear Mick,
Enclosed find a cheque for £6 as requested. I've only just come back from the funeral. I missed the entire first day's business of the Dail on account of it, but so did the opposition man. He waited for the funeral, too; acting under instructions, I would say. I expected a rap from the Minister but when I pointed out my reasons, I was excused. He knows the value of funerals.

Do I detect a certain note of sarcasm in your request to know more about the hunger-strike? You don't know what we went through, boy; sleepless nights, no resting place, our lives constantly in danger.

The hunger-strike took place during the Civil War when every farmer's boy and discontented bastard in the country wanted to be another Michael Collins or Cathal Brugha. Myself and Mick (Razzy) Ferriter were cycling with dispatches from Ballymoney to Kiltubber, when we were captured by the enemy. There were twenty of them and an officer. The officer pointed a Webley at my head when I started to eat the dispatches and told me that if I didn't spit them out he'd let me have it.

I was terrified, said the Act of Contrition – the short Act as I hadn't much time – but I swallowed the dispatches and so did Razzy. One of the enemy, a fellow called Spud Gerraty from Faha, pulled an open razor out of his kitbag and wanted to cut me open but the officer gave him a kick on the shin and told him he'd get a court-martial. I know

many who were castrated by drunken perverts. Maybe
they were lucky. Did you ever see a bullock that wasn't
content and happy.

They took us to their headquarters and tied us up.
They left us in a small room with no light for a whole
day. They then brought us out and questioned us about
the contents of the dispatches. They bullied us and shoved
us around but we held firm. They then took us to a sort
of mess-hall where about a score of men were seated at a
long table. An orderly served them with boiled corned
beef and turnips. The corned beef was lean and the
turnips were steaming hot. Our mouths watered at the
sight of them. I swear I'll never forget them as long as I
live.

We pointed out to the officer that we had nothing to
eat for twenty-four hours and that we had certain rights as
prisoners-of-war. I wouldn't like to tell you the answer
the enemy gave us. Spud Gerraty, the bully who wanted
to cut us open, put his plate under my nose and, when I
tried to take a bite of the meat, he knocked me over with a
push into the chest. 'Twas then that Razzy and I decided
to go on hunger-strike.

After a while the officer asked us if we wished to go to
the toilet.

'For what?' says Razzy. 'We have nothing inside of
us.'

Spud Gerraty gave Razzy a kick in the hip for giving
guff to the officer and when Razzy tried to kick back,
Gerraty fired a pewter pint at him and flattened him out.

They offered us cold spuds that night but we refused.
They brought us hot soup and baker's bread in the morning but we refused to touch it, although our tongues were
hanging out by this time. At dinner time they brought us
mashed potatoes and fried eggs but we turned it down.
That was real will power, boy.

The following night Spud Gerraty arrived with two
cases of pot-still whiskey he fecked somewhere. They fell
at it and after about an hour they were all staving drunk,
puking and piddling all over the place.

The officer was off somewhere with a woman and
there was no one sober enough to take charge. They

started a sing-song – filthy songs like 'The Wooden Bucket' and 'The Ball O' Yarn.'

They fell into a drunken sleep after a while and we crawled, over their bodies, out of the front door. We got on our feet and darted away across the fields. After about two hours, weak and half-blind, we arrived at the house of a widow who was friendly to Razzy. She cut the thongs which bound our hands and put down a pot of spuds and a wedge of bacon for us. We ate it like dogs before it was half-cooked but we regretted it after and got sick, but we had the good of it for a while. My stomach was never the same afterwards. Let me eat bacon now and you'll hear growling and grumbling inside me like a kennel of bull-dogs. The widow has a military pension now and she buried two more husbands since then. They were the lucky turnips to her. Spud Gerraty was blown up a month afterwards at the Scrohane ambush. There's a monument to him in Scrohane. Razzy met him fair and square in the belly with a grenade and his guts were draped like ribbons around the bushes. Civil wars is a curse.

So now you know about the hunger-strike. 'Twas no fun. Razzy died a few years after that in Philadelphia. He was in the rats before he died. He took to the booze and couldn't leave it alone. They say 'twas his conscience that bothered him for the way he killed Spud Gerraty. Anyway, he developed pleurisy and died. Pleurisy is the scourge of all boozers. The tubes won't stand up to it.

Your uncle Tom broke out again at Mayney Haggerty's wake, and had to be lifted into a car and taken home.

Your mother is gone back to bed as a result, but Kate is staying on at Tourmadeedy for a few days. I got her a certificate, so she'll be around for a week at least. We'd be in Queer Street only for the certs.

Our friend, Flannery, was at the funeral, too, and what do you think he said to me inside in the graveyard?

'Don't take it too hard, Tull. We mustn't break down!'

'Go to hell!' I told him.

I'd half a mind to knock him over a grave and hammer the daylights out of him. He'll say the wrong thing one of these days and then I'll make my move. I'm glad you're writing to your mother. She could do with a bit of cheering up.

I have a long week ahead of me. I have several chores in the Department of Lands about drainage grants and there's two Widows' Pensions to be hurried up. Also there's a nasty case of drunken driving. A young fellow from Kilnavarna knocked a woman off her bicycle and crashed his father's car into the pier of a gate. A few fellows drawing stamps were caught working by an Inspector in Tourmadeedy and that will take a bit of squaring. It all depends on the Inspector. Some of the young Inspectors are tricky but they learn the ropes quick enough when they think about promotion. 'Tis easy to bluff them, although I've met a few lately who don't give a hoot about hog, dog or devil. Independent fellows! The sooner they learn that this world can't afford independent thinking, the better. If every fellow thought independently, we'd have a nice rumpus to deal with. You'd never get anything done and no man would be safe in his bed.

I'm sick and tired of asking you about confession. Have you been there or haven't you? Write soon and look after yourself.

Affectionately,
Dad.

★　★　★

Mick MacAdoo writes to his father:

Thursday.

Dear Dad,
Got your letter and the money. The exam. starts to-morrow, so this will be brief. I wrote a long letter to my mother last night. Will you send me £2 by return as I need a new fountainpen. I'll be going to confession on Saturday night.

Your loving son,
Mick.

CHAPTER THREE

Kate MacAdoo writes to her father:

My dear Daddy,
I sincerely hope that you got to Dublin safely. I know
it's not proper to say so, but I never enjoyed a night so
much as I did at Mayney Haggerty's wake. Wake up and
live – poor pun!

May I say that it was your presence which made the
night. Your sense of humour improves, but I fondly believe that if humour wasn't there in the first place, there
could never be room for improvement.

The amenities at Mayney's did not make for first-rate
toilette and the following incident, which you did not
notice, may amuse you. Like yourself, I had several
cups of porter. (Anything for the cause, Dad!) It was
my first time in the house and I asked a woman the way
to the toilet. She issued elaborate instructions and I
wended my way to the spot. It was overhung from
the east by three bastard pines and sheltered from the
west by a declining fence of poxed box. When the brief
business was but barely concluded, I was approached,
one at a time, by several male romantic mourners
who swore fealty to your good self and to the party. I
have the feeling that I was watched the whole time
during my absence from the wakehouse. However, anything for the cause! Does anyone know where enjoyment
lies?

Henry was greatly amused by my account of the
wake. He's really a wonderful man, Daddy, I'll never
forget what you said when I told you he was a Protestant. Do you remember? 'I don't care what church he is,
Kate, as long as he makes you happy!'

I know I can get him to turn before the wedding but
he must think he's doing it of his own volition. You
always said I could charm the hinges off a door.

Sometimes I worry about you, Daddy. You work too
hard and you worry too much and mother is of little help
since she gave in to her 'nerves'. I wish you would let me
give up the Library. I could be of immense help here till

the wedding. I'm not too sure that Henry will take too kindly to my working after our marriage.

The Lawlesses are proud, you know. There was a Lawless in Lislaw Castle during the reign of Elizabeth I. – or did you know that? You hear landed Catholic families boasting of being on the same estate for hundreds of years but if this is true, it means they changed religions as often as they did clothes. At least the Lawlesses stuck to the one faith, whether it was right or wrong. I remember when I was a kid we firmly believed that all Protestants went straight down to Hell when they died. Times are certainly changing. People are becoming more broadminded but the old prejudices are not completely dead, of course. There are country people who still believe that every Protestant is an agent of the devil.

Now, there is something very important which you must do for me. In fact you will have to give it priority. A nephew of Henry's who has just finished secondary school wants a job. He failed his Leaving Certificate but he's a nice boy. He comes from one of the poorer branches of the family but, of course, they are terribly respectable. Is there any chance of getting him a job in the Bovine Tuberculosis Eradication Scheme or the Insemination Scheme or whatever it's called. He has a turn for cattle as his father is a small dairy farmer (twelve milch cows and a horse). I know it's asking a lot and realise how plagued you must be from similar requests but if you succeed it would kill any trace of resentment there might be over Henry's marrying a Catholic. Do your best anyway, and if you don't succeed there won't be any harm done. But please make a special effort in this case.

Come down some week-end if you can at all, and we'll go out somewhere for dinner. Try and get to bed early. I have only one daddy, you know, and I like him far too much to see anything happen to him.

Love,
Kate.

★ ★ ★

Tull MacAdoo writes to his daughter, Kate:

Dublin.

My dearest Kate,
A thousand thanks for your letter. Yes, Mayney Haggerty's wake was enjoyable, but make certain you mention it to nobody outside of Henry. A wake is a serious matter for the person who is dead. Get Henry's nephew to apply for the jobs you mentioned and have no doubt at all but that he will be a salaried man within three months.

You know I'd do anything for you. You never caused me a moment's worry from the day you were born, whereas Mick has my heart broken. He's like his mother's people: you can't depend on them. I always say a prayer before I open one of his letters, never knowing what trouble he might be landed in, with some girl up the pole or even worse.

Would you believe that, in the three years he's been going to the University, he never once asked how I was feeling or never made a comment on my speeches at the County Council meetings. He never writes that it hasn't been a request for money. There's nothing else in his head except women and drink.

I'm still laughing over your story about Mayney Haggerty's toilet. Mayney is another number one gone under the clay.

When the Reclamation Bill is passed, we should see work commencing on the Awnee River. It will mean jobs for two hundred men from Kilnavarna, Tourmadeedy, Glenalee, Glenappa and Kiltubber.

I'll have a major say in the giving of those jobs. In fact I know the chief engineer for the job already. He's one of our crowd and as gay a man as ever you met, fond of a drop of the cratur. He has a red nose from it. He's from Leitrim. The bill should be passed by seventy votes to sixty four. The Independents are abstaining. If work starts on the Awnee before the October elections, I'll be a certainty to head the poll. I would dearly love to see the expression on Flannery's face after the final returns. It could be the cause of his cracking up altogether.

I hear he has a plan for employment for the Awnee Drainage Scheme. Married men with big families to get the first jobs. Then, apparently, he has a list of young fellows of merit for the machines, timekeepers, stewards and so on. He forgets it was I who was responsible for the Awnee Drainage and he forgets it is I who'll be giving the jobs. Anyway, darling, I'll try to get down for that weekend. I have to write to your mother now, so, for the present, God bless you.

Love,
Daddy.

CHAPTER FOUR

Tull MacAdoo writes to his wife:

Dublin.
Monday.

My dear Biddy,
I trust when you get this that you will be greatly improved and up and around. The weather here is windy at the moment and I have a slight cold in the stomach, windy too. It may be the change of food because McFillen, the parliamentary secretary, is confined to the hotel since yesterday with a bad dose of diarrhoea. He blames the grapefruit: says it was rotten. He's always cribbing about something, but he gave me a bit of good news last night. You may have read in the papers about the truce negotiations in Kuraka in North East Africa. It is expected that a three-man team will be sent from Ireland as observers and McFillen has intimated that I might well be one of the three. I think we should go.

The climate is wonderful and we should be there for a month all-told. We would be flying out from Shannon non-stop by jet and the journey will not take more than five hours. Kuraka, as you know, is situated on the

Mediterranean and you will see from the enclosed booklet: '*Kuraka: Its Customs and Peoples*,' what a nice spot it is.

You will see from the photographs that the natives wear little or no clothes, so it must be fairly hot. We might go for a bathe although I was never in the salt water in my life but McFillen tells me that the water there is irresistible. So I hope you'll come. God knows I deserve this trip, but no more than you do. It's a reward for my long years of loyal service.

When McFillen suggested my name to the Minister, what do you think the Minister said? 'By God, if anyone deserves it,' he said, 'it's poor oul' Tull.'

Everything will be scotch free, as they say, and McFillen assures me there's a good fiddle in the expenses if I work my loaf. I'll have to make up my mind by Thursday as the names of the observers will be made public on Friday morning. Also, in Kuraka, the observers can make use of special flights to consult with African leaders in Algeria, Ghana and elsewhere, so it means we would see quite a bit of the world. We can see the gazelles and zebras. McFillen says I won't have to open my mouth, as young Carrol O'Dempsey will be our spokesman. He is probably our most brilliant speaker and is a hot favourite for the Ministry when old Peterson, the Minister for Culture, dies, which should be any day now.

I could have rung you up about all this but I know you're in bed and would have to get out of it to answer the 'phone. Imagine me being selected to go to Africa! Did we ever think it thirty-five years ago when I first stood for the County Council, a raw innocent gorsoon with one suit of clothes and no one behind me, save yourself? Did we ever think I'd be hobnobbing with black chiefs and flying around in aeroplanes? Wait until Flannery hears it! He'll collapse altogether. We'll send him a postcard when we get out there.

Mick's exam started this morning and he sounds pretty confident, if one is to judge from a letter I received yesterday. I have a feeling he may pass this time. If he doesn't I'll have to get a job for him. A third time loser is more than I can afford. If a fellow can't pass one exam after three years he'll never pass it.

I fixed that case of drunken driving. A plea of guilty of careless driving will do and the young fellow should get off with a stiff fine and, maybe, a six month's ban.

I met Judge O'Carvigaun yesterday in the diningroom here at MacMell's. He sends his warmest regards. I remember him when he was a down-and-out barrister without a halfpenny in his pocket and his coatsleeves frayed. His father-in-law is a bosom pal of the Minister for Culture and a black party man.

Judge O'Carvigaun has a fantastic salary now and an Oxford accent to go with it. I had to laugh at him yesterday, touching the corners of his mouth with a serviette and calling for the wine list. He couldn't afford a bottle of cider when I first met him. I often ask myself is it right the way these fellows are appointed judges but then I remind myself that the party knows what it's doing and it is not my business to criticize the actions of my Ministers. There are good reasons for all their actions.

I'll close now, Biddy. Write by return to confirm the holiday in Kuraka.

Your loving husband,
Tull.
XXXXX

★ ★ ★

Kate MacAdoo writes to her husband:

Dear Tull,
You've an awful neck and I inside in my sick bed, asking me to go out to the wilds of Africa where a lion might guzzle me up, or have you no consideration for the state of my nerves, or is it trying to do me in you are?

I wouldn't be seen dead in Koolacky or Malacky or whatever you call it. I was disgusted by the photos of them black devils without a stitch of clothes on them and their tits all over the place. I hear they're out of their mind for white women and that they cut their throats when they're done with them.

I've always been a good Catholic and a good mother and a good wife and you had no right sending me on them immortal books with naked savages all over them. If the party want to do you a favour why can't they make you a parliamentary secretary or a Minister or send you to America where I could call to see my Aunt Bridgey and her family. I never laid eyes on one of them and what harm but they're always inviting me out there. 'Twould be a great opportunity to see my cousins in Pittsburgh, too, the O'Briens, they're very high up in the world out there, but you never think of that or do you want them to make a right fool of you. No one in his sane mind would spend a holiday in Africa where you might wake up with a spear in your back or a black man on top of you. I read in 'Housewives' Circle' that they sell white women to them sheikhs and sultans and chefs and they're locked up in tents until the day they die. What do you take me for, to expect me to go out there? You know the kind I am? I was a virgin when I married you and it wasn't easy with the country full of half-cracked soldiers and raping black-and-tans.

My nerves have me killed altogether. I have a terrible cross to bear and you make it worse, talking about them black maniacs out in Malacki.

Kathleen Stack was visiting us yesterday. She's a great consolation to me and the best friend I have. Her eldest boy is going on eighteen. She'd love if he could get into the cadets. You did it before for another boy, so I told her you'd get him in. You'd better get on to it unless you want the whole lot of my nerves to go. In conclusion, may God guard you.

Love,
Biddy.

★   ★   ★

Tull MacAdoo writes to his wife:

Dublin.

My dear Biddy,
Sorry to hear your nerves are so upset. It's a pity you won't come to Kuraka. It's not what you think out there,

and it was the last thought in my head to upset you. You know bloody well that I would never do anything deliberately to hurt you. I never deliberately hurt anyone as you damn well know and I only got cross with people when they made full sure to upset me as you're trying to do now. No, no, sorry – I didn't mean that. I thought you would be honoured by the offer to go to Africa.

The part we would be in, the seaport of Kulpa-Buhrein on the Mediterranean, is occupied by white people and cultivated Africans. Some of them are priests and surely you don't believe that a black priest is a savage and wasn't that black doctor in Thronane Hospital as fine a gentleman as ever you met. Didn't he remove your appendix for you and made a grand job of it.

I wish there was some pill invented to make black men white or white men black, some pill to end all this fecking suspicion of people or I wish there was a race of green men to put the heart crossways on the blacks and whites and end all this whining.

What you ask for Kathleen Stack's eldest boy is next to impossible. 'Twas different with the other boy. He had a fine education and his father, Jim, R.I.P., was a man of action in the civil war. Jim was a good soldier. He fought by my side with Razzy Ferriter and the boys at the Battle of Glenalee. He was a devoted comrade and a fine Irishman whose equal is not to be found walking the earth to-day. It was no bother to get his son into the cadets. It never is for the sons of veterans. However, I'll do my best for young Stack, but you shouldn't have promised his mother anything without consulting me beforehand. Some people seem to think that getting into the cadets is applepie. If it was the Civic Guards now, I could swing it easily enough. I'm owed a favour from the right quarter and it would be a mere formality. Many's the nervous Superintendent I straightened out and many's the drunken Guard I got out of trouble.

I had another letter from Mick. The exam. finishes to-morrow and he seems quite pleased with his progress. Let us hope and pray to God that he passes. I'm receiving Holy Communion every morning that he'll get through this time.

I heard disturbing news last night. Apparently Flannery is determined to prove that the Battle of Glenalee never took place. It is only my word against his since Razzy Ferriter died. Jim Bennett is dead. Pug Nevin died in Manchester six months ago and Dermot Fiely died in a nursing home in Boston last Christmas. I'm the only survivor.

The world has produced few rats to equal Flannery, but jealousy is the worst disease of all and there's no medicine for it. He must be the lowest and most vile type of insect in the world to-day. He has devoted his whole life to slandering me and criticizing everything I ever did. I'd swear it was he who wrote the song: *'The Bright Young Faces of the Old I.R.A.'* but I have no proof. What has he against me? And why me, of all people? Is it because I didn't pull the State Solicitorship for his son? How could I do that and he an Opposition man? I've nothing against young Flannery but the party comes first. Flannery must think he's God Almighty. He'd never have the school only for the way he kow-tows to the priests.

If duelling was legal, I'd challenge him in the morning and I wouldn't miss. Rats like him are better under the ground.

You never can tell about that trip to America. There's a trade delegation going to New York next summer and although I have no qualifications they might stuff me in. I'll talk to McFillen about it and he'll talk to the Minister, so you may be seeing your Aunt after all and all the rest of your relatives.

I was in the Land Office this morning about the distribution of old Lord Brockley's estate in Kilnavarna. The greed of some people would frighten you. One farmer, with one hundred and forty acres, wants more, but I think my own relations will come well out of it.

Your own is your own any day. I met the Commissioner and we had a booze-up together. He's a Wexford man and has a son who knows Mick in the University.

Your cousin Danny is fixed up nicely too. I saw to that. Fifteen acres of the best of it and bordering his own. I also got ten acres for myself. I have as much right to it as anybody. 'Twas us broke the English yoke.

Lord Brockley is getting well paid by the Land Commission but he insists on holding on to the fishing rights on the Awnee River. I had my eye on those but he knows their value. Twenty pounds a rod for thirty rods is six hundred a year and then there's the netting which runs into £3,000 a year. My idea was to start a company with myself as managing director. We could have bought the rights for nine or ten thousand pounds but his solicitor is a cute buck from Cork. It's too late now and if we went after it, the price would be upped to fifty thousand quid. Another golden opportunity missed, but it can't be helped.

I'm going to go after Jimmy Hassett's farm, the small one on the old Mail Road to Kilnavarna. Keep this under your hat as it can mean thousands in due course. I happen to know that there will be thirty new houses going up there shortly and it would also do as a site for the new School and Garda Barracks. I won't buy it in my own name, of course. Too much talk. I should be able to purchase it for fifteen hundred quid and it should be worth seven or eight thousand for the sites. I have only nine hundred cash in the bank at the moment but it should be no trouble to raise the rest. All I have to do is ask.

I had a letter from my old friend, Timmony Hussey. He wants a job. The only thing I can manage just now is a Hotel Inspector and, sure, Timmony wouldn't know a napkin from a sheet of toilet paper. There are a few weeks' training, so he should manage nicely. He has a big nose so he should be able to smell things.

Some of the Inspectors I know in the racket wouldn't know mutton-broth from dishwater, but it's a cushy job with good expenses. Anyhow, love, I'll try to arrange that trip to America. I hope your nerves are better.

Your loving husband,
Tull.

★   ★   ★

Kate MacAdoo writes to her husband:

Dear Tull,
What do you mean by saying that you want me to go to America in my condition? Do you want to murder me

altogether? God help me, I'm in a terrible state. I told Kathleen Stack about the cadets. If you don't get him in I'll never speak to you again. Nell Fetherington is gone to Limerick to have her womb removed. She hasn't been well since she lost her baby. I've great pity for her, married to that half-idiot, Paddy. Nine babies in eight years, although she used to say herself that her annual visit to the nursing home is the best holiday one could get. The Carneys of Kilnavarna were here last night to know would you get them a grant for the extension they put on to the house. I told them you would, of course. I've a splitting headache and so I must conclude.

As ever,
Biddy.

CHAPTER FIVE

Mick MacAdoo writes to his father:

My dear Dad,
The exam. finishes this evening and I am quietly confident. These have been the most strenuous days of my whole life and I'm really flattened. To make things worse, I haven't the price of a butt, my last pair of socks have holes and I have a splitting headache. I would have sent you a wire for money but I know your hatred of wires. I need £5 urgently. Two pounds of it is for a contribution towards a gift for one of the professors who is to retire shortly. I need the other three to buy a new pair of socks, to buy a summer vest and to buy my ticket home this evening. Would you be a brick and wire the £5. Don't wire it to the digs. Send it to myself c/o The Hideaway Bar, Mangolds Lane, off Jug Street, Cork City. I'll explain the reason for not sending it to my digs when I see you. I hope you're keeping well. I sent a picture postcard to Flannery. It represents a fellow who got stuck in a toilet and I got an art student, a pal of mine, to substitute

Flannery's head for the real one. The finished product is the spitting image of Flannery. You'd get an attack of laughing paralysis if you saw it. Don't forget the £5. or maybe you had better make it six, as I promised the art student a quid as soon as it came to hand. God bless.

Your loving son,
Mick.

★   ★   ★

Tull MacAdoo writes to his son, Mick:

Dublin.

Dear Mick,
Got your letter just as I was going to vote on the Civil List Bill. You'd make a right good candidate for an Honours List. When it comes to reasons for sending you money, you are the finest liar I've every encountered. That's your real vocation.

For quietness sake I am posting you on a cheque for six quid. What business have you got in the Hideway Bar? I know Mangolds Lane by reputation and it is not a spot I'd like to be alone in at night. Between tally-women and Teddy boys a man wouldn't know when he'd be murdered.

That was a great idea sending the card to Flannery, but I've received an open postcard this morning, anonymous as usual. There's no doubt at all about the identity of the sender. It was definitely Flannery and the bother is that it was seen by several others before I got it. What do you think the rat is up to this time? He wants to know: '*Did Bacon write Shakespeare?*' and asked me if I would address the Francis Bacon Society and give my opinions on the controversy.

Who is this Francis Bacon? There are no Bacons in the constituency. There are Beacons all right, but not Bacons. There is Wilberforce Beacon and his sister Amelia in Dry Valley, south of Kilnavarna. They bought Moran's place in 1940. They say he is a retired Methodist minister.

I haven't a clue as to what politics they have. In fact, as far as I know, they never vote and keep very much to themselves. If Flannery wants an argument he should leave religion out of it.

McFillen, the secretary, is a sick man these days. He blames it on bad food but I would say too much booze is nearer the truth. The man has a phenomenal gut for brandy. It's a mystery to me how he can afford it on his salary. Two bottles of brandy a day runs up to six quid. That's over two thousand quid a year and that's his whole salary down the drain. He can carry his liquor, however, and that's the important thing. I was down in his constituency with him last year at the opening of a new Vocational School. He left Dublin at half-past eight and by the time we reached our destination he had twenty-three small brandies thrown back. After the ceremony, the bishop invited us for some refreshments and when he asked Mac to have a drop of brandy or whiskey or something, 'No, thank you, your Lordship,' Mac said, 'I didn't touch a drop with seven years.' The Bishop believed him, because the Bishop said to me later that the country could do with more politicians like McFillen.

It's teeming rain here in Dublin. You'll be glad to hear we carried the Civil List Bill without the opposition we expected, 68 for and 42 against, with thirty abstainers and a few absentees. Cubway, that lunatic Independent from the north, suggested that Paul Singer be the first person to be honoured. He said that any man who could take down the North Kerry farmers deserved the greatest honours the country could bestow. His suggestion didn't provoke the laughter one would expect, which confirms my earlier belief that a number of prominent members were investors. Some of them turn purple when Paul Singer's name is mentioned. I lost a hundred pounds myself, which I invested in Kate's name but, thank God, it was only chicken feed in comparison to many I could name.

Go straight home when you cash this cheque as there are two meadows of hay to be cut and you'll have to keep an eye on the workmen. I won't be down for a few weeks as there is still a lot of business to be concluded and if I asked for a few days off the Minister would have my head.

I look forward keenly to the exam. results. If only you could be lucky enough to pass, I'd be the happiest man in Ireland. Your University education has cost me £920 to date and that does not include the £85 I paid out for your grind before you sat for the matriculation and no exam. passed yet. There's no father but myself would endure it for so long. You have no idea of the value of money. If you had, you would have passed your exam. the first year. However, third time lucky, as they say.

I read in the 'Journal' yesterday where Flannery was re-elected Chairman of the Kilnavarna Development Association. That rat couldn't develop a negative!

There was quite a celebration here in MacMell's last night. Even Mrs MacMell got giddy from booze and wound up sitting in MacFillen's lap. The Minister's wife had a baby boy – the first – and he threw a party. He insisted that I sing a song and I sang: *'The Black Hills of Dakota'*. It's my favourite next to *'The Red River Valley'*. Everybody joined in the chorus.

McFillen took off his shoes and danced a hornpipe at two o'clock in the morning but, as usual, he insulted somebody and there was a bit of a scrap in one of the lavatories. We got him to bed in the end, and, as far as I know, he's presently boozing somewhere down town with members of the Carrigmult Builders' Association who have just returned from Copenhagen. He has something up his sleeve. I should know what it's all about when he shows up.

> Don't forget to go straight home.
> Meanwhile, God bless.
> Affectionately,
> Dad.

CHAPTER SIX

Tull MacAdoo writes to his daughter, Kate:

Dublin.

My dear Kate,
My heart is broken by your mother. I was offered a chance to go to Kuraka, a paradise on the African side of the Mediterranean, but she turned it down because of her *'nerves'*. There isn't a man in the Dail wouldn't give his right hand for the chance I'm getting. If I told the Minister that was because of my wife's 'nerves' I couldn't go I'm sure he would tell me to have my head examined. What a spouse for a politician to have.

She wanted to go to America instead but when I told her that I might be able to arrange it, her 'nerves' seemed to get worse. I can't afford to have 'nerves'. 'Tisn't but I could do with a break but what's the point when she constantly refuses to break with me.

My chief reason for writing this is to tell you that Mick is on his way home. He will probably arrive before you receive this letter. Take very careful note of the following instructions.

Under no circumstances is he to be left behind the counter of the Post Office or shop alone.

Make sure there's always somebody with him or you'll find the cash register acting queerly.

God knows I don't begrudge him a few pounds but he overdoes it and too much spending money is not good for a lad of his age and besides I'm told he has a terrible tooth for porter. The local girls are always throwing themselves at him and he has the antics of a Sultan.

They know he is a good mark should anything go wrong. See to it that he supervises the cutting and saving of the hay in the two meadows. I'm not a slave driver but when my back is turned the men won't work. You know that as well as I do. Oh, they'll drag through the day all right but there's no proper return for the hours they put into it, hours that will have to be paid for whether the work is done or not.

We will never again see a worker like Topper. I will never forget him as long as I live.

You probably don't remember Jeremy Topper. He died of T.B. when you were about three or four. It still plays on my conscience that I might have driven him too hard. In those days we used to get youngsters out of Kilnavarna Industrial School to work as farm labourers. They were usually aged about fifteen or sixteen. You didn't have to pay them much and I know for a fact that most people paid them nothing.

I had several lads but they were better for eating than they were for working. It was a mistake, too, to get fellows who hadn't made their Confirmation because you would have to leave them off every day for catechism.

Jeremy Topper was different. He had made his Confirmation. He was a great worker and a light feeder. He was as thin as a whippet but I never heard him complain and he worked out-of-doors, hail, rain or shine.

I often worry that I might have misused him, but no, that isn't true, because he worshipped me as a son would. He had no father or mother but that was during the Economic War when nobody could afford a regular workman and the dead calves were blocking the eyes of the bridges.

The only labour we could afford were young lads or girls out of orphanages or Industrial Schools. Jeremy died when he was twenty but I think he killed himself. I never touched him, although I know of boys and girls who were whipped and punched like slaves and there were young girls who were badly abused by certain farmers who are pillars of the Church to-day.

May God forgive them and the priests who knew what was going on. I put up a headstone over Jeremy when he died. There was no cure for T.B. in those days and I've lost count of all the handsome boys and girls who died as a result of it, my own brother Dan for one, and my poor mother, God rest her, cut off in her prime.

But to pass from poor oul' Jeremy, the Lord grant him a bed in Heaven, I was with McFillen last night and he came up with a brilliant idea. When doesn't he? It will be a poor look-out for all of us if the booze affects his brains.

As you know, the new housing scheme for Kilnavarna is long overdue and it looks as if the County wouldn't be able to afford it for many a year. McFillen knows how I can get 25 pre-fabricated houses at £250 a house. That's £6,250.

A pal of his will be importing fifty of them from Europe and I can have twenty-five. I'll probably get a friend of mine here in Dublin to buy them and I see nothing to prevent me from flogging them to the county for four or maybe five hundred apiece.

In the name of the sainted mother of God, destroy this letter! Because, if wind of this move got out, I was finished. It would be a front-page scandal. It's a clever move, you'll have to agree. The houses are being imported as an experiment, and, if they are a success, they will be manufactured here. McFillen will be a sleeping director of whatever company gets the concession. If the voters of this country knew one-tenth of the things I know, there would be a revolution to-morrow morning.

However, we are the men who freed the country and we are entitled to certain considerations. Don't forget what I told you about Mick and the shop. He'd have a fiver fiddled while you'd be looking around you. Give my fond regards to Henry. It won't be long more, D.V. He's a fine cut of a lad and, by all accounts, a steady reliable worker. The country can use steady, reliable workers. I wish there were more of them. I'll see to it that there will be a wedding to remember. I have promises from three Ministers that they will attend. Don't spare my purse if you have any ideas which might make the day a more perfect one for you.

Your loving,
Daddy.

★ ★ ★

Kate MacAdoo writes to her father:

My dear Daddy,
Thanks a thousand for your letter. I'll do as you ask with regard to Mick. Last night I went to see Bridgie Teeling.

She's just had her fourteenth child and, believe me, this is a family which is in dire want. Whatever you do you must see that her husband, Sam, is made a road steward. It's an absolute necessity if they are to live any sort of life at all. There are holes in his waders and he has no socks. I made him a present of a pair of strong boots and six pairs of woollen socks. He's been a labourer now for 25 years. Since you first stood for the Dail he has never voted for anybody else and neither has Bridgie.

Number one, Tull MacAdoo, and no number two's or three's either. I told her last night you would do your utmost and I pray that you will succeed. I really do because I know of no more deserving case.

That was a brilliant idea of Mac's about the prefabs. I hope it goes off without a hitch. Don't worry about the letter. It has since its receipt been consigned to the flames and nobody will ever know what it contained. I agree that it would be explosive in the hands of a hungry sub-editor. You know what they can do as well as I do and there's nothing in the world will buy them off.

Give Mac my love and tell him that he's been behaving poorly for a godfather. He hasn't dropped me a line in a year. Tell him to go easy on the brandy, that I said he was too nice to die – from alcoholism.

Your beloved brother-in-law, my uncle Tom, is off the booze since ere yesterday, but he could be on it again to-morrow. It's a small relief anyhow. I'm at my wit's end trying to get him interested in a girl from near Glenappa. She's going on forty but she's sensible and quite a looker. It might be the makings of him if he settled down.

There is little of interest here just now, except that business is booming in the shop since work started on the Awnee Drainage. Most of the workers cash their cheques here and they spend the best part of them before leaving the shop.

Mother is still in bed. Was there ever a time when she wasn't complaining about something. When 'twasn't her nerves 'twas gas and it wasn't gas it was neuralgia or laryngitis.

Mick has just come in the door now looking like an English squire in his suede shoes and sportscoat. I'll wind up now to get all the news of Cork from him. He looks well. In fact he looks downright handsome. A pity he hasn't a brain. I'll end now as he is about to come behind the counter to serve a customer. His willingness to do this surprises me and justifies your cautioning me about the till. Au revoir.

Love,
Kate.

★ ★ ★

Mick MacAdoo writes to his father:

Dear Dad,
Since I am apparently no longer to be trusted by the members of my own family, I feel honour bound to drop you a line so you can regard this letter as a protest. I am not in the habit of begging and it breaks my heart to have to go to my beloved sister when I want a few shillings. It is with great regret that I take my pen in hand to begin this sorrowful epistle since it is not in my nature to stir up trouble under the roof where I was born and reared. I am, however, your only son and as such I feel that I am entitled to certain considerations. I should, I feel, be allowed to go to the cash register without escort. I am not a tramp or a robber and I think that as the only male member of the house, apart from yourself, I should be in charge and not subject to the miserly whims of your darling daughter. Unless you write and tell her that I am to be trusted I feel compelled to demand £15 from you unless you want me in Court where I will be forced with my many obligations. I regret if the tone of this unfortunate epistle is without affection but I am the blood of your blood and I have my pride. I await your reply.

Sincerely,
Your loving son,
Mick.

★ ★ ★

Tull MacAdoo writes to his son, Mick:

Dublin.

Dear Mick,
You write a good letter. It's a pity you weren't around in the time of St. Paul. He would enjoy you even more than me. Speaking about saints, I pray for the day when you will write me a letter where there will be no request for money. As for sending you £15, I have no notion whatsoever of doing so. I trust Kate implicitly and I am quite sure she gives you enough. If you would only remember, Mick, that there are other things in life besides money, or can you think without thinking of money? I'll sign off now and trust that you will take note of what I said.

As ever,
Your affectionate father,
Tull MacAdoo.

★ ★ ★

Tull MacAdoo writes to his daughter, Kate:

Dublin.

My dear Kate,
Rumour has it here that Mrs MacMell is going to marry again. 'Twill be the talk of the city if she goes through with it. She's fifty-five if she's a day and the buck she's marrying is hardly thirty. He's the private secretary to a Cabinet-Minister. He's supposed to earn fifteen hundred pounds a year in his capacity as private secretary. Supposed is right!

McFillen is writing to you to-day. He was all apologies. I think he's gone out somewhere to get you a present of that new perfume: 'Exploda'.

It's very expensive but he's in the chips at the moment – something to do with insurance. It's commonly rumoured that the Minister and himself got a sum of £2,000 apiece for giving the insurance concession on a

certain item to a certain company. No doubt Mac will tell
me all about it in his own good time. He has the diarrhoea
constantly now and, to be candid with you, I don't like his
colour. He gets fits of empty retching and I'm after him to
see a doctor. When he came downstairs yesterday morning
he went straight to the bar and breakfasted on two large
brandies. When you're writing to him, invite him down
for a few days. He might go off the booze for a while for
your sake. He's always telling me that if he had a daughter, he'd want her to be a girl like you.

Seriously, however, he's a sick man and I'm too fond
of him to see anything happen to him. For instance, he
eats little or nothing and he starts off every day with a
large brandy. No constitution could stick that kind of
carry-on. If a person won't eat, that person must take the
consequences. A few of us here – his near friends – are
constantly after him to go and see a doctor but he's so
pig-headed that it is a waste of time asking him any more.
He spent one whole day last week without eating a bite of
any kind, not even a sandwich.

I, myself, still feel the effects of the hunger-strike and,
Kate, for God's sake tell no one, but I'm having night-
mares again about Dodigan, the R.I.C. sergeant we killed
in 1921. I try to dismiss it from my mind but his face
keeps re-appearing in my dreams and I wake up sweating.
I'm still convinced he was a spy, although his family and
friends swear otherwise and maybe they're right. Who's to
say in time of war. All is fair, they say, and I hope it's
true.

Why would he be playing cards till all hours of the
morning with the Tans, and how could the Tans know
where Razzy and I were hiding the night they raided my
uncle Mick's house in Kilnavarna. Still, I can't get him
out of my mind. He must have been alive for hours after
we left him on the roadway. Maybe we should have got
him a priest. That's the part that worries me most, him
not having a priest. I said the act of contrition into his ear
after we shot him, but was it enough?

I wouldn't like the thought of going myself without a
priest, although I never got on with them since oul'
Canon Murkason said we were all murderers. Canon

Murkason was a pro-British hobo. Maybe 'tis him we should have shot instead of a man with a wife and three kids. God pity me with these horrible bloody dreams! It is not right that I should be made suffer for only having done my duty.

I hope Mick is supervising the workmen and I hope you're keeping him well away from the till. Judging from his last letter you seem to be succeeding. The results of the exam. should be out any day now. I'll be down in a fortnight to start the campaign for the October elections. Mac has promised me a week at least and he will address meetings at nine venues. He's a powerful orator, the kind country people fall for. You'll have to start writing out speeches for me shortly. Put plenty of humour in them and a few good stories. They like that.

I hope your mother is well. I wrote to her three days ago but I've had no reply since. I can't figure her out. She should be the happiest woman in the world. She wants for nothing and she knows I love her but she persecutes me every chance she gets. I don't know how I put up with it.

Don't worry about Sam Teeling. I'll see that he's made a steward but remember that Rome wasn't built in a day. Give my regards to Bridgie and the fourteen kids. The bother is that most of them will be gone to England before they're old enough to vote. Well, darling, I'd better dry up and look after the affairs of my constituents. Give my regards to Henry and my love to yourself.

> Affectionately,
> Your loving Daddy.

* ★ ★

Mick MacAdoo writes to his father:

Dear Dad,
Here, at last, is what you've waited for so long, a letter without a request for money. Does it make you happy. But try to remember that St. Paul had to have money to take him on his journeys. Am I supposed to travel the

constituency on wings, or what? The reason I'm not writing to you for money is because I swiped two fivers out of Uncle Tom's wallet when he was asleep up against your manger after a booze which will be spoken about for many a day to come in Tourmadeedy. I could have swiped more but we musn't make pigs out of ourselves. Your daughter is fine. She guards your treasury better than any bloodhound. Your wife has a new disease which deserves mention in medical journals. I'll call it Crowitis. She resents the cawing of crows in the mornings and says they'll be the death of her. You can pick 'em, Tull.

> Cheerio.
> Your loving son,
> Mick.

CHAPTER SEVEN

Kate MacAdoo writes to her father:

My dear Daddy,
I'm afraid I have rather disturbing news. It has nothing to do with Mick or Mammy or Henry. All is fine here, but, since you do not buy or read '*The Demoglobe*', the following report will interest you. I am quoting directly from the leader page:

'LOCAL SCHOOLMASTER TO PROVE THAT BATTLE OF
GLENALEE WAS FICTITIOUS!'

'*Mr James Flannery, N.T., asserts that he has conclusive proof that there was never a Battle of Glenalee. In an exclusive interview, Mr Flannery told our reporter that there may have been a few scraps there between weasels and rabbits, but there was no gun battle. There were battles, he said, between weasels and rabbits and murder was perpetrated but it was only when a sparrow-hawk assaulted a wren. He said the battle was a figment of the imagination of Mr Tull*

*MacAdoo, T.D. He challenged Mr MacAdoo to refute his
statements. 'I am convinced,' Mr Flannery concluded, 'that
no battle was ever fought there, and,' he added, 'I have the
evidence to prove it.'*
I hate to send you upsetting news like this, Daddy, but
isn't there something we can do to make him eat his
words? If he's not made to look foolish quickly, it could
be disastrous in the October elections. Nobody believes
him, I know, and you might think it wiser to ignore it,
but I firmly believe that he must be shown up. It has
come at a critical time. Twenty years ago you could have
shot him and got away with it but not to-day. More's the
pity, because a bullet is exactly what he deserves.

It may all blow over, but, on the other hand, it may
gain momentum and spread all over the country. You
know how people love to see a national hero like yourself
brought into disrepute. Ask Mac what he thinks. Mac's
advice would be invaluable.

I got his bottle of perfume and it must have cost him a
small fortune. I'm delighted you will be able to obtain the
steward's job for Sam Teeling. Fourteen mouths are quite
a number to have to feed. I told Bridgie the good news
and she's saying a novena for you. Sam is praying, too,
that you'll head the poll. 'I wish I had a thousand votes,'
he said. 'I'd give them all to Tull.'

Mick is all right, reasonably dependable, but he fecked
a fiver out of the till while I was having lunch yesterday. I
followed him and made him put it back. He denied it
black and blue at first but I searched him and found it in
his breast pocket. I gave him a pound. That should keep
him going for a day or two. The new girl is dead keen on
him but she is sensible. Thanks be to God for that. The
patient upstairs would want seven nurses to see her wants.
She never stops calling. I turn on the transistor now since
it's the only way to drown her out.

Uncle Tom broke out last night and I'd swear Mick
was drinking with him. His eyes were bloodshot this
morning and he couldn't eat his breakfast. I'll split Uncle
Tom when I meet him. Mick is bad enough without
turning to the booze. Wait a minute! Here's a telegram
and it's from Cork. I'm half afraid to take it. Hooray!

Hooray! Hooray! He's passed! You Merciful God, he's passed his exam! I'll tell the countryside. I'll close, Daddy. Isn't it marvellous? Oh, it's the sweetest news we ever had. God bless him! God bless him!

Love,
Kate.

* * *

Biddy MacAdoo writes to her husband:

Dear Tull,
So-called husband that has his shoes polished in the best hotels and nothing to worry him, with the health of a mountain ram. I'm hardly able to hold the pen in my hand, my nerves are so bad from constant irritation and dyspepsia and neuritis. There's a tingle now in my spine often that'd drive any normal woman insane except myself.

What's this I read about James Flannery? When I opened the paper I nearly dropped dead inside in my sick bed. I always knew you would bring disgrace on top of us but this is the biggest disgrace of all. You always swore to me that there was a battle fought in Glenalee. You said yourself you wounded two Tans although the Tans denied ever being near Glenalee. What are we going to do at all. This will be the death of me. God take me out of my pain and relieve my suffering. I spilt a nineteen and sixpenny bottle of medicine all over you. I'm not eating a bite. I threw up rashers and liver. I couldn't keep it down or does anyone know what I'm going through, even my own husband with his shoes polished above in the poshest hotel in Dublin like a Canon or a P.P. No one thinking about me or will I be taken away in the end when my senses are gone to a nursing home or does the great Tull the T.D., the brandy-nose, forget who his wife is and what ails her. Mick, my own dear son, is a great consolation to me. There's money missing out of my handbag and he's investigating it. Somebody must have come into the room while I was asleep, he said. How would I know and I in the height of agony. Now I know what Our Saviour went through in the Garden of Eden. I wish I was surrounded by serpents the way I feel. And now James Flannery finding out about you to crown my misfortune. We'll be disgraced and Mick going to be a doctor. What patients will come to him, I tell you, after this except the riff-raff. He'll get none of the priests anyway and no convent would let him near them when his father is found out.

I'm starting another novena for you to know would God in his mercy take pity on you and save you from the powers of the devil, that Flannery, that schoolmaster with his row of Biros in his pocket and the tweed suit to crown it. The Latin should be read over that fellow and sprinkled after it in public. The hand is tired. God forgive you.

Your wife,
Biddy.

* * *

Tull MacAdoo writes to his daughter, Kate:

Dublin.

My dear Kate,
That's great news entirely about Mick. It's almost too good to be true. You're sure, I suppose, that it wasn't some other Mick MacAdoo? I'm only joking! It's the biggest surprise since Delaney won the gold medal in Australia. I'm going out to-night with Mac and the two of us will get plastered on the strength of it.

Now, Kate, I made Mick a promise. I told him that if he ever passed that confounded exam, I would stand him a holiday in Ballybunion, but he seemed to prefer Bundoran. Every man to his taste, as the saying goes. I was never a man to go back on my word, whatever my other failings may have been. I want you to outfit him like a hotel manager and give him fifty pounds and also the price of a return train ticket to Bundoran. The poor fellow deserves it after all the doubts we had about him. How did your mother take it? Maybe it will get her out of bed, if such a thing is possible, which I doubt very much indeed.

The second thing I want you to do is to check with oul' Willie Blakeney of Blakeney's Cross about the number of wynds in the two meadows. Find out from him if they are as big as last year and how many wynds there are. I'll need a lot of hay this winter as I intend going in for store cattle. Beef will be high next summer. There is a whisper here about a new agreement with Great Britain.

That's terrible bloody news about Flannery, but not as bad as it sounds. I doubt if he'll go any farther when you hear what I have to say. The moment I got your letter, I brought Mac into the resident's lounge here at MacMell's, opened a bottle of brandy and locked the door from the inside. Mac's first idea was to get sworn statements from the survivors of the battle, but, since there are no survivors, this would not be possible. He suggested we invent survivors and he could get a friend of his to draw up the necessary statements. This friend got four years for forgery some time ago but he's all right now and looking for an honest day's work. There's none of us perfect.

I think you will agree that Mac's idea was a good one, but mine is better as I know certain things that nobody else knows. We will have to move fast, however, before this thing gets out of hand and, since I cannot come down to Tourmadeedy at the moment, I am leaving everything in your hands. I trust you completely.

Follow carefully. The third thatched house on the bohareen that goes over Crabapple Hill is occupied by a woman called Jenny Jordan, two doors down from Kane's place. You know where Crabapple Hill is, but in case you don't, it is seven miles north of Kilnavarna and there's a signpost where the bohareen meets the main road. Jenny Jordan is a useful friend of mine and will do anything for me. I got her an I.R.A. pension ten years ago, which she deserved. She was no Countess Markievicz but she often carried a dispatch in her bloomers and many's the time she brought ammunition from Kilnavarna to Tourmadeedy. She is a good oul' soul and she'll like you instantly when she hears you are my daughter.

Go to see her at once. Do not delay a minute.

Here is the twist in the story. Thirty years ago before Flannery married, Jenny Jordan worked for him as a housekeeper. The inevitable happened and she had a baby daughter whom she called Maud, after Maud Gonne.

Flannery sent her to England – where they all go. She stayed there a year, supported by Flannery. I know he's an unhung scoundrel but he was never mean with money. Jenny came home after the birth and left the baby to be adopted. Flannery settled a hundred pounds on her (worth about six hundred to-day) and there was no more about it. The only persons who know this are Flannery and Jenny, yours truly and now yourself. Oul' Canon Murkason knew about it, too, but he kept it under his hat and wherever he is the secret is gone with him.

Flannery doesn't know that I know. You see, Kate, my darling, there are lots of things I know about people, necessary things in case I ever need them. It's part and parcel of the dirty game we call politics. Don't ever judge a politician outright if he does something which seems underhand. He is only doing his best to survive. Anyhow, between the jigs and the reels, Flannery married Elsie Rice (a grade A snob) who taught in the school with him. Elsie was always a girl who thought her water was Eau de Cologne.

They had four kids, as you know. There's the solicitor. There's the daughter who married the doctor in Ballybobawn. There's the dentist in Kilnavarna and, finally, there's the curate in Cloghauneen parish down south. Explain to Jenny what Flannery is trying to do to me. Point out to her that I might well lose my seat if his ugly lies began to snowball. Get her to go to Flannery and tell him that, unless he publishes an apology, she will make the affair of the child known. He must come to his knees. It will wreck his whole family unless he does and if he doesn't, I'm ruined. Get her to go to him without delay and everything should be rosy in the garden.

There is another woman, married now in Tobergorm, whom he is supposed to have sired but I am not sure about this. Flannery's great weakness was that he was a bit of a ram and I've yet to hear tell of a cautious ram and

I'm prepared to swear that I've seen Flannery's long nose and big ears on a dozen kids, although I couldn't prove it if I was asked.

Well, Kate darling, I leave you to it. I hope to God Jenny succeeds in frightening him. If she fails, I don't know what I'll do, although I don't think she's likely to fail. Flannery has too much to lose, what with his son a curate and the wife and all, not to mention the pupils and the new Canon. The new Canon has no time for rams. I will conclude, darling Kate, and I look forward eagerly to hearing from you. You might say that my whole future depends on you.

Love,
Daddy.

P.S. I went to confession to Father Flannery once when I was serving in a bye-election. (Flannery's son, Father Jack, as they call him down there.) You couldn't meet a nicer confessor, not if you went to poor Pope John himself. But I have to live, too, and I have you and your mother and Mick to think about and Henry on top of you. Mac sends you his love as always. If Mac wasn't stuck in politics he would be a saint. He would do anything for a friend.

Love,
Dad.

★   ★   ★

Kate MacAdoo writes to her father:

My darling Daddy,
Don't worry! Remember those words. Don't worry. Everything will be taken care of and you'll head the poll, no bother. Henry is here with me at the moment and he is giving me the loan of his car to go to Crabapple Hill. He doesn't know what it's all about and he isn't curious. He is a wonderful person. All that concerns him is my happiness. He'll make a good hubby.

I'll contact Jenny Jordan straightaway and let you have a full report of all activities the moment anything conclusive occurs which should be at the precise moment she puts her cards on the table before Flannery. I knew you would come up with something. Tell Mac he's a genius, that I wouldn't dream of having anybody else for a godfather.

I've given Mick the money, and the money for a new outfit, too. When I come back from Crabapple Hill, Henry will drive him to the station. Mick is a new man since he passed. He's beginning to look and act like a fully-fledged doctor. He is meeting a bunch of fellow-students in Bundoran, so it should be lively up there. Let us hope it will not be too lively. We both know Mick. A bill has arrived from his landlady in Cork for six week's lodgings. I expected it.

Mother is much the same – no improvement but no deterioration either. We both know there's nothing the matter with her, but we must put up with it, mustn't we? I won't dilly-dally with more news. There's a job to be done and I'm the woman to do it. I'm going straight to Crabapple Hill, or -- if you like – to Flannery's unveiling. I always suspected he was a bit of a boyo. He pinched my behind once at a social.

Above all, Daddy, you're not to worry about it. have no doubts but that my next letter will be laden with good news and the mouth of one James Flannery N.T. will be sealed unto infinity. He knows where he stands and he daren't do anything now. Remember not to worry.

> 'Bye, Daddy, and don't worry.
> Love,
> Kate.

CHAPTER EIGHT

Mick MacAdoo writes to his father:

Bundoran.

Dear Dad,
Weather wonderful here with balmy breezes, fine-looking women, and all that. A great place to develop an appetite but the food is expensive. In fact, so is everything. It should be an easy passage to the Finals, so you had better become accustomed to calling me Doctor. Money simply evaporates here, although this is only my second day. I paid my hotel bill in advance, £24. I was wondering if you would be good enough to send a few extra quid, say fifteen or even twenty if you can manage. I'll pay it all back to you when you fix me up with a good dispensary some day. Send it as soon as possible as I'm tied to my room without a penny in my pocket. I spent my last sixpence on a blade. I haven't had a smoke in hours. You would think Kate might have stuck a few cartons of cigarettes into my suitcase, but trust your Kate to do the right thing.

Love,
Mick.

★ ★ ★

Tull MacAdoo writes to his son, Mick:

Dublin.

Dear Mick,
At this particular time I-consider it most unfair of you to burden me with your financial worries. I have enough troubles of my own but I have no notion of transferring them to you as I want you to enjoy your holiday. If you would only think about other people and not always be putting yourself first. You're never done with begging.

You should have studied Economics, not Medicine. You're the best warrant I ever knew to screw money out of a person. Kate gave you fifty pounds and your return fare – and already you want more. However, I suppose I can't be too hard on you. You will find my cheque for fifteen pounds enclosed. Holy Mother, fifteen pounds, imagine! It would support a labouring man and his family for two weeks or are you aware of these things at all. I never had a holiday in my life. When I was your age I spent the fifteenth of August in Ballybunion. If I had sixpence for seagrass and periwinkles I was lucky.

Go easy with your spending and go easy with the girls. When your holiday is over I'll get you on as a temporary timekeeper on the Awnee Drainage Scheme. Ten quid a week and damn all to do only make certain your watch is in good order – or have you got a watch? You will enjoy the characters working on the scheme. There's oul' Micky Byrne (Tricky Micky, we call him). Would you believe it that when I told him there would be bulldozers on the river bank, he told me that he always thought a bulldozer was a cow that fell asleep when there was a bull around. You'll really enjoy yourself but it's imperative that you stay awake. There will be enough sleeping on the job without the timekeeper starting it. I don't want any girls around either while you're working. 'Twould be the last straw if you did damage.

Seriously now, son, I want no more requests for money. I have enough worries with the general election drawing near and I have one major worry at this time which could be disastrous but, like I said, I want you to enjoy your holiday. It could be your last one if things go wrong.

I'll close now, as I have an unopened letter here from your mother which I must read and answer so as to have it ready for the morning's post. Enjoy yourself and be sure not to miss Mass. It's all we have, you know – the Faith. Lose it and you lose all. Write to your mother at the first opportunity. Write her a long, funny letter as she needs a lot of cheering up. Drop a card to Kate and to Henry and drop a few cards to as many people you can in the constituency. Votes are votes and I enclose a pound's worth of stamps for the cards. Enjoy yourself and don't do anything I wouldn't do.

Love,
Dad.

★   ★   ★

Biddy MacAdoo writes to her husband:

Dear Tull,
It's ages since you wrote a line to me and I here in bed with my nerves in a bad state and my left breast sore. Maybe 'tis cancer I'm getting or maybe 'tis something worse altogether. There is no disease going but doesn't pay me a visit or how does one human body endure it all. Will you tell me that? You sitting down in fine health in Dail Eireann and me here on my last legs thrown down on the bed. God help me, I'm to be pitied and no word from you to find out if I'm dead or alive or do you care what becomes of me above there and you surrounded by luxury and your meals served up to you by waiters in white coats. There was a time, and I young and plump, that you never left my side.

I suppose 'tis boozing on brandy you are with that fecker McFillen. He's not fit company for anyone and if you knew some of the yarns I heard about that fellow, you would say hell wasn't hot enough for him. He's the talk of all holy Catholic mothers and their innocent daughters. Books wouldn't give down the tales about him. Mick passed his exam. I barely saw him at all on account of you and the fifty pounds you gave him to go to Bundoran. I do like to be beside the seaside. 'Tis far away from the seaside we are, God bless us and save us in the warm weather. Far away indeed from the time I was a slip of a girl walking the streets of Ballybunion in my figure and you winking at me. That's forgot now, is it, Tull? 'Tis me should be going to Bundoran and you needn't mind writing back to say you'll send me as it's too late now anyway. I wouldn't be able for it. I wouldn't be able to travel three times around the house without a black sweat breaking out through me. 'Tis to Lourdes I should be going with a private nurse and a wheelchair. I see where the Minister's wife got an audience with the pope. I never even had an audience with a bishop, not to mind a pope and imagine I a T.D.'s wife or does the T.D. think about me at all, or maybe there's another woman in the T.D.'s mind whose wife is a pity and a martyr to her nerves. I hear Dublin is surrounded by prostitutes, black and all sorts of colours, and houses with the women going around with nothing on them except garters and head-scarves to tease the young men. Scurrilous is what it is, scurrilous conduct in a Catholic country. There's nuns or no one safe the way people are carrying on.

Isn't it lucky I'm in my bed? You'd think Mick would stay a few days after passing his exam but no, he's off to Bundoran. Off to Bundoran and his poor mother with no one to talk to her and her only son that was the difficult rearing with mumps and scarlatina gone off to the seaside instead of staying at home nursing his victim of a mother. There's two charms gone off my bracelet. I wouldn't say I lost them. I hope he's not flogging them off in some pawnshop. The nice rearing he turned out to be – my own flesh and blood. 'Tis from the MacAdoo's he brought it, not from our side, that's certain and sure I may tell you. Fifty pounds no less and when I wanted a new lavatory put up the time Father O'Donnell was coming home I had to go down on my knees to you for a few hundred pounds. My breast is agonising and little you care or do you know you have a wife and mother of your family at all?

I won't be here for the October elections, making tea and firing whiskey into your friends. I'll be above in Lisdoonvarna, D.V., with Maggie Simpson. The two of us have it planned to go if my nerves improve, or is this new attack to be the finish of me? Lisdoonvarna is the last hope for me or do you begrudge me even that? I can't bear it and I eat only a few bites yesterday, and you guzzling chickens and what not up in MacMell's, and other things maybe, behind my back. Sometimes I wish for death to bring relief to my sufferings and what harm but I the most religious woman in Ireland that never missed her Nine Fridays when she had her health, that never did a bad thing to any one or even only had the good word as them that know me will swear in the high court of law. Why is it always the good ones that suffer, or is that the way that God has it planned for us. 'Tis our cross, I daresay, and the cross must be borne by the humble and the suffering and the lamenting in this vale of tears.

Your wife,
Biddy.

★   ★   ★

Mick MacAdoo writes to his mother:

Bundoran.

My dear Mother,
Having a grand time here but it's spoiled a lot knowing how much you are suffering. You're a saint, a pure saint, the way you put up with it. Wait till I'm qualified and the two of us will go to Lourdes. I'll be acting as your personal physician. We'll have a rare old time between us. I visit the chapel regularly to say a prayer that your health might improve, and please God it will. There are new drugs coming on the market every day and who knows but one of these days some chemist will come up with an all-purpose drug to suit you. We will get it at cost price since I am in the medical trade so you see it's worth while having a son who is a doctor.

By the way, mother, a small request. I gave an African Missionary here a few pounds to say Masses for you. I did it on impulse and now I find that I have only ten shillings left to my name. Is there any chance you could send me ten pounds without letting Kate know about it. It will only be a loan and I will pay you back on the treble when I'm qualified. Better still if you could send £12 as I promised a Lord's daughter from England that I would take her to a dress dance and the tickets are £1 each so the extra £2 would cover the cost of the tickets. This is a very nice girl and she often enquires about you although she's English and titled. I make out that the richer people are, the nicer they are. I have her saying a few prayers for you, too. The weather is quite good here and I spend most of the day on the strand. I'm in bed every night at 10.30. I don't go to the dances like the other fellows as I'm short of money. The hotel bill alone will be up to £40, a small fortune. I've given up smoking and hadn't a drink since I came.

Send the £12 by return of post if at all possible as I really need it.

Your loving son,
Mick.

* * *

Kate MacAdoo writes to her father:

My dear Daddy,

There was a letter from Bundoran this morning with curt instructions for the dispatch of twenty-five pounds as your beloved son expressed his intentions of spending a third week there. He didn't even say 'please'. I sent him a telegram telling him where to get off and ordering him home at once. He immediately sent another telegram saying he was in dire straits for cash so I wired him fifty shillings which was quite enough for him. He must be boozing like a fish up there.

Now for the joyful part. I went to Crabapple Hill to see Jenny Jordan and she received me with open arms. She was so excited when I told her who I was. She dabbed her eyes with a handkerchief whenever your name was mentioned and she bawled out crying a few times when I told her that you had such a very high opinion of her. You certainly have a loyal friend on Crabapple Hill and make no mistake about it. Anyhow I put the facts of the case before her and at first she was reluctant but with a bit of pressure she agreed.

I took her in the car to Kilnavarna and on the way into the village who should we see walking along the road, swinging his walking-cane, but the great schoolmaster himself, wearing a white straw hat if you don't mind and a most impressive row of fountainpens, biros and pencils adorning his waistcoat pocket. You will have to agree that he is a fine-looking man, well-preserved and of most commanding appearance.

I pulled up and told him that Jenny wanted to speak to him. He grew flustered and tongue-tied and tried to brazen his way out of it by walking away from us, and a grand majestic way he has of walking. I followed him in the car and shouted through the window at him:

'Walk away if you like,' I said; 'Your wife will do just as well.'

'Wait a minute!' he whispered. 'Leave my wife out of this.'

I swear to God, Daddy, I never saw anyone so terrified, and for a minute I felt sorry for him – but only for a minute, because I remembered what he was trying to do to you. But honestly I felt for him because he knew he was up to his ears in trouble. But it was Tull MacAdoo or James Flannery and that was that.

'Get out,' he said to me, 'and I'll talk to Miss Jordan in the car.' He stood very aloof then and fingered his moustache. I must say that he recovered his composure immediately and I'm sure he felt that he was master of the situation again. God pity him! He didn't know the power of Tull MacAdoo's influence.

I obliged and went for a walk along the road. There was nobody in sight. An hour passed and I got impatient but Flannery made no move to leave. I signalled to him that I wouldn't wait any longer. He pulled down the window and asked me to give him ten minutes. He was as pale as a corpse and the jauntiness gone from him and he chain-smoked the whole time he was in the car. Another half-hour passed and finally he got out. He didn't look at me when he passed me by. All he said was: 'Tull never heard of the Marquis of Queensbury'.

Jenny Jordan was crying her eyes out when I got into the car. It took her a long time to come back to herself but when she did she disclosed the following facts.

Flannery tried everything in his power to force her to

remain silent. He explained about his wife and family and what it would mean if they ever found out. He mentioned his son, the curate, but Jenny held firm. In the end he offered her £250 but she told him that all he had to do was to withdraw publicly what he said about you. He started off again about his wife and family and told her you were a scoundrel and a gangster.

'Ah, but, Master,' she pointed out to him, 'hasn't poor oul' Tull a wife and family too. If your wife and family found out wouldn't you still have your job, but if you published the lies about Tull couldn't he be out of a job?'

Flannery tried every trick he knew for a solid hour and a half, and when all fruit failed he tried to buy her with the money. The upshot of the meeting is that an unqualified apology will appear in next week's paper and so all is well and your honour is no longer threatened.

I will tell you one thing I learned and it is a rather strange thing. Jenny Jordan still loves Flannery. Imagine still being in love with him after all these years and after what he did to her. He must have been quite a man in his day. It's a pity he's opposed to you. He would make an excellent Senator on appearance alone. Then that deep booming voice of his would be another asset.

Now for some bad news. Uncle Tom is on the jigs from whiskey. He spent two days boozing in Kettleton's Bar in Kilnavarna and when he fell off into a sleep, Mr and Mrs Kettleton took him upstairs and put him into bed. They sent for me and I went upstairs to the room. I took his shoes, clothes, hat, everything and locked him in.

What do you think he did? He found a white shift belonging to Mrs Kettleton in the wardrobe and put it on. He climbed out the window and down the eaves-shoot. How he wasn't killed is a mystery to me. Sergeant Keogh caught him going into another pub and took him back to Kettleton's. Luckily only a few old women saw him. It was dark and they thought he was a ghost. One of them fainted and had to be given brandy. I made Uncle Tom go down on his knees and promise me on the bible that he would not touch another drop of whiskey for the rest of his life. If he stuck to the few pints, all would be fine; but the whiskey puts him on the jigs. I'll close now, Daddy. Henry sends his regards and mother is still in bed. I hope you're taking care of yourself. Didn't I tell you that all would be well. You can't whack the MacAdoo's when they put up a united front. Even the cunning of James Flannery will not prevail against them. Give my love to Mac and tell him I have his room ready.

Love,
Kate.

CHAPTER NINE

Tull MacAdoo writes to his daughter, Kate:

Dublin.

My dear Kate,
Thanks be to the Holy God Above that Flannery is going to make an apology in the paper. The worry of him had the sleep robbed from me and I was in a queer way, I may tell you. I swear to you that I would be worse than your Uncle Tom in the end because if Flannery succeeded I would seek release in the whiskey bottle. God bless you, Kate. You conducted yourself better than I ever expected and thanks to you my good name is safe.

Your mother is writing strange letters to me. She is a very demanding woman – always was although she wouldn't admit that part of it to-day. She says she intends going to Lisdoonvarna for the October elections, Lisdoonvarna of all places, when the constituency will be like a beehive. Kate, love, I hate asking you to do this, but is there any chance you could postpone your wedding until the elections are over. You *don't* have to do it and it isn't fair to Henry or yourself but, quite frankly, I couldn't go

it alone again. Your mother was nearly the death of me
the last time. Do you remember the night she put on the
accent when the Minister's wife came in for a cup of
coffee. God forgive me – 'tis wrong to be talking about
her – but she thinks of nobody but herself. I decided not
to answer the last letter she wrote. Shakespeare himself
couldn't answer it.

If she would only behave like other women and give
me a minute's peace. If she was one bit predictable itself.
I'm sure she would love to be hobnobbing with royalty
and ministers and bishops but I wouldn't get many votes
if I hung around with the big shots. They would start
saying that my success was gone to my head. Talk to her,
Kate, and try to drive some commonsense into her. She's
beyond me. She seems to find satisfaction in needling me.
I have been a great husband to her. I've supported all
belonging to her for years without a word of complaint. I
gave her father ('Oul' Scutter Heels') three hundred
pounds to buy two fields in Glenalee. All her nieces are
telephonists and I've forgotten how many of her nephews
I've got into the Guards and, if you don't mind, one of
her nephews, a Sergeant, stopped me once to ask me for
my tax. 'Shag off!' says I to him, 'or I'll have you transferred to the Blasket Islands.' You have no idea of the
number of letters I receive every week from your mother's
relations – all looking for something: money or jobs or
both. Kate, I often think that if I met another woman,
more suited to me, a normal wife, that I might have been
a better man.

About the wedding – postpone it if you can and you
won't be sorry. I'll settle a good penny on you the morning of your marriage. For the present, God bless.

All my love,
Daddy.

P.S. I should be home next week. The session is about to
close before the elections.

★   ★   ★

James Flannery, N.T. writes to Tull MacAdoo, T.D.:

National School.

Dear Tull,

I've just had a session with Jenny Jordan concerning a very human indiscretion committed a long, long time ago. The apology will appear in next week's paper and it should satisfy you. You are a shoddy man, Tull, and a crafty man and you know as well as I do that there was never a Battle of Glenalee. There was a onesided battle all right on the night yourself and Razzy murdered the Sergeant, an unfortunate wretch who was only carrying out his duty and carrying it out rather indifferently at that. Can you explain how no Black and Tan or member of the British Military was killed by you and your so-called fighting men when in every other part of the country they were fighting tooth and nail for a cause that meant death.

Poor Jenny Jordan. Don't you think, Tull, that I often stay awake nights, haunted by the awful fact that there is a child of mine somewhere in England, a young girl who is my daughter and about whom I know nothing. My worst punishment is that I cannot do a damn thing about her. I cannot search for her, and I cannot forget her. I was a young man then, Tull, and young men are virile and hungry. They must be forgiven a lot. Do you ever blush, Tull, when you remember the past or does the past mean anything to you?

There is a stain or two in every man's yesterdays. Mine is Jenny Jordan and a few other women – with others I was lucky. Yours are the Battle of Glenalee, the killing of that defenceless sergeant and the others that only you know about. You are not a fair fighter, Tull. I will concede that a professional politician cannot afford to be, but to defile the basic principles of co-existence by exposing the human failings of a fellow human being is stooping a little too low. However, I have long ago convinced myself that nothing is beyond you when your alleged good name is at stake. How I wish that I were free of responsibility. If I were, I would break you, but you know as well as I do that I am reduced, by you, to the stature of a helpless old man.

Neither you nor I are greedy men, Tull, and we are both reasonably charitable. As a human being, I could probably like you, but as a politician you stink with an odour so putrid that my stomach revolts at the most insignificant of your actions. I got to be a teacher on merit, and merit alone, and you got to be a member of the Dail on merit, a particular kind of merit, yet you consistently betray the trait that made you successful.

To you, Tull, nothing is sacred – not even the dignity of your own daughter, whom you profess to love. You have made her share some of the vileness of your own responsibility. Funnily enough, I liked her because of her intense loyalty to you. For what you have done, you will both suffer yet, she in particular – or do you understand me? I think you do.

The main point I would like to make in this letter, Tull, is that you have corrupted everything you touched. You have damaged everything irrevocably. My only satisfaction is that you are part of the slime which surrounds you. Your legacy will be your ignorance, your crudity and your villainy.

James Flannery, N.T.

★   ★   ★

Tull MacAdoo, T.D. answers James Flannery, N.T.:

Dublin.

Dear Ram:
Listen, Flannery, or should I call you Archangel Flannery? Perhaps I should call you Excellency. It's the sort of salute you expect. Well, you're not dealing with schoolchildren now, Master Flannery. You're dealing with Tull MacAdoo, a grown man who doesn't give a tinker's curse about you. Another reference to my daughter and I'll blow your brains out. Worse still, I might beat you till you hadn't a breath of life left in you. Now you're trying

to tell me that it's unnatural for a daughter to want to help her own father. Well, let me tell you, it's the most natural thing in the world. Your own actions prove it. You firmly believe there was no Battle of Glenalee and you say you can prove it. But you daren't prove it, Flannery, out of loyalty to your own family, or maybe it's fear of your own family. You don't want to hurt them. Please remember that my daughter doesn't want to see me hurt either. And, above all, I don't want to see her hurt. God have mercy on the soul of the man who offends her.

But, of course, you and your family are different – special! Who are you trying to kid! It must be yourself. Yes, that's it! You're kidding yourself. You and your stupid principles: principles, moryah, and principles when they suit you, but only when they suit you. Wouldn't a man of principle have married Jenny Jordan in the first place and say to hell with the neighbours and public opinion. But not you, Principles Flannery, the worthy schoolmaster.

Listen, Flannery! Why don't you go for the Dail? You have a following who think you're God Almighty. You would definitely get in. No bloody fear, Flannery: you leave the dirty work to me and my equals and criticize us with safety from a distance.

You're an educated man, Flannery, and I'm surprised that you don't know more about yourself. I'll tell you exactly what you are, for nothing. You're a cod, Flannery, a pompous oul' cod who never did anything in his life except to criticize when you know it will cost you nothing and when there's no danger in it.

What did you do for the country if you're so concerned about it? Did you ever run for the County Council? If things are as rotten as you say, isn't it the duty of an educated man to stand up and protest? Why don't you do something positive? Don't say that you can't because of Jenny Jordan. You had thirty free years to do something constructive and when you try to do something after your own heart – something destructive – you haven't the courage to go through with it. You spineless, pitiful fool. 'Tis the likes of you that has this country held back with your weak whispers and rumours, terrified of your bloody lives and jobs to come out in the open.

What do you know about politics? I don't tell you how to run your school, do I? You'd perish inside of a year if you were stuck in politics. You're not tough enough and you know it. A man has to have the skin of a crocodile if he wants to survive in politics.

You haven't the strength or the courage, Flannery. But, don't worry – I'll carry on and you can be assured of your salary and pension while you have people like Tull MacAdoo holding the country together in spite of you.

Cheerio,
Tull.

★ ★ ★

Biddy MacAdoo writes to her husband:

Dear Tull,
Loving so-called husband and backbiter that had my own daughter, my own flesh and blood, giving out the pay about me. How long is the conspiracy going on? Do you want me out of the way so bad? So you're coming down next week, and no word to me, or am I only a servant girl or a playabout woman to be put away when your pleasure is done after I bearing you children through thick and thin when there was no maternity homes or drugs to kill the pain. I suppose you're enjoying your four-course dinner and your soup before it and your sweet after. You were always a good head to your belly, or anything that gave you pleasure. You didn't show much control. I suppose McFillen is telling the dirty, filthy stories as usual. Well, he'll tell me no more because I'll throw the holy water on him if he comes within an asses' roar of me. I had a lovely letter from Mick, three packed pages, not like you. I sent him a few pounds. He'll only be young once. He's a good boy only for ye all being down on him so much. He reminds me a lot of my father, the same slow smile and the same thoughtful face by him. A pity my poor father wasn't alive to-day to see him and to see my suffering here in the bed.

Of course you prefer your little pet of a daughter who gave out stink to me this morning and wanted me to shift myself and my bed and I in the throes of mortal suffering. I didn't like to say anything, although I could say plenty about the Protestants that won't even believe that there's an Our Lady, our beautiful Blessed Mother, the spouse of St. Joseph and the Mother of God. Did I ever think that I would live to see the day that the daughter I breast-fed would be half a Protestant. The parsons won't be long getting after the children if they have them. You'll have to get out the gun to see they are baptised in the Holy Catholic Church or will they be half and half, with some Catholics and more Protestants. I knew a woman that committed suicide over she changing the faith. Thanks be to God, there's no fear of Mick, my own boy, that will marry a pure clean Catholic girl when he's a doctor. Georgina Muldowney is a nice girl, an only daughter. She called to see me last week and landed a big bag of pears and oranges up on the bed to me. More than my own ever did, after they being the whole cause of the way I am. Do you think of me at all or even when you say your prayers a person would think that your conscience would move you and that you might remember to think that you have a wife who gave the best years of her mortified life to you and yours. May God forgive you.

Your wife.

★ ★ ★

Tull MacAdoo writes to his wife, Biddy:

Dublin.

My dear Biddy,
What's wrong with my own girl that I love. Why are you so cross with me, or what did I ever do to you only to give you anything you ever wanted. Now, isn't that true? Did I ever refuse you a single thing, or was I ever demanding of you? You'll have to admit that I was always a reasonable man. Ask me to do anything for you and I will

do it but don't ask me to give up politics because I'm good at them and I can do a lot for poor people.

I'll be home next week and maybe the two of us will go off for a few days somewhere. How would you like Killarney? We could spend a few nice nights there in a good hotel, away from it all. I sincerely hope that you will be up and about when I come home. It would be great if we could spend a few days together, and Killarney is beautiful this time of the year. If you say the word, I'll book a double room in the best hotel. It would be a break for me, too, before the elections. I would come back refreshed for the fray. We could do a bit of motoring during the day, see the sights, hire a boat and have a journey over the lakes. I think you'll agree that we should have a most enjoyable time. Write soon, love, and let me know what you think. We fixed Mr Flannery all right.

> Ever and always,
> Your own Tull.

★　★　★

Biddy MacAdoo writes to her husband:

Tull MacAdoo,

So that's your plan for me, is it? Killarney! Don't you know that I know there's a mental home in Killarney? You covered it nicely with the idea for the double room in the hotel.

Is it a girl of sixteen you think you're playing with? 'Twould be more in your line to forget about going for the Dail again and stay here at home in Tourmadeedy and look after your wife. Everyone that comes to see me tells me that I look desperate bad. The breast is painful and I have neuritis. Soup and toast and a few tit-bits is all I can take now.

I'm taking a tonic, too, that Johnny O'Dell, the chemist in Kilnavarna, made up for me. Sixteen and six for a small bottle but he says 'tis good and he says it brought great relief to the Sergeant's wife the time she lost the child. I eat a slice of brown bread now and then and I'm taking honey for my throat. I had another letter from Mick for a few pounds. He met a Lord's daughter up there and she had her purse whipped from her by Teddy-boys. Mick gave her what he had and was left with nothing himself. This Lord's daughter is from England and they're millionaires over there and she asked Mick over for a holiday. She is an only daughter, too. She's mad about Mick. I'm saying a novena to know would my health ever come back to me. If God listens to prayers, He must have heard a great share of mine. I'm never done praying for all of ye. What about Kathleen Stack's son and the promise you made about getting him into the cadets? She's a good friend and she would cut off her right arm for me. I see in to-day's paper where James Flannery apologises to you about the Battle of Glenalee. He's a right mongrel, that Flannery, and his wife thinks she's a duchess or something. The airs and graces of that one and she going up the aisle of the Church on Sunday are enough to sicken a person. You might think she would show some respect in the house of God. It's a pity some one don't write her an anonymous letter about James and the days he spent rutting the countryside. That wouldn't be long knocking the gumption out of her. There should be a lot more letters to a lot of other high and mighty women around here. There's one doctor's wife playing golf that I could mention and other big shots drinking gin and lime and what nots like that. Ah, no respect for God or man. I'm exhausted now from writing this. I'll end.

Your wife, Biddy.

P.S. Rex Feckler was in to know would you fix him up as an auxiliary postman for the Tubbertone area. There's five more in for it but Rex is deserving. He brought me a fine pair of chickens, plucked and all, when he heard I was knocked up. He always gave you the number one and he always canvassed for you. 'Twas him flung the bicycle tube across the wires the night the opposition had the big meeting. Apart from that, his mother and myself are connected. Her father and my father were third cousins.

Biddy.

★　★　★

Tull MacAdoo writes to his wife, Biddy, who is in Lisdoonvarna:

Dear Biddy,
I trust this finds you well. Give my regards to Maggie. Well, the campaign is nearly ended and the voting commences at 8 o'clock to-morrow morning. I'm nearly exhausted but it's a blessing to me that you are improving a bit. I enclose a cheque for £250 in case you're short or would like to buy something for yourself – a dress or a coat, maybe.

I'll be going to bed now as I want to be up bright and early in the morning. Polling begins at 8 o'clock. I have no doubt whatsoever about the outcome but I still have the same old excitement after all these years. There is nothing to beat election fever, win or lose. MacAdoo, the old warhorse, revels in it. He is in the thick of it now and he will emerge at the top of the poll. I'll try to sleep now but it won't be easy with my seat in the balance. God bless you, my darling wife, and may he guard you and improve you so that you will come back to me a better and healthier woman. I think I'll make a mug of cocoa before I turn in. Looking back over the years I have certainly come a long way and I have an awful lot to be thankful for, more than most men. I worked hard and I had you behind me and I never refused a man a favour whenever it was possible. Good-night. I'll let you know the result first thing to-morrow.

Love,
Tull.

CHAPTER TEN

Tull MacAdoo writes to his wife, Biddy, in Lisdoonvarna:

The Courthouse

My dear Biddy,
I'm here at the Courthouse and I can't resist the urge to drop you a line. The votes have been divided at last and

the first count is about to begin. They've just broken off for lunch and will start immediately afterwards.

Take a deep breath, because I am the bearer of great tidings. You will be overjoyed with what I have to tell you.

I think you should be the first to know that I am a cast-iron certainty to head the poll. In fact I confidently expect to poll the highest total ever achieved by anybody in this constituency. You should see the looks of astonishment on the faces of the opposition. Flannery had the gall to come to the count and he is as pale as a ghost. Kate and Mick are here with me and wish to be remembered. My pad of votes is twice as high as the nearest rival and I reckon that I should be returned on the first count with ten or even eleven thousand first preferences. I rang poor McFillen a few minutes ago and it looks like as if he'll lose his seat. I wonder who will be appointed in his stead. It could be a certain chap who is your husband. Poor McFillen. I always told him he couldn't have it both ways. I hope yourself and Maggie are enjoying Lisdoonvarna. I'll come up to bring you home whenever you say the word and if there's anything whatever you want, don't hesitate to ring or write. I'll be home in Tourmadeedy for the next few days at least. I daresay I'll be expected to throw a bit of a shindig to-night. Kate is looking after that for me. We'll bring in all those who worked hard but to-night my house will be open to every man whether they voted for me or not. I'm not a small man and I'm not a begrudging man. Do you need anything. If you do, write at once and it's yours. The salary for parliamentary secretary is very attractive. I will buy a little car for you if you would like and teach you how to drive.

I'm so elated with the results I can hardly write steadily. The most I expected to poll was eight thousand votes but, wonder of wonders, I should have almost 11,000 first preferences. What have I done to deserve it! I had a call from the Minister to find out if there was any news and when I told him, he was delighted. 'Good solid dependable old Tull,' he said. If I'm not made a parliamentary secretary after this there's no justice in the world. The Minister expects to head the poll himself and he was really tickled at my news, especially since I'll bring another man in with me and especially when McFillen is about to depart the scene. I'll fight like a dog to get Mac a seat in the Senate. He deserves it.

Mick goes back to the University to-morrow, a week late, but he worked his head off during the campaign and I'm convinced he got a lot of the younger votes for me this time. I have a wonderful family, I must say, and you yourself the best of them all, my own dear girl.

Big changes from the day I stood for the County Council. Did you ever think that Tull MacAdoo would head the poll or that one day I would be a parliamentary secretary. They would have laughed at the idea, in those days. Aren't you delighted with my achievement? Nobody ever dreamed that any single man could even poll ten thousand votes in this area. Tull MacAdoo fooled them all and when you consider how I scraped in on the seventh count the first time it is a truly remarkable performance. It's a historic achievement. The thing now is to work hard to stay at the top. There are hundreds of people here congratulating me and I find it difficult to write. The quota is only 6,800 so that Din Stack should get in, no bother, with my surplus votes. He only polled 3,000 votes but this surprise poll of mine gives him a right chance because my surplus should be enough to check him in in the second count. In fact I think we could take it that he's a T.D. already. He's over in a corner crying his eyes out with joy. "'Tis all due to you, Tull,' he said a while ago, and I thought he would break my hand with the shaking he gave it. He's still crying with joy but I think that he's fairly boozed. He was up most of the night drinking. He was too nervous to go to bed. Wait till he's been through as many campaigns as I have.

More good news. Rex Feckler will start next Monday as auxiliary postman for the Tubbertone area, so what do you think of the husband who can fix anything for you? I still can't get over my phenomenal votes. I had better close and shake hands with my admirers. There's a crowd cheering now outside the Courthouse, after hearing that I am about to break all records. I wish you could hear it . . .

'Three cheers for Tull!' they're shouting. 'Three cheers for Tull MacAdoo!'

> Good-bye, my darling and God bless you.
> Your devoted and ever-loving husband,
> Tull.

★   ★   ★

Biddy MacAdoo writes to her husband:

> Lisdoonvarna,
> Co. Clare.

Dear Tull,
I got your letter, but I seen it in the papers this morning. You must be pleased with yourself but it's only what I expected. There's a priest here in the hotel, on holidays from the African Missions, and he's a great consolation to us. He says Mass every morning and I swear that I would be a total wreck only for him. He's not well himself, the poor man. He's a pure saint if ever I came across one and Maggie says the same thing. We play a few games of whist at night before going to bed and we have our sulphur bath every day. It does seem to be improving me. By the way, there's one thing I must tell you that you must do for me. There's no pots in the rooms here and we are ashamed to ask for one. Maggie is as shy as me. Would you ever get a good enamel pot and wrap it well and post it on to me. 'Tis an awful trek downstairs to the toilet, so don't forget, and ask Doctor John to post on my prescription for the red nerve tablets as I want to get some from the chemist here. Or is it too much for you to do after I giving you the best years of my life?

> Your unfortunate wife,
> Biddy.

JOHN B. KEANE

Letters of an Irish Parish Priest

The Presbytery,
Lochnanane.

Dear Joe,

I've just come in from the garden where I spent the morning planting daffodil bulbs. The man before me, the late Father John Clement Fitzraymond used to claim relationship with Strongbow. He had a book of sermons published by Shule and Rune, the London firm and he had his suits made in Saville Row. There is a garden in front of the presbytery consisting of one acre and thirteen roods, yet in all his fourteen years as parish priest of Lochnanane he failed to plant one daffodil. Have no fear but he planted the bulbs of doubt in the collective crania of The Lochnanaanites. After nearly a year I am still trying to re-establish contact with the ordinary people.

God in his wisdom has whistled many a strange warbler into the church but did you ever hear of a priest who charged a guinea for saying Mass, who, the year before he died addressed the final year students in Saint Olack's with the opening question 'Stand up all here who masturbate.' Needless to mention no-one stood up. This then is the man in whose wake I must navigate, whose potholes I must fill in, whose hedges trim as it were. This is the man who introduced grapefruit to the parish of Lochnanane. By this he is remembered and by nothing else.

He brought the grapefruit in a brown paper bag from the city of Cork when he was a curate at this place in

1937. He bamboozled poor Norrie Crean who was house-keeper at the time.

'Oh Lord Jaysus,' said she. 'That's the size of an orange. 'Tis as big as an elephant's conundrum.' The same Lord have mercy on Norrie and all the poor inno-cent souls this hallowed month of November. I offered Mass for your mother this morning. I know you miss her more than I although she was my only sister. She is surely in heaven. Yes, indeed. She is in heaven or there is no-body there.

The new curate arrived this morning. He seems a likeable sort, nicely disposed and well-mannered. I sup-pose you could call him self-effacing. Time will tell. His senior, Father Romane is still the same. He has as much integrity as a certain English Sunday newspaper. The last thing I want to be is harsh and on that account I'll say no more. He is due to depart in a few days and please God the memory of him will be shortlived. I don't envy his new parish priest. Mary Teresa was never better. She sends her regards.

Do you want for anything? Let me know your needs when next you don't spare me. This is a good parish in that respect.

Affectionately,
Your uncle,
Martin O'Mora, P.P.

★　★　★

The Willows,
Gurtacreen,
Lochnanane.

Dear Father O'Mora,
I called twice but you were out on each occasion. Let me introduce myself. I am Henry Dring, a native of this place, who is now home to stay after forty years in exile. I bought this fine house some months ago but only took up residence a fortnight back. I am a retired headmaster, widowed and without family. I had better come to the

point and in so doing would have you remember that it is from a sense of duty and nothing else that I am compelled to unfold the following harrowing tale; as you will recall, the second fortnight of October was exceptionally fine. The last Monday of the month, in particular, was more like a June day than an October one. I motored in the afternoon to the beach known as Trawbofin four miles from here and set out for a walk across the dunes. There were few about; an elderly couple as I recall and a mother or governess with some children far up the beach. Suddenly a young couple dashed from behind a sandhill and ran towards the sea. You will say to yourself that they were perfectly entitled to do so. I concur and I would fight to the death for their right to dash into the sea provided they were wearing bathing attire, however immodest that attire might be.

I regret to inform you that they wore nothing whatsoever. They ran past me shamelessly, ignoring me even when I called after them in protest. The only words that escaped the young man's lips were when he administered a half-hearted slap to the girl's bare buttocks – I recall what he said: 'Get moving or get mounted, your posterior has me intoxicated.'

I left the dunes in disgust vowing never to return until they were made safe for God-fearing people.

I naturally assumed that this immoral couple were from some distant city or foreign land forsaken by God, such as England or Wales. Some weeks later I was shocked to discover that the young man is a teacher in Lochnanane. Worse still the girl works in a chemist's shop here. You can imagine my feeling of outrage at this gruesome discovery. My first thought was to report the matter to the Civic Guards but I decided, before doing so, that you should know first. The young man's name is Thomas Cooley. Being a gentleman I will not mention the girl's. I hope to hear from you soon regarding this most serious matter.

Sincerely,
Henry Dring, M.A.

* * *

St. Unshin's College,
Ballyrango.

Dear Uncle Martin,

Many thanks for your letter. Funny you should mention daffodils. The three new girl students here spent all yesterday afternoon planting daffodils and irises with the junior dean, Father Mockessy. The new girls are the talk of the place. By and large the students are in favour of having them but the entire teaching staff, Mockessy excepted, are in a dither and don't even know how to behave towards them. You could call it 'conservatism at the crossroads.' The president, Monsignor Dang, pretends they aren't there at all and I'm sure he's secretly hoping they'll just go away. It wouldn't be so bad if they were nuns but three attractive laywomen out of the blue is a bit much for the college elders.

I had a short note from my father to say that he would be in Ireland for a spell before Christmas with his friend Mrs. Garrett. He said he would like to see me so I told him it would be alright if they wanted to stay overnight in one of the guesthouses here in Ballyrango. I hope you don't mind. Whatever else he is my father. I know you can't stand him and I know you have good reason or you wouldn't treat him the way you do. Don't you think it's time you told me. You are the nearest person I have in this world. There is no-one else really. I have my own reasons for not caring one way or the other about my father. I am more interested in yours as they would weigh more heavily with me. I will be twenty-one in less than a week and I am a bachelor of arts. What I am trying to say is that I feel I can be trusted with any confidence, that I am mature enough and resilient enough to be able to absorb any heavy data which I might hitherto have been incapable of doing.

I got a tip for a horse called Finicky Fencer from a pal of mine here. His father is a trainer and thinks this horse will win a two mile maiden chase at Limerick Junction next Thursday. Have two pounds each way for me and I'll settle up with you in due course. Have a flutter yourself and tell Mary Teresa.

I'll close now. We are rehearsing a show for after Christmas and I have a small part.

Your affectionate nephew,
Joseph.

★ ★ ★

The Presbytery,
Lochnanane.

Dear Joe,

That was solid information about Finicky Fencer. I hold your winnings. Mary Teresa and I had a bet and collected. It's you that's in for the good feeding at Christmas. I have been confronted with a thorny problem since I wrote to you last.

A Henry Dring wrote first and then called to complain about young Tom Cooley, one of my teachers, and a certain young lady. Dring asserts that he saw Tom and the girl in the nude at the strand of Trawbofin in the middle of your noon day. I don't doubt it but so long as no one was scandalised I do not see how it could be the concern of anybody. Dring, who is a retired headmaster and whose mother came from these parts, has threatened to go to the Civic Guards and I may tell you that this would not do at all.

I am very fond of young Tom Cooley and he is also an excellent teacher. This fellow Dring must be made to retract. He had an uncle, his mother's brother, Canon Dring of Killaveg, who had the reputation of being the second meanest parish priest ever to hold office in the diocese. Old Canon Dring died from malnutrition but not before he salted five thousand quid over on the sister. This is how our present Mr. Dring got his M.A.

While oul' Dring was P.P. of Killaveg there was a Tom Kilmartin, a pal of mine, a curate there. Tom told me that there was only one W.C. in the presbytery. It consisted of a cracked toilet bowl and a flush tank that never worked. Tom was never permitted to use the toilet. This was reserved for oul' Dring. Whenever Tom had a call of nature he had to go behind the house. He was lucky in this regard because behind was a large uneven bog which afforded him a change of scenery every time he wanted to release a button. He was often caught in the act by a turfcutter or a stray tourist. To this day when he enters a bathroom or W.C. he looks behind him regularly expecting to be surprised.

Nellie Dwan, the housekeeper, was not allowed to use the W.C. either but she had an outsize enamel chamber pot which she bought at an auction. This she faithfully emptied every morning in a stream about two hundred yards from the presbytery. She was frequently followed by schoolboys who would ask her if the pot was full or if it was to the creamery she was going and so forth and so on. She was often mortified. The people of the parish could always tell by her gait if the pot was full or half full or near empty. If she walked slow, one neighbour might remark to another 'By the Lord but poor Nellie Dwan had a lively night last night,' or if the pot was near empty 'By the Lord but Nellie Dwan must have wet the tick last night.'

Anyhow I have summoned Tom Cooley to render an account of himself. It should be an interesting interview.

So your father is coming before Christmas with Mrs. Garrett his so-called wife. How in the name of God can she be called a wife whose husband and children are still to the good. I'll grant you she is divorced and that her children are grown up and that her ass of a husband married again but she has no religion of any kind. She isn't even a Protestant. Your father is a Catholic and yet he married in a registry office in London. He can say what he likes and she can say what she likes but in the sight of God they are not married. They are adulterers. I'll say no more about them.

I hope all is well with you. Being a Third Divine is a happy time. Soon you will be a Subdeacon D.V. It was my favourite year at Saint Unshin's. Those few girls around the place will do no harm – they'll liven things up – it would have been considered a sacrilege in my day.

Joe, there were many wrongs in my time but the passage of the years, thank God, has set most of them to rights. There is one thing I find it hard to forgive myself for.

When I was a young priest it was fashionable to waylay young courting couples and pairs of lovers in the laneways and out-of-the-way places at night. We often surprised and chastised older lovers in great need of each other. As God is my judge Joe I don't know why I did it? It was the fashion. That's all I can say in defence of myself.

I know why some did it. It was because they were lonely themselves and had natural longings and many found release in this sort of persecution. It still goes on sporadically and it will always go on I suppose but Joe, believe me when I say, it is one of the very few things that I have ever been ashamed of.

You ask me to explain my dislike of your father. You are now old enough to know. It has little to do with his obsession with that grey-haired trollop Mrs. Garrett.

After you were born Joe the doctor told your mother that she was to have no more children. He was most emphatic about it and he pointed out that should she conceive again she would be placing her life in grave danger. Your mother was one of the most perfect Catholics I have ever known. Only God knows how good that woman really was.

It was put to your father that he should sleep with your mother no longer. She was unpredictable in her menstruals which made the risk even greater. He agreed but he broke his word and in a matter of months your poor mother was expecting another child. The doctor was pessimistic but I saw to it that the best specialists in the field were available.

Your father suggested an abortion. I could have struck him. Your mother was appalled. To her and to me such a course was unthinkable. As the days passed and the time of her confinement drew near your father began to insist that there be an abortion. He even went to a solicitor. What's the point in labouring the issue. My heart aches even now when I remember.

She died in childbirth. Everything possible was done to save her. It was all to no avail. I closed her eyes on the bitterest morning of my life. The child died a few days later. Your father threatened to kill me. After a few weeks he left and it was five years before I heard from him. That was when he tried to claim you. He hadn't a leg to stand on.

He is your father. You must never forget that. You must never forget your mother either. Time has dimmed a lot of things for me but the ache in my heart which came after your mother died has never left. It never will. Let us have no more of this particular subject but let us look to the brighter days ahead. Write soon.

Affectionately,
Your Uncle,
Martin O'Mora, P.P.

P.S. (The new curate is a grand lad – more of him anon.)

★   ★   ★

The Presbytery,
Lochnanane.

Dear Dring,
Sorry to have been out when you called. I was on a sick call and while I am parish priest of Lochnanane sick calls will always have priority no matter who may ordain otherwise.

Should you ever feel like calling again it might be a good idea to drop me a note. I cannot be expected to sit inside all day awaiting casual callers. We also have a phone in the house, Lochnanane 2. Why not ring and advise me as to the approximate time of your next arrival. This would greatly facilitate me and anyway I am most anxious to meet the man who makes the most monstrous accusations ever to assail my ears.

I am also anxious to meet the nephew of the late Canon Henry Dring of whom I have heard so much over the years.

Like I say, sir, a note or a ring on the phone would be the intelligent thing to do.

Now let us come to the letter and the apparition you claim you saw on the strand of Trawbofin. Let me tell you that I have not yet acquainted Mr. Thomas Cooley of your accusation. I am not such a fool. I have known Mr. Cooley for three years as a teacher and for twenty-one as a person. Be assured sir that he is a devout Catholic, an excellent teacher and the youngest son of a family of seven distinguished males and four equally distinguished females.

What the hell were you on the look-out for anyway? Are there no birds on the great strand of Trawbofin, no cadaverous cormorants clutching the glinting rocks, no oyster catchers conning the clear shallows, no air-loving plovers ploughing the unimpeachable elements?

What does one look for on an October seashore? I would ask you to think before you answer. It is possible you saw a young couple without clothes. What if you did. By your own admission it was a broiling day and by your own admission the couple you saw were young. You were a mere witness to a classical natural reaction. It is your mind sir that needs to be clothed, not the innocent bodies of God's children.

You say that a man you believe to be Thomas Cooley threatened to mount the girl if she did not get a move on. I am at a loss for words in the face of the other expression you used. I am seeing Mr. Thomas Cooley tomorrow and if you wish you may make the accusation to his face.

Yours in J.C.
Martin O'Mora, P.P.

*   *   *

The Willows,
Gurtacreen,
Lochnanane.

Dear Father O'Mora,
I have no wish to be present when you interrogate Mr. Thomas Cooley. When I call to the Guards' Barracks I will, if he is present, make such an accusation to his face and to the face of the girl.

Before I go to the Guards I want to assure you that I am merely doing my Christian duty and that I am not the dirty-minded person you try to make me out to be. I am a reasonable man, travelled and broadminded. I will postpone my visit to the Guards until I hear from you again. Then I must go and no power on earth will stop me.

Yours faithfully,
Henry Dring, M.A.

★   ★   ★

St. Unshin's College,
Ballyrango.

Dear Uncle Martin,
I read your letter with great interest and I am grateful that you explained your position with regard to my father. How could he have been so monstrous. How in the name of all that is just and holy could he contemplate such a thing. It was as if he deliberately set out to murder my mother. The man behaved like an irresponsible animal. My poor mother. Why did she not refuse him? Why did she not go to yourself or the doctor? He knew it was likely to kill her. I refuse to think anymore about it. It does something to me inside.

I am going to try to forget and as you said in your letter let us have no more of this particular subject but look forward to the brighter days ahead.

I think I mentioned in my last letter that we are producing a play for presentation some time after Christmas. Traditionally when there were female parts in a play the producer would inveigle gullible first year students to fill the roles. These were known as Starlets but they never quite measured up. Fortunately two of the three girl students are taking part this time. Both have already taken their degrees at National but are here doing a year's course in Theology.

Rehearsals are enjoyable. The play we are doing is 'Death of a Salesman' and I am playing the part of Willie Lomax. Make-up will be quite a problem. I must age thirty years if I am to be convincing. One of the girls, Jean Raymond, plays the part of my wife. She was born only twenty miles from Lochnanane in a place called Fahabawn. It appears that you were a curate there for a while during the never-to-be-forgotten reign of Father Donal 'Dynamite' Carey. When I get home for Christmas you must tell me all about him. He must have been a fantastic character. Take care of yourself and try not to expose yourself to the bad weather.

Write soon. Tell Mary Teresa I may have another tip very soon.

> Your affectionate nephew,
> Joseph.

★ ★ ★

> The Presbytery,
> Lochnanane.

Dear Dring,
I am very much afraid you have landed yourself in serious trouble and it could well be that it was a black moment when the thought of visiting Trawbofin entered your head. Trawbofin, or in its translation into English, The Strand of the White Cow, is four miles from Lochnanane. The city of Cork is seventy-two miles from Lochnanane. On the day you presume to have seen Thomas Cooley on the strand of Trawbofin he was seventy-six miles away in the city of Cork on business. His brother Walter who teaches in Cork met him on his arrival and was with him in that ancient city by the Lee for a period of three hours. They spent the time in pubs and it is a known fact that the barmen in the public houses in Cork have most reliable memories.

Thomas Cooley left the city of Cork at seven o'clock in the evening. If it took him two hours to make the journey to Lochnanane it would have been dark on his arrival. As things turned out it was dark when he arrived at his mother's house on the evening in question.

His mother brought eleven children into this world of Drings and other things that go bump on the beach. She assures me that it was dark when he arrived. It is barely possible that you saw somebody who outwardly resembled Thomas Cooley that fateful evening (fateful for you). Mr. Cooley informs me that on a few occasions recently he has been seen at places where he could not possibly have been at the time. He informs me that there is an insurance agent in Castlepellick who is very like him in appearance, a chap of low morals who spent some time in England and who consorts with girls of doubtful reputation so that it could not possibly have been our friend who works in the chemist's shop and who is a veritable paragon by all accounts.

The gravity of your accusation is enormous now that it has been conclusively proved that you never saw Tom Cooley on the day you said you did and at the place you said you did and in the company of whom you said you did and in the state of undress you claim you saw them disport themselves.

You have put two feet in it and all that remains for us to determine at this stage is if you told any others apart from myself. Better a millstone were tied around your neck, etc.

Tom Cooley is not a man for law but he will go to the supreme court if necessary. When I spoke to him he told me he would sue you for every penny you possess. He was shocked beyond belief when he heard the charge against him.

Knowing him to be a reasonable man I asked him if he would consider settling out of court. He told me that he really wanted no material gain if you were prepared to withdraw the charge and say no more about it. An apology naturally would be in order as well. Drop me a line as I hate having callers in November.

Sincerely,
Martin O'Mora, P.P.

★   ★   ★

The Willows,
Gurtacreen,
Lochnanane.

Dear Father O'Mora,
I must have been mistaken although, in truth, if I were in
a courtroom I would feel justified in swearing that
Thomas Cooley was the man I saw in the nude at Trawbofin. The insurance agent you speak of would want to be
an identical twin to make me do otherwise. However,
there seems to be overwhelming evidence against me. I do
not accept it but I will go along with what you suggest. I
have no choice. I am the victim of circumstances. You will
find the apology enclosed. You will not hear from me
again nor indeed would I ever dream of calling to see you
about anything ever again.

Yours faithfully,
Henry Dring, M.A.

* * *

The Presbytery,
Lochnanane.

Dear Joe,
All is well that ends well. Our friend Henry Dring has
withdrawn his charge against Tom Cooley. He also sent
a letter of apology. I doubt if he will bother us again.
I could never stand these self-appointed moralists.
Anyhow I told Tom that I wanted to see him at the
Presbytery and he called. He had no inkling of what I
wanted him for.

I sat him down and gave him a drink, poured one for
myself and for openers asked him if he knew our friend
Henry Dring. The drink nearly fell from his hand. He
admitted being at Trawbofin but said it was the heat and
that there was nothing more to it. He also insisted that the
girl wore a flesh-coloured panties and covered her breasts
with her hands but that Dring must not have noticed in
his agitation.

So Tom Cooley was guilty as charged or almost guilty. What was I to do? I like Tom and I happen to know that the little girl who works at the chemist's shop is a decent type at heart. It was a hot Autumn evening. They had neglected to bring togs. They saw nothing wrong in it. Tom admitted that he passed the remark of which Dring accused him but assured me that he often said the same to other girls with no harm intended. He promised it would stop.

I had to ask myself which was the more important; satisfaction for Dring or the future of a nice lad like Tom Cooley and the utter ruination of a girl's character.

It was then we composed the letter which brought the apology from Dring. He himself had given me the clue. You remember he wrote that no power on earth could stop him from going to the Civic Guards. There surely, said I to myself, is some drop of the Uncle's blood in this man's veins. No power on earth would stop his uncle either when the late canon made up his mind about something, no power, that is, except money. The late canon would do anything for money. That is why I suggested to Henry that Tom Cooley would sue him for every penny he possessed.

Knowing the seed, breed and generation of Henry Dring I guessed that the thought of losing one penny would be sufficient to make him abandon his course and see the light. I judged my man's weakness to a nicety. The only thing I regret is that he saw fit in his reply to say that he would never trouble me again. I have done him no harm, nor have I ever done any man deliberate harm since the day I was ordained. He may need me yet. For this reason it was foolish of him to say that he was burning his boats. I enclose a tenner. Don't ever refuse money unless you are certain it comes from an evil source. If you want any more let me know by return. Did you hear any more from your father? Write and let me know all.

Your affectionate uncle,
Martin O'Mora, P.P.

★   ★   ★

c/o Mrs. Joseph Mellington,
Castle Avenue,
Lochnanane.

Dear Father O'Mora,
I would call to see you but I am ashamed of myself and I
am afraid people would put two and two together. I am
pregnant and the man who I allowed to do this to me
cannot marry me as he is married himself. I don't know
where to turn or what to do. My father would beat me up
if I told him. He would also want to know the name of the
man and this would not be possible for me to tell as it
would cause nothing but trouble to a whole family that do
not deserve it. If I told my mother she would tell my
father she is so much afraid of him.

You know my father yourself. He is nearly always
drunk. What am I to do Father. I am in terrible despair
and I have thought of the river. Please do not ask me who
the man is as I cannot tell. Will you please help me. I
have heard from a girl who is my best friend that you
never turn a person away. Please don't turn me away. I
have made my mistake and it will last me for a lifetime. If
you fail me it will mean I must go to England or do
something dreadful.

Sincerely yours,
Bridget Day.

★　★　★

St. Unshin's College,
Ballyrango.

Dear Uncle Martin,
Many thanks for your letter and the tenner. My father will
be coming with Mrs. Garrett the second week in December
for two days only. I have told him I look forward to seeing
him. He said in a letter that he would like to talk to you.
It's purely a matter for yourself. All goes well. It's only a
few minutes to six a.m. but a few of us are catching up on
our correspondence so we rose rather early. There goes the

Vox Dei. You heard that bell often enough yourself to know that it is a summons that m..st be answered. Let me know about my father. That tenner wasn't really wanted but I appreciate it as I do all the kindnesses you have always shown me since my mother died. I hope I shall be able to repay you some day.

In haste,
Joe.

★ ★ ★

The Presbytery,
Lochnanane.

Dear Bridget Day,
Put England from your head this instant minute. England is ninety per cent pure Pagan and you have no business there. I'll grant you there are a few Catholic institutions there which would accommodate you but I fear for you afterwards. Enclosed herewith you will find twenty pounds and a letter to a good friend of mine, Mother Amabilis of the Convent of the Winged Servants of Saint Sonia in Clonleary. I am, today, writing to her. I assure you that you will be well taken care of and do not worry about your father or indeed about anyone. Just do as I tell you and leave the rest in my hands. You poor girl. You have suffered your share as it is.

Pack your bag this very evening. The twenty pounds will help you buy any knick-knacks you may need. Follow carefully. Be at the main gate of my church at seven thirty on Friday morning. Father Raymond Tubridy, the parish priest of Lockeen, will be waiting for you. You know him by sight. He is the tall, redhaired man with the cross face. He will drive you direct to Clonlea. It's two hundred miles away and you can have your baby in peace and comfort when the time comes. I will look after everything else. I will write to you from time to time. Want for nothing. Be sure to write regularly and let me know your needs. Do not think you are without friends. The Virgin

Mary will befriend you as she did so many others. Pray regularly and say one for me sometime.

> Your Parish Priest and friend in J.C.
> Martin O'Mora.

★ ★ ★

> Loafer's Lane,
> Lochnanane.

Dear Father O'Mora,
I am no great spelerr. The agonys of the damd has me presued since the day I married the Monster. That's what we calls him now myself and the kids. He won't do a stroke of work and but for the family alounce we would starve. I am the mother of fourteen childeren and there is five more went to heaven. I have to work six days out of the seven and keep one of the older children inside from school. He stands all day with his back to the corner in the village woching the cars pasing and scraching himsef. You would nevver think wit his inocent face he was the same man woke this morning with a weapon would beat a ass out of a feld. He wanted his chips on the spot. I ran from the bed into the kichen an he arter me shoutin stand stand for me, steady you bludy bich. I had to go in the road in case he knoc me up agin. I culd not have no more not if you gev me a millon. My helth wuld not stand it.

Culd it be cut of him some way. I stayed in the rode in the cold a hole hour and he roaring come in you effin skiv for the rich. The childeren wok for school so he went back to bed.

Save me from the monster, Father O'Mora. All people says you have a grate hart. Keep this sex manac offme no wuld I enjy one sumer wit a slack belly.

> Your fateful servaent,
> Rosie Monsey.

★ ★ ★

Convent of the Winged Servants of St. Sonia,
Clonleary.

Dear Martin,
Just arrived. Our little friend is in good hands. She has
gone to watch television with another girl. I'll stay on a
few days. I'm tired after the journey, a good deal more
tired than I thought I would be. What can you expect at
sixty four. I felt very honoured to be able to help Bridget. What a charming little girl she is. You know what
she said to me when we were having lunch in Ballinasloe.
'Father,' said she, 'you're not cross at all. You're very
nice.'
    Good God, I never felt so complimented. It occurred
to me more than once that the father of her child
would be the head of the house where she worked.
Maybe I'm wrong but we both know him well enough to
know it is most likely. If it were a normal boyfriend she
would name him. Why shouldn't she try to get a father
for the child. Who would blame her. It has to be our
friend. How many has he already in his own family? Five
or six?
    I played golf with him a month ago. You could not
meet a more likeable fellow. Every man has his cross and
he has his but I feel, Martin, that he should be made to
do something for Bridget. He must not be let off scot
free. No better man than yourself to figure it out.
    I haven't been well lately. I haven't told anybody but
yourself. It may be the heart. Goodness knows the pains
are bad enough across the chest. I'll see a doctor when I
get home. Not to worry. Our friend is fine, thanks be to
God. I'll call on my way home and you had better have
a few bottles in. What's your new curate like?

                                        Yours in J.C.
                                        Ray.

*   *   *

The Presbytery,
Lochnanane.

Dear Joe,

The Vox Dei Bell. I was often drugged in the deepest sleep when it roused me. I swear, that for us students, it made the Bells of Shandon sound like the rattle of an aluminium Rosary Beads. I will not see your father. I have forgiven him long since but I cannot be expected to condone his alliance with Mrs. Garrett. If I spoke to him I would be doing just that. He has betrayed his Catholic Faith deliberately. God knows we are all weak but God gave us the gifts of life and faith to cherish till we expire and I would be betraying my most cherished beliefs were I to speak to a man who married in a registry office. I'll say no more. You asked about Father Dan (Dynamite) Carey. God grant him a special place in heaven. He spent some years in America, before being appointed to the parish of Fahabawn. He brought two things from America. One was a heart of gold and the other an insatiable appetite for whiskey. The latter killed him. I was his first curate and I can say without fear of contradiction that Father Donal Carey was the finest priest and the decentest human being I have ever known. There is a story told about him when he dropped dead in Killarney all that was found in his pockets was a corkscrew. This is true.

You may wonder why he was called Dynamite? Simple. He would often say to me when he would come in from a sick call: Martin, my ole buddy, pour me a shot of the goddam dynamite.

The dynamite was his undoing. He gave me my first car as a gift. When your mother died he found three hundred pounds somewhere for specialists. The people loved him. They would do anything for him. In all his time in Fahabawn, although he drank all round him, his name was never associated with drink. Woe betide the man who would dare to put a hard word on him. He died penniless. He had no possession of any kind except of course the corkscrew and the grace of God. It was he coined that immortal phrase about Ballybunion-by-the-sea. 'Ballybunion,' said he, 'where parish priests pretend to be sober and bank clerks pretend to be drunk.' I'll say no more for now. I have too much respect for his memory and I would only laugh out loud were I to recall his deeds. It was Dynamite who told me that every month the late Canon Dring would give a bundle of old newspapers to his altar boys with instructions that they be cut into pieces of a specified size. The pieces were used in the toilet. Apparently he would count them every day to ensure that nobody else was using the toilet. For the moment, farewell.

Your affectionate uncle,
Martin O'Mora, P.P.

★ ★ ★

Loafer's Lane,
Lochnanane.

Aha if twas the rich youd have them ansered long go. How is it not the poor. The keeping down of the poor is the wurk of the priests thes days I see for sure. The Monster struk agin las night an I sleeping. The docter said the las time it was tech and go. I'm lucky I'm not in the famly way. It wasent my time. His polci is strike first and ask qestens arter. Will you cum to my aid or I'll get the brednife to him soon. They shuld be cut off all the men. I will rite to the bishop.

Your fateful servant,
Rosie Monsey.

★ ★ ★

The Presbytery,
Lochnanane.

Dear Mrs. Monsey,
I'm genuinely sorry for not answering your letter. What you say is probably true. It it was a rich person I would sit up and take notice at once. Forgive me and thank you

for telling me the truth. I will speak to your husband very soon. If you would tell him I need him for some odd job I'm sure he would call. Meanwhile mind yourself as best you can.

Yours in J.C.,
Your friend and P.P.,
Martin O'Mora.

★ ★ ★

The Presbytery,
Lochnanane.

Dear Ray,
A thousand thanks for driving our little friend to Clonleary. I would not have asked you had I known you weren't feeling well. I'm glad you're going to see a doctor. I'm sure all you need is a good, long rest. Stay in Clonleary as long as you can. That's a great curate you have. About my own. He began like a new broom but as time passed the fibres lost their bristle and rigidity. He does not like work. He likes the company of women. I am all for being friends with women so long as there is no discrimination but the type he prefers is the young married one or the unpredictable nubile sort. He is never available to talk to older women. Any time I see him publicly at functions or in the street he is either giggling or whispering with some empty-headed girl. It has come to such a pass that I'm afraid I'll have to take him aside and talk to him.

I have received a few pointed anonymous letters. His liaisons with these feather-brains are quite harmless. He favours none openly as far as I know and this is good because there is safety in numbers. Inevitably the bishop, who has the cuteness of a pet fox and the long distance eye of a starving gannet, is bound to hop a ball. 'Father, your curate would seem to be a great boon to the ladies,' then the pulling of the earlobe. 'Father, let us see what he can do for the ladies of the southwest.'

By the southwest, of course, he would mean the remotest outpost he could find. All very fine but new curates are getting scarcer and scarcer. It will have to be a talk.

I considered very carefully what you wrote in connection with the father of our little friend's expectation and there was no doubt in my mind but that you were on to the right man. I discovered from Sister Daphne of the Presentation Convent here in Lochnanane that Bridget Day passed her leaving certificate with two honours but failed to get a decent job. She took רים temporary work with Mrs. Mellington, something to pass the time and earn a few quid while she waited for a break. Bridget's father is a bully and a drunkard. Her mother is a weakling, although not by choice.

Sister Daphne knows nothing about Bridget's trouble. I carefully covered all tracks, inventing a story here, planting a hint there with the result that everybody now believes Bridget Day stole away quietly to study nursing in England.

In view of what you said I decided to approach Mr. Joseph Mellington. Easier said than done since I wanted the climate for our conversation to be nothing less than ideal on account of the subtleties involved. I thought of a number. I haven't caught a consistent club in five years but I remembered that when I was in my heyday it was Joe Mellington's burning ambition, and many another patsy, to beat me over eighteen holes. They never came remotely near it and they greatly supplemented my income when I was a curate in various pauperised places. I gave Joe a buzz and asked him for a game some morning when he would be free.

We were on the phone together at nine a.m. and we were on the links at ten. He knew I was rusty and he wanted quick vengeance. I played better than I thought I would but he had a shot over me to the sixteenth. The bet was a tenner and, all things allowed, I was prepared to lose if it would advance my cause. On our way to the seventeenth we stalled for a smoke. I always find when I am trying to get my pipe started is an ideal time to shoot a pertinent question.

'How's Irene?' I asked innocently.

'Fine, fine,' he said, 'never better.'

I expressed my delight and enquired after the children. They were in excellent form as was he and all connected with him. I said no more till after the seventeenth which we halved.

'God knows,' said I, 'you're a great man entirely the fine family and the fine happy home you have and the great business you built.'

This buoyed him up no end and he approached the eighteenth with confidence. I might have beaten him but I knew if he lost my case would be a hopeless one. He won by a stroke and I handed over the tenner. We strolled back to the clubhouse for a drink before lunch. I dawdled and began to frame my next question. Circumstantial evidence never hanged a man and that was all I had anyway you looked at it.

'Did Irene succeed in getting a new girl?' I asked.

'Who told you that she was looking for a new girl?'

'Ah I heard it just by chance. It could have been my housekeeper Mary Teresa. You know the way women are when one of them is looking for a girl. Word spreads.'

'She hasn't got one yet,' Joe Mellington said. 'Do you know of someone?'

I told him I didn't but that I would be on the lookout, that we often heard of girls looking for work.

'Where did the last girl go?' I asked. 'What's her name? Bridget Day wasn't it?'

'Yes,' he said, 'that was her name. She went to England to study nursing. I told her myself that she would be better off although I knew it would be hard to replace her.'

This convinced me that he was the man and from the way he spoke that he was a very relieved man. Without having to exert himself in the least he had disposed of a most serious problem. That he had dismissed the matter completely from his mind was also evident. I lost pity for him at this stage.

'Well, Joe,' I said, 'Bridget Day is not gone to England to study nursing and you did not tell her that she would be better off if she were to do so. She could not do so, Joe, for the simple reason that she is expecting a baby and that baby, please God, will be delivered in this country.'

He was flabbergasted but, by God, he came round like a shot. He wouldn't have got to where he is if he wasn't tough. I waited a minute before I delivered the next one. 'Why did you say you advised her to go nursing when we both know you didn't.'

'I did tell her,' he said.

'I have her word,' I told him, 'that you did not and whatever else that little girl may be she is not a liar.'

To this he made no immediate reply. He may have won the curtain raiser but I was winning the main bout.

'Maybe I did. Maybe I didn't,' he said.

'Alright,' I said, 'but let me tell you a few interesting facts, Joe. I happen to know that the father of the child is a married man with a family. I happen to know that he is a native of Lochnanane and the reason that Bridget Day refused to expose him was because she was afraid of the effect it would have on that man's wife and children.'

'Was this what you brought me out here for?' he asked, 'to tell me this?'

I admitted that it was.

'Are you implying that I might be the father of the child?'

'Joe,' I said, 'one of my parishioners is in trouble. I have no desire to see two of you in trouble.'

'Is that supposed to be a threat?' he asked, 'because if it is you're talking to the wrong man. I take threats from nobody. I am my own man.'

'Joe,' I said, 'don't come the heavy with me. You are the man responsible for Bridget Day's misfortune,' I shouted, 'now what are you going to do about it?'

'For God's sake,' he begged, 'keep your voice down. Do you want the whole country to hear?'

'What are you going to do about it?' I shouted.

He begged me not to raise my voice. I told him I would lower it when he told me what he planned to do for Bridget Day.

'What do you want me to do?' He was a changed man. The fear showed in his voice.

'I want her to have a university education,' I told him, 'and I want you to pay for it.'

'You're mad,' he said.

'Give me a thousand pounds,' I told him, 'and I'll see that she gets that education when her troubles are over.'

He told me he could not lay his hands on that kind of money.

'This is a girl,' I said, 'who may well want to keep her child. She must have the means to support it. She must be independent. You owe it to her.'

'A thousand is ridiculous,' he said. 'I haven't got it.'

'Joe,' I said, 'you drive a three thousand pound plus car. You recently bought two farms. You are the biggest contractor in these parts. My patience is coming to an end. I'm really doing you a favour.'

'It's blackmail,' he said. I told him I did not like the word blackmail, that it was unfair, that justice was the word. 'You'll have my cheque tomorrow, Father,' he said meekly.

You can tell Bridget the news. Don't say where the money came from. Tell her it's a private fund long since created to help girls in distress who have this capacity for university education. The money will be in the form of a trust. You, Bridget and I will administer. I got a present of a turkey from a friend. Let me know the day you are coming home and we'll try the bird out.

Your friend,
Martin.

* * *

St. Unshin's,
Ballyrango.

Dear Uncle Martin,

Many thanks for your letter. I had guessed that you would not see my father. Enough said. All goes well here with the production of the play moving smoothly. The elocution classes are an immense asset especially if a person wants to act. I loved your stories about Dynamite and

Canon Dring. Any more? It can be very dull here in November. Did you plant any more daffodils? How is Mary Teresa? Tell her she is very slow about answering my letter. How about the new curate? What's he like? I want to know all.

Affectionately,
Joe.

★   ★   ★

Loafer's Lane,
Lochnanane.

Dear Father O'Mora,
Hel be doun to see you Fridey. He compland of a pain in the back when I sed you wantd him but hel be doun Fridey for sure. Oh chastis him the low hound that give me no peace. Im dead if i have another child. Chastis the monster get him operate on by some surgin. Whip the fako off him. Don't siy i sed nothing whatever you do.

Your fateful servant,
Rosie Monsey.

★   ★   ★

The Presbytery,
Lochnanane.

Dear Joe,
All goes well. Glad you enjoyed the stories about Dynamite and Dring. There are still some great characters in the diocese. I refuse to answer any questions about my new curate beyond saying that he is opposed to work. He doesn't like it and he is never around when he's wanted. He would want to catch on to himself. Mary Teresa is fine. She is a great housekeeper in all respects, unique in fact.

She always minds her own business yet she knows enough to run the parish in case of emergency. I planted another hundred of daffodil bulbs and a score of copper beeches, ten at either side of the presbytery. If my predecessor, the late Father John Clement Fitzraymond had planted in his time we would have trees now. I still get his bills. I honour them. They are mostly for intoxicating drink and tinned delicacies such as crab, lobster etc. The parish clerk was once examining empty bottles to see if there was anything left when Fitzy popped out of nowhere.

'They are all dead you fool,' said he.

'Thank God they didn't die without a priest,' said the clerk.

Another time the parish clerk was chasing ducks out of the presbytery kitchen.

'Go on. Shag off outa that,' he was saying when he was surprised by Fitzy.

'Listen,' said Fitzy. 'You shouldn't tell those ducks shag off. Never use rotten language in front of ducks. Just say cush, cush and they'll shag off themselves.'

You heard me say often enough that Canon Dring was the second meanest priest in the diocese. It's time I told you the who the meanest one was. He was Father Tom Winder of Tubberdarrig. His first curate was a meek man called James Dee. On the occasion of their first breakfast together the housekeeper delivered one boiled egg to Father Tom Winder but nothing to Father Dee.

Dee waited expectantly for some addition to his meagre allotment of one slice of bread but he waited in vain.

'Do you like eggs, Father?' asked Winder.

'I love 'em,' said the curate.

'So do I,' said Winder. With that he took the cap off the egg and placed it in front of Dee.

'There is more nourishment in the cap of one hen-egg,' said Winder, 'than there is in a pound of meat.' After that Father Jim Dee ate out whenever possible. One of our late lamented bishops was once dined by Father Winder. There was buttered bread and roast beef. The bishop lifted a slice of bread and examined it.

'The man that buttered this bread,' said his Lordship, 'would grease the road from here to Dublin with one pound of butter.'

'Have you anything to say about the beef?' said Father Dee hopefully.

'Can you see through yours like I can through mine?' asked Dee.

'I can,' said the bishop. 'With a roast cut as thinly as this I could cover the walls of every bedroom in my palace.'

The only effect that this unkindly banter had on Winder was that he released a huge guffaw and slapped the bishop on the back.

'You're a gay and airy man my Lord,' said he. 'May the good God leave you gay and airy for many a day to come.'

You may wonder Joe about the hardness of my attitude towards your father. He married outside his Faith which means he turned his back on a true authority. For a man of his age and education to do this was irresponsible. Authority is what holds the world together. I accept the Pope as the be-all and end-all in authority. There are no deviations on my part from this complete acceptance. It is natural for me and nature is not easily checked. Your father failed when he ceased to accept the teachings of the Catholic Church. He thereby turned his back on the real meaning of authority, of respect for and maintenance of it. Without authority there can be no order. Without authority there can be no love or no peace. Abandon authority and you invite anarchy to your dominions. That is why I utterly reject and utterly detest anything which is opposed to authority. Authority is God.

If I seem adamantine about the Catholic Faith in regard to your father it is out of respect for authority. You see about you today what this lack of respect is leading to. In a sense the Pope is my father. I obey him and accept him as a child accepts the dictates of its parents. To defy the Pope is to destroy the meaning of authority with its attendant virtues such as the idea of peaceful co-existence, the idea of a true and lasting love, the rearing of a family, in fact all the virtues.

Those who oppose the laws of the Catholic Church oppose authority. In their youth or ignorance or plain fecklessness there are many priests and people who question the Pope's authority. They question his infallibility. They question traditions. What they are doing, whether they are aware of it or not, is rebelling childishly against authority because they find the necessary strictures of the Church too binding.

In or out of the Church these types will wreck community effort and order. They may be right in part. So what? We are all right in part even when we differ. None of our ideas are identical no more than our faces and bodies are, but there are no two ways if you are a member of the Catholic Church. It is the first and last authority. It is universal. Remember too that if I ever seem unbending in matters of Canon Law that I was suckled on the Code.

To return to Father Tom Winder. He lived to be ninety-two and in so doing survived most of his curates. Some day, some far-seeing curate or P.P., who knew him better than I, will do a book on him. 'He was so mean,' said poor Jimmy Dee, 'that if he was a ghost he wouldn't give you a fright.'

Here is what his housekeeper said about him: 'He was that perished,' said she, 'that he'd begrudge you the steam of his water.' Once during a confirmation breakfast he made eleven sandwiches out of two ounces of ham. That's one for the Guinness Book of Records. His parish clerk Dickie Molyneaux looked like Uriah Heep. He was paid a pittance and even the station money he received had to be divided with Winder. Dickie carried the altar wine around in a Baby Power bottle which he kept in his waistcoat pocket. He would produce the bottle during the Offertory. There was no bell but Dickie had iron tips on the heels of his boots and he would click those heels together whenever necessary. The sound was as good as that produced by a bell. The congregation took it for granted.

You may ask what Winder did with his money. No one ever found out. He disliked bishops and once when he saw several together was heard to remark: 'Will you look at the corpulent wretches strutting among the novices like drunken colonels in the Mexican army.'

Even when he was a curate he was mean. He once got a present of a case of Scotch. First of all he tried to sell it but he was so unpopular that he could get nobody to buy it off him.

He locked it in his chest. Every curate had a chest in those days. The housekeeper had a notorious tooth for the hot stuff and because of this Winder kept a close eye on the chest. As close as he watched it the whiskey began to disappear. Rightly or wrongly he suspected the housekeeper. What did he do but put a rabbit trap on top of the whiskey case. He cleverly fixed the chest so that it could only be partly opened. In other words whoever rifled inside would not see the trap until it was too late. He then told the housekeeper that he would be gone for the day. The day passed and when he arrived home it was dark. The housekeeper was sitting on a chair by the fire in the kitchen. Her hand was bandaged.

'Wisha what happened you girl?' he declared full of mock sympathy.

'Kiss me arse,' she said and no more. He was a hard and a merciless man.

When Father Dee first came to Winder he had a horse which he rode to his sick calls. When he went on a fortnight's holiday Winder did not give the horse a solitary sop of hay, blade of grass or grain of oats. The horse was hardly able to stand when Father Dee returned from his holiday.

At once the curate fed the poor animal with a large bucket of oats. Then he brought the horse indoors. Inside he led the animal around Winder's study several times until it had fully discharged itself.

I could go on all day but I have to hear confessions. Take care of yourself and write soon.

Your affectionate Uncle,
Martin O'Mora, P.P.

★ ★ ★

Loafer's Lane,
Lochnanane.

Dear Father O'Mora,
The Monster is a lamb. He havint come near me since.
You mus hav give him a grate talking to. He don't try
cum aroun me no more. You mus hav pourin the blessed
water on his fako. He still doun at the corner scratchin
hisself and countin the cars passin. What the cars do if he
not there.

Your fateful servant,
Rosie Monsey.

* * *

The Presbytery,
Lochnanane.

Dear Ray,
There is a character here called Jack Monsey who is
nicknamed the Monster by his unfortunate wife. She has
babies year in, year out and often every ten months. Apart
from this Jack does nothing except to hold up the village
corner from morning till night.

For weeks now she has been pestering me to talk to
Jack. Anyhow I got him into the Presbytery on the
grounds that I had some odd jobs for him. I have no
doubt whatever but that Rosie Monsey would die if she
was to have another baby. Jack Monsey is an ignorant
man and you will agree that if you want to get anywhere
with ignorance, ritual is the answer.

I put a white smock on Mocky Dolan the parish clerk
and held him in readiness while I interviewed Jack in the
sitting room. First I put Jack sitting down and then I
looked out the sitting room window for a full ten minutes.
You could almost hear the sweat oozing from his pores.

'Jack,' I said, 'it is my painful duty to inform you that
the Jesuits are on to you,' I let this sink in and watched
his face turn ashen grey.

'What did I do?' he asked.

'Something terrible indeed,' I told him, 'because the Jesuits never bother ordinary sinners.'

'Is there no hope for me?' he asked with a crack in his voice and the tears beginning to show in his eyes.

'Don't despair,' I advised him.

'There is a hope for every consostasite who is prepared to recant although in your case the situation may have gone too far. First of all you must give me your sacred word that you will refrain from having intercourse with your wife.'

'I never done that,' said he. 'I never stooped to that.'

'Jack,' I explained, 'intercourse means mounting your wife.' He nodded solemnly.

'You must give me your most sacred word that it will stop until such time as she can have no more babies. Nothing less than your sacred word will do.'

'Will you call the Jesuits off me if I do?' At this stage he was bawling.

'That I cannot promise,' I said, 'until the following obligations are fulfilled.' Again he nodded solemnly.

'First,' I told him, 'you must be resuminated and properly contracted. You must also be filtrated and fumigated and in order to do these things properly the bishop will have to be written to for a loan of vestments and the college of cardinals contacted for oil of olives.'

'Good God,' Jack cried out as he crossed himself. 'Help me Father,' he begged. It was precisely at this moment that I called in the parish clerk. He was well rehearsed. He liberally sprinkled Jack with holy water (which will do him no harm anyhow) and muttered some mumbo-jumbo under his breath. Jack was impressed. The parish clerk walked round him till he had made three full circles. He sprinkled him with more holy water and walked round him a second time till three more full circles were completed. Then the parish clerk withdrew walking slowly backwards, head bent, still muttering for all he was worth.

'Stand up,' I ordered Jack. He leaped to his feet. By this time he was trembling like a leaf but I reminded myself that watching a trembling ignoramus was better than looking at the mother of fourteen laid out on a slab.

'Jack Monsey,' I addressed him in a stentorian tone. 'You have now been made ready for consalmination.' He nodded eagerly.

'Do you promise,' I asked him, 'never to touch your wife's body until the doctor says it is safe to do so?'

'I promise,' he said. 'I promise. I promise. I promise.'

'Alright,' I told him, 'I will see what can be done for you. The final word will rest with Rome but be assured that the Bishops of Ireland will not be dumb when your case comes up.'

He clutched my hands in his and went on his knees thanking me. I sent him on his way. I had a letter from his wife a short time ago to thank me for what I had done for her. Apparently he has left her alone since. Only yesterday I sent Mary Teresa to fetch Rosie Monsey to the presbytery. We gave her a cup of tea and made her feel at ease. The poor woman never had a day off in her life apart from her confinements which never lasted more than two days believe it or not. One for Ripley surely.

We discovered that she has a sister married to a soldier in Cork. The sister's husband is a decent sort of man and on numerous occasions they asked her to the city for a few days. Between one thing and another she never got there. She once managed to put aside six pounds but the Monster found it and spent it on drink.

While the Monster is still recovering from the shock of our interview and conducting himself in an exceptional fashion by his standards we have decided to send her off to Cork to the sister. Her oldest girl can manage the house. I gave her enough for a decent holiday and enough to buy some new clothes. The poor woman was overcome. Ray would you believe it when I tell you that never once in her twenty years of marriage did she or one of her children eat a plate of rashers and eggs in that house. I may tell you that they will eat them from now on and I will personally see to it that she has a holiday every year. I do not want you volunteering to drive her to Cork, let her go by bus. It will be a bigger treat for her. My curate is gone to the dogs. He has women on the brain. He spends all day and all night chasing them. It looks as if I'll have to chat him up. Speaking about dogs. I was once a curate with Father Dick Hobbs. Dick, as you know, was a great man for the greyhounds.

He could never be found for parish duties when the track season started. The result was that the letters began to pour in to the bishop from well-meaning souls in the parish.

One day his Lordship arrived and took Dick aside.

'Dick,' he said, 'you know me. The last thing I want to do is interfere with the running of the parish but Dick you are rocking the boat.'

'In what way would I be rocking the boat my Lord?' said Dick innocently.

'I have it on good authority that you are more interested in greyhounds than in your parishioners,' said the bishop.

'There may be a grain of truth in that,' answered Dick, 'but my Lord it is not by choice. I am addled with thoughts of beautiful women. It is a terrible cross but I find that my interest in greyhounds negatives my interest in women.'

'Is that a fact?' said the bishop and he pulled his left earlobe.

'As God is my judge,' said Dick.

'Look,' said the bishop, 'don't worry any more about my visit. Try to train your dogs without attracting too much attention and everything will be alright.' With that the bishop departed and Dick trained his dogs with his head in the air from then on. A month later he had an urgent letter from the bishop requesting a greyhound pup.

As ever,
Martin.

★   ★   ★

St. Unshin's College,
Ballyrango.

Dear Uncle Martin,
There is little news from this place except that the play goes well and that I am progressing with my studies. I

love your stories. Was there ever a book of clerical anec-
dotes gathered from round the diocese. I'd love to do it
some time. I might even get an M.A. for it. I'm not
serious of course but it has the germ of a good idea. I
daresay the bishop's approval would be needed.

Last week we had a guest producer for a few days.
This man has a very original approach. Afterwards he
spoke to us about the modern theatre and modern poetry.
He made a scathing attack on the likes of Shelley and
Keats and said that their work was childish and idiotically
romantic. Jean disagreed with him but he made some
novel points.

How is Mary Teresa? That tip failed to materialise
but there should be others. Take care of yourself. I
look forward to Christmas. I need your advice on a few
matters.

Affectionately,
Joe.

★   ★   ★

Randle's Terrace,
Cork.

Dear Father O'Mora,
Just a line to let you know Im having a marvless time here
with pitchers every night and holy mass in the morning.
We go an we have chips after the pitchers and they are
luvey. I pray for you. Its a luvey time.

Your fateful servant,
Rosie Monsey.

★   ★   ★

St. Philomena's Nursing Home,
Lochnanane.

Dear Father O'Mora,
Your will find no name signed at the end of this letter but
please do not ignore it. Every word I say is true but I

dare not become involved. I am one of the staff here and I hope you will keep it a secret that you were put wise by one of the staff. This is very important to me.

One night last week a girl from the parish was rushed in by Doctor Mick Moffy. It was all hush-hush and instead of being put into one of the wards she was taken to Mrs. Clavey's private quarters. About two hours later she was taken to the labour ward and not too long afterwards a pair of twins was delivered. What makes me suspicious is that all the babies were taken down to be christened last Sunday at two o'clock but the twins were not taken at all. The mother of the twins left yesterday and it would seem that Doctor Claffy is now in control. The mother has gone back to work as if nothing happened. I do not wish to stir up trouble but I hope I am a good Catholic.

This summer I was in the lounge of a certain hotel in a certain seaside resort and near me were Doctor Moffy and his wife with two English visitors a husband and wife as well. From the conversation I gathered that he and Doctor Moffy had gone to the same university in Galway and that he was an engineer. They had no family and I think they had no religion unless maybe they were some sort of Protestants. During the talk I learned that the pair had no family and she made Doctor Moffy promise he would be on the look-out for a nice child with a good background to adopt.

'Maybe twins,' she said and she clapped her hands.

'Oh, I would love to adopt a pair of twins,' she said. If you put two and two together Father you will see what I mean. Are these twins destined for a non-Catholic home in England and who gives Doctor Moffy the right to hand them over.

I think this is a case where you should stop at nothing to save these Catholic infants from a faith worse than death.

Sincerely,
One who tries to be a
good Catholic.

★   ★   ★

The Presbytery,
Lochnanane.

Dear Joe,
Great to hear from you and glad that the studies and the
play go well. November is a lonely time everywhere in the
Catholic world. We are remembering our dead. It is a
month of mourning. I am amused by this new producer
especially since he knocks Shelley who was a great friend
to Irish Catholics in a time when friends were few. The
first verse of the only decent poem I ever learned in the
seminary at the age of thirteen was from Shelley's Cloud:

I bring fresh showers for the thirsting flowers,
From the seas and the streams;
I bear light shade for the leaves when laid
In their noonday dreams.
From my wings are shaken the dews that waken
The sweet buds every one
When rocked to rest on their mother's breast
As she dances about the sun.
I wield the flail of the lashing hail
And whiten the green plains under
And then again I dissolve it in rain
And laugh as I pass in thunder.

Ah well. Maybe that producer knows more than I do. I
look forward to Christmas too and to seeing you. I'll be
glad to give you any advice you want although, quite
honestly Joe, you always struck me as a man who needed
no advice from anybody. Speaking about advice I am
reminded of the advice the tinker gave to his son:
    'Mount away,' said he, 'but marry at home.'
    'Be sure,' said he, 'always to stand your horse in the
middle of the fair and to always take the morning price.'
    'Never go between a husband and wife for that is to go
between the bark and the tree. Most of all be sure to test
your friend before you need him.'
    The tinker hadn't much else to give but maybe what he
gave was better than money. I like the last piece. Test your
friend before you need him. It's worth remembering.

Joe I'll tell you something. When I was at the stage where you are at now I had problems, serious problems. I went to friends for advice but they had none to give. It is a tough and trying time with your subdeaconate coming up and celibacy to boot. Anyhow write and let me know what's troubling you, why wait till Christmas?

Your affectionate Uncle,
Martin O'Mora, P.P.

★   ★   ★

The Presbytery,
Lochnanane.

Dear Doctor Moffy,
I have come from Saint Philomena's Nursing Home where I have had a long and profitable chat with the proprietress, Mrs. Clavey. I have given instructions that those twins be baptised on Wednesday next. I'll countenance no objection. I have also been to the mother of the twins and I have got her to agree to sign a document transferring the twins to my care i.e. to a Catholic Orphanage of my choosing where they will remain until they are adopted by worthy Catholic parents. I would hereby ask you to refrain from visiting the twins again.

Yours in J.C.
Father Martin O'Mora.

★   ★   ★

The Dispensary,
Lochnanane.

Dear Father O'Mora,
I would like to remind you that we are not living in the middle ages when a superstitious and benighted peasantry believed that priests could turn them into goats. Your letter is a monstrous insult to my profession and to my personal integrity. Here is the full story of what happened.

One night last week I was called by the girl's mother to her home. She told me she feared that her daughter had an appendix and that she should have it out. Poor innocent woman.

I went upstairs to examine the girl and discovered that the appendix pains were not appendix pains at all. They were labour pains. I came downstairs and reported my findings to the mother whose only reaction was to scream selfishly and invoke the aid of that greatly overworked trio Jesus, Mary and Joseph. In an inkling she calmed down. 'She can't have it here,' she shouted, 'she can't have it here. Her father would strangle her. Her brothers would crucify her. What would the neighbours say. Oh Jesus doctor get her out of here.'

I did as this fine Christian parent told me and took the girl to Saint Philomena's where in order to avoid publicity I placed the girl in Mrs. Clavey's private quarters. Shortly thereafter I delivered the twins. Those twins are my responsibility. The day after I delivered them into this world of dictatorial clergymen and cowardly parents I rang a friend of mine, a professional man with a fine home and a good job not to mention a lovely wife.

To fulfil a promise I made to him some time ago I told him that he could have the twins. His wife came on the phone and begged me not to allow them be baptised until she found sponsors and arranged for a christening in her own town.

After I received your letter I went to the mother of the twins. She was at home with her own mother. I asked both the mothers to remember that it was I who helped them in their hour of need, who saved a reputation and arranged everything. They agreed that they owed more to me than to you.

The result was that I drew up a document declaring the note she gave to you to be manufactured under duress and that forthwith I was to be the sole and rightful guardian of the twins.

Sincerely yours,
Michael Moffy, M.B.

* * *

The Presbytery,
Lochnanane.

Dear Ray,
After Moffy's last letter I decided there was no point in further writing so I went and bearded the scoundrel in his den. 'You are here,' he said pompously, 'after dispensary hours.'

'I am here on God's business,' I told him.

'What do you want?' he asked.

'I want,' said I, 'that you stop interfering with God's work and keep away from those twins.'

'The twins are in my care,' he bellowed like a bull.

'The twins are in my parish and let's see you try to take them out of it?' I told him.

'I can see you have been talking to people,' he said. 'What about the reputation of the mother?'

'Which is more important,' I asked him, 'the reputation of a girl who is a known maleficent or the souls of two innocents? Will you damn them forever by allowing them to be brought up in another faith or maybe no faith at all?'

He laughed at this.

'Christ Almighty,' he said, 'why don't you pop back into the nineteenth century and stay there this time? What difference does it make what religion they have as long as they are happy and content?'

'They will not be baptised Protestants,' I warned him.

'How do you know they won't be Hindus?' he scoffed.

'Listen doctor,' I reminded him, 'maybe you don't care whether they are Catholics or not but they might when they are old enough to know.'

'Fine,' he said, 'let's wait till they're twenty-one and we'll ask them what they want to be. Maybe they might like to be Quakers or Lutherans or Mormons or Presbyterians. If they have any sense they'll have nothing to do with any of you. Now I'm a busy man Father and I have important reports to make out.'

'Those twins,' I told him finally, 'were born of a Catholic mother in a Catholic Nursing Home. The laws of God and State command that they be baptised Catholics.

Do not interfere further,' I warned him, 'or you will bring the wrath of God and the full force of the civil law on your head.' With that I slammed the door on him and walked off.

> I'll report further,
> As ever,
> Martin.

★ ★ ★

> The Elms,
> Loughnanane.

Dear Father O'Mora,
I have never troubled you up to this but I feel that you are the only one I can turn to. I am, as you probably know, a spinster and I live in retirement here at the Elms with my housekeeper Josephine Lalor.

Recently a local drunkard, Sammy Seller has been causing me some annoyance and embarrassment not to mention the embarrassment he causes other people. I cannot quite bring myself to tell you what it is wrong but I suppose I had better begin somewhere.

On his way home he persists in urinating at the entrance to the avenue leading to my house. He exposes himself for long periods and even when the children are on their way home from school or old ladies are passing he refuses to button himself. It is all dreadfully embarrassing and I am afraid to go to the Guards in case they might expect me to act as a witness to this sordid and revolting business. You are the one person I feel I can trust.

The other evening he was there so long that my housekeeper Josephine went down the avenue. I feel I oughtn't tell you how she addressed him but it has to be told.

'Get out of here you tramp,' she screamed at him, 'and stop showing off your dirty oul' drumstick while you're urinating.'

'That's what it's for,' he called back at her, 'for urinating. That's what I got it for. It helps get the water out.'
What are we to do, Father? Please help us.

Sincerely yours,
Cliona O'Gairea.

★   ★   ★

The Presbytery,
Loughnanane.

Dear Joe,
How goes it? I have been fairly busy with important matters and that is the reason for the delay in writing. I won't trouble you with some recent happenings here except to tell you that that ruffian Sammy Seller has been up to his old tricks again. He must have been fined in the local court at least twenty times for indecent exposure or urinating in public places. I never interfered until the other evening. I got a report that he was piddling publicly above and beyond the call of duty at the gate leading to O'Gairea's old house just outside the village. I wrote to Miss O'Gairea and told her to give me a ring on the phone if he troubled her again.

The following evening the phone rang. It was Miss O'Gairea. She informed me that our friend Sammy was up to his old tricks. I hopped into the car and in a minute I was at the scene of the crime. There he was with one hand resting on the wall in front of him and the other holding his lightning rod. I did not wait to see whether he was piddling or showing off. I got out of the car and approached him noiselessly from behind. I had on my strong boots. When I found myself within range I drew back and I let him have a mighty kick in the posterior. He jumped five feet in the air.

'My bum is burst,' he cried out. I let him have a second dose of the boot on the same target. I am prepared to lay you odds that he will never expose himself publicly again.

I suppose you could say that it was just another incident in the daily routine of the parish. Reports about like happenings come in all the time. Once a week without fail there is a plea from some unfortunate wife to come and talk to her husband. It follows a pattern. There she is, at maybe three or four o'clock in the morning in her nightgown, huddled up with the cold against the doorway having been ejected for no reason by a drunken husband or maybe 'tis how the poor creature would have her bag packed to go home or if there was no home then anywhere so long as there would be a respite from the blackguarding she receives. It is the function of the priest to resolve these problems. There is nobody else to do it.

You have heard the expression, man's inhumanity to man, but believe me Joe there is nothing as awful as the inhumanity of husband to wife. Much of it may be the wife's fault and it is my task to find out where the blame lies and to apportion the blame fairly. Most couples want reconciliation desperately and it is a pleasure to steer them on a proper course. With others it is a waste of time. In nearly all cases it is the fault of the husband. Drink is a wonderful thing in moderation but drink in the belly of an inconsiderate or selfish husband means misery for his unfortunate wife. We Irish have many virtues and many faults. If I was asked to list our worst fault I would point a finger at the drunken husband.

Yesterday I planted twenty chestnut trees, ten at either end of the drive. When I'll be dead and gone some priest will remember me kindly, far kindlier than I remember Father John Clement Fitzraymond. He never planted a shrub not to mention a tree.

Here's one for your collection. When Canon Dring received his first parish he was visited by an old woman who told him that she wanted Mass said for her late husband.

'That will be a guinea, missus,' said Dring.

'I haven't any money, Canon,' said the old woman.

'High money for high mass,' said Dring, 'low money for low mass and no money for no mass.'

'But,' said the old woman, 'all the new priests oblige me by saying a free mass for him.'

'How long is he dead?', asked Dring.

'Thirty years, Canon,' said the old woman.

'Missus,' said Dring, 'a Mass won't make the slightest difference to him at this stage but that is not to say I would turn you away were you to come back with a guinea.'

My new curate is a pain.

'There will have to be a raise,' he announced at breakfast yesterday. There is a law which says a curate is entitled to eleven pounds ten shillings a year. The law was never repealed. According to this law he is entitled to free firing from the first of November to the first of April. He can keep mass offerings and he gets his cut (quite substantial) from the November offerings. At the stations he gets Petrol Money. This was known as Oats money when there were no motor cars. In short he gets plenty and if he works his loaf he can put himself in the way of many an offering. With the right approach he could treble his income.

'I am not obliged to give you a raise,' I informed him.

'Fair enough,' he said.

'Are you short of money?' I asked. 'I have been short of money since the day I came here,' he said.

'Don't be smart,' I told him, 'I know how much you're knocking down.'

'Look,' he said, 'I want a new car.'

'So do I,' I told him.

'I should have known what to expect,' he said.

'Listen here now my boy,' I started, 'I will take no lip form you. Is it how you think I don't know you're out till all hours chatting up dames? Is it how you think I wouldn't know the smell of stale brandy as good as the next man? I was a curate too remember. You would do well to change your tack,' I told him. I was about to continue when he rose from the table. 'You're as big a bore as Pope Paul,' he said, 'and that's some bore.'

That was his curtain line. He has been dining out since, no doubt with those eejits of women in the upper crust here. I'll close now. Take care of yourself.

Your affectionate uncle,
Martin O'Mora, P.P.

* * *

The Presbytery,
Lochnanane.

Dear Ray,
The drama of the Terrible Twins, as I will call it, is all
over and I am sorry to have to say that victory went to
Doctor Moffy. I'll start at the beginning. Last Saturday
morning I got a call from Mrs. Clavey, proprietress of
Saint Philomena's Nursing Home. She told me that Doctor Moffy had stolen the twins and was on his way to
Shannon Airport, presumably to take them to England
and place them in the hands of his Protestant fellow-con-
spirators.

I rounded up the curate and ordered him to ring every
presbytery between here and Shannon. Then I went
straight to the Guards' Barracks and notified them. There
was an immediate alert. The local patrol car set out at
once but broke down after three miles. The only patrol
car available within a radius of thirty miles set off in hot
pursuit but a puncture soon put an end to her daring bid.
The spare was soft and there was no pump so she was
rendered hors de combat too.

It was now up to the Church alone and the Church
was not found wanting. Like chain reaction one parish
notified its neighbour and the upshot was that there were
a hundred pairs of eyes between Shannon and the village
of Lochnanane on the look-out for the Doctor's Mercedes.

He never showed up in this route so I became suspicious. Was there a middleman. I had to wait till nightfall
to discover the truth. Here is what happened. After ab-
sconding with the twins he changed cars a mile from
Lochnanane. He transferred his little charges to the other
car and hit for Cork. You will have to agree that nobody
knows the backroads better than a dispensary doctor.
Anyhow he got away and handed over the children to a
couple in Cork. The couple are Catholics, well thought-of
and well-off. He might have told me that he wasn't hand-
ing them over to Protestants. He now wants an apology. I
did what I thought best. He will get no apology from me.
He is going around the pubs accusing me of bigotry. I
have my sources. Here is what he said at one pub:

'O'Mora,' said he, 'is suffering from an overdose of racial memory aggravated by religious bigotry.'

Let-him alone. He'll prove to be his own undoing one day. He'll never get an apology from me. Call when you get a chance.

As ever,
Martin.

★   ★   ★

Church Street,
Lochnanane.

Dear Father O'Mora,

I don't know am I doing right or wrong in writing to you. God knows I have been on my knees long enough trying to come to a decision. The notion to let you know what's going on has me possessed this good bit but I decided that after what happened last night I would have to inform you.

Sometimes my line of work keeps me out late and I see things that I am not meant to see. I live a few doors from the house of Daisy Redlap in Church Street. A fortnight ago the piano was going in that house till half-past one in the morning. From half-eleven till one o'clock Miss Redlap herself did the singing but from one on she was joined by a male voice. He was a tenor, quite good and I was most anxious to find out who it was as I hadn't heard the voice in the Lochnanane Church Choir.

The night's entertainment ended with the song, 'Beautiful Dreamer.' After that there was silence for several minutes. Then I heard a door bang in the street so I tiptoed downstairs to see who was the owner of the excellent voice. As I opened the street door your curate Father Carrity was just passing by. There wasn't a sign of another Christian on the street. It must have been him that was doing the singing.

'Good-night, my child,' he said to me very sarcastic in tone.

'Good-night, Father,' said I, 'you're out very late.'

'A sick call,' he said gaily and went off towards the presbytery whistling. That was a fortnight ago. He has been at Redlap's every night since but last night crowned it. They sang till half-past four and as the night wore on the singing got worse. Very uneven and a trifle harsh. As soon as I heard the door bang I went downstairs for a breath of fresh air. Your curate was coming up the street taking the two sides of it. 'Good-night, Father,' I said, 'you're out very late again.'

'God's work,' he stammered and he nearly collapsed at my feet. I steered him towards the presbytery. I will say no more as I know you will take care of the matter. It is not for us to judge.

Sincerely,
One who tries to be a good Catholic.

P.S.: I'm past 40 and when I first went to Secondary school, Daisy Redlap was doing her leaving.

O.W.T.T.B.A.G.C.

★   ★   ★

The Presbytery,
Lochnanane.

Dear Joe,
Enjoyed your letter. I am indeed glad that you hit it off so well with your father. As I have told you so often you must never allow my opinion of him to influence you. I will be at Mallow to meet your train on Saturday week. Eight days is a goodly spell and I look forward to having you. I enclose twenty-five pounds in case you decide to buy your Christmas presents early.

Now about this girl Jean. I understand your feelings. There was a girl in my life too. Under no circumstances must you withdraw from the play. There is an old Greek saying: 'it is not by running away from evil that we overcome it but by going to meet it.' Not that Jean is evil in the sense implied or indeed in any sense but if you fail to come to terms with this problem what chance will you have against the harsher and weightier problems that will beset you as the years go by. No Joe. Withdrawing from the play will not help you dismiss Jean.

Anyhow you are doing no wrong. You think of the girl a lot. You favour her beauty and seek her company. She intrudes on your meditations and capriciously she invades your studies. This is all natural and you must not think that yours is an isolated or even an exceptional case.

Let us face squarely up to the problem. You say your friendship with Jean is something special. I would expect it to be nothing else. She is a beautiful and intelligent young girl. You are a handsome and brilliant young man. You became attracted to each other inevitably but you must now ask yourself what is the value of such an attraction. You must ask yourself if it has a spiritual worth. To the latter I would answer yes because it is a pure friendship. It will ennoble you at least and properly cultivated the ultimate outcome must be sublimity.

Let us take the phrase 'properly cultivated.' By this is meant the effort to knock the last ha'porth as it were out of a friendship and so develop it into something worthwhile. Your best efforts then should be directed towards adapting this fine friendship so that it will not harass your vocation but rather strengthen it.

If the girl causes you anguish or pain, if there is a spiritual ache then you must succumb or you must adopt a tough and resilient approach. You must find a pocket for this girl in the mental apparel of your vocation, a pocket which will contain her until time erases the charm she holds for you.

There is no shame in succumbing. She is a devout and pure girl and would make a splendid wife. Indeed purely from a selfish point of view I would favour this. I would like the company of children and love to have you and your wife near me in my declining years but I think Joe that you were cut out for priesthood. I cannot see you truly happy in any other situation. I think we both know this.

Anyhow think on what I've said and we'll talk further at Christmas.

> Your affectionate Uncle,
> Martin O'Mora.

★ ★ ★

> Church Street,
> Lochnanane.

Dear Father O'Mora,
Since I last wrote to you the postition has not changed. The banging at the piano goes on till all hours every night. If you care to look into the dustbin at the back of Redlap's any Thursday, that's the collection day, you will see the empty brandy bottles.

I don't mind a person having a drink and a bit of a sing-song but this whacks all. It was half past two this very morning of the day I'm writing. It was fine outside and she came to the door with him when he was leaving. Talk about laughing and skitting. As he passed up I said 'Good night, Father.' 'Ah 'tis you is it,' he said cheerily, 'you can go to bed now. I'm going home.'

> Devotedly,
> One who tries to be a good Catholic.

★ ★ ★

> The Dispensary,
> Lochnanane.

Dear Father O'Mora,
I await your apology. I do not want to write to the bishop but if the apology is not forthcoming by return post that is exactly what I will do.

> Sincerely,
> Moffy, M.B.

★ ★ ★

The Presbytery,
Lochnanane.

Dear Ray,

I've just left the courthouse where the dance-hall extensions were reviewed by Cormac O'Lunaigh, the circuit court judge. I'm afraid I fared badly. Grattan, the proprietor of the dance-hall, applied for twenty-four extensions till the hour of one o'clock in the morning. On the instructions of the bishop I opposed.

'Why do you oppose?' O'Lunaigh asked.

'Because the bishop instructed me to do so.'

'And why did he instruct you to do so?'

'Because the hours are too late.'

'What is your personal opinion?' he asked.

'I think that any boy or girl should have enough danced at twelve o'clock. It really is a question of morals.'

'What,' said he with a sneer, 'is the difference between the morals of the diocese of Limerick and your diocese, Father?'

'No difference,' I said.

'Then how is it?' he asked, 'that it is permissible to dance all the year round in Limerick till one o'clock in the morning but not in Lochnanane, or so your bishop and yourself would have it.'

'I'm afraid,' I said, 'I cannot answer that.'

'I see,' he said and he peered at me for my reactions. He also peered at Grattan for his. I must say that Grattan looked aggrieved and despondent. He wore a coat with frayed sleeves, a ragged shirt without a collar and a week's beard. There was a suggestion of a tear in one eye. He was a sorry sight. You would never think that a month before he offered forty thousand pounds for a farm.

'This poor man must not be deprived of his livelihood,' said O'Lunaigh. 'I hereby grant the extensions.'

It was Grattan's demeanour and dress that carried the day for him plus of course his reactions whenever the judge peered at him in that penetrating way that judges have who keep their heads down during most of the trial.

I don't care who the judge is or how learned he is or even if he was appointed on merit (that'll be the day) he will be deceived by reaction. A witness of Grattan's sort is masterly in cunning and has his reactions carefully rehearsed. The judge knew too that it would be a popular decision. He cutely cautioned Grattan that if he abused the privilege that Grattan would suffer for it. In this way O'Lunaigh was hugging the shores of authority and exhibiting the same sort of duplicity as the knaves who put him where he is. See you Friday.

As ever,
Martin.

* * *

Church Street,
Lochnanane.

Dear Father O'Mora,
I see that the hours get later by your curate. There is no singing now. All is quiet and one gets suspicious about what is going on. What can they be doing all alone together for four and five hours at a time. Is it right or natural? I thought in writing to you that it would stop. At least when they were singing we knew what they were at but what are they doing now?

I think the bishop must be made to know of this carry-on since you seem not to care one way or the other.

Obediently,
One who tries to be a good Catholic.

* * *

The Presbytery,
Lochnanane.

Dear Doctor Moffy,
I will never apologise. It would be the same as apologising for my religion. Anyhow I would not dream of bending the knee to a cur.

Yours in J.C.,
Martin O'Mora, P.P.

* * *

The Presbytery,
Lochnanane.

Dear Joe,
All is back to normal here after Christmas. The curate
would put you off your breakfast with his eyes back in his
head from being up all night. When I attempt to say
something he raises a hand reproachfully and motions me
to silence. For the sake of harmony I say nothing till
lunchtime. Yesterday I told him he was keeping very
erratic hours, hours that might be injurious to his health.
'We must not think of ourselves,' he answered mockingly
and sanctimoniously, 'I always put parish duties before
my health. That is what the priesthood is all about.'

So saying he rose unsteadily and in a series of moves
something like those of an attacking Fijian rugby fullback
negotiated the door. I saw no more of him till supper time
when he appeared fresh, sober and in excellent fettle. He
went off to hear confessions. I'm sure that's where he gets
the money. He is a great hand with the ladies but to me
are left the hundred and one duties that make up the
successful running of a parish. Today it might be the
giving of a pledge to a drunkard who beats his wife.
Tomorrow could find me knocking at the door of a house
to break the news of a traffic accident. The father of a
young family may have been killed while cycling home
from work or a mother and child killed when their car was
struck by a lorry. The day after I might be consoling the
mother of a son who has just been jailed for theft or
violence. This very moment the phone might ring with
news of a disaster for some unfortunate family. I often ask
myself why does God let these things happen and I am
stymied for an answer. Accepting God's will is never easy
for those who suffer. God is the only scapegoat who does
not defend himself.

You asked in your letter for the story of the Castle-
killingham Come-Uppance. It's a long story; perhaps during the next few months.

Speaking about confessions reminds me of our late
friend Canon Dring of Killaveg. Canon Dring would
never hear confessions for the good reason that he did not

benefit financially in the box. The result was that the curate Tom Kilmartin was always stuck and could never go home to nourish himself over a long week-end. Eventually he thought of a number. After leaving the confessional one night he went into the presbytery kitchen where the house-keeper Nellie Dwan was sitting by a pale fire. In Nellie's presence he started to take bundles of pound notes (bor-rowed) from his pockets. Then half to himself he said 'I'll never get all these masses said.'

Needless to say Nellie reported at once to Canon Dring. Father Tom was relieved of confessional duties there and then and Canon Dring took over.

I must raise seven thousand pounds shortly. The National School needs to be extended. There is no doubt but that the Department of Education has right hares made out of the Parish Priests of Ireland. I am a school manager. In addition I am expected to build schools. I inspect schools regularly yet I receive no salary from the Department although I am worth to them at least three thousand pounds a year. I don't know why I do it unless it is in the best interests of the children.

We are expected to appoint teachers, to interview them and often provide houses for them, yet not a penny in return. All I ever made by appointing teachers was a dangerous huddle of enemies in the persons of those I didn't appoint. A teacher in the sulks is a deceptive and unpre-dictable adversary as you will find out all too soon. I would sooner wrestle an orang-utang than face a deluded school-master. There was once a teacher from Castlepellick with the mad eyes of a sparrow-hawk who threatened to shoot his parish priest. Apparently the priest appointed somebody else to be school principal. The priest died suddenly. Some said he died from the fright but the mother of the losing candidate said he was struck down by the hand of God.

Two daffodils have just shown their orange ears at the lee of the house. I expect that they shall be followed shortly by hundreds of others. Write soon.

Your affectionate uncle,
Martin O'Mora, P.P.

* * *

Bishop's House.

Memo. to Father Martin

Martin,
Two disturbing letters to hand. One has to do with your
curate. Speak to him or I will. Have it out to the end with
him and no pussy-footing. The other is from Doctor
Moffy. I cannot make you do anything against your will
but I suggest you do the big thing and apologise.
     You are doing great work. When the extension is built
I may have something in mind for you. Keep up the good
work.

In haste,
Mick.

★   ★   ★

The Presbytery,
Lochnanane.

Dear Doctor Moffy,
I apologise unreservedly for my recent behaviour towards
you. I sincerely hope you will see your way to forgiving
me.

Sincerely,
Martin O'Mora, P.P.

★   ★   ★

The Dispensary,
Lochnanane.

Dear Father O'Mora,
All is forgiven.

Moffy, M.B.

★   ★   ★

The Presbytery,
Lochnanane.

Dear Ray,
I am after a session with my curate which beats all I ever
experienced. The session was not initiated by yours truly.
There was a sharp memo from the boss, a sort of do-it-or-
else injunction which could not be ignored. I decided to
wait for him this very morning. At two-fifteen I heard his
key in the lock. In the hallway he shook the hailstones
from his hat and from the shoulders of his overcoat. He
could and should have disposed of these hailstones before
coming indoors but he is of a very perverse and vexatious
nature. He headed in the general direction of the kitchen
singing 'Beneath thy Window.' After a few minutes I
followed him to the kitchen where he was eating tinned
salmon and a few slices of bread and butter. He produced
a bottle of beer from his trousers pocket, opened it and
poured it into a glass. It was then he saw me for the first
time.

'Come in, come in,' he called expansively. I was already in at this stage.

'Have a seat,' he invited. Then he motioned to the
victuals. 'Help yourself,' he said. I took a seat and said
nothing for a while. I could see that he was nicely although he was far from being drunk.

'This is a great little country we're living in,' he announced. I decided to wait a while longer before acquaint-
ing him of my purpose.

'Where would you get butter the like of this,' he said
and he held a lump aloft on his knife. 'Or tell me,' he
went on, 'where would you find a curate drinking beer
and eating tinned salmon at this hour. I tell you we don't
half appreciate this country. You are very serious looking,
Father. Is there to be some sort of confrontation?'

'Finish your snack,' I advised him.

'Oh I would be doing that anyway,' he said with a
shake of the head. 'I never let anything interfere with my
eating. No future in it. There are too many honest men
suffering from ulcers.' He was enjoying himself immensely
at my expense. Finally he finished off the salmon, the

bread and the beer. He then wiped his mouth with a dishcloth.

'Well, now,' he said, 'let's hear from you.' With that he folded his arms and closed his eyes. 'I can concentrate better with my eyes shut,' he explained.

'There have been letters,' I said.

'I know,' he said, 'and what is more I know from whom.'

'You know more than I do,' I told him. 'Anyhow,' I went on, 'there have been letters from other sources.' He laughed at this. 'I didn't realise I was so famous,' he said.

'The bishop,' I said, cutting in on him, 'has asked me to talk to you.'

'About what?' he asked.

'About your comings and goings at all hours of the morning,' I said, 'about keeping company with a woman when the whole village is in bed. About staggering on the village street blind drunk on occasion.'

'What woman?' he asked.

'Miss Daisy Redlap,' I told him. He rubbed his jaw at this, opened his eyes and pursed his lips. It was obvious that he had more drink taken than I first thought.

'Miss Daisy Redlap,' he repeated.

'Yes,' I said.

'Does this mean I am not to see her again?'

'It would look like it,' I told him.

'Who is going to prevent me from seeing her?' he asked.

'The bishop,' I said.

'It's a free country,' he said, 'and if the bishop don't like the way I come and go that's tough cheese on the bishop.'

I must confess, Ray, that I was shocked at this. 'Do you realise what you are saying?' I entreated him.

No better man,' he said and he rose from the table. 'You can tell the bishop from me,' he shouted, 'that if he don't mind his own business I might jack the whole thing up.'

'You are drunk,' I said, 'you don't realise what you are saying. We'll talk in the morning when you are sober.'

He pushed me back on to the chair.

'We will talk now,' he roared at the top of his voice. 'If I hear as much as another word out of you or the bloody bishop I'll blow the hell out of here to England and get a job teaching. I might even take Daisy with me.'

'You're mad,' I told him, 'you realise I will have to report all this to the bishop.'

'Man dear,' he laughed, 'I don't give a tinker's curse about the bishop. This is a free country. There is nothing you or the bishop can do to me. I wish I had another bottle of beer.'

I tried a change of tune.

'Daisy Redlap,' I advised him, 'is twice your age.'

'Lies,' he roared. 'Lies.'

'She is over fifty,' I told him. 'You are only twenty-seven.'

'You're jealous,' he said. He then grabbed me by the throat.

'If you so much as mention her name again,' he threatened, 'I'll guzzle you.' He was obviously out of his mind on the occasion so I said nothing. He released me suddenly.

'Sorry,' he said, 'I shouldn't have done that.'

Without another word he went upstairs to bed. Over the breakfast table I told him that I would forget about the night before if he promised to keep fairly regular hours and cut down on his drinking.

'I'll do what I can,' he promised. He seemed to mean it but then his attitude changed.

'Dammit,' he said, 'I want to be honest with you. It was my mother the bitch who made me into a priest. I hadn't the guts or the manliness to stand up to her. She used to boast about me. Lies every word. I lived a lie all the time. I'm living a lie now.'

'We've all had our problems,' I tried to console him. 'Yours could turn you into a great priest. Problems solve themselves as the months go by.'

'I still have mine,' he cried almost in tears. 'Do you think that I don't know that Daisy Redlap is older than I. I still want her and I can't drive her from my thoughts. I've always wanted women. I loved their softness, their bulging whiteness. I've craved for them, I've screamed in my anguish for them. That's what I see in Daisy Redlap. She's bulging and plump and white beyond words, beyond my wildest dreams. Sometimes when she barely stirs she shudders and shivers all over. Her trembling tortures me when she moves from one place to another.'

'You will have to go on retreat,' I told him, 'there is no other way.'

He calmed down at once.

'I suppose you're right,' he said.

'I'll arrange it,' I told him.

'Yes, yes,' he whispered, 'do that for me Father.'

He arose and withdrew. I presume he will re-appear at supper. I heard through the grapevine that you are having chest pains again. Take care and rest. I will take you to see a friend of mine in Cork next week-end. Good men are scarce. Be ready early on Sunday afternoon. I'll ring tomorrow or after.

As usual,
Martin.

★　★　★

St. Unshin's,
Ballyrango.

Dear Uncle Martin,

The play opened last night and went well. We started shakily which is understandable since we had time only for one dress rehearsal. As the night wore on, however, we really got to grips with it and afterwards everybody agreed that we had done an excellent job considering our limitations. A few of the lads here have varying accounts of the Castlekellingham Come-Uppance. I promised I would ask you for the correct version. When did it happen? Who was involved? Is it considered a scandal etc.? I realise how busy you must be with your curate the way he is but if you got a chance some night I would really appreciate if you sat down and wrote us an account of it. Give my fond regards to herself.

As ever,
Your affectionate nephew,
Joe.

★ ★ ★

The High Valleys,
Lochnanane.

Dear Father O'Mora,
I am a married woman whose family is done for and all gone their ways abroad in the world from their home in the High Valleys. My husband and I were always united and happy until two months ago he got a parcel from his brother Martin in Chicago. First I thought the contents was a rubber boat or the like but I found out in time it was a rubber woman that could be pumped up with air or filled with warm water until it became the size and shape and colour of a fine figure of a young woman exactly the same in appearance as Dolores Viago, the famous film star that was in voyage to mars. She has glass eyes, dark with long lashes exactly the same as the real Dolores and when she is squeezed she sighs like a real person from some gadget under her oxter. My husband has gone crazy over her and buying the like of a watch for her and some nice clothes and underwear. I do not know what to do Father. There are more cases than me here in the High Valleys which was always a holy and contented place where the Rosary is never missed in any house even still but he puts Dolores Viago in the trimmings and puts her alongside him and says a decade in a woman's voice, by the way it would be her talking. He answers in his own voice and I answer too for the sake of quietness. Others have their false women too but it was my brother-in-law Martin that sent the first one. Then they all started writing for one. I only saw one other. She is the image of Mrs. Freddie Fox-Pelley who rides the horses on T.V. except she hasn't a stitch of clothes on her.

Will you guide us Father out of this evil pass. Pray for us Father. Our men are shoving into the years and are turning a bit foolish. Frighten them Father so they would forget this nonsense.

> Yours faithfully,
> Noreen Hannassy (Mrs.).

★   ★   ★

> The Presbytery,
> Lochnanane.

Dear Joe,
Always great to hear from you. The greatest poker player that ever lived, in the opinion of those who ought to know, was the late Father Fonsie Lynd of Lackira. A few others preferred the late Dynamite Carey who was an authority on the finer points of the game. Dynamite was often consulted where there were no rules of the house. Fonsie was a tight-fisted man but you could not call him mean. He had great points. His is another instance of a missing fortune. When he died there was no trace of his money save for a few hundred pounds in his bank account. I'll tell you something which I was once told by the administrator of a certain diocese in Germany.

She assured me that a certain Swiss Bank was bulging with the money of more than a few Irish P.P.s who over-estimated their lives' spans. In answer to your major question let me assure you that the 'Come-Uppance' was not a scandal. Every diocese has its scandal but this is not ours.

Anyhow Fonsie Lynd was one of the Principals of the Castlekellingham Come-Uppance. Jim Lollery, the County Engineer was another. My dear friend Father Ray Tubridy was a third. Ray is not well by the way. His chest pains continue, growing worse all the time. The fourth was a close friend of mine, a shopkeeper named Neddy Lackin. The fifth was Doctor Petey Wyse and the final member of the once famous Castlekellingham poker school was your beloved uncle whose hand is to this letter.

During the long winter months we would meet, the six of us, in the Castlekellingham C.Y.M.S. Hall where we would play a modest game on Monday and Thursday nights. We did not play in the common room of the hall but in the caretaker's office, a cosy place with a bright turf fire. It was at the rear of the building. The game was usually of the two-shilling-up-the-dealer variety but some of us would skip deals if the action was dull. Often we would have a last pot for a pound-up-the-dealer. A loser might recoup all his night's losses if he won this, the last and most valuable pot. The night of the Come-Uppance as it is now called was the fourth night of January nine years ago. We had not met since before Christmas and we were anxious for a game.

I won the first pot. I won it with a flush of clubs against Doctor Petey Wyse who had two pair and Neddy Lackin who had small trips. It was the hottest game of poker I ever played from the third hand on. Every player was involved all the way through but steadily, surely the money started to drift towards the maestro, Father Fonsie Lynd. The heaviest loser was Jim Lollery, which was a pity, because he was a poor loser, being notoriously short-tempered and tightfisted. It is also a part of diocesan poker history that he hated Fonsie Lynd's guts. He had lost too much to him over the years.

It wanted five minutes to twelve so we decided to play the last pot. It was Fonsie's deal. He paused for a moment and then he threw a five pound note on the table. 'The dealer makes it a fiver,' he announced, 'and I am skipping.'

He handed the cards to Lollery who threw up a fiver and also skipped his deal. Out of sheer bravado we all skipped so that there were thirty pounds in the pot. It was Ray's deal. Kings were openers and as he dealt his hands trembled. Slowly he counted out the cards. Every face was pale except that of Father Fonsie Lynd. Fonsie was the same as always. He belonged at where he was at. He was master of the situation. After an agonising two minutes the cards were dealt out. Every man clutched his allowance of five and slowly each prized his apart.

'It's open,' said Father Fonsie with a ring of triumph in his voice. He produced his wallet and extracted fifteen pounds. 'Anyone who wants to play,' he said, 'plays for fifteen pounds.'

Slowly, almost painfully wads and wallets were produced. All of us signified our intention of playing with him. We placed our stakes in the pot. All looked in the direction of Jim Lollery who had made no decision or had given no indication of any kind that he was playing. He looked at the pot and moistened his lips. He repeated this gesture over and over until he had fully surveyed the terrain.

'Alright,' he said in a tone which it was difficult to associate with him in normal circumstances. 'I am hardening this pot to thirty quid.'

Some sighed but all showed their willingness to participate. Duly the pot was filled until in the centre of the table was a heap of notes totalling two hundred and ten pounds.

Discards were thrown to one side and the filling of hands commenced.

Father Fonsie Lynd bought three cards to a pair of kings. I bought one card to a nine high straight. Neddy bought one card to four of a flush. Doc Wyse bought three to a pair of knaves. Jim Lollery bought two to three deuces and Ray who was dealer and last for cards bought one card to sevens and eights. Carefully he put the remainder of the cards aside. It was up to Fonsie Lynd. It was he who opened the pot. Fonsie was never a man for beating about the bush.

'I'll bet a hundred,' he said. So saying he produced his cheque book, took one out, signed it and threw the blank cheque on top of the pot. This was teetotally unprecedented. It was frightening.

All threw in their cards except one man. That man's name was Jim Lollery. He placed his to one side and rubbed his hands together. A smile showed on his face.

'Did you say a hundred?' he asked.

'I believe I did,' said Fonsie without batting an eyelid.

'I'll tell you what I'll do,' said Lollery. 'I'll make it two.'

'Four,' said Fonsie as if he were passing the time of day. I felt like pinching myself. A four hundred pound pot on a two-shilling-up-the-dealer game of poker? Was I dreaming. 'Boys,' said Ray in a shaking voice, 'let this be the end of it. The fun is gone from our game. Withdraw the bets and let the better of the two of you take the pot. Divide it if necessary.'

'Keep out of this you fool,' Lollery directed at him.

'Sorry Ray,' said Fonsie cutting in sharply on Lollery. 'But a bet is a bet. I am making it four hundred pounds, Lollery. Are you looking or aren't you?'

'I am making it eight hundred pounds, Father,' Lollery said coldly and with this he located his cheque book. He signed the cheque and wrote out the amount. He placed the cheque directly in front of Fonsie.

Fonsie never batted an eyelid. 'That's a lot of money,' he mused without showing the slightest sign of emotion.

'Fill the amount in your cheque if you want to look at my hand,' Lollery told him. 'It's getting late and I can wait no longer.' He pretended he was about to sweep in the pot. Fonsie withdrew his cheque from the middle of the heap and filled it in.

'Declare,' Fonsie ordered.

'Two pairs,' said Lollery with a grin.

'Too bad,' said Fonsie. 'I have a full house consisting of kings on the roof.' He put down his cards and was about to draw in the pot when Lollery intercepted him.

'You mustn't have heard me right,' he said.

'I heard you loud and clear,' said Fonsie, 'you said you had two pairs. I have a full house and a full house beats two pairs anytime.'

'I accept that,' said Lollery with a broad grin, 'but my two pairs are two pairs of deuces.' So saying he threw down the four deuces where everybody could see them. Then he proceeded to haul in the pot which at this stage totalled one thousand eight hundred and ten pounds.

'Hold it right there mister,' Fonsie announced suddenly. 'You declared two pairs. I declared a house. I don't care if you have four deuces. I am judging your hand by what you declared. You declared you had two pairs of deuces. You therefore lose the pot.' Someone muttered approval although the rest of us felt that Fonsie's assertion was outrageous and ridiculous. 'Absolute rubbish,' Lollery laughed and he made a second attempt to gather his winnings. It was then that Fonsie stood up. He spoke slowly.

'That pot is mine,' he said, 'and anybody who thinks otherwise is asking for trouble.'

Lollery looked for redress from one of our faces to another and although most of us felt that the pot should be his we showed no sympathy. There was a stalemate. Lollery was nonplussed.

'Look,' he said, 'will you stop doing the fool and let me rake in my lawful winnings.'

'They are not lawful,' Fonsie insisted. So the argument wore on for over an hour. At length it was agreed by both parties that the issue should be decided by Father Donal (Dynamite) Carey. Lollery was confident that he would get the verdict. So was I. So were the others excepting Neddy. It was exactly three weeks to the day before Dynamite dropped dead. We found him in his study at 1.30 a.m. reading Honore de Balzac. There was a bottle of whiskey by his side and a half filled glass in one of his hands. He was surprised to see us but he received us warmly.

'Martin,' he said to me, 'pour the boys a shot of the Goddam dynamite.'

I filled drinks all round and on his instructions replenished his own glass. We sat down. From my pocket I withdrew the stake money. I placed it on a table and laid bare the facts of the case as best I could. Dynamite listened carefully and when I had concluded he put me one question.

'Does the C.Y.M.S. Hall have house rules, Martin?' I told him no.

'Are both parties fully agreed to accept my verdict?' he asked. Both assured him that they were.

'Boys,' said he, 'I played poker in half the states of the Union. I saw a man shot dead for falsely declaring a flush of hearts. The flush had one diamond. Still that is not a precedent for judgment in this case. Be that as it may there are thousands of precedents. In the absence of house rules the declared hand is the lawful hand. Mr. Lollery, you found yourself with four deuces yet you declared that you had two pairs. The reason you did this was that you wanted Father Lynd to believe, however temporarily, that two pairs was all you had. Not satisfied with winning you also wanted to play a game of cat and mouse with your victim. This is precisely why there is a little-known but internationally accepted rule in poker known as the come-uppance. Where it began I cannot say but it is a fact that gentlemen everywhere abide by it. I have played poker since boyhood but at no time in my life did I ask a man for a look at his cards. I always accepted what he declared. A gentleman's word is his be-all and end-all so that if you declared two pairs of deuces to Mr. Lollery it would be final and I would take it for granted that you had two pairs. Acceptance of declaration is a hard and fast rule where men of honour foregather to play poker. Those who break the rule must pay the price. I therefore award the pot to Father Lynd.'

Lollery protested but it was pointed out to him that he had agreed to accept the findings, whatever they might be. He left without a word. As far as I know he never played poker thereafter. I hope this true story of the Castlekellingham Come-Uppance pleases your pals.

> Your affectionate Uncle,
> Martin O'Mora, P.P.

★ ★ ★

> The Presbytery,
> Lochnanane.

Dear Ray,
The following is the short history of what I will lightly call the High Valleys Heresy. A few weeks ago I received a distraught letter from a Mrs. Noreen Hannassy about which I told you. It concerned a rubber woman as you will remember. First I was going to enlist the aid of a few Redemptorists and let them loose in the High Valleys but those days are gone and more's the pity. I arrived at Hannassy's not long after receiving the letter. They were just finishing the midday meal.

At the table was Mrs. Hannassy, Mr. Jack Hannassy and his friend Dolores Viago, the rubber woman. I must confess she looked very lifelike and in all respects that I could notice resembled the famous film star of the same name. Dolores sat upright with both hands in front of her on the table. She wore a purple trouser suit, bought for her by Jack. Jack and the wife stood up as soon as I entered but he made no attempt to hide Dolores. Mrs. Hannassy invited me to take a seat and at once she started to cry. She attempted to dry her tears with her apron but lost control of her weeping, stood up and turned towards the door.

'You're not like that,' said Jack to Dolores, 'always crying and stinking.' So saying he gave Dolores a kiss on the cheek.

'Destroy that evil image,' I roared at him, 'or I'll have you excommunicated.'

To this he made no answer. Instead he lifted Dolores Viago in his arms and took her to the bedroom. There he proceeded to strip her. I intervened and further warned him about excommunication but he roughly pushed me to one side. Stripped of her garments this rubber object turned out to be as fine a physical female as you could behold. In every manner imaginable she resembled a naked woman. He drew back the bedclothes and laid her down gently. He then drew the clothes over her body. Then he proceeded to undress himself. He ignored my presence. I pleaded with him to have respect for his wife and religion but his eyes were glazed with lustful longing. I left him to his devilish work and went from the room to console his unfortunate spouse.

She informed me that many of the men of the High Valleys had rubber women which resembled famous female personalities and film stars. Here was a pretty kettle of fish. I could think of nothing in the civil law to stop them unless alone a charge of cruelty could be brought against them. But then we would be the talk of the civilised world as they call it and that would never do.

Mrs. Hannassy gave me the names of the other miscreants and I spent a fruitless evening trying to make them see the light. If word of what was going on ever got outside the High Valleys we would never live it down in the parish of Lochnanane. Towards the end of my journey I came to the house of an octogenarian whose name was Alaphonsus Maclir. It was he who owned the image of Mrs. Freddie Fox-Pelley, the famous horsewoman. Up to the time I arrived he had not been able to blow her up to lifesize or fill her with warm water. He hadn't sufficient vessels for the latter or the car pump required for the former. When I arrived he was pumping away with a pump which had been loaned him by a neighbour. The job was near completion as I entered. Remember that the scoundrel was eighty-three years of age. His old woman, Tessie sat doting in the corner while the neighbour, a man in his fifties, looked on. They ignored my presence despite my pointing out to them the evil they were manufacturing.

When Mrs. Freddie Fox-Pelley was blown up I must say she was a breath-taking sight. The neighbour flung his hands about her abdomen but Alaphonsus Maclir with a vicious blow to the mouth drove him back. 'Bide your time, bide your time,' he shouted, 'you'll get your turn.' The old man looked every bit as hideous as a West African, rib nosed baboon when he bore her to the bedroom. I left in disgust wondering how I would combat this dreadful plague. I was hardly fifty yards from the house when the neighbour called after me frantically. 'Come quick. Come quick Father,' he shouted at the top of his voice. I returned to the house. There in the arms of Mrs. Freddie Fox-Pelley lay the corpse of Alaphonsus Maclir. The effort had been too much for him or maybe it was God in his wrath.

When word of his sudden demise spread every rubber woman in the High Valleys was burned or cut into pieces. I think they have learned their lesson. Can you, by the wildest and most vivid use of your excellent imagination, hazard a guess at how the Protestant-owned English Sunday newspapers would treat a story like this? I shudder to think of it. I cross myself hourly and thank God for our narrow escape.

I hope you are obeying the specialist's orders. Plenty

of rest and no excitement. I will be out to see you some time Sunday night.

As ever,
Martin.

★ ★ ★

St. Unshin's College,
Ballyrango.

Dear Uncle Martin,
All goes well and I have now dismissed Jean from my mind although there are vestiges of pain and thoughts that nearly wrench out my heart. We still meet and have chats from time to time in the debating hall. Your advice was invaluable. Summer draws near and there will be five of the lads for ordination. My turn next year D.V. I think I will go to England and get a job this summer if it is alright with you. A pal of mine will come with me. It will be good experience apart from the money we will earn. One of the professors here told me part of a yarn about the funeral rehearsal of a Father Bosco McNelly. You must tell me all about it when I get home. There is no news from this place, so for the present I will close. I look forward very much to hearing from you.

Your affectionate nephew,
Joe.

★ ★ ★

Church Street,
Lochnanane.

Dear Father O'Mora,
The lull is over. They are at it again till two and three in the morning. Long, long mysterious silences that baffle a person. This curate is walking on the razor blade's edge. I hope you told him Daisy Redlap's age while you were at it. I knew their parting couldn't last. I would swear in a

court of law that she made him take Coaxiorum. He has
the look of it in his eyes. I wouldn't put it past her. I
heard there was no cure for Coaxiorum except some sort
of psalm read in Latin by the bishop. I never see two that
wanted the Latin so badly. It was half two this very
morning when I heard the door banging. I went downstairs for a breath of air.

'Nice night, Father,' I said as he passed by.

'Ah yes, my child,' he said sarcastic like, 'it surely is
for half two in the morning.'

'I didn't see you this long while, Father,' said I to
him.

'I know,' he said. 'I know and you can be assured that
it will be a thousand times as long before you will see me
again, you or anyone else in this prying place.'

I'm just tipping you off, Father. When he's under the
spell of Coaxiorum there's no telling what he'll do.

> One who tries to be a good
> Catholic.

★　★　★

> The Presbytery,
> Lochnanane.

Dear Joe,
As a rule mine is a lonely life although a happy one in the
spiritual sense; being the busiest man in the parish does
not make it less lonely. It is now but four o'clock in the
afternoon and here is a list of what had to be attended to
this day so far.

First a visit from one of the greatest thieves in the
diocese, a gentleman with twenty convictions for larceny,
requesting a reference for a job as cashier in a Limerick
supermarket. I sent him about his business quickly. Next
came the post with a letter from a parishioner who wants her
name and names of her children and husband changed to her
maiden name. I suggested she visit a solicitor. A second
letter from a woman who signs herself 'One who tries to be
a good Catholic'. I hope she doesn't try any harder.

Then there was a visit from a mother whose son would not get up for mass on Sunday mornings. I advised her to starve him for a while. It always works. Next a visit from the secretary of the local cumann of the Fianna Fáil Party for permission to hold a church gate collection. I agreed. That was a great song, that 'Forty Shades of Green'. I wonder if the political parties are included, each one trying to be greener than the next. Then a visit from a young married woman who told me that her husband would not make love to her. She brought him along and he declared that he had been promised two heifers by the girl's father the day after the marriage. The months passed but the heifers never materialised. I advised him to go home and to make love to his wife and forget about the heifers.

'No Father,' he said, 'blast the button will I open till I get my two heifers.' He left satisfied when I told him I would talk to his father-in-law. I presume the wife has no complaints now.

Next a visit from a girl home from England wanting me to marry her to a Protestant who was not prepared to change his religion, which he never practised anyway. I showed her the door and told her I would pray for her. Marriage is tough enough without mixing it. Next a visit from a mother who told me that her daughter was doing a line with a married man. I promised to talk to the girl. Next came a farmer who claimed that some person with the evil eye was working pishogues against his stock. His calves and fowl were dying mysteriously. He isn't the first bad farmer to blame pishogues. I promised to visit his place, and now on top of all I must go to the convent and hear the nuns' confessions. You mention the famous funeral rehearsal of Father Bosco McNally. Joe, it was no yarn. I'll tell you all about it in my next letter. Meanwhile the very best to you in everything. You will find a tenner enclosed.

Your affectionate Uncle,
Martin O'Mora, P.P.

* * *

Church Street,
Lochnanane.

Dear Father O'Mora,
More than me now knows about the carry-on. Man,
woman and child in the street knows that he is courting
Daisy Redlap. She is a hard creature to be egging him on
and wearing minis that would suit someone the third of
her age. She came to the door the other night in a bikini
when I knocked to find out the time. My own clock is
stopped.

'What are you wearing the bikini for?' I asked.

'Himself is helping me pick out one,' she said, 'I got
eight pairs altogether on appro. I think I'll keep this one,'
she laughed and she hit herself a slap on the belly. 'He
likes it the best.' The next thing she did was to bang the
door in my face.

What do you think of that, Father? Is there a sacrilege
being committed in a Catholic Street?

One who tries to be a
good Catholic.

★   ★   ★

The Presbytery,
Lochnanane.

Dear Ray,
The inevitable has happened. My curate, Father Carrity, has succumbed to the prodigious guiles and quaking
white form of Daisy Redlap. Caveat emptor. He started
the shenanigans less than a week after he came home from
his Retreat. In the face of a growing storm by pious
layfolk who were witnessing his gradual and carnal downfall I called him aside and spoke to him as follows.

'Father,' I said, 'why persecutest thou me? Have I not
given you a fair break? Have I not been the epitome of
paternity and the very soul of indulgence? I placed my
trust in you Father and you failed me. I appealed to your
nobler nature and you betrayed me.'

He yawned and pandiculated himself on the chair. 'I'm tired,' he said. 'For that reason I will not elaborate on the tidings I have for you.'

'What tidings?' I demanded. 'What nonsense is this? You show scant courtesy to your Parish Priest.'

'I'm jacking the whole thing up and going off with Daisy,' he said. 'As of now I am one of those pious layfolk you so often refer to.' With that he whipped the collar from his neck and threw it on the table.

'Dogs who wear collars have my sympathy,' he crowed. He stood up and fondled his double chin.

'The noose is gone from around my neck,' he declared.

'It could be that you are swapping one noose for another,' I warned him. 'Anyhow you just can't walk out of your ministry in a flash. There is more to leaving than that, a lot more.'

'There may be,' he said, 'but not for me. I have no qualms of conscience whatsoever. I have lived in an arid and musty world for most of my life, from seminary to college to parish. I am no longer the lapdog of Latin lunacy. I'm a free man.'

'Your mother,' I reminded him. 'This will be the death of the poor woman.'

'Amen,' said he.

'Stand right where you are,' I commanded him, 'and I will ring the bishop this very minute.'

'The bishop is in Lourdes,' he said, 'and damn well you know it. Now I must be off. My bags are packed and Daisy awaits me.'

'If you refuse to think of yourself,' I pleaded, 'think of the unfortunate wretch you are dragging into the mire with you.'

'What mire?' he shouted, 'you talk like a mad missioner out of the starving thirties. You offend me when you call my wife-to-be a wretch.'

'You are both mesmerised by lust,' I answered him. He laughed loudly upon hearing this.

'We have given it a lot of thought,' he said. 'We are agreed that many people are born into this world for the express purpose of suffering so we have decreed that we shall not be of these. Daisy's house is up for auction next week. My worldly goods are in my two suitcases which I deposited in the boot of my car yesterday. I'm sure you have work to do, Father,' he concluded, pulling a heinously coloured scarf from his trousers pocket and knotting it loosely around his neck. He then placed the key of the door on the table, shook my hand and skipped whistling to his car. That is the last I saw of him. I will say no more about him. I have yet to get over the shock of his departure. Church Street is still astounded.

The new curate is twenty-four years of age. He was ordained last year. His name is Michael Greary. I like him. He loves work, takes a pint or two with the local lads and is a very cheerful sort withal. What is more important is that Mary Teresa likes him and she has yet to be wrong. Father Carrity was only here a week when I asked her what she thought of him.

'He has the gamese of a latchico,' she said, 'the archrump of a finished idler and the soft neck of a Polly bull.' She has always been a great judge of character. She asks for you regularly. See you Sunday night.

As ever,
Martin.

    ★ ★ ★

Church Street,
Lochnanane.

Dear Father O'Mora,
I am not going to start and say I told you so. The harm of the year go with the pair of them. Wait till he gets a right look at Daisy without her make-up some morning. The reason I take up my pen is to inform you that your new curate is to be seen drinking pints regularly at the Five Poplars with the local lads. What are priests coming to at all these days? The Five Poplars is a low and common pub often open for business till all hours of the morning. Another evening I saw him wear a green jumper on his way to the ball-alley with Tricky Micky Cade who is a

wife stealer. It's well known that he sleeps at Rita Sinnon's all the year round except when her husband is home from England for a few weeks in the summer. I wonder will this curate turn out like the last. God knows he has made a good start.

One who tries to be a
good Catholic.

★   ★   ★

The Presbytery,
Lochnanane.

Dear Joe,
I promised I would write and tell you about the funeral rehearsal of Father Bosco McNelly, parish priest of Tooreenturk. Before I do let me tell you something about the beginnings. There might have been no funeral rehearsal if Bosco had not delivered an extremely crude sermon on the occasion of the bishop's visit to Tooreenturk for the confirmations of 1943. The funeral rehearsal is often confused with the German invasion of Tooreenturk which many local people say took place on the same day. Army authorities and the Department of Foreign Affairs strenuously deny that there was an invasion.

Anyhow the Catholic church of Tooreenturk was crowded to the doors when the bishop arrived. In the presbytery the bishop, together with several canons and Bosco donned vestments. The distinguished party then made its way to the church. It was a fine occasion and the procession was a happy one with much banter flowing back and forth. At the entrance to the nave the party halted for a moment and looked with disgust at a freshly discharged portion of human faeces. No word was said but Bosco was livid. When the bishop had delivered himself of his sermon Bosco went into the pulpit.

He began with Mesopotamia and told the congregation of the respect the people of that faraway, forgotten land had for their places of worship. He praised the Greeks and the Phoenicians for the same qualities. He also pointed out that none of these people were Christian. It was then he decided to address himself to the folk of Tooreenturk proper but in particular to the scoundrel who had relieved himself at the entrance to the church. He dwelt on the man's antecedents at great length, likening them to apes and gorillas. He cursed the seed and breed of the monster who had desecrated his church and accused him of sacrilege. He ordered him to stand up but needless to say nobody was foolish enough to do so. By this time the bishop was thoroughly annoyed by the long and unpleasant harangue. A half hour passed and people started to squirm but still Bosco extended his diatribe. Finally he approached the end. He pointed a finger towards the doorway.

'Let me say,' said he, 'that I take no exception to a man relieving himself if he is caught short. I have no objection to a sick person who cannot restrain himself but,' and here he was vehement, 'I had a good look at the heap outside the door of this church and I can safely say that it was the result, not of a sickly misfortune but of a mighty strenuous effort.'

The bishop who was a sensitive man made a mental note never to attend at any ceremony in the parish of Tooreenturk until such time as Bosco had departed from it.

He conveyed his sentiments to his administrator and in due course word reached Bosco that he had truly incurred the wrath of the bishop.

In many respects Bosco was a simple man and the one thing he looked forward to most was his own funeral. Already he had selected a grave at a special corner of Tooreernturk Graveyard and already it was dug to a depth of six inches. He had also erected a huge Celtic Cross which bore his name, his year of birth and a quotation from Francis Thompson: 'Look For Me In The Nurseries Of Heaven.' Now all his hopes were dashed because he was certain that the bishop would never attend his funeral. He conveyed his worries to his parishioners who had a great regard for him whatever the bishop might think. They were agreed that without the bishop it would not be much of a funeral. Encouraged by his friends Bosco decided that he would take no chances. 'Look,' he said to a special committee which he had appointed to examine the matter, 'since I will not be here myself to supervise it we had better have a dress rehearsal.'

The committee was agreed. Word spread and the parish entered into the spirit of the thing. Tooreenturk was a quiet backwater and this was a great opportunity for the people to show that they were more than mere oafs. The rest is a fairly long story so I will postpone it for a few weeks when I will give you the final chapters, as it were, of the German Invasion of Tooreenturk.

Do you want for anything? Be sure to let me know. I think that going to England is a good idea. It is a Pagan country but there is much to be learned if you keep your eyes opened and refuse to be drawn.

As ever,
Your affectionate Uncle,
Martin O'Mora, P.P.

★   ★   ★

The Presbytery,
Lochnanane.

Dear Ray,
I hate to have to tell you that I noticed a decline in you on Sunday night. You will have to take things easy. Good men are scarce. My new curate is a great lad entirely. He has great patience with elderly people and invalids and this is most important as we both know. He is a man who can carry his drink. When I arrived home on Sunday night after leaving you we polished off the best part of a bottle of whiskey while we reviewed the work of the Parish and re-established our priorities. I showed him the letter I received from our friend who is still trying to be a good Catholic and he informed me that he knew who she was.

'She is probably very lonely and bitter,' he said, 'and needs more attention than most. From now on I will go out of my way to be nice to her.'

Joe has gone to England with a pal for the duration of the Summer holidays. It is hard to believe that he will be a priest this time next year who was a small boy only yesterday. Time passes quickly as we age.

An idea occurred to me a while ago. How about a trip to Lourdes, just the two of us? Think on it and let me know, but above all, for the love of God, take things easy.

As ever,
Martin.

*   *   *

The Dispensary,
Lochnanane.

Dear Father O'Mora,
I believe that we both have the interests of Mrs. Rosie Monsey at heart. Since you exert a great influence on her I would ask you to encourage her to use contraceptives, especially as her husband has become himself once more. I will gladly supply these and all that remains is for us to work out the form they should take.

Sincerely,
Moffy, M.B.

*   *   *

The Presbytery,
Lochnanane.

Dear Joe,
The missioners have come and gone but the number of confessions shows a sharp drop. Neither were there the usual throngs at the evening services. It could be television. Whatever it is the mission is losing its appeal. I went to my first mission with my father at the age of fourteen. We were there a half hour beforehand in order to be sure of our seats. The church was mobbed every night because there hadn't been a mission in the parish for years and

anyway it was a great diversion in a country place. Our parish priest was a very outspoken sceptic who had no time for missions or missioners. He was Canon Mocky Leen. He would stand at the back of the church taking in every word. The missioner was a fat, red-faced man from Limerick. His first two sentences terrified us. He gave a description of hell that had us shuddering with dread. His voice was like thunder, almost deafening. Suddenly Mockey interrupted him.

'You'll have to lower your voice my good man,' he called, 'or you'll break the windows.' The missioner was astonished but he lowered his voice.

On the third night of the mission which, incidentally, is known as dirt-track night among missioners, the sermon was about company keeping. Canon Mocky as usual was at the back of the church holding a watching brief.

The missioner warned couples who kept company that it would have to stop, that he would not give absolution to those who courted alone on dark nights. Again Mocky interrupted.

'You'll never put a stop to it,' he called, 'better than you tried it and failed. 'Twill always be going on. Sure if it doesn't go on,' he proceeded, 'there will be no missioners because there will be no one left to make them.'

The missioner went on to deal with the dangers of close dancing. 'Do not let your bellies touch when you dance,' he warned.

'He wants ye to dance back to back,' Mocky explained.

On the final night when the devil was denounced by a thousand throats the missioner announced that he was going to speak about vocations.

'Pray for a vocation,' he pleaded. 'Get your brothers and sisters and your fathers and mothers to pray for vocations for you. The church needs you.'

'Hold it . . . hold it right there,' called Mocky who was listening intently at the back of the church.

'What's this I hear?' he shouted. 'Listen to me,' he lowered his voice. 'If you want to be priests pray for your vocations yourselves and be sure 'tis a vocation you have and not a foolish notion put into your head by your mother.'

The missioner was about to continue but Mocky lifted his hand indicating that he had more to say.

'There are two kinds of priests,' he declared. 'There are the priests who make themselves and the kind who are made by their mothers. The second crowd are no use to God or man. I've seen them myself meggegging like puck goats around Ballybunion and Bundoran.'

Mocky was great fun. Next week or so I'll finish the funeral rehearsal story.

Look after yourself.

Your affectionate Uncle,
Martin O'Mora, P.P.

*   *   *

Loafer's Lane,
Lochnanane.

Dear Father O'Mora,
The Monster arter striken agen. I lucky not my time. I die for sure if I carry anuther baby. The doctor tell me he has pils and other thins make it safe. I sed I ask you first. You the best friend I ever had. The Monster afraid of you but wont go next or ner the presbry for a millen.

Your fateful servant,
Rosie Monsey.

*   *   *

The Presbytery,
Lochnanane.

Dear Doctor Moffy,
What madness have you been putting into the head of Rosie Monsey. She is in her forty-fourth year with fourteen children hale and hearty and yet you want to come along and destroy the morals of a good Catholic mother after this length of time. Have you no sense of righteousness that you should want to make this good woman no better than a streetwalker?

It would be more in your line to fill her in thoroughly on the tried and proven rhythm method without resorting to unGodly and non-Catholic devices. She will never use your murderous concoctions.

Sincerely,
Martin O'Mora, P.P.

★   ★   ★

The Dispensary,
Lochnanane.

Dear Father O'Mora,
I am gravely concerned about Rosie Monsey. You forget that her husband is an ignorant lout who does not know the meaning of rhythm methods. He couldn't even spell rhythm. He is a classic case of 'penis erectus non conscientiam habet.' Total sexual abstinence is also out of the question for I happen to know that he threatens her with violence. Please see your way to using common sense.

Sincerely,
Moffy, M.B.

★   ★   ★

The Presbytery,
Lochnanane.

Dear Joe,
Glad to hear you are getting along so well over there. There is little from here except that Father Ray has had another series of attacks. Anyhow he has recovered and is resting at present. The new curate is an excellent fellow. He remembers you from Saint Unshin's. He is a great help to me and loves hard work. We get along marvellously.

Let us now return to Bosco McNelly's funeral rehearsal or, as others call it, the German invasion of Tooreenturk. All was carefully rehearsed for weeks under various committees but a sizeable firing squad could not be found. When all fruit failed Bosco went to the nearest army garrison and was received by a young lieutenant who told him that such a thing was out of the question. The young officer who is today one of the country's leading industrialists was intrigued and when he finished duty that evening drove straight to Tooreenturk. He promised Bosco that he would have a firing squad of four army men under his command ready on the day but that if word got out about it he would probably be courtmartialled. He insisted in paying the men out of his own pocket. He would arrange to be hidden with his contingent in a clump of laurel near the grave and would emerge with the order to fire at an agreed signal.

Eventually all was ready. It turned out to be a day that would never be forgotten in Tooreenturk. First came a riderless horse in the shape of a jackass. Bosco was riding the real horse to ensure that the rehearsal went off smoothly. The jackass, representing Bosco's riderless horse, was led by the parish clerk who wore surplice and soutane and carried a large brass crucifix. Next came two altar boys carrying incense thuribles. These wore mauve soutanes and yellow surplices. They were followed by the local football and hurling teams in togs, boots and vermilion jerseys. Then came the Children of Mary dressed in blue. They were followed by the Legion of Mary. Thereafter came several nuns and hot upon these the village sergeant and his force of two Civic Guards.

Next came the bands. The first was the local fife and drum and the second an imported brass and reed from the city of Cork. The fife and drum wore tartan kilts. The brass and reed wore peaked caps and uniforms which were sky blue in colour.

After the bands came the people of the parish of Tooreenturk and there were also large numbers from adjoining parishes who, having nothing better to do, came along in case they might miss something.

Here, there and everywhere was Bosco on his horse. At one moment he would be at the end of the parade. The next he would be at the front. The bands were silent since they had only one function which was to play the Dead

March as soon as the main body of the huge procession
was in the graveyard.

All moved smoothly and according to plan. The riderless horse, i.e. the jackass was very well behaved considering that his nether quarters often came in for a belt from
the swinging thuribles of the altar boys. As the gates of
the churchyard hove into view one could feel a sense of
mounting excitement.

First in was the jackass led by the parish clerk. Unit
by unit the others followed until both bands were inside
the gates. Father Bosco McNelly spurred his mount to the
head of the column and with uplifted hand brought it to a
halt. There followed two minutes of absolute silence when
suddenly Bosco lowered his hand and pointed imperiously
to the leader of the brass and reed band. The drums of
both bands rent the silence asunder. The jackass at the
head of the column became uneasy and proved difficult to
control. At the first sound of the brass he reared and
brayed knocking the parish clerk to one side. The clerk
rose bravely and endeavoured to contain him. He was
knocked aside once more. Bosco caught hold of the bridle
but the creature was too strong. He broke from Bosco's
grip and galloped madly across the graveyard.

'Hi . . . Hi,' Bosco shouted after the crazy animal. Mis-
taking this for the signal the young lieutenant and his
party of four uniformed soldiers leaped forth from their
hiding-place in the laurels. Sharply the officer's commands
rang out. The long procession was paralysed. The guns of
the firing party were pointed in the direction of the leaders.

The members of the Children of Mary screamed. Fear
and alarm showed on every face. Vainly Bosco tried to
convey to the soldiers that the time had not yet come. It
was all to no avail.

In the background a man's voice shouted hysterically
'it's the Germans.' Word spread like wildfire that there
was a German invasion.

'Fire,' shouted the lieutenant. There was a thunderous
and ragged volley of rifle fire. The horse bolted with
Bosco in the saddle. Shrieking and screaming the great
mass of people erupted from the churchyard on to the

roadway where hundreds of others joined the retreat. In a matter of minutes the churchyard was deserted save for four bewildered soldiers, a puzzled lieutenant and a jack-ass, who was now grazing serenely near the Celtic Cross erected to the memory of Father Bosco McNelly. So ended his famous funeral rehearsal, or as many country folk still prefer to call it, the German invasion of Tooreenturk. When Bosco died a few years later he had a very modest funeral indeed but please God we shall look for him and find him In The Nurseries Of Heaven.

There are a thousand great stories if only I could remember them. I will try to recall a worthwhile one from time to time. For the present God bless and keep you. Want for nothing.

Your affectionate Uncle,
Martin O'Mora, P.P.

★　★　★

The Presbytery,
Lochnanane.

Dear Martin,
I am now wherever God saw fit to place me. I left instructions with my solicitor that you were not to be given this letter till death visited me. In my life you were my closest friend and this, in a sense, is my farewell to you. My worldly possessions consist of four hundred pounds and my small library which is worth considerably more. You will pay for my funeral out of the cash. Give what is left to the girl Bridget Day who once confided to me that I wasn't cross at all. The library is yours. I would want nobody else to have it. My car goes to my curate. He deserves it. I have no living relatives therefore no dependants.

I can think of nothing else to say. Goodbye old friend.

Yours in J.C.
Ray.

★　★　★

The Dispensary,
Lochnanane.

Dear Father O'Mora,
Rosie Monsey died a few moments ago. I realise you could
not be here. Your curate rendered every assistance. I want
you to know that she would be alive today to care for her
children if she had been allowed the use of contraceptives.

Hers is not an uncommon story but it is a tragic one
and a heartbreaking one for her children. She found herself
pregnant again and was terrified. Poor ignorant creature,
she visited her vagina with slippery elm bark in an effort to
arrest the development of the child. After some time there
was a slight haemorrhage. Next day she complained that
she wasn't well, that she thought she had a temperature but
which of her family could she tell what she had done. If she
had only sent for me.

During the night she raved with fever but still no
attempt to call me. The following evening she went into a
coma. It was then they decided to send for me. Her eldest
daughter came and I guessed instinctively that Rosie Monsey was lost.

The minute I put my hand on her distended stomach I
knew that there was no hope. Her death certificate will say
that she died from widespread peritonitis but that is not
altogether true because the Catholic church had a hand in
it too as indeed it had a hand in the passing of many a fine,
decent girl over the years. I am too sick at the thought of
Rosie's death to say more.

Sincerely,
M. Moffy, M.B.

★   ★   ★

The Presbytery,
Lochnanane.

Dear Joe,
What a terrible week it has been. First Ray and then
Rosie Monsey. I hardly know where I am. There was a

letter from Moffy reproaching me for my attitude towards
contraception. Even the curate looks at me askance.
Maybe it's my imagingation but I feel he would have no
hesitation in permitting Rosie the use of contraceptives. I
could never do this. It would be opposed to all I ever
believed. There is a natural law and to flout it is to flout
God. Most of Rosie's children must go to an orphanage. I
will do what I can but all the clergy and all the institutions in the world will not replace one mother. This fact
will always haunt me. It is a terrible cross to carry but
then I did not become a priest just to make decisions that
might be transiently popular. God will judge me and I
will fully accept that judgment.

I could go on about Ray and about Rosie but it would
be pointless.

What I would like to say to you Joe is that it is never
easy to be a good priest but it is doubly difficult at the
present time with true values diminishing day by day,
non-stop assaults on celibacy and every corner boy in the
country criticising the Church's attitude on one thing or
another. Time was when the corner boys would run from
us at sight. They are but a few of the village curs that
snap at the great caravan of Catholicism.

Over the past few years our authority has faded till it
has almost disappeared. No one knows for sure when the
rot began. I believe it all started with Pope John XXIII
although it was not started by him. I think old John knew
what he was doing when he adopted a liberal attitude. He
knew that many would see this attitude as an opportunity
to press claims for a softening of the Church's attitude on
many controversial matters. John knew that his liberality
and candour would blow through the corridors of the true
faith like a fresh wind, driving before it in the fullness of
time the weaklings and the wasters who do not belong so
that while there may be smaller numbers only the strong
and the resolute remain. Remember that if the position of
the Church seems weak at present it is merely purging
itself of malcontents and biding its time, as it were, for the
re-assertion of its authority. That authority was never
weaker than it is presently. That is why old, frosty fellows
like myself have to stand firm in the face of what must

often seem to be reasonable demands. That is why we dare not yield to catchcries.

We are the hard core Joe, brought up on the Code. Our mission is to stand fast and to hold on no matter what. We may seem out of step right now and there are many who would say that the world shall not look upon our likes again. They are wrong for believe me Joe the world will whimper for the likes of us in the fullness of God's time.

JOHN B. KEANE

Letters of a Love-Hungry Farmer

To Sean Feehan

INTRODUCTION

Herein you will find an account of the troubled and unfortunate love-life of one John Bosco McLane, a fair-sized farmer resident in the hill country which divides the counties of Cork and Kerry. We find him in his early fifties making the ultimate bid to procure a suitable wife. In appearance he is a jaunty, bald-headed fellow of low size, rosy-cheeked, perhaps too rosy, addicted to the wearing of bright tweeds, suede shoes and white caps. This mode of dress has not altogether set him apart from his neighbours but it has given rise to the opinion that, because of it, a boarding school education and an over-indulgent mother, John Bosco might seem to be possessed of grandiose or Ascendancy notions.

John's father, Ulick Micky Ulick McLane, died, according to his neighbours, from repeated massive doses of wifely tattle at an early age and John's only brother was taken from his mother's reluctant arms at the age of ten by the scourge known as scarlatina. Consequently, for the want of another, the mother's influence was to be the decisive factor in young John's upbringing. When the mother died John was a grown man of twenty-eight years with little knowledge of the opposite sex. His mother, because of her reclusive habits and distant manner, was unqualified to prepare him for the guiles and the wiles of the slyer females in the world at large. Therefore, at twenty-eight John Bosco McLane was what the astute

161

farmers of the border country would call an 'innocent sort of a man'.

There were some who held that his christian name was against him, that it suggested a spoiled priest or brother or worse still a Chastitute i.e. name given by the local parish priest Father Kimmerley to those without orders who chose celibacy before marriage, love affairs or promiscuity and who were peculiar only to country places in Ireland, Spain, Portugal etc., where the Catholic tradition of lifelong sexual abstemiousness was encouraged by the Catholic Church and where free-range sex and sexual discussion were absolutely taboo.

It was John's mother who chose his Christian name. At the time of his birth a world-wide campaign was afoot for the canonisation of John Bosco the Turinian priest who founded the famed Salesian order which was later to have several communities in Ireland. John Bosco McLane was thus christened after John Giovanni Melchior Bosco as part of the canonisation effort in Ireland. Twelve years after the birth of the Irish John Bosco, the Italian John Bosco was canonised a saint. Nellie McLane, who overrode her husband's wishes that the boy be called Ulick after himself, was clearly vindicated by Saint John Bosco's elevation to sainthood and on her death-bed murmured that this action alone had given her the right to the kingdom of Heaven. She expired with a smile of triumph on her face.

Be that as it may it is with her son that we must now concern ourselves. At fifty-two we find him writing to Frank O'Dell, an old schoolmate and farmer in the southern part of County Dublin. Frank is a married man with several grandchildren to his credit. There will be other letters, to his solicitor, his aunt and others who might be said to have an influence on his life.

Despite having unusually rosy cheeks, an addiction to gentry-type attire and a boarding-school education it must be made clear at once that John Bosco is not an uncommon fellow. These superficial characteristics serve only to distinguish him, in a personal sense, from his fellow countrymen. Basically, he suffers from the same ailment that afflicts many of his age group in country places. That is to say he is without a wife, mistress or regular copulatory companion. Thus he shares a common bond, a peculiar agrestic and religious legacy that has consigned him and thousands like him to nights of stark loneliness and endless futile dreams.

He himself seems to think that he is the last of his kind and it is on this despairing note that he opens his correspondence.

Tubberganban House,
Tubberganban.

Dear Frank,

I write to you in despair. Outside the January wind howls and whines and the windows of this lonely room are never done with rattling. In the wide, open hearth my cat and my dog are serene in their slumber, their bodies lecherously stretched towards the heat of the dying fire. It is time to go to bed but the cat and dog, mute as they are, are better company than a bed which is empty and which is not now likely to suffer from mine and jostlings of another softer body. I feel like going out into the wind and the cold and crying out my loneliness to the night such is my overwhelming need for female company. It is not a sexual need alone. There is far more to it than that. There is a desire to share the mind and the heart as well as the body, a craving to communicate at a spiritual as well as a physical level. Since my mother died this place is lonelier than the grave during the long, callous nights of winter. There is nothing for it but the pub, the singing lounge, the dance-hall and the bingo. Even the television palls when there is no one near to share it with.

I have the odd feeling Frank, as I write this, that I am the last of my kind, that this district shall not hear such mournful sighs of sexual hunger again, that the world is catching up with me and my equals. No longer will single men inhabit these bleak, desolate, hilly places where snipe and curlew are more plentiful than people, where there is no diversion for the crusty bachelor like myself, where a man is a lost soul who has not a wife or family.

Oh how I envy you, your wife, your children and your grandchildren. What is there for me at fifty-two years of age? Is there in some remote corner of the earth the ideal companion who languishes as I do, ever-hopeful, ever-constant to the romantic ideal. I fear not. My experiences away from home lately have taught me that the seasoned, unattached females of today are the most dreadful predators since the dawn of time. They burn up vodka and gin as if they had jet engines. You wouldn't mind if it softened them out but the opposite is the case. They become more hardened and crafty with every dollup. Many of them will drink your gin and your vodka all night and then disappear with some other fellow without a razoo to his name who has only to lift a finger. I have been led on countless times by these gold-diggers and often when I felt I was on the point of conquest I was always foiled by some sharp, sly, handsome, semi-illiterate son of a gombeenman. Whatever the formula is I don't seem to have it and yet it is possessed by seemingly retarded, ignorant hulks who have extraordinary powers over the opposite sex. There is, of course, no accounting for the tastes of women. No matter how intelligent they are a man should prepare himself for a pattern of behaviour that is mule-like in its unpredictability.

I think I'll advertise for a housekeeper. For better or for worse she'll be another human soul and this might in some small way help to alleviate my long martyrdom. The bother is that it will be next to impossible to persuade a woman to live in. This house is miles from the nearest town and the nearest neighbours are nearly half a mile away.

You wouldn't by any chance know any cute oul' doxie up there who would cater for a single gentleman. Ask Flora to be on the look-out. Meanwhile I'll advertise in the papers here.

All jokes aside I need someone around the house to keep the place tidy and provide a decent meal now and then. From a purely financial point of view I'm fairly sound and could offer a good wage. The farm takes up most of my free time and I find if I don't go out by night that I succumb to long bouts of depression. I don't want her too young or too old. Somewhere in between would suit nicely. Surely there's a fair cut of a woman somewhere who wouldn't turn her back on a good home, a childless widow or some unfortunate creature who has been deserted by her husband. That sort of business is rampant these days. If I had a woman I wouldn't run away from her. I'd fetter her in case she might run away from me.

Sorry for these mournful outpourings. I'm sure you have enough troubles of your own. Try to spare a thought for an old friend.

Sincerely,
John Bosco.

★   ★   ★

Advertising Dept.
The Southern Bugle,
Loughlee,
Co. Cork.

Dear Mr McLane,
We have to hand two replies to your ad. Box No. 238. When you call to settle your account, same may be had after payment.

Yours faithfully,
M. Power.

★   ★   ★

Ballycolleen,
Co Dublin

Dear John Bosco,
It is always good to hear from an old school friend. What a great pity it is that you never married. You would have had fine young grandchildren now like me and you

wouldn't know yourself. I take the younger ones everywhere with me and better company you would not find anywhere. I was thinking over your case the other night. Flora and myself were out for a meal with a neighbour of mine here, an architect by the name of Dargy. I brought up your case but, of course, never mentioned your name not that Dargy would know you anyway and even if he did he is not the kind of man who would talk about a person. He put it like this to me. I often was near druv out of my mind says he looking for new ideas and I would travel far and wide says he in search of what I wanted but always I never found it till I came home again for there it was under my nose all the time.

Do you see my meaning? There you are gallivanting round to pubs and halls in search of strange birds when the best plucking of all might be right under your hands. It was a wise man that said beauty lies in your own backyard. Have a final sweep round and go over all the old ground again and I'll lay you odds you'll find something you overlooked the last time you searched. I'll put you on a better line still. Last summer the eldest grandson, Jerry, used to dig the spuds for the dinner every morning of the week. I'd be alongside saying nothing. By Janey after the fifth day the first drill was dug out and Jerry says to me we'll start a new drill. Indeed we won't said I. And what will we do for spuds says he. We'll go back says I on the old drill and we'll see what we'll find. Back he went and he picked up spud after spud only barely earthed, till we had the finest dinner of spuds of the whole bloody week. God Gran he says to me, I'd never think of that but for you.

See what I mean John. That's a right home-made parable now for you to remind you of the girl you might have left behind and if you know what I mean and so forth and so on. Look us up next time you're in the city. Don't forget now. There's nicer roses agin your own back wall than ever was found in a nursery.

Your old friend,
Frank O'Dell.

★　★　★

Tubberganban House,
Tubberganban.

Dear Frank,

I am just after digesting your letter over a tumbler of
steaming punch and find much wisdom in what you have
to say. However, in relation to that piece about beauty
lying in one's own backyard I must ask you now to try
and picture Tubberganban Parish Dancehall, cradled between two bare hills where you wouldn't meet a snipe, nor
a hare not to mind a human being, with four whitewashed
walls like a French Foreign Legion outpost, no windows,
no fire escape and only the front entrance to come and go
by and you'll readily understand why I travel out and
about in search of the opposite sex.

The patrons here range between the ages of thirty and
sixty. The men have black-lined, thorn-torn, horny hands
and dirty nails that you wouldn't whiten with a cannon-
hose.

Mostly they stand around the headlands of the hall,
hands in their pockets scratching and adjusting their
under-worked undercarriages when they aren't picking
their noses or scouring their ear-drums for deposits of
wax.

They lewdly ogle the younger women and, in whispers, boast to each other of how they would ravage these
females if the opportunity were to present itself.

The women, for the most part, are stiff-backed and
solid with mighty rumps and heavily-fleshed ankles with
the occasional moderate looker who is nearly always
shifted early.

I am told repeatedly by tradesmen and businessmen in
the nearby town of Bannabeen that there are fast pieces to
be found here, right in the very backyard which you are
so fond of extolling, yet on any occasion when I have
approached one of these they have shied away from me
with looks of disgust and revulsion. My approach has
always been polite and restrained and I have never given
the slightest indication either by word or deed as to what
my intent might be. In spite of all this and in spite of the
fact that I am rightly regarded as a good mark I have

never succeeded in making the slightest impression on any one of these likely prospects.

I have drawn a conclusion from these constant and unreasonable rebuffals and this is that they must have acquired an exclusive taste for the bucks of the town. There was one in particular named Juleen McCoon:

Juleen McCoon with her face to the moon,
She'd hardly gainsay a well-tackled baboon.

By all accounts Juleen was supposed to be the last word at the jig-a-jig caper as serious lovemaking is lightly referred to around these parts and I am ashamed to say that it was with this in mind I accosted her in Tubberganban dance hall on Saint Patrick's night. She must have guessed my ultimate intent because when I asked her to dance she cocked her head in the air.

'Go 'long you cheeky ting,' she said scornfully. She doesn't pronounce her haitches. However, I'd rather hold something else against her than that. Later I saw her dancing cheek to cheek with a whiskery bookie's clerk from the nearby town of Bannabeen. This particular fellow is a long, slimy, cadaverous type who cannot and will not look people between the eyes.

For the space of two reels, two old-time waltzes and a gent's-excuse-me foxtrot they were missing from the hall. This gave him adequate time to flatten a concrete wall not to mind a woman. When they returned her face was flushed to the colour of a rooster's comb and the puddle of the roadside was starting to cake on the fringes of your man's beard. Some session. All around were honest rustics like myself who would have been as good to her if not better than this wretched townie.

It was ever thus with fast countrywomen. Let a murderer or a rapist or an arsonist come from the town and he's preferable to the local man who has the same credentials and would:

Be handy too
If his aim was too true,
Who would not bolt
If she bore a filly or colt.

So what price Tubberganban where the native is denied access to the most desirable resources of the community, deprived of the basics on his very own doorstep but it was always the same wasn't it, since the dawn of time. Do you remember 'Eileen Alanna'?

Then one night a stranger came
And stole Eileen Alanna.

You may be sure and certain that the stranger in question was from the nearest town or city, a polished performer with a good suit, a tie-pin, head well plastered with the dearest hair oil, dancing shoes and whatever else was the go at the time.

Do you remember 'Nellie Gray'?

Oh my darlin' Nellie Gray
They have taken you away
And I'll never see my sweetheart anymore.

God be good to her and to poor Kathleen that wouldn't be pining for home all the time if she wasn't taken away from it in the first place.

I say to you Frank O'Dell that there should be a union in every rural parish in this country, that its members should unite to keep out urban and metropolitan Casanovas and that we, the rustics of Ireland, should be the first served in the event of there being certain commodities on the market if you get my meaning. After that we would begrudge no man his fair share of whatever is going.

Personally speaking I would be for far stronger measures. Bluntly and quite pitilessly I would be for the total demolition, genito-urinarywise, of all invaders of our female domain. In other words I am saying that these foreign gentlemen should be deprived of their procreative faculties and that these same faculties should be tacked to or pinned on to telephone poles, electric light poles, roadside trees or, in the absence of these, draped over convenient bushes. Best of all, of course, like they used to do long ago with the heads of usurpers and unfortunate rebels, they should be spiked outside public places for all to see where they would serve as a warning to would-be fornicators and seducers from towns and cities.

If you think this is rough treatment you should remember the injuries and indignities that we, the natives of the place have suffered down the long years and remember too the legions of unfortunate bastards that these interlopers left in their wake. I will ask you as one friend to another.

What happens when a man steals a priceless gem, a hoard of gold or a fortune in money? Is he not convicted of a major crime and jailed for several years? Yet these purloiners of virtue have been free to pillage the purest possessions of our womenfolk for generations. A time has come to cry halt, a time to stand up and be counted. What other nation in the world would tolerate a situation like this. Even in darkest Africa, those parts that are still dark, interference with native women by those outside the kraal is a crime on a par with murder.

Some years ago in Cork I met a sea-captain by the name of Cooney while having a late drink in the Atlantis Hotel. We were both alone in the residents' lounge and it was inevitable that we should join forces. During the drinking session which followed he told me a story about a young sailor who went ashore at the port of Iquique in Chile in order to spend a few days outstanding shore leave while his ship was discharging cargo.

To make a long story short, this young lad of nineteen, who hailed originally from Tipperary, was fond of strolling along the edge of the forest which crept right up to the suburbs of the town. One day he ventured a little further than usual and after a short while in the forest came across a clearing where he saw an indian woman bent over a cooking pot, gently stirring the contents. The rhythm of her buttocks under her tight-fitting dress excited him. Overcome by passion he bore down upon her. He had only barely completed his lustful act when he was seized by members of her tribe who emasculated him straight away and put him in a cage where they kept him for three weeks, feeding him on high grade nuts and berries till he became as fat as a fool. They then roasted and consumed him entirely.

Yet this coming Sunday night the country dance-halls of holy Ireland will be invaded by cunning townies armed with all the subtle arts of seduction and all the low suggestive craft that only experience and practice can acquire. They will escape scot-free while our innocent sailor boy had to pay with his life for a perfectly natural reaction. Since the townies and city slickers always seem to escape punishment in this world one must presume that they will go straight to hell in the next. Otherwise, God is a townie too. Next time I have business in Dublin I'll call without fail.

Your old pal,
John Bosco McLane.

★ ★ ★

St Regina's Hospital,
Leeside Place,
Cork

Dear John Bosco,
Received your letter this morning. I will only be too glad to help you select a housekeeper. As matron of one of the country's leading hospitals you may be certain I will see to it that you have the best candidate available. If you would prefer to wait for two more years until I retire I would be perfectly willing to housekeep for you myself. I'll see you in the Atlantis then at twelve noon on Saturday. If you changed your hairstyle I'm certain you would have no bother getting a wife.

Your loving auntie,
Frances.

★ ★ ★

Ballycolleen,
Co Dublin

Dear John Bosco,
You are very hard on the townies and city slickers. I agree that there is a lot of truth in what you say. However, let you take heed by what I have to say now.

The grandson Jerry was on his way home from school a few weeks ago when he was attacked and belted for the seventh time running by a gang of youngsters who live in a new housing estate just down the road. He came home crying his eyes out. He was wrongly advised by his father who told him to stand up to them and to have a go at the ringleader. He tried this and he ended up sitting on his arse every time. I called him aside the last evening and we had a man-to-man chat. Look says I to him. Let you give the ringleader a few bob or if he smokes give him a packet of fags and tell him you want to join his gang. He followed my advice and now he is on the best of terms with his former enemies. Are you getting the message, old chum?

Next time you see this bookie's clerk you go out of your way to be nice to him. Buy him rounds of drink. Pay his way a few times. You can afford it. Then watch his style. Find out what makes him tick. Find out what it is he has that seems to impress the ladies. Hang around him. Be a jackal if you have to and pick up his remains. You must stoop to conquer. Beggars can't be choosers. Learn his style and mark you my words you'll be no stranger to the weigh-room when you're out of your apprenticeship. That's how Jack Dempsey became world champion, watching others when he was a gorsoon. How do you think Roger Bannister did the first four minute mile? He watched the styles of others and learned the hard way. I hope you'll be said by me.

Watch out for yourself.

Your old friend,
Frank O'Dell.

★   ★   ★

Spiders' Well,
Ballybarra,
Co Kerry.

My lovely boy,
You don't know me but I know you. I am the Richard O'Connor (Dicky Mick Dicky) that makes the matches. It has come to my attention that you are in the market for a

wife. If this be the case I might be able to meet your wants. Tell me your means, your age and your size, your preferences and what not. Would you fancy lean or thin, rangy or butty, old or young? I give you my guarantee that you'll get nothing put over on you. Whatever the age I swear she'll be sound and firm.

> Courtesy and Civility assured at all times,
> Your obt. servant,
> Dicky Mick Dicky O'Connor.

★ ★ ★

> Tubberganban House,
> Tubberganban.

Dear Frank,

I took good note and careful stock of your recommendations which as usual are sound and to the point. The name of that bookie's clerk from Bannabeen is Sylvester Brady. Sylvie for short. Next time I am in the same public house as he I'll make it a point to buy him a drink, that's if he'll have it. Much has happened since I wrote the month before last. The flowering cherries are in bloom along the bohareen which leads to my house. Every bush has its own share of green and spring grass is starting to take the bare appearance from the fields.

I have a brand new housekeeper and I have placed myself in the hands of a matchmaker, a sly rogue from a place called Spiders' Well in Ballybarra which is in the heart of North Kerry. I have a new car and finally the bad news, another let-down. First the housekeeper. It was the aunt who chose her, a black-haired, sharp-featured lady with a trim enough figure. There were only two candidates despite the fact that I advertised in several provincial papers. The aunt interviewed them both in a room in the Atlantis Hotel in Cork. I saw them go in and go out. The first was a stout fair-haired lady in the mid-thirties. The aunt didn't keep her long although to tell the truth she would have been my choice and I'll tell you why. As she went towards the hotel exit one of the porters

happened to be walking by her side with a suitcase belonging to some guest or other. Casually he gave her a
lingering pat on the posterior and all she did was smile at
him. She had disappeared by the time I thought of calling
her back. My aunt's choice has to be the best in the long
run. She knows her business when it comes to hiring and
firing staff. The woman's name is Eva Kishock. She seems
a hard nail but she's good at her job. She was only here
two days when I accidentally brushed against her as I was
sitting down to lunch. I must have brushed overlong because she sat down opposite me and claimed my attention
by holding an upraised soup spoon in front of me.

'Listen lover-boy,' she said, 'if I wanted that jazz I
could clean up in Cork by floggin' it on the streets.'

I apologised profusely, explaining that it was purely
accidental. She nodded her head and went about her business. The aunt knew what she was doing alright although
her mind is inclined to wander somewhat lately. Sometime
ago she wrote and advised me to change my hair style
forgetting that I haven't had a rib for ten years or more.
Eva Kishock once had a husband but he abandoned her a
few years ago and is now shacked up with another woman
somewhere in England.

About my most recent let-down. I happened to be one
day last week at the Killarney cattle-mart on the lookout
for a few cheap calves when I met a friend from our
schooldays. You must remember Dugs Devine. Anyway
we had several drinks together and the nett result in my
case was that I was too boozed to drive home. I walked
around the streets looking at the shop windows and the
passing tourists of every hue and nationality. Bit by bit I
started to sober up but just to be on the safe side I
decided to have a feed somewhere. I picked a pleasant
hotel with a view of the lakes and took a seat at the bar
where I ordered a glass of beer and a menu. Duly my
orders were filled and I sat sipping the beer and scrutinis-
ing the menu. I decided to gamble on a sirloin. As I
waited the arrival of a waiter to take my order I noticed
three people sitting in a corner of the lounge, one male
and two females. With the aid of a mirror which faced me
from behind the bar counter I was able to study all three,

the ladies in particular. Your man was a handsome scoundrel with an agreeable face and the ladies who would be but barely out of their twenties were extremely attractive. While I sat looking into the mirror the two females rose and hastened in the general direction of the ladies' room. They were hardly gone a minute when the gentleman arose and approached me.

'How about making it a foursome?' he asked, without parley. I looked around thinking that he must surely be addressing himself to somebody else.

'Those two are sisters,' he said with a wink. 'I'm with the darker one.'

I still couldn't believe my ears. Was he speaking on behalf of the girl in question or was he merely asking me as one man to another to temporarily even the odds for him?

'She likes you,' he confided and at once I knew by the way he said it that he was telling the truth.

'But I'm over fifty years of age,' I protested. 'This one likes 'em older,' he explained. 'She has a father complex and anyway she's teetotally kinky.' 'Come on,' he said, 'We're in this together,' and with that he led me to the table at the same time ordering the barman to furnish a repeat of drinks.

I sat at the table tongue-tied waiting for the return of the girls with mounting disbelief. Was this really happening to me or was I dreaming? The girls re-appeared. They looked absolutely stunning. The stood for a moment framed in the lounge doorway exchanging light-hearted comments. Then they advanced gracefully towards us. As they neared us the fairer of the two waved at me and threw a most engaging smile in my direction. Then she sat down alongside me so that our bodies touched.

'I hope you don't mind,' she whispered. I was too paralysed with disbelief to answer her at once. She was easily the most ravishing girl I had ever sat near.

'Say so and I'll go away,' she pouted.

'Please. Please stay,' I entreated. After that drink followed drink. The girl's name was Dolores. The other girl, Olwen, was her sister. Both were the daughters of a famous Dublin surgeon. It transpired that they were taking a well-earned holiday having just qualified as nurses and Olwen's boyfriend who was a barrister was acting as their chauffeur.

I won't bore you Frank with all the details. We had an excellent meal for which the girls insisted on paying. After the meal we went for a drive round the lakes. Olwen sat in front with her barrister boyfriend. I sat in the back with Dolores. She places my hand round her waist and nestled close to my side. With dark, swimming eyes she looked adoringly into mine. Darkness had fallen but there was a pale moon which highlighted the fragility and profundity of her beauty.

'Kiss me,' she whispered urgently. I kissed her.

'Again,' she whispered, 'and again and again after that. Kiss me forever.'

'How's things back there?'

It was the barrister's deep voice coming from a million miles away. I made no answer. I could not. Neither did Dolores.

'You dog you,' the barrister said without rancour and he quietly slipped an arm round the lovely shoulders of his Olwen. The car slowly slid to a halt and we found ourselves at a lovely lakeside glade. Silence descended and there was no sound save the breathing of the car's occupants and the faint mystical rhapsody of lapping lake water. We kissed again. I knew that I was within an ace of fulfilling my great romantic dream. She trembled and shuddered in my arms. I stroked her hair, her face, her breasts. I heard her sigh. A sort of sublime gurgle arose from her throat. Her body heaved ever so slightly. It heaved again and again. More noises. But were they sighs? I knew that I had heard these noises before and I was certain that they were unrelated to the scene being enacted. Then the horror of the whole business dawned on me. She was giggling. It was all a game from the beginning. She had led me along just for the crack. Without a word I disengaged myself from her arms and left the car. Behind me I could hear both girls giggling. Then came laughter, loud and uncontrolled, the heedless laughter of youthful abandon. I hid myself in a convenient grove of sallies and cried. After a little while the car was started up. I heard my name being called by the barrister and then by the girls. For nearly half an hour they drove up and down along the margin of the lake still calling my name. I knew from the way they called that they were sorry, genuinely sorry. I knew that if I hailed them they would make it up to me in some way which would assuage the guilt on their consciences. After some lengthy period the car left and I emerged from my hiding place. I was several miles from Killarney. By the time I reached the town the place where I had left my car I was stone, cold sober. This was the greatest humiliation to date.

Don't breathe a word to anyone, not even to Flora. I'll be in touch. Take care.

> As ever,
> Your old pal,
> John Bosco McLane.

★   ★   ★

> Spiders' Well,
> Ballybarra.

My lovely boy,
Yours to hand in the strictest confidence. I have noted your form and I will study my list of approved mares, if you follow, this very night. I think I have the right lady for you but she don't surface at once. The main trouble with fellows of your age is that they are too choosy. Would you credit it but that I have applications from neighbours of your own hither there in the hills, scraggy bucks as old as them same hills and they wanting things of eighteen and twenty. When I offer them likely dames nearer their own age they cock the noses. As Mike Moran used to say

'what get, don't want.
What want, can't get.'

In reply to your question about my fee, not a copper do I charge till after the first flake in the marriage bed. Don't worry about a lady of around the fifty mark not having children. There was a neighbour of mine here Jackeen Walton married the twenty-two year without raising a flag. He was sixty, the wife forty-seven. Twenty-two solid years of it and no sign of a swelling. A new curate comes and he gives Jackeen's wife copies of prayers to Saint Jude and Saint Colette in the hope that holy intervention might make her pregnant.

What do you think happens? Doesn't she become pregnant. Of course, the minute the curate hears it he comes tearing over to congratulate him. He meets Jackeen in the doorway.

'We should be on our knees,' said he, 'thanking Saint Jude and Saint Colette.'

'For what?' said Jackeen.

'For your wife's pregnancy,' said the curate.

'And what about my twenty-two years of constant flaking?' Jackeen reminded him.

Anyway, my lovely, decent boy it won't be long now till you be hearing from me and please God I will have bright accounts for you and your single days will soon be at an end. If you could leave your Sunday nights free for the next few weeks it would greatly facilitate. (I saw that in a solicitor's letter).

> Courtesy and Civility assured at all times,
> Your obt. servant,
> Dicky Mick Dicky O'Connor.

★ ★ ★

> Tubberganban House,
> Tubberganban.

Dear Frank,

Since you last heard from me my cup of sorrow has been added to if such a thing is possible. Our matchmaking friend arranged to meet me in the Bannabeen Arms Hotel on Sunday night last. With him was a buxom dame of fifty or so. He introduced us and quickly cleared himself away. He came back after an hour and asked if we had any news for him. The answer was in the negative. If I was

trying till Doomsday I could not get the woman to speak.
She would hum and haw alright whenever I asked her a
question. She seemed most agreeable and anxious to
please but she was too tongue-tied to impress and far too
old into the bargain. The following Sunday night he
brought along another. This one was younger. She kept
calling me sir.

This would not be a sign of servility, rather it is an
innate roguery designed to boost the ego of the person
being thus addressed. She was a good conversationalist,
fairly attractive and it occurred to me more than once
that it was strange how a girl of her manner and appearance had failed to find herself a husband before this.
After the usual space of time our matchmaking friend
returned and asked if I had any news for him. We told
him all was well, that we had decided to meet again on the
following Wednesday night at a singing lounge situated at
a nearby crossroads. After we parted I decided to investigate. The girl's name was Norry Macey. I rang Edward
Corr the solicitor and asked him if he knew anything
about her.

'Ah,' said Edward, 'you picked a winner at last.'

I asked him to explain.

'Norry Macey,' said he, 'is what we in the legal profession call a seven-day wonder.'

'And what would she be called,' said I, 'by those who
are not in the legal profession?'

'Not over the 'phone,' said Edward. I met him an
hour later and he told me that Norrie was known as a
seven-day wonder because she had a child for every day of
the week.

'The trouble is,' said Edward, 'that she never bothered
to get married but this could be because she did not know
the fathers of her offspring. It is said that she has a poor
memory.'

Well Frank, so ended my relationship with Dicky
Mick Dicky O'Connor's second nominee. The third was a
widow, not a bad-looker with an excellent figure. She was
the most presentable so far. She was refined and ladylike
and would not touch intoxicating drink. My hopes soared
as the night wore on. Here was the best prospect so far.

When Dicky Mick Dicky returned I expressed satisfaction. The widow and I arranged to meet again the following Sunday night. As I was leaving the matchmaker called me aside.

'Do you strip good,' said he. I was puzzled by the question.

Seeing my embarrasment he adopted another tack.

'What are you like in the pelt?' said he. I was still puzzled.

'Is your natural belongings intact?' he asked.

'Will you not be trying to confuse me,' I said, 'and come to the point.'

He then unfolded an astonishing tale. The widow had been married for several years to an elderly tailor who had been somewhat remiss in the matter of satisfying the physical needs of his partner. He was what country people call a cawboge which more or less means that he was impotent. For this reason Dicky Mick Dicky pointed out that it would be necessary for me to submit a nude photograph of myself to the widow's father and an independent referee (a well-known quack) who would be able to tell from examination of the photograph whether or not I was possessed of the equipment to fulfill my side of the marital bargain.

''Tis only the same as an ordinary bull inspection,' said Dicky Mick Dicky without batting an eyelid. 'And can you blame the woman,' he went on, 'after the suck-in she got the last time.'

I refused to be party to such an agreement. I told him that they would have to take my word, that while I was no Samson I was no dead duck either.

They wouldn't agree and so ended the third chapter of the matchmaking saga. I have no luck with women. If I were to give you an account of my misfortunes with the opposite sex you would agree that I was born under the wrong star in this respect. I am not alone. The countryside is tainted by slowly withering blossoms like me. At the creamery in the mornings I see them with black overcoats and unwashed faces, many of them smelling of the very milk which they have come to deliver, except that, like themselves, the milk has gone sour. They have missed out in the game of love. They are consigned to eternal loneliness. Someone once said that every ould shoe finds an ould stocking. Of us this is not so. We just cannot be matched. We are in excess of the quota but there is no one to whom we can be transferred. We are the subject of debates, of books, of plays but our plight is still the same. The marriage bureaux have settled a handful of us but the great majority are without hope of ever getting married. I believe if we were to leave the land and go to England or to Dublin we might find some sort of acceptable partners. A half-wit who used to work for me on this very farm is happily married to a Pakistani girl somewhere in Camden town. The bother is if I left the land I would be leaving my livelihood, the only thing I'm good at. I would be like a duck out of water. Here I am a sort of squireen and even though I am without a woman I am still a man of consequence. All I would be fit for elsewhere is manual labour. I would no longer be my own boss. The milch cow is my bread and butter. I would have to take my land and my herd with me if I were to retain any trace of my dignity or independence. Fifty-two years of age without raising a flag, without a kill you might say. My confidence is almost sapped away. I'll write as soon as I have any screed of important news. I have struck up a nodding relationship with Sylvie Brady, the bookie's clerk. He seems friendly enough. Only time will tell whether he will be an asset or not. For the present take care.

> Your old pal,
> John Bosco McLane.

★　★　★

> St Regina's
> Cork

Dear John Bosco,
Go ahead and tell me it's none of my business or call me an old gasbag under your breath but I have to say my piece in view of what I have been told about you. I hear you have been keeping the company of unseemly female

companions lately and in particular a certain Norrie Macey who has as many illegitimate children as there days in the week.

Your mother was a lady. I have always tried to be one. I would ask you to have no more to do with women of this kind or if you must please remember that it can only lead to damnation. I am not being snobbish. It's just that I have always regarded you as a gentleman and would expect you, therefore, to keep the company of real ladies. One is never born a lady so it's not a matter of caste. It takes a long, long time to learn how to be one and, once one is one, one will never fall out of character till she draws the last breath. I have no more to say to you for the present except to remember the stock you came from.

Fondly as always,
Auntie Frances

★　★　★

Knackers' Crescent,
Bannabeen

Dear John Bosco,
About what we were talking about the last night I have two lined up for Saturday night. I know one of these already and her credentials are sound. I am, unfortunately, low in dough so if you could bring an extra tenner I would be obliged. It's only for a week or so till I get my annual bonus which is nearly due. Not a word to anyone. Call for me at the Arms at six o'clock.

Quietly, Sylvie.

★　★　★

Ballycolleen,
Co Dublin

Dear John Bosco,
Sorry to hear that the matchmaking venture fell into the soup. These things are only going through life and you

shouldn't let them get you down. You write as if you were the only man in the world who was ever left down by a bird. In the name of God man how many times was I left there but I saddled up again no matter how hard the fall and I cleared my fences 'till I saw the post in sight. I've lost count of the girls who made me look foolish and you can take it from me every mother's son has the same tale to tell. How often did I find myself on the crest of a womanly wave only to find myself in the troughs the next minute. Listen to me now. The grandson Jerry was trying to join a children's badminton club here some time ago but for one reason or another, principally too young, he was turned down so he started his own club with a few others. See what I mean.

You might not have a wife but you have a fine cut of a housekeeper from what I can read between the lines. Start your own club with her. You know the name of the game yourself. Don't take any notice of that first rebuff. That's all part of the game. As the man said a faint heart never won a fair lady nor a dodgy hen never hatched an egg.

As always,
Your old pal,
Frank O'Dell.

★ ★ ★

Tubberganban House,
Tubberganban.

Dear Frank,
I am off to Cork tomorrow evening with Sylvie Brady for better or for worse. He says he has two clients lined up. The point I tried to make in my last letter is that there is some sort of curse down on top of me as far as women are concerned. I know other men have lonely stories to tell and that you yourself have had your share of misfortune but believe me there is no man walking the earth at this time who has gone through what I have gone through as far as women go.

Not long after my mother died I started to do a line with a draper's daughter in Bannabeen. Her name was Peggy. She was smaller than I am which was a good start for as you know I am a little below average height. She had blue eyes, good teeth, auburn hair and a good figure. She was respectable and what my aunt would probably call a lady. In all respects she was a fine decent girl but it didn't work out.

I was told afterwards in confidence by her father when I was buying a corduroy trousers one afternoon that she thought I was a nice sort alright but too conservative and even dull. Peggy was a cheerful soul right enough as I recall. She married beneath her station. He was a tall, curly-haired working man with a tooth for porter but every time I see her wheeling her pram through the streets of Bannabeen I know she is happy and that she would not change places with anybody. She has a big houseful of children and they seem to be happy too. She suited herself did Peggy.

Then there was Kitty Catrell from Cork city. She came on holidays to Tubberganban to her uncle Michael Catrell who has a valley farm about two and a half miles from my place. Kitty worked in a confectioner's shop in the city and she was as pretty a girl as one could wish to meet although her hands and wrists were a little bit redder than the rest of her. She had a kind face, blonde hair and a fine figure. On top of all this she always wore a smile.

During her fortnight's holiday I took her everywhere and we got on famously. Her uncle approved and his wife Maggie approved and so did every man, woman and child from Tubberganban to Bannabeen. Then I suddenly recalled as I was milking the cows one evening that I had also got on famously with Peggy, the draper's daughter and yet she had left me without so much as a goodbye. Was it possible for the same thing to happen again? Was I to be thrown over once more when all seemed to be going well? Was I to be suddenly struck by an unexpected squall just as my craft was about to enter the harbour? I resolved not to allow it.

On the second last night of her holidays we were sitting in my car looking down at the patchwork farms in

her uncle's valley. We were content. A chip shop, the first
in the district, had been opened in Bannabeen and we had
sated ourselves with chips, peas and sausages. There was a
full moon and the stars never danced as gaily or shone as
brightly. Now and then from the valley's depths came the
faint barking of a watchdog. Near at hand crickets chirped
and frogs croaked mutely. The faintest of summer breezes
played with the roadside greenery. The moon's rays which
shone discreetly through the car window dimly lighted her
lovely face. Her lips were moist and her eyes seemed to
laugh when they looked into mine.

I took one of her hands and squeezed gently. She
responded and my heart soared with a new-found hope.
What is the next move? I asked myself. What must I do
now to ensure that she remains mine? I cannot go on
holding her hand forever. There has to be an end and a
beginning to everything. In addition my palm was starting
to sweat and I was beginning to get a cramp in my
shoulder.

I shall never know what evil force prompted my next
move. The awful act was perpetrated before I realised
what an abomination I had committed. I had suddenly
and without warning of any kind thrust my free hand
under her dress as far upward as it would go. There was
an unholy shriek from Kitty Catrell. My face was slapped
and my hand was scratched till nail met bone. The car
door was loudly banged and I found myself sitting with
only the pale moon for company. Years were to pass
before I found the neck to salute Michael Catrell her
uncle. For a long time I thought I would never live down
the embarrassment of that fatal moonlight encounter. The
simple truth is that I had not wanted to do what I had
done. It was against all my training and instincts. I know
now that I should have taken her lovely face in my hands
and kissed her gently, ever so gently, I should then have
told her I loved her. Hindsight is worst of all when it
revolves round lost opportunities.

I daresay I was too anxious. I had failed with Peggy
because I was too dull and too unexciting. Fear of losing
out a second time forced me to take drastic action with
Kitty. One particular thing I will never forget about that

harrowing, shattering and soul-destroying night was the fact that Kitty Catrell carried a rosary beads inside the gusset of her knickers. There I was at the edge of thirty with two dismal failures weighing me down and my confidence badly shattered.

The next line I did was with a nurse from Waterford. Her name was Jane. She was introduced to me in Cork at Saint Regina's Staff Dance by my aunt who was her matron. I took her to dinner one night and to a show after at the Opera House. We seemed to be ideally suited to each other and we would meet frequently at weekends, not as often as I would have liked but the cows had to be milked and there were all the other chores around the farm. One night after three months of steady dating we found ourselves sitting in the car in a secluded parking spot overlooking the River Lee. The light from the street lamps was reflected in the placid water and now and then stately swans swam silently by like white faery barques out of the mists of long ago.

Beside me Jane sat still, breathing gently, serenely aware of the pleasant scene outside. I could feel that there was something between us, that it was not a time for words. Time passed, a half-hour, a whole hour and then another. Suddenly Jane spoke.

'Sweet John Joseph Jesus,' she said crossly, 'are you going to sit there forever?'

I was stunned beyond words. I seized my chance quickly and kissed her gently. I did not know what to do next. Mindful of past experiences I tried desperately to size up the situation. I decided to wait for some sort of cue. Time passed and this was my downfall.

'Shag you from a height,' she said viciously, 'you God-damned statue.' Then came the all-too familiar sound of a door banging and the awful quiet thereafter. So you see my dear Frank there is some evil genie lurking in my immediate vicinity. What I have revealed to you is but a synopsis of my whole love-life. I'll write when I have news.

Your old pal,
John Bosco McLane.

* * *

Spiders' Well,
Ballybarra.

My lovely decent boy,
I'm going back over my lists these nights and 'tis only a
matter of time you may be sure till I turn the right trump.
We will forget past failures and start fresh. We'll stop for
nothing. Slash dunkey, slash car and rise the white dust
till the journey is ended. Don't ever worry about the age.
The raw egg and the greens is your answer and if I come
with a lively piece have no doubts but you'll be able to
handle her.

There is a woman in Toordrumagowna by the name
of Nonie Brack or Nonie the Speckles as the neighbours call her out of the goodness of their hearts. You'll
know the house no bother as there is a Marian Year
grotto a hundred yards to the west of it and an elegant
duck pond outside the front door. Go into Nonie and
order a half hundred of her green duck eggs to be taken
raw at the rate of nine a day and if you don't spark
after downing the full dose you'd want to get your engine
looked after. Another thing 'tis a pure fool that turns
up his nose at oldish women or widows that know the
course and wouldn't balk at a Regulation. Young ones
are alright but for any man past the fifty there's more
soot to be knocked out of the oul' warriors. I see a
lady lately at the Bannabeen G.A.A. Social and she wearing what looked like a butcher's apron. She was bare
along the whole broad of her back from where the thighs
do rise to the butt of the neck and straps holding it up.
'Twas no apron. I was told 'twas the latest make of a
dress.

There was another one there and the breasts only
half-covered and they fit to pop out if she got a decent
slap on the back. The likes of you would be no way
far-to-go against the likes of those. When you would be
thrown down exhausted they'd be getting anxious for the
caper to continue till cockcrow. You stick to the older
women. Drive on the port wine and you'll end up with as
game an article as ever drew breath. I won't be in touch

with you now till I have my hay saved and turf drawn home. Please God I'll have the right accounts for you.

Courtesy and Civility assured at all times,
Your obt. servant,
Dicky Micky O'Connor.

★ ★ ★

Ballycolleen,
Co Dublin

Dear John Bosco,
After I put down your last letter I thought about your case and I am forced to agree that you have met bad luck in your love life but this don't mean you're in for a dose of sympathy or that I'm going to let you cry on my shoulder. That would be the wrong medicine for you my old schoolmate. What you need to do is to tackle the problem from a different angle. I am most pleased that you are going on the outing with this fellow Sylvester Brady. This could easily be the most fortunate outing of your entire life. Let me put it to you this way.

Quite recently, as you know, my grandson Jerry started to play badminton. He was slow to learn and no matter how hard he practiced the poor little fellow could never win a game even when he was facing the most moderate of opposition.

It wasn't for the want of trying. God knows he put his heart into every game but heart alone wasn't enough. Now there is a thing in badminton called doubles where two people play on each side rather than one.

'Join up,' I told him, 'with the best partner of the lot and stick with him. You may be no good on your own but with a good man at your side you have every chance of success.'

Fair play to the lad he took my advice and joined with a bigger and more athletic boy who was an excellent player. They didn't win many games at first but as time went by they became unbeatable so you see John there's many a man who is useless on his own but join him up with the right partner and you have a potential world-beater. So here's what you'll do. You latch on to this bookie's clerk like I told you and watch every move he makes. He'll be flattered that you should take such an interest in him and want to turn out like him. You'll be his protege. You see what he's done already; a brace of birds lined up waiting to be flushed and bagged. Even if things don't work out in Cork don't let it be a cause of worry to you. Rome wasn't built in a day and there's always tomorrow. Constant dropping wears a stone and ice is only ice till 'tis melted, if you get my meaning. Look to the future with new hope John. Let this man Brady be your new star and I'll be raising my eyebrows at the likes of the letters you'll be writing to me. Take care.

> Your old pal,
> Frank O'Dell.

*   *   *

> Tubberganban House,
> Tubberganban.

Dear Frank,
The Tubberganban Expeditionary Force has just withdrawn from Cork. From the beginning I had a deepseated presentiment that the business would be a failure but acting on your advice and knowing the powerful stratagems of my commander-in-chief, Sylvester Brady, I decided to finance the expedition for better or for worse. On Saturday evening I collected Brady and after a drink at the Bannabeen Arms we set out for the city. As we left Bannabeen the rain started to fall. It grew denser as we drove and aided by a strong southern breeze it reduced visibility to twenty-five yards and less in the mountainous areas. After a demanding and exhausting journey we eventually arrived at our destination. Brady insisted on a meal, a sirloin steak with chips, mushrooms, onions and peas. I couldn't eat a bite. Brady devoured the contents of his plate in minutes. He eats like a horse. Afterwards he borrowed a tenner from me. We had a few brandies and I

felt better. We then proceeded to a public house known as The Three Roosters. There was a plaster effigy of a woman holding three roosters to her bosom just over the entrance. The time was near midnight. Carefully Brady looked up and down the dismal street where the pub was situated and satisfying himself that there was no police-man in sight rapped four times on the fanlight with a coin.

'Who's out?' a male voice asked at once.

'Sylvie Brady and a friend,' came the reply.

'Come in effendi,' said a small, swarthy youth with a pock-marked face. He shook hands with Brady and with me when I was introduced to him as a Captain Cogan of the United States Marines.

'We have an appointment with some ladies,' Brady informed the youth whose name was simply Banger.

'I believe they're on the premises effendi,' said he with a wink. We were ushered through the main bar into a snug where two ladies were seated. The lights were low and I could hardly see my hand with the smoke. Brady seemed to be well-known to the females. Both shook his hand enthusiastically. He introduced me and we paired ourselves off. From what I could make out in the dim light, my partner whose name was Heather was heavily made-up but otherwise she looked attractive. I called for a drink and the conversation started to flow. Heather sat as close by my side as was physically possible. In whispers we spoke of many things. There was a warm and exciting air of intimacy in the snug. Brady cracked joke after joke and it could be said that we were all well on the top of our form. Heather told me of her life, why she never married because she was the sole support of an invalid mother and a demented brother, about her job in a bacon factory where she was supervisor in the sausage depart-ment, about a cruel foreman who never ceased to make passes at her, about girls of weaker character who surren-dered to his whims, about the general manager, a suave character who was always offering her lifts in his car and generally about the dangers that continually beset a decent girl who chose to remain single out of loyalty to her mother and brother. She told me of a doctor who was madly in love with her and who threatened to poison himself when she refused to marry him. Then there was a barrister who was insane about her. There was an engineer, an assortment of company directors and a handful of wealthy businessmen. There was no mention of menaials and I could hardly be blamed if I later suspected that she was suffering from delusions of grandeur. At the time it all sounded very factual and acceptable.

The hours wore on and the four of us grew progressively drunker. At length the youth known as Banger informed us that they were closing down but that if we wanted anything to take away they would gladly accommodate us.

'We'll have a bottle apiece of your best gin,' Brady told him. 'put them in separate bags and stick a few bottles of tonic in with each.' The parcels were duly delivered. I paid for both.

'See you back at the hotel later,' Brady said. With that he collected his parcel and left with his partner. It was now my turn. I felt the old excitement stirring inside. How many millions of times have the pulses of manking quickened at the prospect of the great encounter. I waited for a moment or two for some sort of clue. It was as well that I did, otherwise I might have said the wrong thing.

'Let's go,' she said. Arm in arm we walked through murky, gloom-ridden alleyways and lanes 'till we came to a narrow street. Conspiratorially she placed a forefinger on her lips and inserted a key in the lock of the run-down, two-storied house which was her home. In the tiny hallway she pointed the same forefinger at my shoes indicating that I was to take them off as she was doing. She then led the way up a creaky stairs. Never did so many steps protest so loudly and for so long. When we reached the top a female voice rang out loud and clear. 'Is that you Heather?' it said.

'My mother,' Heather explained in a whisper. 'Let me have a few pounds to keep her quiet.' Feverishly I withdrew my wallet and extended it. She extracted two fivers and returned it. She then disappeared into one of the three rooms on the landing. I stood idly, clutching the parcel which contained the gin and mixers, awaiting developments. The hair stood upright on my head when the figure of a man clad only in a short shift suddenly appeared in the doorway of the room next to the mother's.

He had a shock of wild dark hair on his head and for what seemed like an age he stood there silently without taking his eyes from mine. He started to tiptoe towards me. I would have run but my feet were stuck to the ground with the glue of mortal terror. He stopped when he was only a foot away from me.

'Have you e'er a smoke?' he asked civilly enough. I told him I didn't indulge.

'Would you have the price of a package itself?' he said. I was only too happy to oblige. If he was demented as his sister had said the proper thing to do was accede to any reasonable request he might make. Again I withdrew my wallet and was about to extract a pound when his fingers beat me to the draw and neatly lifted a fiver from the sheaf of notes inside.

'This will be plenty,' he announced. Like a flash he was gone. Almost at once Heather re-appeared. She opened the door of the third room and beckoned me to follow her. In her hand she carried two tumblers. Inside there was a bed, a ewer and basin with a rickety stand, a picture of Blessed Martin de Porres on the wall near the window and an ancient wardrobe in the corner near the bed. There was also a decrepit bamboo chair. She bade me take a seat while she poured two respectable dollups of gin into the tumblers. We added a little of the mixers. She swallowed hers at once and re-filled. She also swallowed this and re-filled again. She did no more than sip the third tumblerful. She placed it on top of the wardrobe and took off her coat. As she proceeded towards the bed she staggered and fell across it. She recovered quickly enough. It was only then I realised how drunk she was. I found the old excitement getting the better of me.

Just then the brother appeared in the doorway. He wore torn wellingtons and a tattered posteen. I am certain that he wore nothing underneath.

'I'm going out for awhile,' he informed Heather.

'Fire away,' she said drunkenly. He left after bidding me a most civil good morning. From her seat on the bedside she extended her open arms.

'Come to me,' she said. I went at once and we both lay on the coverlet with arms round each other. Then she emitted one of the deepest and most startling snores I ever heard and when I looked at her again she was fast asleep. I touched her but the snores came deep and even. I shook her but to no avail. Her mouth opened and her false teeth fell on the coverlet. I looked at her closely and I could see that she was out for the count. Silently I tiptoed down the stairs. At the foot I searched for my shoes but they were nowhere to be found. The brother's wellingtons were there alright. Thankful to have any sort of footwear I pulled them on. They were at least three sizes too large for me and I must have presented an odd picture as I plopped painfully back to the hotel. I had some difficulty in convincing the porter that I was a legitimate resident. In the end he let me in.

Brady was in the bathroom when I entered. He was entirely in the nude. He was crouched over the toilet bowl retching his guts up. He was a well-built fellow and it was there and then that I discovered what might have been part of his attraction for certain types of women. He was extremely well-developed in the netherlands. In fact there was a seam at the back of his pendants like you'd see on a sliotar which as you probably know is a hand-stitched hurley ball.

We both slept far into the following day and arose refreshed for the journey home. Brady wanted to spend another night in the city but the man I had hired to look after my cows had asked me to be home early on Sunday evening so that his wife could catch her Bingo bus. We arrived at Tubberganban at five o'clock in the afternoon. Brady insisted that I introduce him to my housekeeper, Eve Kishock and although I had warned him that she was as hard as nails he nevertheless insisted. Against my will I brought him into the house. Miss Kishock was reading a Sunday newspaper in the sitting-room. We stayed in the kitchen. I offered Brady a drink out of simple courtesy which he accepted. At once he made himself at home.

After ten minutes Eva Kishock came into the kitchen to enquire what time I would require the evening meal. I availed of the opportunity to introduce Brady. She received him coolly and was about to leave when he offered her a drink. She refused firmly. He held her there by pushing the conversation for all he was worth. You should see the transformation that took place in him. A more fawning, grovelling, slobbering wretch you could not imagine. Her every answer to his servile, cringing questions was a rebuke yet he persisted with a hangdog look about him which was disgusting to behold. The odd thing was that she seemed to take a perverse pleasure out of forcing him into the role of ingrate. He literally exuded servility accepting her insults with an instant 'yes miss' or 'no miss.' It was the first time since I came to know her that I saw Eva Kinshock enjoying herself. She did everything but spit on him and every time he came back, begging for more. When it was apparent that he could sink no lower she left him with a triumphant leer on her face.

'You should be ashamed of yourself,' I told him when we were alone together. I noticed, however, that he was his old self too quickly.

'Ashamed of myself?' he laughed.

'Yes,' I said, 'for behaving in such a degrading manner, allowing her to treat you like muck.'

'John Bosco,' said he, 'there are horses for courses and courses for horses and if I didn't know by now how to handle the likes of Miss Kishock I would have failed in my life's mission. She is a man-hater,' he continued, 'which means that she likes to get in the old heel at all times which is why I acted the way I did. Some dames like to be swept off their feet. Others like to be taken by force. More like a romantic approach. With this type you have to crawl.'

'You're wasting your time,' I told him.

'Maybe so. Maybe so,' was all he said. I drove him to the Bannabeen Arms where there was a new barmaid and where he borrowed two extra pounds from me. 'We'll rise again,' he said as we parted. I must go to confession soon Frank. I feel contaminated and in need of shriving. As soon as Father Kimmerley comes back from his annual holidays I'll face his confessional and tell him all. I'll try to get up for the Spring Show and will call to see you without fail. Meanwhile, take care.

As ever,
Your old pal,
John Bosco McLane.

★　★　★

Spiders' Well,
Ballybarra.

My lovely decent boy,
I have news at last. Three candidates for the job. One of these is only after leaving the convent after twenty-two years. She's fresh, shiny and firm and you may be sure would be a good bargain. I'll be approaching her with an account as soon as she gets more used to the outside. A likelier prospect is after arriving from America and by all accounts she is anxious to settle in a good farm and has a boodle of dollars. I'd say she's a bit long in the tooth but then there is none of us getting any younger. There is a third lady I met in the market when I was buying a trousers in the standings. I takes a fifty inch bellyband and the standings is the only place I can get what I want. This third one is from this locality and is a good sort of a mare in appearance and temper. She comes from good stock, a crowd that wouldn't turn their backs on a day's work. She knocks around a good bit but we musn't fault her on that. She do have a lot of callers and this can't be a bad sign. You may hear reports after you meet her that she's a flyer but this is jealousy as she is a fine ball of a woman with a noble stand and a head of red hair that would turn a man's head. What are we looking for anyway but someone nice to keep us company for all the rest of our days and boil our kettle and make our bed and all that. 'Tis not someone that's after being canonised we want. Am I right or

wrong? When I write again be ready to meet your future missus.

>Courtesy and civility assured at all times.
>Your obt. servant,
>Dicky Mick Dicky O'Connor.

P.S.: The name of the red-haired dame is Susie Lispie. She is one of the Redbelly Lispies that used to keep the Station Cock long ago if you ever heard of them.

>D.M.D.O'C.

★   ★   ★

>Knackers' Crescent,
>Bannabeen.

Dear John,
I would have hitched a drive to Tubberganban but I don't trust the drivers, not that they might crash the car or anything like that but I always sense an overpowering resentment whenever I am in the vicinity of yokels, no disrespect to yourself who I find to be one white man. The new barmaid here at the Arms is a dead loss. She's engaged to a carpenter from Galway and she's keeping it for him. The reason I write is to find out if by any chance you might be going to the Spring Show in Dublin. I understand there's plenty hoofla going the rounds during that week. If you are going I would be free to go with you as I have a fortnight's holidays coming to me. I have a gift for you. It's not from me personally but from your Cork girlfriend, Heather. It's a pair of shoes. I'm certain they'll be the right size.

Let me know about the Spring Show as soon as you can as I will have to give a week's notice if I am to get my holidays.

>Quietly,
>Sylvie.

★   ★   ★

Tubberganban House,
Tubberganban.

Dear Frank,
There have been a few interesting developments since I wrote last. Sylvie Brady wants to accompany me to the Spring Show. What do you think? The Cork travesty was not altogether his fault and maybe he deserves a second chance. Things have a habit of happening when he's around. Desperate ills require desperate remedies but I'll wait to hear what you have to say before finalising anything. The housekeeper seems friendlier of late but she is still the same, cold, detached female at heart. I must confess I like and respect her. I daresay I could grow to be fond of her if she gave me any encouragement. Your suggestion that I start my own club with her is out of the question. She has a resistance like stressed concrete and a general contempt for men which is quite frightening. There is a barely perceptible change of late but a false move on my part and I can see her reverting fully to her old self. A few weeks ago I took the bull by the horns and asked her if she would like to come out with me some night to the singing pub. The answer was no. I asked her if she had anything personal against me.

'Nothing,' she said, 'it's just you're such a manky little runt.'

I have been to confession. Father Kimmerley came back from his holidays on Saturday and I went to him Saturday night. I told him about my sinful expedition to Cork. Kimmerley spent the early years of his ministry in Pittsburgh before being recalled by his bishop.

'Why do you unburden these harmless sagas on me?' he asked.

'Because you are my confessor,' I said simply, 'and besides I have sinned.'

'Sinned,' he echoed scornfully. 'There isn't the makings of a dacent sin in the entire doings of the lot o' you. In God's name,' he continued, 'how would you commit a sin in Tubberganban unless 'twas buggery. There's no one to adult with and who would you rape?'

'I'm not talking about Tubberganban,' I said testily.
'I'm talking about Cork.'

'Okay,' he said irritably, 'so you're talking about Cork.
I just told you about Cork.'

'No, you did not,' I put in.

'You want me to be clinical,' he scoffed. 'Is that it? If
that's it please answer the following questions truthfully.
Did you have intercourse with this woman?'

'I did not.'

'Did you in any way interfere with her private part?'

'I did not.'

'Or she with yours?'

'She did not.'

He laughed scornfully. 'My poor man,' he said, 'you're
still a chastitute. This whole countryside is reeking with
chastitution. What am I going to say to you? Should I tell
you go forth and fornicate properly before confessing to me
again or should I castigate you and send you from this
confessional without absolution.'

He remained silent for a while and so did I. When he
spoke again it was in rhyme:

Good Luck and success to the Council of Trent,
Who put fast upon meat but not upon drink.

'Doggerel,' he said 'but the Council of Trent should
have taken places like Tubberganban into account. Canon
law should have made special provision for the situation
here where marriage is a luxury. What right have I to
condemn a man who is plagued by physical hunger for the
opposite sex? Is this not the natural law? Is it not good? Is
it not a thousand times better than buggery or self-indul-
gence? Sometimes I think the Church is blind to the real
needs of places like Tubberganban where enforced chastity
is stifling life itself. Three Hail Marys and get out of my
sight.'

That was the end of the confession. Father Kimmerley,
to give him his due, is an honest sort of man. He knows
what is basically amiss. He knows that sexual sin, as the
Church defines it, is the road to normalcy.

Write soon and let me know for sure about the Brady
situation. By the way, I had a brief visit from my aunt. The
housekeeper and she toured the house together and the

aunt expressed satisfaction at the state of things. I have a
sneaking feeling that she does not want to see me marrying.
I suspect that she wants to spend her retirement here. It
would be an ideal set-up for her and why should I complain when there seems to be now no likelihood that I will
marry. Where would I find her equal as a housekeeper? She
chose the Kishock woman to suit herself. She knew that a
no-messing, no-nonsense woman would hold the place
intact till she herself was ready to take over. She senses that
these are my most desperate and vulnerable years. She's
right of course. Roll on the Spring Show. Hope springs
eternal. Where would we be without it? I still dream the
erotic dreams. I still long for the great fulfilment. Hopeless
though my prospects may seem today I am more determined than ever to carry on the campaign. It has to be now
or never and if I fail I cannot reproach myself. My utmost
shall have been done.

Your old pal,
John Bosco McLane.

★   ★   ★

While John Bosco prepares for the Spring Show let us
take a look at the environs from which he evolved. Wholesale emigration, stemmed alas too late, has taken a terrible
toll of Tubberganban. The haemorrage began during Black
forty-seven at the height of the potato famine and for over
a hundred years extracted its dues out of the human crop
that sprang forth from each generation. The population of
the parish declined with every passing year until its all-
time-low of this present time. The truly tragic characters
are the middle-aged and more advanced bachelors who
walk the land like shadows as if they knew they were the
last of their kind. They are peculiar to the time and to the
countryside where they eke out a living from their milch
cows and small government supplements. The womenfolk
have deserted them for the towns, for the irresistible call of
the five-day week, the annual holidays, the modern houses,
the urban amenities, the steady wages. The bigger farmers
were luckier. They married their own kind but there are

only a handful of these so that there are only handfuls of children where there were hundreds. Those crusty fellows who hung on to their small holdings were for the most part obliged to wait for an independence of sorts till their aged parents passed on. By then it was too late. The younger women had fled the place and only a few suspect spinsters remained.

A lucky few found women to marry them but the moment their offspring were capable of engaging in a day's work they could not get out quickly enough. It is true to say that there are more men and women from Tubberganban in England, Australia and America than there are in Tubberganban.

Let us look briefly at the eligible girls who flowered in Tubberganban during John Bosco's young manhood. They numbered twenty four and if they had married in the parish the population would have surged upwards and restored life to the hills and valleys. What happened was this. Only one married locally. She was the daughter of one of the bigger farmers and she naturally married into a similar situation. Twelve of the remainder emigrated to England and America and those who remained married products of the nearby towns and cities. They married men with the following occupations: trousers-maker, teacher, shopkeeper, doctor, commercial traveller, bank clerk, fitter, lavatory attendant, hardware assistant. They married anybody in fact who was not a product of the Tubberganban hill country. The two remaining became brides of Christ which means they entered convents. There was nobody left.

As for John Bosco, it might be said that he remained overlong with his mother. If he had sought a wife in his twenties or early thirties we might not see him as he is today. There are many like him who waited or were forced to wait. Cruel mischance turned them into love-laggards. When they found themselves free to enter the lists of love their lances were blunt and their armour rusted. They are not, however, without hope and are, as Dicky Mick Dicky O'Connor might say, game to the tail.

'If I could personify this area of rural Ireland,' Father Kimmerley once told his bishop, 'I would see it as an unshaven lout, fifty-five years old, wearing a long black coat and a cap. He would be standing at the door of a public house in Bannabeen with porter stains on mouth and a bloodstained parcel of boiling beef under his oxter. He would be futilely waving after the bus to Tubberganban which has just departed the terminus. In short, he has missed the bus of life and now he must straggle home on his own.'

'I see it in much the same light,' said Bill Carey, who was a curate in Bannabeen but was familiar with the Tubberganban countryside because it was no more than a replica of the parish where he was born.

'I see it,' said he, 'as a dark, dull, dour man on a bleak mountain road leading an old cow into the teeth of blinding hailstones on the way to market. The cow drops dead but the man goes on and on to nowhere.'

The bishop heard these contributions in silence.

A young curate spoke. 'I see the place,' said he, 'as a jaded old woman fit for nothing but the corner of the hearth, waiting for the cold hand of death to touch her on the shoulder.'

The bishop coughed uneasily. This sort of thing could get out of hand.

'I'll set up a commission,' he said.

'For what?' Father Kimmerley asked.

'For the purpose of investigating the problem and finding a solution,' said the bishop.

'You're a generation too late,' Kimmerley told him. 'The best thing now is to let the poor aingisheoirs expire naturally and peacefully.'

It was as well that John Bosco McLane and his bachelor neighbours did not hear this conversation. It would have eroded the slender hope that remained to them.

Let us proceed now from this juncture and look over the shoulder of Dicky Mick Dicky O'Connor, an inevitable product of the aforementioned environment and curiously enough a man, although often maligned, who has done far more than Church and State together to ease the marital situation. He believes that he has at last found the ideal partner for John Bosco in the person of Susie Lispie of the renowned Redbelly Lispies who once kept the famous

Station Cock of Rhode Island extraction. Susie Lispie is approaching her thirty-fifth year but it is strange to comment that she has not, until this time, felt the urge to settle down. When Dicky Mick Dicky O'Connor informs her of the availability of John Bosco McLane she jumps at the opportunity.

★   ★   ★

Spiders' Well,
Ballybarra.

My lovely decent boy,
Soon you'll be throwin' the leg over as sure as there's bristles on the back of a boar. I was yesterday at the Redbelly Lispies and I spoke to the father and mother who know well your breed and the comfortable place you have and they have no objection so long as Susie herself won't cock her nose at you. You may be sure she'll do nothing of the kind for she's as anxious to settle down as you are with all the oats sown by her and a brother who's for the place thinking of bringing in his own woman. She has a very winning way with her has this fine young Susie Lispie and the sooner you meet her the better for all parties. I'll have her at the Arms Hotel in Bannabeen at nine o'clock next Sunday night and praise be to God and his holy mother you'll be calling off the search by the time the night is over.

Courtesy and civility assured at all times
Your obt. servant,
Dicky Mick Dicky O'Connor.

★   ★   ★

Tubberganban House,
Tubberganban.

Dear Frank,
Many thanks for your letter. On the strength of what you say I'll bring Brady to the Spring Show. On Sunday night

last I met a girl, through the agency of Dicky Mick Dicky O'Connor, at the Bannabeen Arms Hotel. Her name is Susie Lispie. I told Brady I was meeting her and he informed me he was acquainted with her. I asked him what he thought of her.

'In the whole of Europe,' said he, 'and that's a wide place, there is nothing on two feet to match Susie Lispie.'

It was not till later that his meaning was made clear.

In the bar of the Bannabeen Arms dark-eyed Susie Lispie awaited me. As soon as I appeared Dicky Mick Dicky, in whose company she had been, excused himself and promised that he would be back later. Susie opted for whiskey. I decided to stay on safe ground and ordered a gin. After the third round the barriers of reserve were raised and we began to talk about each other. She would have married sooner but it had not occurred to her. An extremely popular girl she was forever going to parties. She had had scores of boyfriends but had never done a serious line, at least not yet. I spoke about the house and farm, my aunt and Eva Kishock. I carefully avoided mention of Brady and was pleased to note that he was patronising some other establishment that night. She mentioned the problem of her brother who was planning to marry. This would necessitate her having to leave home and the finding of alternative accommodation. As soon as her brother's intended handed over her dowry to his parents they, in turn, would hand it over to her. She confided that she would probably go to America where she had an aunt who would be glad of her company since the husband of said aunt had succumbed to a coronary a short while before. She had no intention of making me rush my fences but she would have to make a decision very soon and it would help matters if I was to declare my hand. We parted and arranged a meeting for the following Tuesday night. I collared Brady and asked him to define exactly what he meant when he declared that in the whole of Europe there was nothing to match Susie Lispie.

'What do you want me to do?' he asked evasively, 'give the girl a bad reference. I only knock women,' he went on 'in the physical sense. I never knock them otherwise.'

Susie and I met, as arranged, at the Bannabeen Arms. She wore a smart navy blue trouser suit and a huge brooch on one of its lapels. The brooch, she explained, was a gift from the American aunt. We started off on Irish whiskey and after the third the conversation took an intimate turn. We discussed her situation on the home front. The brother, it appeared, had announced the date of his marriage. It was to be soon, less than six weeks.

'I suppose,' I said with calculated carelessness 'that if a fellow was to propose you might not say no.'

'That,' said she 'would depend on who the fellow was.'

'Suppose it was me,' I said.

'I'd marry you alright,' she answered after a while, 'but I couldn't leave down my regular clients.'

I took a quick swallow of whiskey and pretended I hadn't heard.

'Would that suit?' she asked after another while. I could not believe my ears. I rose and excused myself on the grounds that I had to visit the toilet. I met Brady in a pub near the market place. There was a fat woman in his company. She turned out to be a Mrs Lapwing from the United States, who was holidaying in the district with distant relatives.

'I'm home and dried here,' he said in an aside, 'why the hell do you want to cut in?'

'Why didn't you tell me about Susie Lispie?'

'Because,' he returned in a whisper, 'the same Susie is as straight as they come and would not conceal anything from anybody, least of all a prospective husband.'

I was forced to admit to myself that what he said was true enough. My ill-luck with the opposite sex continues. I knew decent girls when I was in my prime but every one of these is married. What sort of woman can I expect at my age. She would have to be flawed as I am.

A minor flaw I would not mind
But oozy Susie loves mankind.

Brady and I have decided to stay at the Royal Brigade Hotel during the Spring Show. It was he who selected it. I don't know what the rates are but since it is I who will have to pay the bill I have no doubt that it is the most expensive available. I'll be seeing you soon then. Take care.

As ever,
Your old pal,
John Bosco McLane.

★ ★ ★

Tubberganban House,
Tubberganban.

Dear Frank,
Before I say anything let me first of all thank you for the splendid dinner Flora set before us before we left your place for Dublin proper. Brady wishes to convey his thanks also and assures me that he will be writing himself as well as sending a small token of his appreciation. It was a princely reception you gave us Frank and as far as I am concerned it was the highlight of my itinerary. Brady maintains it was the best week-end he ever spent anywhere. We booked into the Royal Brigade at ten o'clock and from then on it was a non-stop jumble of unrelieved boozing. I had the most extraordinary time, a conglomeration of tragedy, comedy, farce and burlesque. I found myself in the strangest situation. I won't bore you with all the details but I'm sure you'll be interested in how we fared at the Show itself. On the Saturday morning after our arrival we set out for the showgrounds having put away a hearty breakfast. The night before was uneventful. We had a lot to drink and chatted up several women but all to no avail. At the showgrounds we inspected the various stands. This country has certainly come on since my first Spring Show twenty years ago. The displays of sophisticated machinery were simply bewildering. There were huge crowds in all the enclosures and luckily the weather held fine. Brady left several orders under a false name for machinery and other odds and ends. We were treated to a variety of drinks by the salesmen, many of whom were continental and quite clearly impressed by Brady's offhand manner.

I begged him to return to the stands and cancel the orders but he wouldn't hear of it. In nearly every stand we visited we were offered a drink because of his obvious interest in the wares. He wore a bright tweed suit and a jaunty tweed hat with a feather in its hand. He looked like a respectable businessman and wherever we tarried to inspect interesting machinery he would whisper meaningless phrases to me concerning the items we were inspecting. All I could do was nod my head and try to look serious. He did not have to approach anybody. Always they approached him. Whenever we happened upon a stand where there was a good-looking girl employed he would ask for a date but nearly all were married or engaged. They seemed to enjoy his proposals, however, and I was under the impression that, given the time and the right place, there was at least one who might have succumbed to his wiles. I nearly said charm but that would be a grave misapplication of the word. Give him his due he never tries to be charming. He is uncompromising, blunt, suggestive and often deliberately nasty but these combined characteristics never fail to impress certain women. I have heard them insult them to their faces and get away with it. He never, under any circumstances, treats a woman like a lady unless it is for an evil purpose. If I were asked to describe Sylvester Brady in one sentence I would say that he was the very opposite of a gentleman. Paradoxically, this is his trump card when he sets his sights on somebody he fancies.

Towards midday we had lunch in the restaurant and after a second inspection of the grounds we adjourned to the bar where he immediately became involved in a serious row with three farmers over the price of cattle. I dragged him away to the other end of the bar and called for two whiskies. He took a sip from his and surveyed the scene. Nearby there were two ladies talking loudly about showjumping. Their accents were highly cultivated and it was apparent from their clothes and jewellery that they were women of means. Their talk was without let-up and without real meaning. They were a reasonably attractive pair although somewhat past their best and were, from a showgrounds point of view, in prime condition.

Brady interrupted the conversation and addressed himself to the nearer of the pair. 'I beg your pardon,' he said with an imperceptible doff of his hat. The woman looked at him vaguely.

'Were you addressing me?' she asked disinterestedly.

'Correct me if I'm wrong,' Brady said superciliously, 'but I have the feeling we met last Easter at Fairyhouse.'

Before she had a chance to reply he took her hand and kissed it deftly. He then introduced himself.

'Hugo Sinclair,' he announced imperiously, 'of Sinclair's Seeds.'

'Oh' both women said simultaneously. Through the bar window could be seen a mighty hoarding which advertised the seeds in question.

'I just dashed over for a drink,' he explained, 'to get the chaff out of my throat.' Nobody spoke for a while. We stood as if by arrangement in complete silence as if we were waiting for a definite cue.

'Let me introduce my friend,' Brady spoke after the best part of a minute. He had used the intervening silence cunningly. He had given the impression that it was probably shyness and respect which held up his furthering the conversation.

'This is Colonel McNab of Melbourne,' he said, 'he is the chief mule-buyer for the Australian Army.' I could see that we were making an impression. He ordered a round of drinks despite their protestations but he neglected to pay for it.

'In a moment,' he said to the barman. The barman moved away and subsequently made several unsuccessful return trips for his money. I paid him in full when I ordered a second round of drinks. The ladies turned out to be Mrs Evelyn Purson and Mrs Joy Berry. During the conversation it was revealed that Mrs Purson was a widow and that Mrs Berry was separated from her husband. Of the two Mrs Berry was the more attractive. Somehow I found myself partnered with Mrs Purson. This, of course, was solely due to a choice bit of manoeuvring by Brady. In no time at all we were on first-name terms. Brady had insisted on this and the women had not objected. We drank steadily, exchanging views and confidences till six o'clock. The ladies were natives of the west of Ireland and were staying at the Elmlands Hotel which was situated on the same block as the Royal Brigade. When Brady offered a lift they accepted gladly. On the way from the showgrounds to the alley where I had parked my car Brady sang incessantly. His companion, Mrs Berry, whose hand he held in his, hummed her approval. I dared not risk taking Evelyn's hand in mine although I had the feeling that she would not have minded. I was later to be proved correct in this. I won't bore you Frank with interminable details. We stopped at the Elmlands where we had several rounds of drink and a meal, all at my expense. I didn't mind in the least. The evening was turning out to my liking. Immediately after I had paid for the meal Brady, in the presence of the ladies, insisted in reimbursing me. He thrust a sum of money into my coat pocket with a lavish flourish which impressed his partner considerably. When I examined it later to find out how much he had given me I discovered that it wasn't currency at all. He had duped me with three or four crumpled sheets of crisper-type toilet paper. I had partly guessed that it wasn't genuine money. I wasn't in the least put out. For one thing he did not have the resources to pay for the type of meal we had enjoyed.

At about ten o'clock Mrs Berry and he had vanished from the scene. Neither Evelyn nor I had the faintest idea where they might have gone. I certainly knew where Brady would have liked to go but somehow Mrs Purson did not strike me as the type who would become promiscuous overnight. I was stunned when my companion turned to me and suggested we withdraw. I had entertained certain hopes I confess but here she was making all the running. Silently I rose and let her lead the way. I was too overwhelmed to speak. Anyway, I dared not trust myself to make a comment of any kind.

In her bedroom she turned on the radio and at once the strains of a string quartet set the atmosphere for a romantic interlude. We danced cheek to cheek and on our second time round the room I kissed her gently on the brow. She responded by pressing her body against mine. We danced for some time. Suddenly she stopped and studied my face for a long moment.

'Get your clothes off,' she whispered, 'I won't be gone long.'

So saying she entered the bathroom. I stood dumbfounded for a moment but then I stripped to my pelt as I had been told. I sat on the side of the bed with my back turned to the bathroom door. I am most modest by nature. I sat waiting for her to re-appear. Outside the bedroom window the leaves of a giant elm fluttered in the evening breeze. Dusk had fallen. Somewhere in the world of trees and shrubbery outside an owl called faintly. Then there was silence. Had he called to wish me luck or was his muted salute a hoot of derision. For better or for worse the great confrontation of my life was almost upon me. I thought of Juleen McCoon's coarseness and poor taste. I thought of my mother and my father and of the dancehall at Bannabeen and of Father Kimmerley seated in the awful darkness of the confessional. He might not react so smirkily when I next visited him. I thought of everything and anything except the woman who would presently lie in my eager arms.

Suddenly there was a shaft of light behind me and I knew that when I turned my head she would be framed in the open doorway of the bathroom. Slowly I looked round. I was right. She stood there smiling, bulging and roseate, tender and inviting, the moisture of love glinting on her full, red lips. She advanced a step but I was still too shy to turn round. She stopped a few feet from the bed. There was an overwhelming odour of delightful scent. Then she extended her open arms towards me and I knew that my time had at last come. I was about to rise when there sounded on the bedroom door the most thunderous knocking I had ever heard. It was absolutely deafening and when it persisted I decided it would have to be answered. What if it was her lover? My life wouldn't be worth a quenched match. Covering my loins with my shirt I opened the door. Outside stood a young porter with sweat shining on his forehead.

'Run for your life,' he shouted, 'there's a bomb about to go off at any minute.' With that he knocked on the next door with all his strength. A pink and white form whistled past me and careered along the corridor. It was my partner, in her birthday suit, making good her escape. Snatching my trousers I followed suit, I passed her on the second landing. It was every man for himself at this stage. Screams and shouts came from the rooms and I cursed the fiends who spread such terror amongst innocent people. As we erupted into the foyer Mrs Purson took the lead for a second time. Neck and neck at the front of the disorderly field we poured into the street. Outside a large contingent of onlookers had gathered. We were greeted with loud cheers. I distinctly heard the voice of Sylvester Brady above all the others. I paused in the middle of the roadway to pull on my trousers. I saw him standing on the roof of a motor car applauding wildly.

Later that night in my room at the Royal Brigade, while recovering from shock, I was visited by Brady. He was stewed in drink but incoherent as he was he heaped a wide selection of colourful curses on the Elmlands Hotel. Apparently one of the night porters who he had earlier insulted for no reason followed him to the door of Mrs Berry's room and, as he was about to enter, accosted him and told him that he could not occupy a single room with another person. When Brady protested and told the porter that he would fling him out of the windows if he didn't go away the man called a number of his colleagues and booted Brady unceremoniously out into the street. A running fight followed in which Brady was an easy victor. He would run twenty to thirty yards to lure his assailants away from the hotel door, stop suddenly and haul out viciously with a combination of accurate punches, then sprint off again in another direction lest he be outnumbered. I could well believe this because if you ask anyone in Bannabeen about Brady they will assure you that the only way to beat him in a fight is to kill him.

'Will you give me a straight answer,' I requested him, 'if I ask you an honest question?'

'Ask the question,' he said with a deep laugh.

'Was it you who rang the hotel and told them there was a bomb about to go off?'

'Yes' he said after a while. 'I hope it didn't inconvenience you.'

That is the story Frank of my trip to the Spring Show. I have a notion of changing my whole way of life. I'm going through a crisis and I cannot say what the outcome will be. Say a prayer for me.

Your old pal,
John Bosco McLane.

* * *

Spiders' Well,
Ballybarra.

My lovely decent boy,
I heard you were at the Spring Show with Mr Brady. I hope you enjoyed yourself. 'Tis a place I was never in is Dublin. I hear they have great spuds there, pure balls of flour by all accounts. I have a lady for you. She's nice and firm. It's fair to tell you that she has the false teeth, upper and lower but this don't take from her. She was going with a man by the name of Kearney for years but the heart gave out on him and he spreading manure. She's free now is Miss Daisy Mongey which is the name she goes by. You might know her father, Dan Jack Pats Mongey from Cappafaudeen that always wears the Clydesdale Navy on Sundays. Fond of his drop too. I pulled him out of a scairt of briars one evening and he coming home from Bannabeen horse fair. He was like he'd be sand-blasted. A fine decent man you may be sure with that bare fault and no more. The daughter Daisy is a decent girl, never had a harness on her I swear not like more of them that was over the course a hundred times. I can have her planked at the hotel this coming Sunday night if you are still inclined towards the twosome way of life. See you unless otherwise stated.

Courtesy and civility at all times.
Your obt. servant,
Dicky Mick Dicky O'Connor.

* * *

Knackers' Crescent,
Bannabeen.

Dear John Bosco,
Why the coolness? Is it over the bomb scare? Listen to
what I have lined up. There are a set of identical twins
staying at the Arms here in Bannabeen. I was introduced to
them yesterday by the manager and they looked game
enough to me and I, as you know my friend, am no bad
judge of game. I told them I had a bachelor pal and they
agreed to going out for a night to Cork or some place. I'll
expect you on Saturday night. I'll have them ready and
waiting.

Sincerely,
Sylvie.

★   ★   ★

Tubberganban House,
Tubberganban.

Dear Sylvester,
I won't be coming in on Saturday night. It has nothing to
do with the bomb scare and it has nothing personal to do
with you because I must admit that bad as my luck was
with the opposite sex there was never a dull moment while
you were around. I am going through a puzzling time just
now. You won't be seeing me for some time. I wish you
every success.

Sincerely,
John Bosco.

★   ★   ★

Tubberganban House,
Tubberganban.

Dear Dicky Mick Dicky,
Enclosed find my cheque for fifty pounds in part recompense for the efforts you have made on my behalf. I will

be unable, for personal reasons, to be present at the hotel on Sunday night. In fact I will no longer need your services.

Sincerely,
John Bosco McLane.

* * *

Tubberganban House,
Tubberganban.

Dear Frank,
You would think that with so many defeats and total routs in the sex war I would have the good sense to surrender and become resigned to bachelorhood but no. I muster my jaded, battered resources time after time and chance my arm in fresh combat. From the age of puberty to this present time it has been a forty years war. What other motive would send a man forth, bloody but unbowed, for the best part of a lifetime, not gold, nor silver nor precious stones, not land, nor scholarship, nor God nor all your Everests, only womankind. Be sure the great urge passes for a while and seems to fade but this is merely dormancy. You can no more keep it permanently at bay then you can reap the stars of the heavens or turn back the flowing tide. But for my faith in Christ's goodness I would sometime call a halt to it all. When I am out amongst humanity I sometimes feel like a hare. That's what all men are whether they like it or not, hares who are being constantly hounded by their own kind. We are forever fleeing the results of man's progress and we end up by fleeing ourselves. Such is the competition of the world that I sometimes feel the currents of evil swirling and boiling all round me as I walk the country and town. These countries are the hostilities, the jealousies, the indignities, the resentments and futile, consuming hatreds of life. If they had a physical shape they would be horrifying to behold. These are the real devils my friend, these harassing fiends whose aim is to mutilate mentally and physically.

I have come to the conclusion that Christ is the only answer, the only hope. Subconsciously I knew this all along but so avid was I for the pleasures of this life that I forgot the only real goodness that exists. As the sun is the source of power so also is Christ the source of goodness.

This is a known fact but it has to be repeatedly revealed to a person before he gives it the priority it deserves. As you can see I am in a philosophic mood. Philosophy is a great balm for the wounds inflicted by a cruel world. I announced this lately to Brady and do you know the answer he gave me. 'A good screw,' says he, 'would leave all your philosophy in the shade.'

He's a hard case. 'You'll never see Heaven,' I told him.

'Heaven,' says he, 'is for eunuchs and holy josies.'

I daresay this new-found philosophy of mine is the result of a recent fit of depression after my experiences at the Spring Show. You are the only person Frank to know what I am now about to reveal and I would ask you to keep silent till certain arrangements have been made. I have decided to join an order. I have the matriculation from our school days and with five or six years study I would have no difficulty in being ordained a priest. With the present world-wide scarcity most orders would jump at the opportunity of acquiring me even if I am past my prime. I have thought of the Franciscans although they seem to be a far cry from the innocent mendicants of Saint Francis's time and their worldly possessions would seem to be a far cry from the pitiful Purziuncola of Assissi but for all that I regard them as a brave and dedicated company devoid of nonsense and frills. I believe they would be my best bet. There is so much to be done, many a slip between the cup and lip if you follow. That is why I must insist that you keep this divulgation to yourself. Do not look upon this proposed action as a retreat from the fray. Rather look upon it as the entry into a new life. I am no bullock seeking lush and peaceful pastures. I can still feel the red blood thumping in my pulses when a nicely-designed posterior waggles within my ken. I have dreamed all my life of fair women. I have suffered many an agony in my lovely bed conjuring up impossible encounters. I have longed for the bouncing and bobbing of nicely turned tender buttocks in my lustful palms and yielded to every conceivable fantasy. I have thirsted for the incomparable symmetry of smooth young bellies. I feel as deeply and as strongly as any man. This is no plaster saint who is holding forth. This is a sinner, a man of the world who confides in you. I confess I fell in for some deflation a few weeks ago when I first thought of the idea. The end result, however, of this deflation was the strengthening of my determination. I went to Father Kimmerley to have my confession heard. After he had given me absolution and a nominal penance I asked him if he would give me some assistance in solving a personal problem.

'That is exactly what we are here for my good man,' said he.

'I have a notion' I said 'of entering Holy Orders.'

'So long as it remains a notion,' said he with a chuckle, 'we'll be alright.'

'I didn't expect you to be facetious at my expense,' I said hotly.

'Sorry,' he said. 'You see I am a product of Salamanca who was case-hardened in Pittsburgh and you might say I am something of a sceptic. What precisely have you in mind my son?'

'The Franciscans,' I replied.

'There is no accounting for taste,' he returned, 'and we are told that it takes all kinds to make a world and I daresay if there weren't Franciscans we would have some other gaggle in their stead. So you want to be a priest,' he lowered his voice and spoke half to himself, half to me. 'This could mean that the Italian monopoly of the Holy See is in jeopardy at long last,' he said with mock seriousness. I could hear the barely restrained laughter from the inky blackness of his compartment.

'You refuse to take me seriously,' I said bitterly.

'Aren't you McLane?' he said, 'that has the farm back the road?'

'My identity doesn't matter,' I replied.

'It matters to me,' he shouted, 'for without a reference from me you can go and whistle.' His voice grew softer all of a sudden. 'Maybe I've been too hard on you,' he said.

'You seem to be serious. If you want me to do so I'll write to the Abbot and enquire what the position is with regard to chaps like yourself. I'll tell him that as far as I know you're sound in mind, limb and sconce. You're not drunk by any chance are you?'

'I assure you I am not,' I replied.

'Very well,' he said. 'Drop round to see me in a week or so and I'll let you know where you stand.'

'Do you think I'm doing the right thing?' I asked instead of keeping me mouth shut.

'When all fruit fails,' he said, 'we must try haws mustn't we?'

With that he slid across the small shutter of his compartment and gave his attention to some unfortunate sinner in the other box. All he did was strengthen my resolve. I am determined to quit this awful bloody world and find happiness in holy surroundings where there is neither mockery nor scorn, where brother loves brother and all love God.

Pray for me.

Your old pal,
John Bosco McLane.

* * *

Ballycolleen,
Co Dublin.

Dear John Bosco,
Go off it for a few weeks. Better still join the A.A. You can come here if you want to and rest up.

Your old schoolmate,
Frank O'Dell.

* * *

> Tubberganban House,
> Tubberganban.

Dear Frank,
Dammit and blast it man I haven't had a drink since the
Spring Show.

> Your old pal,
> John Bosco.

* * *

> Ballycolleen,
> Co Dublin.

Dear John,
If you're not drinking then you're out of your mind. If I
don't get a coherent reply to this letter I'll have to presume
you are not yourself. I'll have no choice but to make the
journey to Tubberganban to ensure that all is well with
you.

> Your old schoolmate,
> Frank O'Dell.

* * *

> Tubberganban House,
> Tubberganban.

Dear Frank,
For the love and honour of God can't you get into your
head that there is nothing whatsoever the matter with me.
I am not the first man to be blessed with a late vocation.
It's a commonplace happening. You'll just have to get
used to it. Some day, several years hence, you'll be calling
me Father John. Maybe I'll be the priest to marry your
grandson. I'm touched by your solicitude for my welfare.
It's only what I would expect of you and you know I
would do the same for you. Please give me a fair hearing.
I am determined to join the Franciscans and there is no

power on earth that can stop me. It's no use trying to dissuade me. No more will I suffer at the hands of ruthless females. I'll be safe from all that sort of thing soon. My priesthood will bring me immunity from the wicked wiles of the opposite sex. I will not hate those who spurned me. I will pray for them. Do not be concerned about me. I am travelling the right road at last.

> As ever,
> Your old pal,
> John Bosco McLane.

★   ★   ★

> Ballycolleen,
> Co Dublin.

Dear John,
Very well. I'll bear with you 'till this thing is over.
    Take care.

> Your old schoolmate,
> Frank.

★   ★   ★

> Tubberganban House,
> Tubberganban.

Dear Auntie Frances,
The contents of this letter will come as a surprise to you. Actually I don't know where to begin. I'd better begin at the beginning I suppose. For some time I have found that life has not been as kind to me as it should be. That is to say I am not getting my fair share of the pleasures which all human beings have a right to expect. Also I feel ashamed and degraded at many events in my past life. For this and other reasons I am turning to God. Staying with me here at the house for the past few days is a Father

restraint and only partial involvement. Sex, I concede, is only one of many aspects of marriage but it can assume proportions which dwarf the others into insignificance.

Your nephew and others like him have no way of escaping at this stage. Security has to come first when you pass fifty and because of this they refuse to pull up roots and transfer themselves to climates where there would be a greater awareness and a solution to their particular problems. You can almost feel the guilt of these unfortunate people. A world without guilt would be unimaginable to them. Let me conclude by saying that John Bosco McLane will never wear a round collar. Let your worries in this respect be at an end. Many thanks for your substantial offering. I will say the masses at the earliest opportunity.

> Respectfully yours,
> Patrick Kimmerley, P.P.V.F.

★　★　★

> Ballycolleen,
> Co Dublin.

Dear John,

I'm indeed relieved to hear that you have given up the idea of entering the priesthood. You were never cut out fot that caper. Suppose you wanted to go on a skite? Where would you come by the money. Attached to an order like the one you had in mind you wouldn't get a bloody razoo. Anyway you haven't the appearance for it. I'm not saying that you're ugly or anything like that but fair play to you that kisser of yours does not inspire confidence. Man dear you wouldn't even make a tolerable Christian brother. Not even a brown monk would you make. Stick to what you're at. There is no friend like the land. You can go off and leave it behind but it will still be there when you get back. You don't leave the land down and it won't leave you down. It won't deny you or it won't renege on you. So now after all is said and done the world is your oyster again and I'm hard put to know what

Alaphonsus Plugg. He comes from Warwickshire and is the Vocational promoter for the Pioneers of the Holy Word who are endeavouring to establish an up-to-date missionary movement in Latin America. Plugg is an amazing man. For years before he was visited by God he was a strong man in a circus but when the call came he abandoned the road and entered a seminary. His speciality is the late vocation and that is precisely what I have.

There would have been no need for me to apply to the Pioneers of the Holy Word if my own parish priest, Father Kimmerley, had taken me seriously or even accorded me the common respect that one human being owes to another. He is a dyed in the wool cynic. Even his own bishop cannot stand him. When he failed to negotiate on my behalf with any of the Irish orders I answered an advertisement which I saw in *The Southern Bugle*. It simply said: 'Have you a late vocation? If you think you have consult us. Write to Father A.X. Plugg, Pioneers of the Holy Word, Thope-on-the-Resin, Warwickshire.'

Image my utter astonishment when Plugg arrived by return post as it were. What a difference there is between a man like this and Father Kimmerley. Father Plugg and I go for long walks at night and afterwards share a bottle of whiskey while we argue or rather debate theology and other matters relating to my future. Plugg is a most virtuous and saintly man and if he has a fault it is that he takes a drop or two over and above on occasion. Kimmerley with typical disparagement has christened him Cut Plugg. As you well know I have my matriculation which means there will be no preliminary examination or test of any kind apart from suitability before I enter the mother house at Thope-on-the-Resin. The main reason I have in writing is to ask for your blessing and prayers. Miss Kishock sends her regards. I have explained to her that there will be a bonus to compensate her in lieu of her enforced retirement from my employment. Write soon.

> Your loving nephew,
> John Bosco.

P.S. I propose to sell the house and farm at the earliest opportunity.

John Bosco.

* * *

St Regina's Hosp.,
Cork.

Dear John Bosco,
I will pretend you did not write that last letter and put it down to your time of life. There is no other explanation. Your lodger Father Plugg will drink you out of house and home if you don't get rid of him quickly. I'll be up over the week-end to drive those foolish notions out of your head and I'll see to it that Plugg goes about his business as well.

Your loving Auntie,
Frances.

* * *

Tubberganban House,
Tubberganban.

Dear Aunt Frances,
My mind is made up and there is nothing in this world that will change it. You're always welcome here but do not put a needless journey on yourself. For your information Father Plugg is due to leave on Saturday morning and will not be coming again. I will be joining him at Thope-on-the-Resin in a matter of weeks.

Your loving nephew,
John Bosco.

* * *

The Presbyte
Tubberganba

Dear Miss McLane,
As I predicted in my first letter to you there is now fear that your nephew will be inflicted by the house of th Holy Word on the long-suffering innocents of Lati America. The first signs of recantation appeared when h discovered that a vow of poverty would be mandatory i he survived long enough to be ordained. I understand tha he was always a man who liked the best in food and drink. Your nephew is no fool. He chose the good times before the lean and clearly proved what I have always believed about men like him who are indigenous to outbacks like Tubberganban that the nub of the crux is sex. They are simply men without women. I'm afraid that the Irish have always taken sex too seriously. In this vale of tears sex is the one thing that should not be taken seriously. At times I am at odds with my bishop over this very issue. Your nephew and others like him are the victims of an unnatural and unhealthy clause in the basic teachings of the Catholic Church which proscribes any sort of natural relationship between man and woman other than the marital one sanctioned by the Church. I go along with the Church's teachings because my calling forces me to do so. I do not, however, agree with them.

I have also heard much dissatisfaction expressed about the sexual side of marriage in this remote place. The men say that the women are casual, careless, frigid, withdrawn etcetera. The women seem to believe that if they over indulge their menfolk with eroticism and any involvement, display or otherwise, above and beyond the call of duty, the men will regard them as sluts or even whores. This fear of total sexual commitment is deep-seated and is even proof against the immoral trends of to-day. I feel free to reveal these facts to someone like yourself who is used to clinical discussion. The result, of course, is that the full life which the Church condones is not possible with sexual attitudes the way they are in Tubberganban and places of a like nature. I would go so far as to say that there is acute mental agony in many cases arising from excessive

to say to you. The one possibility, I believe, that we have not fully investigated is your housekeeper who you say hates men. No woman hates men except some women who hates them for the want of knowing them.

'Tis like my grandson Jerry. He wouldn't eat tapioca if you put a collar of gold around his neck. The appearance of the thing put him off. One day I made him close his eyes by the way to give him a spoonful of ice cream. Instead I gave him a spoonful of tapioca and I declare to God he opened the eyes and asked for more. Do you get my meaning? There's many a man stayed out of the water and woman too that might have won an Olympic gold medal. Not knowing a thing would turn you against a thing. Remember this about that housekeeper. First of all she's right there under your hand, in the theoretical sense, and number two she's unattached. So what if she has no form card. There's no way of knowing her time when she never had a trial. Good God man she could have twenty nine thirty potential if you follow. Many a good bitch shied at the water till she was caught by the scruff of the neck and thrown in.

Another thing about these men-haters is this. Their fear of men could well be a fear of themselves. I remember your account of Brady's encounter with her. As I recall she treated him like the dirt under her feet. She has never gone that far with you so what I recommend is this. Bide your time. Do nothing to offend her. If as you say she has thawed a little bit would she not thaw further if the heat was to rise, ever so slightly, unknown to her. Do things to make her think well of you. Do not, however, make it too obvious. It might be no harm if you enlisted the aid of Brady. According to what you say she seemed to take a perverse pleasure out of insulting him. Be that as it may the important thing is that she was prepared to make converstion with him for better or for worse. She takes pleasure out of his fawning so why not use him as a sort of mediator. He would have to be subtle about it. He could be putting in a good word for you hear and there as if he was doing it subconsciously. It's worth a gamble. You have nothing to lose. Put your cards on the table with him and let the two of you draw up a plan. Two heads are better than one. This Kishock woman intrigues me. There has to be more to her than meets the eye. Think on what I say let you and what I always have maintained will come to pass.

Full many a gem of purest ray serene
The dark unfathomed caves of ocean bear.
Full many a flower is born to blush unseen
And waste its sweetness on the desert air.

You need go no farther than Gray's *Elegy* to find the answers to life. Let Brady be your diving suit, if you follow, when you look for the gem in the dark, unfathomed caves of Tubberganban. Think on what I say and your number has to come up sooner or later.

Your old pal,
Frank O'Dell.

★   ★   ★

Tubberganban House,
Tubberganban.

Dear Frank,
Your letter certainly gives me food for thought. Only last night I revisited Tubberganban dancehall. I assure you it was for the want of something better to do. I was working late repairing fences and when I came home I felt drowsy so I lay down for forty winks. It was almost eleven o'clock when I woke. There was no point in going to Bannabeen as all the pubs and the hotel would be closed so I shaved and headed for the dancehall. The band consisted of three aged musicians from some distant town. They looked downright feeble and the oldest of the three, who was the drummer, was barely able to lift his drumsticks. One played an accordeon with his eyes closed. He must have been seventy if he was a day and the last played a saxophone. Not a rib of hair on his head. Far worse than myself which is saying something. As usual there was the music of a foxtrot. There were several couples on the floor but the vast majority of the patrons were congregated near the door commenting on the form of the female dancers.

The saxophone player stopped playing and wiped his lips with the back of his hand. He stepped forward and started to sing. He was also billed as a crooner. For thirty years he has been singing the same songs:

You can hear the whistle down the line,
I reckon its the engine number forty nine.
It's the only one that sounds that way,
On the Acheson to Pecos and the Santa Fe.

I just stood there with the rest and waited for him to break into 'South of the Border' which is a waltz. More important I know the words of the song and if my partner turned out to be uncommunicative I could always join in with the vocalist and so avoid embarrassment. The foxtrot ended somewhat abruptly and it was then I noticed Juleen McCoon seated near the bandstand with a cigarette in her mouth. Her eyes were narrow slits behind the uprising cigarette smoke but I could see quite clearly that they were focussed on me. I waited for her attention to be diverted but unwaveringly she continued to keep me in her sight. This was unusual. Slowly she took the cigarette from her mouth and crushed it with the heel of her shoe. Never once did she take her eyes from me. She folded her hands and crossed her legs. She pursed and unpursed her lips provocatively and I was certain I detected a lustful appraisal of my humble self in her long, speculative stare. There was nobody in my line of vision nor was there anybody directly behind me so that it had to be me. Suddenly there was a weak rolling of the drum. The bandleader who was also the vocalist and saxophonist announced that there was to be an old-time waltz. At once there was the usual scramble for partners. Screwing up all the courage I possessed I made a bee-line for Juleen McCoon. Would she spurn me or would she be swept away by somebody else? These were the questions I asked myself as I made the stort excruciating journey to where she sat.

I had known Juleen McCoon since she was able to walk. I am not going to say that I watched her career with interest or anything like that. She was one of eleven children, all of whom had been acutely deprived in their childhood. The father was an ignorant lout who rarely worked and the mother a backward, resigned woman who accepted the pregnancies of her unmarried daughters as her rightful and proper due. There had been ten daughters and one son. The last I heard of the son was from Sylvester Brady who was reliably informed that he was bannerman for several streetwalkers in Dublin's dockland. Who would ever have thought that Tubberganban could produce such a prodigy but then as Brady said, 'They have to come from somewhere.'

Pudge McLoon as he was called once beat me up after a dance at the Tubberganban dancehall. I refused to give him some cigarettes. That was a mistake on my part as I should have known that he would have no means of acquiring even the slightest luxury unless through misappropriation. Although he gave me a thorough beating I never held it in for him. Vengeance and retaliation are man's most useless ploys. A stitch in time saves nine so I never refused anyone a cigarette after that. Juleen McCoon accepted my offer to dance with alacrity. We had danced together before but always she would keep her body away from mine and devote her attention to new arrivals. Her eyes would continually sweep the headlands of the hall in search of any diversion till her purgatory with me had ended. This time it was different. She concentrated on her steps so that it was a joy to dance with her. I held her closer than ever before and so successful was our combination that we seemed to drift rather than dance. The bandstand and the faces of the onlookers went by in a swirl and I was as close to being transported as ever I had been. The first waltz ended and the band struck up the opening notes of 'Sweet Rosie O'Grady'. Still in absolute terpsichoreal harmony we sang the words of the song together. Everybody else seemed to be singing too. The dance ended and I asked her if I might have another. She nodded her blonde head demurely and we stood together in the centre of the hall waiting for the music to begin.

'I haven't seen you with a long time,' she said.

'I rarely come here now,' I told her, wondering at the change in her attitude towards me.

'Not swanky enough I suppose?' She said it provocatively.

'You should know me better than that,' I returned. I stood tapping a foot against the floor trying to think of something to say. She made it easy for me.

'I'd love to have a car,' she said, 'tisn't here I'd be, I assure you, if I had my own little mini.'

'I'm always available,' I said, trying to force a laugh.

'Available for what?' she said giving me a mild dig with her elbow. We both laughed and sought each other's arms as the band resumed with a slow waltz.

Can I canoe you up the river?
Can I canoe you up the stream?

I could feel her warm throbbing body go limp in my arms as she surrendered her every movement to my control. Now and then my nostrils were faintly assailed by remote whiffs of Californian Poppy and I wished fervently that the dance would never end. How long had I known her as a likely candidate for the ultimate caper. Fifteen years? I would never dream of marrying a girl like Juleen McCoon and she would never dream of marrying someone like me. It would be ridiculous and we both knew it. That maybe was why, in the past, she saw no future in dancing with me. It was different now. In her eyes I was probably beyond marrying and I felt that this would weigh in my favour as the night wore on.

The night is like a lovely tune,
Beware my foolish heart.

We danced again and again until the bandleader announced that the end was at hand.

'Is there any hope of seeing you home afterwards?' I had it blurted out before I realised what was at stake.

'You never know your luck,' she replied coyly. I took her in my arms as the familiar strains of 'Loch Lomond' alerted one and all to the charms of the old time waltz. I held her lightly, not wishing to spoil my chances with any premature display of intimacy. In the middle of the waltz she looked at me and smiled wistfully. I sensed that she was making up her mind and I silently prayed that she would decide in my favour. I was at that awful stage in time and place where I might have gone so far as to sell my soul to the devil in exchange for a woman. That's how bad I was. Juleen was looking at me steadfastly now and I knew that she had decided in my favour. My head reeled as the blood surged through my veins. Then suddenly she tensed in my arms and I knew something was amiss.

'Is something the matter?' I asked. She seemed not to heed my question so I repeated it. Still no answer but her face had hardened and there was a different look in her eyes. They no longer met mine. They were now fixed on an area near the door where stood a tall dark-haired new-comer with a moustache, dazzling teeth and curling, flow-ing hair. I knew him by sight. He was a part-time window-cleaner from Bannabeen who spent most of his time lounging around the street corners with others of the town's loafers. Juleen steered me, against my will, in his direction but as we drew near I spun her suddenly and waltzed her away from the newcomer. Safely out of reach I endeavoured to restore myself to my former state of favour. Alas the climate had altered completely and when I received a gentle touch on the shoulder I knew that fate had intervened to thwart me once more. I turned and there was the window-cleaner displaying every tooth in his head in a disgusting array of glinting white. 'Excuse me,' he said with that greasy, easy, oily, obscene, confidence that I could never acquire.

'It's not an excuse-me,' I told him firmly.

'I have something here that says it is,' he said raising a bony fist towards my face. I looked to Juleen for direction but there was nothing forthcoming apart from the hint of a wry smile on her face. The window-cleaner brushed me aside and took her confidently in his arms. In a matter of moments she had both hands around his neck and you would swear that they had been dancing together all night. Truth to tell one could hardly call it dancing. A better definition would be to say that they were grappling. Disil-lusioned and disgusted I stood on the hall's headland, my hands thrust deep into my trousers pockets, my ever-de-clining spirits at their lowest ebb. Defeat after defeat, disaster after disaster, blow upon cruel blow had not yet rendered me impervious to the thoughtless, vicious va-garies of the opposite sex. Would a time ever come when I could declare myself immune from the jilting germs of infected romance. Disconsolately I left the hall. I had not brought a car. Under a bright moon I wended my way homeward. The stars flickered brightly above me and my mind went back to futile moonlight encounters. The faces of countless desirable women I had known passed fleetingly before me. Tragically I remembered how my whole romantic life had been a totality of downs unrelieved by a single, solitary up. In the dreary arid expanse of my sex life there had not been a single oasis where I could slake my thirst. As I walked up the avenue towards my home I saw coming towards me a great bird, flying but a few feet from the ground. It was only a night-owl but in its ominous approach I saw the ruthlessness of life, the chilling, murderous, preying of one creature upon another and I knew that a foolish romantic soul like myself had no chance of fulfilling his fanciful dreams in this blighted world. The creature with a silent, powerful dipping of wide wings raised itself aloft and exited through a gap in the trees. The instant it disappeared I felt a lifting of the gloom which was pressing down upon me. Could it be that this wraithlike, feathered hunter was the physical manifestation of my misery and did its departure mean that my days of misfortune were at an end and that an improvement in my situation was in the offing. I dared to hope that this was the case. In the kitchen of the old house there was a light and when I entered I was astonished to see none other than your friend and mine the duke of Bannabeen himself, his Grace Sylvester Brady. He was seated at one side of the fireplace with a glass of my whiskey in his hand. At the other side knitting some sort of woollen garment was Eva Kishock. Brady smiled upon my entry and shouted a welcome. It was plain to be seen that he was fine and drunk for himself. Eva Kishock's face was a mask.

'He said he wanted to see you on business,' she explained, 'and I had no choice but to admit him. The whiskey he located for himself and he sits where he is without my invitation or consent.'

'Yes miss. Of course miss,' said Brady slinkily with a downcast look that was pitiful to behold. He was up to his old practise of grovelling again. He nodded his head furiously to signify his complete surrender. Eva Kishock gathered her knitting and excused herself.

'Please don't go. Please don't leave us,' he whined.

'I wouldn't dream of interrupting your business,' Eva said with a hard laugh. She looked at Brady with mounting contempt until I thought she would savage him but no. Instead she asked us if we would care for sandwiches. Brady slobbered his gratitude like a hound and with an amused look she went about preparing a bite to eat.

'I never saw bread sliced so artistically,' Brady commented with a fawning face.

'Shut up you half-wit,' Eva told him.

'I mean it,' Brady said in cringing tones.

Eva ignored him and applied herself to her business. When she had finished she placed the sandwiches on the table and left without a word. Immediately Brady wolfed down the likeliest-looking one.

'Eat the lot,' I told him. 'I'm not in the least hungry.'

In a matter of minutes there was nothing left on the plate.

'Now,' I said. 'Will you tell me what brought you traipsing out here this hour of the night.' Before answering he finished his whiskey.

'I have a proposition for you,' he said. I waited knowing that he had his own inimitable way of presenting things. The gist of what he had to say is this. An elderly bookmaker in Bannabeen had gone to collect his heavenly winnings and his office was vacant. Brady had taken up the lease but did not have enough cash to start off on his own. His widowed mother was willing to mortgage her small home but four hundred pounds was the very most he could hope to raise by this method. Could I see my way towards becoming his partner by investing four hundred pounds in the firm? We would divide the profits down the middle and from the figures he submitted it looked as if these would be quite substantial. We would engage a solicitor to draw up the agreement and to make sure that all would be square and above board. The fact of the matter was that I didn't have any cash on hand but I knew I would have no problem raising it. I told him it was out of the question but then I remembered what you said about using him to win over the Kishock woman.

In a nutshell here is what happened. I promised him the money on condition that he would use every wile at his disposal to present my case favourably before Eva. He asked for time, arguing that she would be a hard nut to crack. I gave him time, three months to be exact. He wanted the money the following week, however, and I promised to consider the matter further during the interim.

'When I'm finished singing your praises,' he promised earnestly, 'she'll be eating out of your hand.' He vowed he would start his campaign the following day and he has positively assured me that she will soon be mine. I wouldn't mind at all for she is a fine-looking woman and a wonderful housekeeper, spotlessly clean and extremely efficient. I suspect that she has a lot to give and that once the barrel of her womanhood is tapped the kindness, the goodness and the love will flow freely.

I'll say no more for now. I'll be in touch regarding developments.

Sincerely,
Your old pal,
John Bosco McLane.

* * *

Knackers' Crescent,
Bannabeen.

Dear John,

No time to call out at present. We won seventeen pounds yesterday, lost nine the day before but won forty the day before that. We can't go wrong with my experience of the game. If you could manage to clear away for a few days I would be able to do a better job on your case. Without company of any kind in the house she would be glad to have someone to talk to. I am delighted that she is changing in her attitude towards you. I really built you up big the last time I spoke to her. I left her with the impression that you were the answer to every girl's prayer.

Do the disappearing act for a few days as soon as you can and I will have her fully lined up when you get back.

Quietly,
Sylvie.

★　★　★

Spiders' Well,
Ballybarra.

Dear Mr McLane,
I heard in the lavatory of the Cattlemart in Bannabeen that you were in the market for a partner again. I think I have the woman for you. She is Nellie Cant of the Tooreengarriv Cants, a shy, nice sort of a girl that never raised her skirt except to answer a call of nature. Her brother Willie was in court once over the rape of a hen and there was talk of some other unfortunate creature but that's all behind him now and I'm after finding a woman for him, long in the tooth and grey as a goat but all Willie wants is a woman and he doesn't care whether she's grey or black, fat or thin, supple or brittle. I promise you she'll earn her oats because the same Willie is diverted out of his mind for the want of someone to leather.

Nellie Cant is a lovely-looking girl and I swear to you that you will never meet her likes. The shyness that kept her in her own corner is gone from her on account of the father buying the television. They wouldn't have bought it at all but he was dying with the flu last January and he told them where the money was, thinking that he would have no more use for it. Nellie can milk cows and knows what's to be done as regards the fattening of pigs, the rearing of calves and all matters that has to do with the running of a farm. The Cants make their own butter and with what she makes out of eggs she could keep a man in strong drink without he ever having to dip in his own pocket from one end of the year to the other. She has her faults the same as you or me or any other man that's thrown together out of flesh and bone. The kind she is 'tis myself wouldn't be long in making lanes to her door but for I being fettered by a woman of my own. She has all her own teeth and not a grey rib. There is five hundred pounds going with her direct from the father and there's no telling what she has put aside herself because 'tis well known that she was never seen spending money only on the bare needs.

I know that you will say to yourself now that there has to be a catch. You will naturally be saying if she's all Dicky Mick Dicky cracks her up to be why can't she do better for herself. Why can't she land herself a young hardy fellow that would be off his mark like a racehorse and not be consorting with chaps that has passed the half-way mark. The answer is to come and see for yourself. I'll have her hobbled to the leg of a chair at the Bannabeen Arms on Sunday night next. Be there at nine and you'll have no regrets.

> Courtesy and civility assured at all times.
> Your obt. servant,
> Dicky Mick Dicky O'Connor.

★　★　★

> Tubberganban House,
> Tubberganban.

Dear Frank,
Brady has disappeared without as much as a solitary word of farewell. Eva Kishock has gone with him. So has my four hundred pounds but I do not mourn after that. It was the dirty way they double-crossed me that really infuriates me. Father Kimmerley married them on Saturday morning at nine o'clock and at ten they were seen boarding the morning bus for Bannabeen. You will ask where I was. I was far away in that lovely spot known as Lisdoonvarna where the sulphur water bubbles and men of my ilk are ever on the lookout for likely partners. It was Brady who insisted I spend a week-end there. He was to pave the way for me towards a lasting union with Eva Kishock. All he wanted was to have me out of the way to embark on his dirty scheme without interference. I'll never again

trust a woman even if she comes with the credentials of a saint and the beauty of an angel. Brady turned out to be a nice friend. I am not altogether surprised. I knew what kind he was the first day I made overtures to him. It is Eva Kishock who astonishes me. I would have thought that Brady would be the last man in the world she would marry. There is no accounting for female behaviour after what she has done. No one knows where they have gone. When they arrived in Bannabeen they boarded the train for Dublin and I think we can safely assume that we will not see them in these parts again. There is one consolation to be drawn from this latest setback and it is that nothing worse can happen. All that can possibly happen to me has happened. Before I close let me tell you what happened to me last night. On the instructions of Dicky Mick Dicky O'Connor I presented myself at the Arms Hotel in Bannabeen to be introduced to one Nellie Cant of Tooreengarriv. Dicky Mick Dicky and she sat side by side in the lounge awaiting my arrival. She seemed a nice enough girl and after the introduction Dicky disappeared for awhile to enable us become better acquainted. Port wine was her poison and mine, at least for the night, was Irish whiskey to help me get over the disappointment of Brady's betrayal and that arch-witch of deception, Eva Kishock. Nellie Cant opened up after the second port. Her sole topic of conversation was the enormity of her brother's evil doings. If ever there was a sex maniac that man is Willie Cant. The cause, of course, could be that he was an only son and was pampered by the mother and father from an early age. Only that night he had come in from the fields in a bad mood. Two boiled eggs were placed in front of him by Nellie. He cracked one and then threw it over his shoulder. 'Too soft,' he said. He cracked the other and threw it over the other shoulder. 'Too hard,' he said. Poor Nellie boiled two more eggs. Again he threw them over his shoulder announcing that one was too soft and the other too hard. She boiled a total of eight eggs and all were either too soft or too hard. Poor Nellie. We conversed away meaninglessly until closing time when Dicky Mick Dicky appeared. He asked us bluntly if we had come to any arrangement and when I answered in the negative Nellie blurted out that if there was to be an arrangement it would have to be soon.

'Why so is that?' Dicky Mick Dicky asked.

'I'm gone the three months,' Nellie said.

'If you are,' said Dicky, 'it wasn't us that made you gone.'

'I know that,' she said, 'but 'tisn't too bad when 'tis one of your own is the cause.' I looked at Dicky Mick Dicky and he looked at me. We both realised that further comment was unnecessary. The girl rose quietly and went into the foyer where she stood with her hands folded and her head bent. The matchmaker scratched his dark jaw and shrugged apologetically. I told him that I did not blame him, that he had done his utmost and that I was there and then dispensing with his services. The disappointment showed plainly on his face.

'You're a man,' said he, 'that needs a woman and deserves a woman and all I can say is that I'm downright sorry for your trouble.'

That's all for now. It's a bad time for me. For too long now I have had to swim against the current but I have gone on in spite of never having had the wind to my back. I miss Brady for all his perfidy. Somehow he always gave me hope, in my darkest hours and even now I smile when I recall some of our times together. If he were to come back in the morning I would forgive him instantly. He is one man I never heard apologising for himself. Ah well, we must carry on regardless. I may be up for a day or two during the Spring Show, that is if I can whip up the enthusiasm to travel. Take good care of yourself.

Sincerely,
Your old schoolmate
John Bosco McLane.

* * *

The Presbytery,
Tubberganban.

Dear Miss McLane,

I am writing to you because I feel that you should come home for weekends more often. Your nephew John Bosco seems now to have resigned himself altogether to a state of chastitution. There's no need for alarm as I am sure it is the time of year more than anything else. Winter in a hinterland like Tubberganban is no joke. He has stopped coming to mass and from what I gather in the Station-houses he no longer goes to the Arms in Bannabeen. Neither does he go to Tubberganban Dancehall. Since Miss Kishock left he has allowed nobody near the house and I have noticed a carelessness in his dress and a slackness in his appearance on the few occasions I have encountered him coming from and going to the creamery. Company is what he most needs. I would call to see him myself but I feel he would not allow me in. He never returns my salutes so I can only conclude that he has, probably quite rightly, a very poor opinion of me. I must finish now as I have an evening mass to say. This is the latest thing on Sundays here. Be sure to come next weekend if you can at all. It is my experience that when crustiness sets in men like your nephew they become entrenched in their attitudes and begin to harbour a dangerous hostility for the outside world. He is, in short, in danger of becoming a sad man. Your company, on occasion, would solve the problem quite easily.

Respectfully,
Patrick Kimmerley, P.P.V.F.

* * *

Spiders' Well,
Ballybarra.

Dear Mr McLane

My lovely decent boy what am I to say to you that has no partner at this time of your life and that has pulled up without finishing the course? I know that some of the clients I presented to you had their flaws and blemishes and that others were odd in their ways but there were a few genuine enough and if they were given a long slip after a staggy hare might turn in to decent respectable women that no man need be ashamed of. 'Tis for the want of a chance or an even break that has left a lot of women to the mercy of nature. Christ man I knew the makings of powerful women that were trampled down from the minute they were able to think for themselves. I have seen brave and free women beaten into slaves and ending up not right in the head. I do have to laugh too at the antics of some of the dolled-up ladies I see on my visits to Bannabeen and other towns. I see fine-looking women and they stroking dogs and cats and they cuddling them and calling them by Christian names, tickling them and squeezing them, tickles and squeezes a lonely man would die for. People say love of animals is a good thing. Maybe so. I would never kick a dog myself unless he was after earning it no more than I could flog an ass or a jennet that would be half dead with the weariness. There is a society I hear for the care and love of animals. Great adorable Christ will they not realise that a man is the truest animal of all. Why don't they have a society for the love and care of lonely men or are they gone clean raving mad squandering their favours on cats and dogs. Let cats love cats and dogs love dogs. Let woman love man and man love woman. A dog is a fine thing in his own place and so is a cat. I wouldn't be without a dog for the world but you may be sure 'tis like a dog I treat him and not like a child that would be after making its first holy communion. There's some of those same women wouldn't part with it for love or money and there's more often gave it up for a currant-top biscuit or a package of fags. 'Tis hard to know what to make out of it all. I do be often at my wits' end wondering at the ways of women. There's no two of them alike. There's more of them goes in for love-biting like pony mares and asses and some that's afraid to smile for fear someone might benefit out of it. I tell you my lovely decent boy that those of them that like the love bites are those that were used to flea bites and they in their fathers' houses. But where does all this leave you and you not settled nor likely to settle.

These few lines I write in order to say goodbye to you and to tell you that I found you an honourable and decent sort of a man that deserves the best. 'Tis like anything isn't it? When you leave a thing go too late you can't expect too much. 'Tis like the dinner in a hotel. If you come last you'll get the bottom of the pot. The best of the spuds will be ate and the cabbage gone sour. 'Tis like the morning bus to Bannabeen. If you don't arrive on time you'll have no seat. 'Tis like the lavatory in the cattle mart at Bannabeen. If you don't do your business early all the paper will be gone.

I could say more but maybe 'tis better to leave well alone. If ever you happen to be up in this quarter knock in and see us. I am truly sorry you have decided to close your account. Every tide washes up something new but we'll say no more. Let the last hour be the sorest. Let the hare sit.

> Courtesy and civility assured at all times,
> Your obt. servant,
> Dicky Mick Dicky O'Connor.

Dicky Mick Dicky was not to write to John Bosco again. The account was closed. In the evenings as he drove his four cows from the Long Acre to the straw-thatched byre the matchmaker would ponder on the apparent callousness of an order that allowed decent men to go to seed and condoned the sexual scavenging of louts and scoundrels. Much as Dicky Mick Dicky had learned from his dealings with men and women there were a number of situations and conditions in his very own domain which were utterly beyond his comprehension. Why, for instance, did women persist in marrying failures when they might avail themselves of eminently successful men under their noses? Why, for instance, did they persist in marrying gawky youths, untrained and immature, when more mature and reliable men were for the taking? Why, for instance, punch and abuse them for the rest of their lives when they might have chosen gentle, withdrawn men who would never raise a hand in anger?

There would be no point in telling Dicky Mick Dicky that the answer was love and that love is blind and that this accounted for the aberrations of otherwise normal women. He knew that obsession with well made figures and handsome faces was not love. He knew that marriage was the price that obsessed women paid to find out what love was all about. He knew that there were many silent wives who would testify to this in private.

Dicky Mick Dicky knew that love was partnership. It was the art of consoling, of being concerned, of being loyal and of being true unto the death. He knew that John Bosco McLane had the capacity for love. That was why he shook his head in sadness when later he lifted the latch of his kitchen and saw his own woman darning socks by the fire. That was why he frowned so often when he saw the plover flocks alighting on the snow-fringed fields or listened to the high honking of geese in winter skies. This was why his eyes moistened when he saw the shadows of torn clouds racing over the uplands behind his house. This was why he sighed when the wind howled and groaned amid the spruces in the small plantation at the side of his home. There were times when a man simply had to have a woman. There were times when it became so unbearable that no man could go it alone. There was a breaking point. This was why he shook his head silently in front of a blazing fire when he saw the pathetic figure of John Bosco McLane in his mind's eye.

So what of John Bosco. It happened that after the leaving of Sylvester Brady and Eva Kishock and after his encounter with Dicky Mick Dicky's final nomination for the position of housewife he decided to pull in his horns for a time in order to take accurate stock of his position. For the first time in his life he was no longer to feel the resignation that resulted from his failures. Instead he was to feel resentment and shame. Days would pass and he would not shave. He became careless about his appearance. He no longer felt the urge to go out at night and consequently he hugged his own hearth. He drank more than ever before. He bought his whiskey in cases which contained a dozen quarts. His purchases were made discreetly in various cash and carry stores throughout the area. He drank alone, never sparingly, always consuming as much as would convey him into a state of stupor. He never drank during daylight hours but made up for this as soon as he had bolted a supper of sorts.

We find him one evening in late January in the early stages of a whiskey session when he is at his most coherent. He has stowed the cows and replenished his turf box. He locates his writing implements and arranges them on a table near the fire. He breaks the seal on a bottle of whiskey and pours a stiff measure into a deep glass. He adds a spoon of sugar and a few cloves. Then he fills the glass with boiling water. After this is swallowed he will dispense with cloves, sugar and water and drink the whiskey direct from the bottle. He does not drink merely to dull the senses. He savours and enjoys every mouthful for like all his breed before him he has what the natives of Tubberganban call a true tooth for the cratur. Lovingly he lays out the notepaper which will transmit his feelings to his old friend Frank O'Dell.

Outside the wind freshens. The fire in the hearth responds. The cat and dog lie still.

Tubberganban House,
Tubberganban.

My dear Frank,
I am going to seed. I no longer care. I no longer worry. Before me is a bottle of whiskey and whatever the night may bring. We have been long-time friends you and I and one of my great regrets is that we did not see more of each other since our schooldays. The cold wind of winter howls without and harries the wedge and willow and I dearly wish that I had sons to share my fireside and a sweet wife to share my bed. To-day I gave some schoolgirls a lift as far as Killarney where I went to purchase whiskey. I wonder if they will ever know how deeply they gashed my last vestiges of pride. I doubt if they could ever grasp the extent of my humiliation as I listened to them titter and giggle in the seat behind me. None of the three would sit in the front seat. You would swear I was some kind of dirty old man. Sometimes the tittering and the giggling erupted

into unbridled scoffing and laughing. I was glad when they left the car. I watched them as they threw backward looks at me and covered their open mouths with their palms. I hope the days hold fine for them. So this is what I now am, the butt of schoolgirls who know my plight and who are too young to have pity. They see me as I am. They know but they don't know everything.

They don't know the crying, whimpering loneliness of nights without end, the barrenness of summer days when all the world is singing but one has no note left to join in. They don't know the woeful futility of trying to grasp the evasive wisp which is the loveliness and beauty of women. Only my God and I know what my hell is like.

Oh woman why are you so merciless, so heedless, so thoughtless? What heinous crime have I committed that I should be sentenced to misery by your lack of concern, your lack of compassion. What awful unknown misdeed have I unwittingly perpetrated to incur your eternal failure to understand a man's need. Oh the good you could do with the slightest effort. You hold the key to the happiness and hope of outcasts like myself. Without you there can be nothing. The door to love is barred and bolted by your lack of comprehension.

And now Frank the flames in the hearth reach into the chimney. A lone bright spark is swept upwards by the draught.

Oh sprightly bright spark retain your fire and mount the midnight wind. Ride the heavens and circle the seas till you alight upon the lap of a lonely heart like mine. Somewhere, somehow, there has to be someone who would understand and care. The whiskey is gone to my head. The truth is I don't care anymore.

I don't matter anymore. I don't count and if I don't matter nothing matters, nothing whatever. If I don't count nothing counts. I hope you understand Frank. I will not be writing to you again. My deep love to your good self and to all your care.

> Your old schoolmate,
> John Bosco McLane.

So ended the last letter written by John Bosco McLane to his friend Frank O'Dell or to any other person. In the local newspaper known as *The Southern Bugle* there appeared the following news item a few days later:

> *At an inquest on the death of John Bosco McLane, a fifty-three year old unmarried farmer of Tubbergan-ban House, Tubberganban, the jury returned a verdict of death by misadventure. It is believed that the gun which he was cleaning accidentally discharged itself. Sympathy was extended to his aunt and other relatives.*

JOHN B. KEANE

Letters of a Matchmaker

To Mary Feehan

INTRODUCTION

Poets, they say, are born not made. The same cannot be said of matchmakers. As will be seen from the following correspondence they are not created overnight. Only circumstances can make a matchmaker. In an ideal world there would be no need of such a person. Men and women would be paired off, the brave deserving the fair and, at the other extreme, every old shoe finding an old stocking.

There would be no surplus on either side, no left-overs, none left out in the cold. Rather there would be a man for every woman and a woman for every man. Alas and alack such an ideal climate is far beyond the hope or vision of mortal men. We must look, therefore, to our hero Richard Michael Richard O'Connor, otherwise known as Dicky Mick Dicky, to remedy insofar as it lies within his power this bleak and unhappy situation where men are often without women and women are often without men.

Dicky Mick Dicky O'Connor resides in that place known as Spiders' Well which is situated in the townland of Ballybarra which lies in turn in the midst of that wild and mountainous countryside along the borders of Cork and Kerry. Here he wrests a livelihood from five small fields and a haggard. The total extent of his holding amounts to fourteen acres. Two of the fields are meadows. They provide fodder for his five milch cows and pony

243

across the lean seasons of winter and spring. The other fields are devoted to pasture and in the haggard the common vegetables and root crops which sustain man and beast are grown. The fields are wet and soggy for the greater part of the year but they are firm and fruitful in the long dry days of summer and autumn.

Dicky Mick Dicky is married to Kate McIntyre, a product of the misty westlands of the Dingle peninsula. She was ever a gay and cheerful woman who always took a firm hold of misfortune and fearlessly moulded it so that it enriched the lives of her husband and herself and strengthened their partnership. The pair are without issue having forfeited a young son to a raging plague of diphtheria and an even younger daughter to the diabolical blight of consumption.

Seven years have passed since they trudged arm in arm, wan and disconsolate, from the small mound in the Ballybarra graveyard under which lay buried the frail body of the little girl they had both loved. There she had joined her brother in eternal rest. There are many who would have succumbed to the grief and despair that arise from these lamentable, personal tragedies but Dicky Mick Dicky and Kate were moulded from finer clay. Other couples might have surrendered to the combined forces of scraggy soil, pitiless and uncertain weather, pestilence and death but it is fair to relate that the indomitable pair thrived rather than pined in this unlikely climate.

Dicky Mick Dicky's induction into the delicate business of matchmaking was caused by a number of factors. Small farmers of his ilk who peopled the hills and mountains around him were fast fading from the scene. There were no young folk left to take their places. The government was at pains to equal the opposition's record in afforestation and all available holdings were purchased with this in view. There would be trees in plenty but no people. There would be birdsong by day and at night the mooning vixen would call to the dog fox. The wind would howl and moan and carry the scent of pines to far-off places. The rain would whisper to the matted grasses but there would be no laughter, no crying, no playful shouting, no human sound at all.

Dicky Mick Dicky was determined that the people should stay in the hills and mountains. Life was brighter, better and longer. Men would come to see this in time. Soon unless something drastic was done a way of life would vanish forever. At this juncture we find Dicky Mick Dicky writing to his brother Jack who is a saloon-keeper, sole owner of the Shamrock Inn, Shillelagh Ave, Philadelphia. Dicky Mick Dicky has other brothers and sisters scattered all over England and the United States of America but of all these only Jack has kept in touch. The truth is that he needs the news and the feel of his distant source to make living more palatable. Like millions of his race he has never fully pulled up his roots nor has he been able.

Spiders' Well,
Ballybarra.

My dear Jack,

I hope the weather over there is not like what we're getting here. We're all but drowned and what harm but I have five acres of hay down these nine days and the Pattern of Ballybunion staring me in the face. If the weather don't come fine soon it won't come fine at all and if it don't come fine at all my cows and pony will walk the Long Acre trying to nose out their pick across the coming winter. Since I wrote to you last I've turned my hand to matchmaking. There is a fostook of a man by the name of Cud Muldoon living alone in the holding next to ours. You will remember the mother and father Cornelius and Maynan Muldoon. Cud is bordering on fifty and he has Kate addled these past years buying socks and shirts and the odd suit of clothes for him. Too shy to go into a shop, a man with no woman, like many another around this place. The disease of the single life is a curse beyond curing when it catches hold.

Now over in Glenamoon there is a well-blossomed damsel living alone with her brother and she going by the name of Circes Fee. The brother Tom is anxious to bring in a woman but Circes has no notion of taking to the high road and she facing for forty. Word went abroad that she would not turn her back on a likely man with a roof over his head and the means of supporting a wife. I got to work and soon, barring an accident, Cud Muldoon won't be turning and twisting in his bed as much as he used to. There was any amount of delving and digging to be done beforehand. Cud was never married before because he never set foot outside of Ballybarra in all his born days saving a trip to Cork for the Munster Football Final and he hardly married in the space of one July evening, not with a dial like Cud's with every tooth in his head as black as the ace of spades and the hair on his head standing up like the bristles on a coarse brush.

With Circes Fee 'twas different. She gave a tamaill in England but for sure she never married there. What took here there is another matter. Some say 'twas to leave a legacy to the Sisters of The Little Ones Lost. As the man said it do coincide. That was ten years ago. She left here eight months after the night of the Greyhound Coursing of Ballybarra and came back three months later much in the better of her visit with her natural shape restored and the pasty look gone from her face. So small blame to the friends and neighbours if they said she left a legacy behind her.

A man should always be careful of marriageable birds a certain distance of time after events like the Ballybunion Pattern, Ballybarra Coursing night and Listowel Races where you have all-night dancing, earousing and all makes of carryon that priests and missioners does be always giving out about. There does be any amount of anxious dames with all their possessions intact, if you follow, what thinks they have carried their burden long enough and who does be well-tilled and seeded in those times and occasions I draw down. 'Tis after these outings you would find women softening in their attitudes to men they would cock their noses at before. There does not be many like these but there's enough to make a man wary. There's others then what often parted with it for a few pence worth of Geary's currant tops, what would think as little of giving of it as they would a mug of tay or a jug of

colourin'. It all depends on the value you place in a thing
and demand, of course, do have something to do with it
too.

When word got out that I was tending to the wants of
Circes Fee of Glenamoon who suits Cud Muldoon fine by
the way, legacy or no legacy, didn't I get a letter from a
lady anchored in a place called Coomasahara to the east of
Caherciveen. She's tagged with the name of Fionnuala
Crust, an only daughter burning oil I'd say but with a
fortune of five hundred pounds. A man was what she
wanted and she aisy about age as long as he had a house
and a way of living and the natural faculties in fair working order if you follow me. I got on to Mickeen Snoss of
Doonaleama who has a good place with seven cows and if
he's long in the tooth itself he's still a fine lump of a man
and some says what knows that he has a haft like the shaft
of a dunkey's car. Once a good man they say always a
good man. I arranged a meeting for Teddy O'Connor's
public house in Killarney. We had a drink, small ones for
myself and Mickeen Snoss and a port wine for Fionnuala
Crust of Coomasahara. I left them at it and went down
town to make out a dozen buns for Kate. They're to meet
again and who knows but we'll have new blood in Ballybarra in no time at all. You'll hear from me no more now
till the fall of the year and say a prayer let you that we'll
get the weather fine or my cows and pony will go without
hay.

> Your dear brother,
> Richard.

★   ★   ★

> Coolkera,
> Coomasahara.

Dear Mr O'Connor,
I have a lonesome tale to tell after landing you my fat fee,
twenty pounds that left a nice hole in my purse. I'm back
at home again after a month married to Mr Mickeen
Snoss of Doonaleama. If I was teasing and tearing him till

doomsday he wouldn't come to life. What mi-ah was on top of me to quit my fine home here.'Tis cursed I was to travel the seventy long miles from here to Doonaleama with five hundred pounds of a fortune in my bosom and the same Mickeen Snoss not having a tack of the dick. What harm but I was looking forward many the lonesome year to having a man of my own and what do I wind up with only a lifeless latchiko with as much spark in him as a taovode of spairt.

I wanted him to go to a doctor to see after his apparatus but he told me he'd let no man living look at it till they were washing him for the clay. So you see I would be well entitled to a refund of my twenty pounds. You contracted to supply me with a partner who would be well-geared to fulfil his part of the bargain. As I recall you boasted that he was a fine example of manhood. Well he fell down on the job entirely so I will thank you now good sir for my twenty pounds and I may tell you that you'll spare yourself time and money and maybe the back of Shaws to boot if I hear from you by return of post.

Yours faithfully,
Fionnuala Crust (Miss).

★   ★   ★

Shamrock Inn,
Shillelagh Avenue,
Philadelphia.

Dear Dicky,
Got your letter. Tough shite about that chick from Coomasahara. You want to cover yourself from dames like that. Here in Philly we got what they call marriage parlours where a dame's got hundreds of guys to choose from. They got files and computers and they got headshrinkers who conduct what they call compatability tests. You get a feedback from a computer says a guy aint suitable for a certain dame and that's the end of it. It saves a helluva lot of time and nobody gets hurt. Say you gotta guy aint got all his marbles or say a dumb guy who's

a flop with the fancy talk and say this guy wants hisself a permanent piece of ass what does he do? He kicks in maybe fifty bucks to the dame or guy that runs the parlour. That's for openers. I think they call it preliminary pairing. He waits awhile until they come up with a number of dames that cotton to his kind of kicks and sorta general lifestyle. He kicks in maybe another hundred bucks and a meeting is arranged. They hit it off and get married or they just don't in which case there's no beef and the guy is introduced to another dame. The more dames the quicker the guy runs outa dough. There's one of these parlours on the next block. It's called the Cumangettum Love Parlour. I had a long spiel with the guy who runs it and he told me you're just plain nuts to be working the way you do. He says you oughta get out a circular advising prospective clients about charges and get them to reveal as much as possible about themselves. When you got all this dope you start figuring who suits who. The other way you're gonna have floozies coming up with decent Johns and nice dolls paired off with maybe hoods or nuts.

This guy realises you can't have no set-up like he's got over here and that they aint heard tell of computers in Ballybarra but he figures your business oughta double if you take his advice. I hope the weather's improved over there. Here in Philly we got ourselves a twenty carat Indian summer that's expected to last all Fall. You take care now and give my love to Kate. You tell her Marge and me's gonna come for that holiday real soon now.

Your loving brother,
Jack.

*   *   *

Hunter Hall,
Ballyninty,
Co Limerick.

Sir,
It has come to my attention through hearsay that you operate some sort of marriage bureau. I am a single man.

I still hunt. I'm in perfect health although sixty-eight years of age. I am in need of a wife. For some reasons the local girls round here or those of my own class won't accommodate me. I am quite well off. I confess I sowed some wild oats and was interested in nice boys for awhile but which of us isn't human sir.

I was married but she left me nearly twenty-seven years ago for a professional tennis player. I would like a lass of twenty or so with good points, good health, good teeth etc. Must be of sound stock. I require no dowry but if one is available I would not be averse to taking it.

With regard to your fee sir. I shall pay according to quality i.e. ten guineas deposit if you accept the commission and a proportionate extra amount if she comes up trumps in performance. There is no point in your trying to pawn a flawed piece of material over on me. I'm as good a judge of a filly as ever drew rein.

> Yours cordially,
> Claude Glynne-Hunter (Hon).

★ ★ ★

> Spiders' Well,
> Ballybarra.

Dear Miss Crust,
As you call yourself. Although by laws of God and man you are no other than Mrs Michael Snoss and no man barring alone the Holy Father has the power to unfetter you. With regards to your twenty pounds the bargain is made and it can't be broke no more than you can make yourself a miss again.

Before you go engaging the law and maybe pauperising yourself into the bargain wait till you hear this. As I was letting go a grain of water at the back of a public house in town a few days ago who should arrive with the same complaint but your beloved husband Michael Snoss esquire of Doonaleama or, as he is affectionately known to his late wife, Mickeen Snoss.

He promised me faithfully that if you come back to him he'd go to see a doctor. Well now what have you to say to this?

I look forward to your reply.

Courtesy and civility assured at all times.

Your obt servant,
Dicky Mick Dicky O'Connor.

★   ★   ★

Coolkera,
Coomasahara.

Dear Mr O'Connor,
I won't give you a dose of the law this time. I'll bide my time and wait the outcome of Mickeen Snoss's visit to the doctor. I'm afraid that there is no cure for what ails Mickeen bar alone a transfer from some fellow who would be going in the priests or brothers and would have no use for it.

Yours faithfully,
Fionnuala Crust (Miss).

★   ★   ★

Spiders' Well,
Ballybarra.

Dear Mr Glynne-Hunter,
Your two names will do you no good in these stakes nor your Hon. but as little but all the same you have as much rights as the next man and I'll take note of your wants. I takes no deposits but if you end up with what you want on my doing I'll bill you well for my dues. No doubt there is some women in cities or towns would be well pleased with an Hon. or a Lord or the likes but what good is such a thing in the country? Will it hurry your milking? Will it save your hay? Will you be the better the rutter for it? No my man it don't make no difference here no more

we'll say than one blade of grass is more honourable than another or one bush better than the next no more than one grey goose is more honourable than another grey goose nor one crow more than another nor a cat. However, you seem well fixed in material ways and this is always an advantage. A lone man in his own house is a powerful attraction. Say if you had an old sister now or the mother was alive it would be held against you. I enclose a circular which I would like you to read and a form to fill in to the best of your ability leaving out nothing as the priest said to the fornicator. The luck is with you as I say over you having no woman in the house for I'll tell you true that if you were to build a house from here to Australia it wouldn't be big enough for two women. Where you have two women under the same roof the marriage is under fire from the start. Two can make a nest but three can make hell. So my fine honourable man I'll be spotting form for you. You're a horsey man. You must know that outsiders seldom comes up and you're a thirty-three to one shot if ever there was one but the bookies were caught before and in this old life anything can happen. Where there's life there's hope. The dick don't give the men of this world no rest. He's a monster what lurks in wait from the first shave to the last. He's the world's greatest disturber and I seen sane men turned into idiots and wise men into fools by him. There is no connection between him and love. He stands for one thing only and that's the flesh whether 'tis triggered off by the rustle of a skirt or the whisper of a dropping knickers, whether 'tis the cocking of a leg or the bulge of a breast. Love is a fine thing, a noble thing but the other is a crazy fiasco and yet the two goes hand in hand like beauty and the beast or Sodom and Goodmorrow. Love won't drive a man to drink. Only the lad we spoke about can do that. Love won't put a man in a mental home but the other thing will keep him there maybe a lifetime. Love will make a home but the bucko will break it. Man you would want a harness of iron and a reins of steel to guide him from his first outbreak of his final one. There is no trusting him, no taming him and them what think they have him subdued is in for the biggest land of all for there is

no bull nor lion nor no shark nor no serpent nor anyone
of God's creatures one tenth as treacherous. I'll say no
more to you now my honourable man but I'll be mindful
of you and please god the thing we were talking about
won't be troublesome for you any more.

Courtesy and civility assured at all times.

Your obt servant,
Dicky Mick Dicky O'Connor.

* * *

Dead Man's Lane,
Ballylittle.

Dear Mr O'Connor,
I am a widow aged forty and something with it with own
cottage and nestegg but the nights does be lonesome and
I does be afraid with times the way there are. I want to
know would you be on the look-out for a man for me.
He must be under sixty and over forty with means. I
don't care about anything else as 'tis company I want in
the nights. I met you and your missus a few times and
seen you at the mixed mission in Ballybarra Parish
Church. Was there the night Father Scalp made the attack on the backs of motorcars and what goes on. More
bastards he said comes out of them than all Paris or New
York. My children are reared and the nice rearing they
turned out. All in London without so much as a card
from anyone of the five of them in the past two years not
even at Christmas. Two of them married Protestants and
I don't know about the others are they living free or
what. I'll be good to a man, am good cook and tidy.
That's all for now.

Yours sincerely,
Lena Magee.

* * *

Spiders' Well,
Ballybarra.

My dear Jack,
The weather picked up great since I wrote to you last. I
have the hay in the shed and the spuds dug. The turf is
ricked and we have no dread of winter. Kate is fine. She
is preparing for the Christmas and is now as I write
mixing the groodles for the plum pudding. She says
yourself and Marge is always welcome. Don't drop no
line or nothing just come. I took your advice about the
circular. We must await results. You will remember Lena
Magee. Of course you would that married oul' Jack
Magee of Dead Man's Lane. Well Jack turned over on
his belly this Christmas five years ago and gave up the
ghost. Lena is on the market again. She gives her age as
forty. That would be true of her oldest daughter who
was born prematurely a week after the marriage going on
forty years ago. She has a nice cottage I must say, with a
fine selection of ware and cutlery stolen from pubs,
restaurants and hotels all over Cork and Kerry. Your cup
might be stamped by the Great Southern Railway and
your fork by the Imperial Hotel or your knife saying
'twas belonging to the Chinese Restaurant in Cork City.
More power to her. 'Tis one way of making a home and
she never made any attempt to rub off the names of the
original owners. She'll tell you she was admiring a salt-
cellar one day in the Great Southern when the manager
arrived and made her a present of it. The same with the
pepper-casters, mugs, jugs and bowls. All presents from
managers.

About the circular. I had a job making it out. Some
of the spelling might be better. I'm no professor. Ask me
to dehorn a bullock or castorate a bonham and I'll do it
blindfold but the pen is for men with soft hands what
minded their books when I was looking out of the class-
room window and thinking about the Woodbine butt in
my trouser pocket that I'd be lighting once I left the
school. Still for a man what quit after the fifth book I
make a fair fist of driving a pencil. Read the circular and
see what you think.

ANNOUNCEMENT

Take notice that I Dicky Mick Dicky O'Connor being of sound mind in this year of our Lord am willing and able to perform services for those in a single or widowed state to wit the making out of a marriage partner for those as require same of their free will and consent, regardless of colour, creed or class with respect to the constitution.

Please advise as to weight, age, height, colour of eyes and hair. If widow number of offspring with ages and sex. If illegitimate please state for record purposes only. If deprived of natural faculties please state to felicitate my job and speed selection of suitable partner. Way of living. State full details, wages etcetera. If short a leg or hand or two or afflicted physically please state. Dependants if any. Drink heavy, moderate or teetotaller? Also state if randy or sexmad etcetera. Frank answers earnestly required to felicitate enquiries. Set out below is rate of charges.

Farmers: One pound on head of cattle. Two pounds for horse or bull. Half crown on head of sheep or pigs. No charge on goats, asses, dogs, fowl but ponies, mules and jennets a half note.

Civil Servants: Including guards, postmen, pensions officers etcetera, one pound in every hundred of yearly income.

Professional Men or Women: Fifty pounds

Buttermakers: Two and a half percent of annual income

Shopkeepers: According to turnover

Tradesman: all sorts, flat rate twenty five pounds

Counterhands, Floorwalkers, Dressmakers, Clerks and Labouring men, etc.:   By arrangement

Other Matchmakers: No charge

Widows: Half price

No reduction in above rates no matter what.

Well my brother what do you think of that? 'Tis easier than having to be searching the countryside looking up chimneys and behind doors for partners to suit the odd misfortunes what calls on me these days since my name is gone out as a matchmaker. 'Twill give me more time to study the nature of my clients and come to better conclusions as the saying goes. The thing that worries me is will they tell the truth and they answering the enquiry. They're not in the habit of telling the whole truth here at all like they do in America. Them computers of yours would be set astray in no time by some of the answers you'd get here to innocent questions. Most of them wouldn't answer at all only with another question. You ask a man you might meet at Ballybarra cattle fair where he came from and he'd ask you where you came from yourself. Even the priests asking questions at the confirmation does have a job with the simplest questions. A Doonaleama man was asked who made the world by the parish priest of Ballybarra.

'Whoever 'twas', said the Doonaleama man, 'they made a right balls of it.'

So you see my dear brother what I'm up against. Still they're so anxious to get women that they'll hardly go making a fool of me on account of 'tis themselves they'll be fooling in the finish. What I used to do up to this was to go to Ballybarra Bog during the springtime cutting or to the football matches between the parishes. 'Tis there you'd often see a likely man. Say you had the lone daughter of a farmer with no brother for the place and she hankering for a sturdy fellow to handle herself and the farm. Some of these would go so far as to take a farmer's boy if all other fruit was failing and the same boy was a good physical specimen but mostly 'tis for farmers' sons with no place of their own they'd be looking. 'Tis looks and size that matters here and money of course having a big say too. You may say there is no courtship and no romance but the marriages work well and that's what matters. They work better than most of the town and city marriages where its all cronawning, smahawning and pawdawling beforehand and none after. What I am you might say is the worm that curdles the loam of love.

We'll have the Christmas down on the door before we know it thanks be to God. Love from Kate and self.

> Your dear brother,
> Richard.

★ ★ ★

> Coolkera,
> Coomasahara.

Dear Mr O'Connor,
I tried your recipe and went back to Mickeen Snoss. He was with the doctor and he was told there was no cure for his ailment and 'tis me that knows it for didn't I give the past three weeks under the one quilt with him. I'd be better engaged sleeping with a corpse. Now like a good man will you forward my money by return of post.

> Fionnuala Crust (Miss).

★ ★ ★

> Spiders' Well,
> Ballybara.

Dear Mrs Snoss,
Am I supposed to go around like a vetinary surgeon examining and inspecting candidates or like a department man passing bulls. Did you try poitcheen on him internal and external? You're not doing your job right. Isn't it well known that doctors have no cure for what ails Mickeen. If they had they'd be millionaires. You'd be better off going to a nurse or a chemist's shop.

There is pills. There is bottles and lotions. There is blisters and whatnot there for taking that would improve his condition. Where there's life there's hope. There's roundy yokes called oysters what is swallowed alive out of their shells and what fills men with taspy what was only fit for the grave before. The poitcheen is your handiest remedy of all. I remember Nell Tobin's turkey cock Patsy what she used to stand on market days at the back of Emery's pub. After servicing three hens in a row the cock would be inclined to fall back and stagger and there would come a glassy look into his eyes. From under her shawl Nell would bring a black bottle. Inside would be a half-pint of poitcheen. She'd throw the cock on the flat of his back and pour a crawful down his piobawn. She'd follow this with a pill and in five minutes the cock would be anxious for more hens. If turkey cocks can be got going with pills and poitcheen why not old men?

Lamp oil or petrol rubbed into the backbone is another good way and there is them what swears by a turpentine blister applied to the afflicted area. Another way is coaxiorum. There is nine different ways of using this but two is all I know. One is to prick holes in an orange and put it between your breasts for two days and then give it to him to eat. By all accounts there will be no ram or no boar or no puck the bate of him after this. Another way is to fire a grain of your water on the back of his poll and he asleep. There is reported to be seven other ways and if there is any old woman handy she may know a few. Don't write to me no more letters now like a good woman but go back to your lawfully wedded husband and apply yourself to the job you were armed for.

Civility and courtesy assured at all times.

> Your obt servant,
> Dicky Mick Dicky O'Connor.

★   ★   ★

> Hunter Hall,
> Ballyninty,
> Co Limerick.

Sir,

Many thanks for your letter. I note what you say about the difficulty of procuring young wives these days. Perhaps I was a bit too choosy. You may now widen the net in the hope of attracting marriageable dames from the age of thirty-five downwards. This should not be too difficult. I am well endowed in every way. Meanwhile would you know of any nice boy who would like a good home. The work would be light and I promise to be very fond of him. Any sweet boy under forty would suit nicely.

I will be spending Christmas with my married sister in England but will be back for the New Year when I hope you will have some cheering news for me.

Yours cordially,
Claude Glynne-Hunter.

★　★　★

Spiders' Well,
Ballybarra.

Dear Lena Magee,
I am in receipt of yours and I would ask you to pardon the delay in answering but the truth of the matter is that I was casting about looking to know would I find a man what would be suitable for you. There is an honourable chap I have in my books that will be inclined to settle for a lady in your age bracket shortly but he must be given time. We wouldn't want him to think we were forcing the pace. That's a sure way to spoil your chances. This man I have in mind is a very well-bred sort of fellow and I'm sure you're a lady what has a lot of taste. All belonging to him were lords and squires and gentleman jockeys. He is a man of ideology, psychology, archaeology and bollixology and a great man too to fix a crack on a ceiling. He bulls his own cows as well. You might say what the poet said long ago that he's a man for all sessions. I hear you have a lovely home with antiques and other valuables that you were presented with over the years. They say you are a woman of great taste and you tell me your age is a bit with the forty. What size of a bit if you please as my client will be anxious to know all these matters. Most men like him with farms of his size would be enquiring after laying hens such as district nurses, schoolmistresses, hairdressers, lady doctors and the likes so we must consider ourself lucky indeed. I will be in touch in the very near future.

Assuring you of our continued attention.

> I remain,
> Courtesy and civility assured at all times,
> Your obt servant,
> Dicky Mick Dicky O'Connor.

★   ★   ★

> Shamrock Inn,
> Shillelagh Avenue,
> Philadelphia.

Dear Dicky,

First Marge and me send our love to you and Kate. Business is good right now but the number of muggings in this so-called City of Brotherly Love is on the up every day. I enclose a few bucks. Let it go as far as it will as the guy with the small penis said the night he got married. That circular of yours sure oughta work wonders. I was assin around Fairmont Park in Philly last week and I got to thinking. Suppose you and Kate was to come out here for a holiday. Boy you sure would pick up a lotta knowhow in the Cumangettum. The guy owns it is going to be a millionaire. Two more years and he can tell the world to kiss his ass. What about it? You could stay with us. We'd love to have you. You'd meet all the guys from home. Man they sure would like to see you and hear the news. Don't worry about the dough. I can fix that. I got a pile stashed and I got buddies from home would throw you a benefit. You let me know man. You never gimme no news about the old place since you started on this match-making jazz. What gives? Who died and who buried 'em? Man I get crazy for news of home. I gotta go now. Joint's filling up. You tell Kate take care and how me and Marge would love to have the two of you.

> Your loving brother,
> Jack.

★   ★   ★

Menafreghane,
Tullylore,
Co Cork.

Dear Mr O'Connor

I am what people call a cripple. All that's wrong with me is that I have a wasted leg and a bit of a permanent stoop. I swear to you I haven't spoken to ten women in my lifetime. I am no good to converse with them and I am not a success at dances as you can well imagine on account of my disabilities. I am a small farmer and I live alone here in the high country in the townland of Menafreghane which is the Gaelic name for the Hill of the Fraochan berries which blacken the bushes here in the late summer. You know my trouble. I need a wife and have almost despaired of ever getting one. In my time I have been ridiculed by a few women I fancied. I have been pitied by others but alas I have been loved by none. I am aged forty-one and you are the last straw as far as I am concerned. I have a nice little farm, a good house but very little money as I had to give a fortune to a sister of mine when she married a year ago. I have my own bog, black as coal after the third sod and my piece of land is fertile. My creamery book would be a good witness for me if my appearance itself would be a hostile one. I like books and magazines and I have a keen interest in gardening.

In God's name Mr O'Connor can you do anything for me? I am all but driven out of my mind with the need for a wife. I often considered abondoning my way of life to commit myself to the mental home and other times I all but done myself in. All I want is a decent woman around my own age or a little bit older. I am not worried whether she has money or not. I am not worried about looks. What I want is a good woman, let her be plain as the gable of a house so long as she wouldn't laugh at me or pity me. Please show this letter to no one and I beg of you to do what you can for me.

Yours in hope,
Cornelius J. McCarthy.

*   *   *

Spiders' Well,
Ballybarra.

Dear Jack,

Spring came yesterday but you wouldn't know it for all the change it made. 'Tis wild and wet still after the winter. We had a good Christmas and I drank them dollars of yours on Christmas Eve. Kate had a jorum too.

I'll start with the news. Cud Muldoon that I matched with Circes Fee sired a second time, a daughter hot on the heels of a foxy-haired son. There is a servant boy working there and there is talk over he having a red head too. But do it really matter in the long run I ask you who took the shot once the flag is raised and the goal is allowed. You remember the damsel from Coomasahara what I matched with Mickeen Snoss. Well she's after leaving him again for the third time. She do maintain that he has no spark of life at all. She gave him a big dose of poitcheen on Saint Stephen's Day and it flattened him altogether. The hair turned white on him and what little of it he had but no other result and we all living in great hopes. I have made a few more matches since I wrote last but there is some poor wretches in the hills and there is no match on the face of this earth for their likes. The hills are rightly empty now boy. The rabbits and hares would hardly get out of your way there and the crows and magpies stand in the roads with no gorsoon to pelt a stone at them.

We were going great here till the Economic War when the unfortunate farmers had to pay the price for De Valera's notions. I remember a daughter of Nell Quade's by the name of Noney took off for England and came back in the space of six months covered with powder and lipstick with a new coat and hat and shoes and a handbag the size of a horse's collar and two big suitcases full of face lotions and slips and knickers and other finery. She drove the poor neighbours out of their minds with envy and the bitch had a highfaluting accent like poor Parson Roberts God be gracious to him the same as He would to a priest. When Noney was going back she took the daughter of a neighbour with her, a handsome girl of twenty by the name of Madge Heighery. The bother about England was that you needed little or no money to cross over and there was great houses there mad for cheap servants would pay the fare. 'Twas different with America. You needed dough to cross the Atlantic and not dough alone but medical tests and intelligence tests and references and you had to satisfy the American Consul and you had to have connections over that would claim you. 'Twas England scoured all the young women out of here. The boys followed. What better could they do except to mope around the crossroads or sit by the hearth with long faces and they scratching theirselves and thinking all the time of the fine women that went over the sea.

Whenever a girl came home for a holiday whether she was flying her kite for coin or in honest service she was sure to be better dressed than the aingisheoirs at home with her purse full of money and high-heeled shoes. She was a walking advertisement for the other side of the Irish Sea. They followed her back in dribs and drabs, in ones and twos and threes and finally in scores till there was more from the parish of Ballybarra in the city of London than there was in Ballybarra itself. Mark me well my brother but they'll be glad to come back yet. When that time will come I can't say but as sure as cocks crow and dunkeys bray they'll face this way again.

I have no blame to the girls that went. They hadn't powder nor decent dresses only hand-me-downs of passion-killers to their knees tied with giobals or hempen cord and knickers made by their mothers out of Sunrise flour bags with sex-starved fostooks of men breathing down their necks what knew as much about paying court as a stallion or a bull. Who in the name of God could blame them for leaving this black land as it was in those days. Times were tough and bellies were slack. There was no diversion because everything that had to do with women was a sin. Thinking about them was a sin. Courting them and kissing them was a sin and sweet adorable Jesus loving them was supposed to be the biggest sin of all. Ignorance was everywhere, smothering us like the mist falling down from the hills. We couldn't see our way with it only grope like blind men not knowing whether we were going the right way or the wrong way.

By God there was slavery at the start of the thirties in this poor countryside. If a girl was knocked up with the fattening sickness she had no place to turn. She was shamed and scorned and damned and they searched high and low and begged, borrowed and stole for her fare to America or England rather than show love and understanding and what chance had the daughters of the poor unless they were made of steel and good Christ Jack no woman or no man is made of steel. A girl going in service to a farmer would want her legs fettered because in the dark of the night and she exhausted after her long day there were hard hands would go groping for her in the dark of her room. Many the good, innocent, hard-working girl that was wronged. 'Twas the time of the shut mouth and the closed eye and the hardened heart. There was two big black clouds covering the pleasant face of this country. One of them was the Church and the other was the State. They made prisoners of our minds and bodies and 'twas that bleak for awhile we were afraid to take note of the beating of our own hearts.

I'm not saying we were teetotally without good priests or brave men. It was worse for them, the creatures, than for us. It was no time and no place for softness or charity. All we could do was turn to Christ in the quiet and wonder was He the son of God or was He the monster what the missioners roared about what sent the weak-willed and the unlucky scurrying like rats down the dirty road to Hell, with no come back for all eternity, no mercy, nor no allowance made for the fire in a man's body or the thoughts in his mind.

There is a few priests around here what gives out about my matchmaking as though 'twas an evil thing. Well my brother 'tis better than buggery and that goes on here and 'tis better than acting alone and that goes on here. They say there is no love in it. Is there talk of no love when the royalty and the lords and ladies are paired off or the high business houses? Man dear I will never know why the poor people of Ireland stayed so quiet in those times. Maybe they had their fill of fighting.

I don't know why people sing about love. Love is a disease that only time can cure and love is given to few so what is the singing all about. It's not natural for a man to sing when he's hurt or wounded so we may take it that he's not right in the head when he's bitten by the love-bug. Otherwise the poor whore would be lamenting and not making songs.

I saw a girl once and I twelve years married to Kate what mothered my two dead children and as loyal and as generous as ever shared her life with a man, a woman what stands back in the shadow of her man and compliments him with everything she says and does, a woman you just can't lose with and yet I saw this girl and I making for a bus in Killarney and she struck me the way a bolt of lightning strikes a tree and I was paralysed. She came on the same bus and she sat next to me and if I was there yet I couldn't manufacture two sentences to say to her although she passed weatherly remarks from time to time. I saw her often after that. She was a music teacher and she taught for a while in the convent in Ballybarra. Often and she out by way of Spiders' Well she would stop and talk to Kate or myself if one of us was showing on the roadway or in the door. You could see by her open face that she was eager to learn about the countryside and the ways of the people. By God I would teach her a lesson or two for no charge. Ah but sure I shouldn't be talking like this. Anyway if that was love, this thing I had for her, all it ever brought me was pain and sorrow. The image of her is faded now but in the odd time her face with all that young eagerness taunts me. But you must put these things to one side for mental diversion only and proceed onwards like the Civil Guard, at a steady pace.

Have I news enough given to you now? Kate is good. Neither of us is anxious to go to America. We're happy and contented here and what we loved is in the clay here where we'll finish up ourselves as sure as there's paps on a heifer. We're thankful to you all the same and we'll be forever mindful of your kindness.

Your loving brother,
Richard.

*   *   *

Coolkera,
Coomasahara.

Dear Tricky Dicky,

Ah you scoundrel for there is no other handle suited to you. I went back to him again. I'm like a yo-yo between the two places. I dosed him and blistered him left, right and centre till I nearly done away with him. I poulticed his posterior with nettles but you would swear 'twas a tickle for all the notice Mickeen Snoss took of it.

There is no way to cure him. The battery is ran down too far by him and if you were to charge it for a week not a gigs nor a miocs would you get out of it. What mortification was on top of me in a country famous for the tackling of its menfolk that I should land a glugger. You will be good enough to return my twenty pounds. I got the law after Mickeen for the return of my fortune and I have no doubt there will be a cheque soon in the post. If the money don't come I'll put the law for sure on you.

Yours faithfully,
Fionnuala Crust (Miss).

★   ★   ★

It was thus as stated that Dicky Mick Dicky O'Connor turned to the trade of matchmaking. As the first few years passed his fame grew so that he became known in distant places. In Clare and Cork, Limerick and Kerry if a man were to announce that he hailed from Ballybarra there was sure to be someone listening who would say: 'Isn't that where the matchmaker lives?' and in the breasts of others the hearts would flutter with hope and they would secretly vow to put a day aside for calling on the one man who could help solve the greatest problem in their lives. During these years Dicky Mick Dicky was not the only person involved in the marriage business. There were fathers and mothers, greedy and unscrupulous who cajoled, encouraged and forced young daughters to marry men twice and three times their age. Needless to mention these old men were well-heeled financially and had outsize farms to boot.

These parents were well rewarded for the sacrifice they were supposed to be making. The truth of the matter was that the young brides were making the real sacrifices, sacrificing their splendid young bodies to the wrinkled hands of elderly lechers. Parents would argue that there was no harm being done as a healthy young woman would be too much of a handful for an old man and that after a few short years he would succumb to the demands of youth leaving her free to choose a fine young man from the many landless bucks who would sell their souls not to mind their bodies for a farm of land. In some cases this was true but in the majority it was far from being the case and there were many young women who ended up in mental institutions as a result. There were others who duped their senile husbands and took lovers. These would be servant boys who worked in the same house but these deprived and frustrated women were not above setting tender traps for postmen, insurance agents, agricultural inspectors and any other likely prospect who would have legitimate access to the house. Those made-marriages rarely worked. Matchmaking was different. Dicky Mick Dicky was a man who knew his countryfolk. He knew instinctively when couples were not suited to each other. When this happened he terminated his contract with the parties involved and advised them to look elsewhere. His great problem was finding matches for the physically deficient, for the over-sensitive, for the excessively sheltered, in short for all those who did not wholly correspond with the average picture of mankind and who because of this are often wrongly regarded as misfits and sometimes referred to by ignorant critics of the rural scene as mountain weirdies. Dicky Mick Dicky saw no weirdness only the grim reality of finding suitable partners for the maimed and the deprived among God's created men. If there was an over-riding policy to be found in his approach it would be this: that every sane and well-disposed man was entitled to a woman of his own in accordance with the laws of God, man and nature and likewise every woman entitled to her man. This inherent philosophy was to be the force that guided him when he was saddled with too many hopeless cases and there seemed to be no prospect whatsoever of marriage for the more benighted of his clients. Dicky Mick Dicky never gave up and even where anticipations were dimmest he managed always to keep hope alive.

Frequently he would be asked to defend his position. In pubs and in the market places of nearby towns coarse men in search of butts for their crude jokes would attempt to pillory him. He took it all in his stride and when hardened old toughs asked him jocosely to find a woman for them he would put them in their places by asking: 'Is it how you can't handle the one you have?' or 'Is your own one getting tired of you?' Underneath the jokes there would be an element of truth and there were many of the jokers who secretly regretted not having gone after the services of a matchmaker in the first place so unhappy and unsatisfactory were the marriages they had rushed into themselves. Dicky Mick Dicky knew that there were some husbands who would cheerfully unload their wives if there were a legitimate way of doing so. They secretly suffered their entanglements for the sake of their children or not to give it to say to the neighbours or to relatives. Underneath the banter was a great yearning for the love of an understanding woman. Dicky could afford to laugh if he so chose at his public detractors but he chose silence or a harmless reply for he was not a cruel man and he knew, if any man knew, how some women became careless after a few years, how they let themselves go so that they are no longer capable of attracting or exciting a man. He knew there were many marriages which were mockeries. The slightest of hints or clues were sufficient to fill him in on the whole sorry tale. A word or two, a look, an act unnoticed by most were for him, more than adequate. He saw beneath the acting and the bravado and the pretence but he kept his counsel. Where was the glory in deflating a man who had already given a hostage to fortune. There was one occasion when one of the jibers went too far and passed a derogatory remark about his wife Kate. At once he smashed the man to the ground and there was another time when a beefy cattleman became too truculent and seized him without provocation by the lapels of his overcoat. In a matter of minutes the fellow was sitting on his well-cushioned rump with a rapidly swelling jaw. Dicky was not easily ruffled nor was he prone to violence but he was never a man to be bullied or cowed.

As time passed whether they liked it or not most men began to take him seriously as he intended they should. He believed in what he was doing. He felt as a man does who has a true vocation and he knew that without his services or the services of somebody like him the rural scene would fall further into the decay to which emigration had consigned it. We find him now writing to Jack of the Shamrock Inn in Philadelphia. It would seem as if he wished to justify his vocation.

★ ★ ★

Spiders' Well,
Ballybarra.

My dear Jack,
I hope this finds you as it leaves me with enough to eat and drink, yourself and Marge in good working order and all other things going as well as they can for you. I have now put together nineteen couples and only two of them discontented. One is the Crust Lady from Coomasahara and the other is a Mackessy man from Tubberdarrig West whose woman will only canoodle with him once in a year, that time being Saint Brigid's Day as she says there is no luck under a roof where you have that kind of disgraceful conduct going on all the time. No fun for Mackessy but once a year is better than no time at all which is what he was used to for close on forty years. The Crust lady is at her own home these past months but she'll be coming to Mickeen for the final time when the moon is in the last quarter as she was told by some old man down in that part of the world that this was a great time for the love caper. To my eyes Mickeen Snoss seems to be failing. There is a stagger in his walk and 'tis not drink is the cause of it and there is a stare in his eye so that I'm thinking it will take more than a quarter moon to extend his lease. He always made a bad fist of women for want of understanding their nature and their ways. If you asked

Mickeen what love was you'd only dumbfound him and yet he knew a kind of love, love for the land and for the produce of the land. These things he understood and felt. If you saw the gratification on his dial and he rubbing the rump of a fat bullock or note him and he feeling the quality of grazing or meadowing the way he'd stroke the blades of grass or fiddle around for clover with the tips of his fingers or best of all to watch him with a fist of yalla wheat ears and he twiddling the seeds or letting them pour through his fingers feeling every single grain to know was it ripening proper. There is men like that what has the love knots tied the wrong way with them. Through no great fault of his own Mickeen always went withershins with women. Yet he was a powerful man in his heyday. I done my best for him and for any man what ever came to me and my best for any woman.

So we have remaining a total of seventeen working marriages that has all the signs of happiness and contentment with a half dozen toddlers and babes bawling and calling from one end of the day to the other. There is no other sound what guarantees so much the future of this countryside. 'Tis music to me to hear the cry of a child. So there you are. Without releasing a single button I'm after fathering six children for you may well say that only for me the craturs would not be there at all. What is a house without a child? Happy I'll grant like my own is but too many houses like mine could kill a countryside and what is a countryside without children? If marriages won't make themselves then I say we must go out and make them. Sure I would hardly be married at all myself if it wasn't for a matchmaker.

My wife Kate came from the West to work for a farmer by the name of Morrissey in Knockmaol. They're still there the Morrisseys with twice the amount of land for the whores never spent a copper nor never gave to charity and they worked their servants half to death. Kate came there as a milkmaid, a handsome cut of a girl, full of life with all sorts of mischief and roguery dancing in her eyes. My mother was in the house with me at the time but she was ailing and you may say the engaging of a partner was the highest thought in my head. I was the last of my family, yourself and all the others being scattered like feohadawn to the four corners of the world.

Morrissey was a slave driver. A boy or girl needed no reference to get a job from him unless alone 'twas a certificate to say they ate nothing and worked hard. Farmers were always on the look-out for boys out of orphanages who weren't used to the world or for big stupid fellows what would be wanting in the head, fools what settled for praise instead of pay for overtime. Farmers had no time for poetic chaps or gay men or sports or handsome fellows but the worst of all was a man with brains. Brains was the worst reference a fellow ever had because he was liable to read the papers and entertain notions of equality with his master which was a sin according to the missioners and the ranchers and a fearful notion worthy of hell to go carrying around in their pagan heads.

I saw Kate first at a crossroads dance on Snapapple Night and she dancing with one of Morrissey's workmen, a black-haired dullamoo with hair-oil and a tie-pin. I was taken by her at once and I danced with her a few times but I put no spake in about what I had in mind. Instead I went to see Falsetooth Riordan of Ballinruddera who was a kind of matchmaker. He demanded a pound down and three more if she agreed to marry me. I had three pounds spared and not another copper to my name. I handed him the pound and a week later he told me that the girl had no notion of marrying, that herself and her parents were dead set against and that she was sparing her service money to go to America. The next I heard was that Falsetooth was matchmaking on behalf of a strong farmer from Knockmaol itself by the name of Hognose Hogan and that he was given a five pound note down if he could inveigle Kate to settling in Knockmaol. I tried a new matchmaker by the name of Keating from the Stack Mountains, an honest class of a man who would take three pounds when and if I was latched to Kate. This was a silver-tongued loveable man with sentences that ran from one minute to ten and lovely long words like you'd hear in a poem. He took my account to Kate and he made a strong case for me. Meanwhile Falsetooth was working like a demon for Hognose but his man was well into the fifties if he was rich itself whereas I was only twenty three and a lively, likely make of a man. We went west in a jennet and trap on the first day of June taking Kate with us to the home of her parents. They spoke bad English but their Irish was fast and free. Keating produced a bottle of whiskey and Kate's people produced glasses. Then Kate and her sisters took off for the shore while Keating made my case. He was the most marvellous liar I ever heard and while he talked about me I was so carried away that I thought I was listening to the life story of some saint. Then when he came to describing my few cows and bit of land you would swear that it was the Garden of Eden itself. The main thing on my side was, of course, that Kate was for me. The parents spoke about America but Keating said he gave seven years there as a potato-taster and that hell was a pleasanter spot. He was never beyond the town of Tralee till that very day but to listen to him you would swear he knew America like the back of his hand. He had a great run of talk for a man that was used only to bog and mountain. Bit by bit he won my woman for me and finally 'twas settled. The best they could offer in the line of a fortune was ten pounds but 'twasn't a fortune I wanted but Kate. We drank more whiskey and Kate's father and Keating started to talk about oul' times. Then I saw Keating's eyes narrowing as he looked out of the window along the white ribbon of road what went for miles in a long loop above the sea.

'Christ Almighty', he whispered to me, 'that's False-tooth and Hognose. I'd know the gait of Hognose's cob if he was as far away again.'

We made our excuses and collected Kate. She hadn't much belongings save a silk shawl what her grandmother willed her and she has that same shawl to this day. She had a pillowslip full of clothes and an old sciath full of odds and ends the mother gave her. On the road we passed the pair inside in the cobtrap. Hognose was pouring sweat and so was his cob with white foam like suds all over him. Hognose Hogan had small black eyes like currants stuck in his pudding of a face. He knew he was done when he saw the three of us together. 'Tis certain that Kate's parents would never consent to myself if they knew the extent of Falsetooth's farmlands and his name for being rotten with money.

'I'll give you a hundred pounds', Hognose shouted to me, 'and the service of my bull 'till the day you die if you draw out of this and leave the girl to me.'

'Not', says I, 'if you give me a million and my cows', says I, 'are no fools and they in and out of the Long Acre since they were heifers. They know the gaps and they knows a bull when they sees one and a bull knows them.'

Hognose swore and he cursed and he spat but we were first off our mark. I married Kate the following December. 'Twas a frosty time and I was caught short of money having to fork out five pounds to the parish priest and another pound to the parish clerk and to land up thirty shillings for a firkin of porter for them what would come sopping.

I went to the town of Listowel to a turf dealer a week before with a pony-load of heavy turf for 'twas by the weight they bought it. 'Twas so wet it froze the night before and I had to sell before the noon of the day so that the sun wouldn't come and melt it. It made four shillings for me. The following day I sold another rail to a schoolteacher before it thawed for four more shillings because 'twas my aim to hire a motor car for a visit to Limerick on the day of our honeymoon. We would go to the pictures what I longed to see since they came out and maybe have a mouthful of tea somewhere at an eating house before coming home. In Listowel I went into a public house for a bottle of stout. At the back there was a clothes line of clothes that had two white shirts drying on it. I took these and I'm sure I didn't leave the owner short. There was plenty others.

We had a great day in Limerick where neither of us never was before. In the pictures we sat on very high seats. We found out later that they were what are known as tip-ups. We never thought to lower them down as we didn't know anything about such seats and thought they were made that way on account of city people being smaller and having such narrow bottoms. We had ham and tea in an eating house followed by buns but the charge was saucy although we enjoyed it. We came home happy and nature took over then. The Lord have mercy on Keating that kindly Prince of men. He was a gay man and a great matchmaker. 'Twas the drink that killed him. Only for his handsome talk and his wiles and his roguery I would have been no match for Falsetooth and Hognose. In time Falsetooth made out a woman for Hognose, a bouncer with fat red legs, an almighty rump and fingers like sausages. But she done him fine and when he buried her he stood a grand cross over her grave. I'll leave you now and bless you. There is fine days coming soon according to Old Moore and there will be great times for all makes of people. Give our love to Marge.

Your loving brother,
Richard.

★   ★   ★

Spiders' Well,
Ballybarra.

Dear Widow Crust,
I got your letter and I will come to its contents later. First of all I must sympathise with you on the loss of your beloved husband, the late Mickeen Snoss. The Lord be good to him and grant him a silver bed in Heaven. He is at rest now have no doubt amongst the angels and saints for God knows the poor man suffered his share of purgatory in this world and no disrespect intended to yourself for you played your part nobly and in no way can you be faulted. God knows you acted above and beyond the call of duty and there is few women with the patience and perseverance shown by you in your misfortune and misery and when your own time comes to join Mickeen there will be a silver bed for you too in the halls of Heaven for although the horse that earns the oats don't always get them in this world he won't be left short in the next and there is many the waster resting on his oars in this vale of tears will have his rump well singed when he passes over to the other side. Now for the contents of your letter. You must remember that no daisy has appeared over Mickeen

yet and it might be too previous if you were to put yourself on the market right away although no one has a better right. I think you would be well advised to bide your time till the fall of the year or at least until the summer is down and the grass has a chance to show itself over your husband's last resting place.

I have in mind for you an uncommon man, a blacksmith and a small farmer with the strength of a horse and he barely gone the forty-five years with a curly head and all his own teeth and no fear of he failing with we-all-know-what for didn't he leave his curls on several and he sowing wild oats while he was working as a journeyman hither in Clare. Carrolane is his name from Coolnaleen and the reason he never married was because his name for calefacting bastards went far and wide and the parents of likely women were wary of him poor fellow. I think he might be the man for you. Now no one knows better than me that there is a lot of luck in the making of matches but I assure you that lightning will not strike twice in the same place as far as you are concerned because I can assure you that this is one horse of a man in all departments.

So my advice then to you is calm yourself till the fall of the year and I'll go matchmaking for you. Please God you'll be Mrs Carrolane in due course and there is more good news for you. I only charge half the fee for widows.

Courtesy and civility assured at all times.

> Your obt servant,
> Dicky Mick Dicky O'Connor.

★ ★ ★

> Menafreghane,
> Tullylore,
> Co Cork.

Dear Mr O'Connor,

I suppose you could find nobody for me. Remember me! I'm the man with the wasted leg and the stoop. I knew it wouldn't be easy on account of my disability. I know how busy you must be so I'll just remind you again to be mindful of me should you come across any kind of decent girl for me. For God's sake do what you can for me as I can find no words to tell you about the loneliness.

Hoping to hear from you at your earliest convenience.

Yours in hope,
Cornelius J McCarthy.

★   ★   ★

Hunter Hall,
Ballyninty,
Co Limerick.

Sir,

I was hoping to hear from you but no doubt you are kept going. In your last letter you mentioned the difficulty in finding young wives for old fogies like me. You may recall I wrote and told you to widen the net and I suggested we try an enlarged area from the age of thirty-five downwards. Obviously you have had no luck. Since I live alone I have given much time and thought to my particular problem. Here I am sixty-eight years of age with most of my allotted span foolishly squandered and nothing whatsoever to show for my time. How vain of me to expect young women to come flocking to me at my time of life. My wrinkles grow more pronounced and the infant scholar would not be hard put to count the hairs on my head. Yet I am not altogether wasted. I am a sprightly fellow for my age and I could still be of service to a woman. It's dashed lonely here most of the time. I now suggest that you widen your net further. Say we extend the age to under forties or say you were to come across a well-preserved firm type of woman a little older be she widow or spinster I would be well pleased. I am fully aware of the fact that I am not getting any younger and that my chances grow slimmer every day. I would ask you, therefore, to expedite the bally business and make allowances for my impatience. Every day that passes is another black mark against me. There is another thing I would like to bring up. On each occasion on which I have written you I have asked if you might be aware of the whereabouts of a nice boy under forty, preferably under twenty but again beggars cannot be choosers. I should imagine that there should be little difficulty here as the demand seems always to be for women. Consequently I am somewhat surprised that you have never mentioned the matter in any of your replies. Please give the matter your kind consideration and I shall not be unmindful (financially) should you succeed.

We are agreed then about the age extension in respect of my future wife. There will surely be somebody interested now that the post is open to all-comers as it were. I hope to hear from you soon.

Yours cordially,
Claude Glynne-Hunter.

★ ★ ★

Spiders' Well,
Ballybarra.

Dear Cornelius J McCarthy,
I have not forgotten you my honest boy and there is no day that passes that I don't think of you and your lonesome situation up there in them deserted hills. It is not easy to place you and we both know why so I won't go into that. I promise you this, however. You won't be forever without a woman. Rome wasn't built in a day. It is only a matter of time, a matter of persevering till we get what you want. I never takes note myself of ailments like you have. There is more to a man than hands and legs if people would only see. A good heart is everything and I know from your letters that you have that same heart. I would judge you too to be a man of mettle what would not be afraid to defend his corner. Don't despair. There may be nothing on the horizon now but in this game it's when you least expect it that the sun comes out. One day there might not be a single woman available in the entire countryside and the next you'd find yourself being

knocked down by every sort of a long hair. Like all businesses there is ups and downs. Keep your fingers crossed. You may be small and thin as you say and you have your own place and you sound like a decent man so compose yourself and be content to wait. You may be sure and certain that your turn will come too when you least expect it.

Courtesy and civility assured at all times.

Your obt servant,
Dicky Mick Dicky O'Connor.

★   ★   ★

Knockbrack,
Tubberdarrig West.

Dear Dicky,
I am now well married and scalded thanks to you. This wife of mine must think she's a cow or something. She'll only leave the bull near here once a year. What am I to do? All my pleadings is in vain. I told the curate and I told the parish priest and they spoke to her and the answer she gave was that no one came to our Divine Mother Mary and she did fine regardless. I busted in then and said I was flesh and blood and the oul' parish priest told me conduct myself and not be making a bashte of myself and to know was there no other thing in the world except corpulation I think he called it and asked me why we weren't saying the Rosary at night and know when was I at confession last or did I know the value of Sanctifying Grace. I turned to the curate and he only shrugged his shoulders the poor fellow and I could see that if he put a spake in there would be trouble for him. I got no law from the parish priest save to conduct myself and be mindful of my wife's health and feelings and to thank God for the two fine healthy children I had and not be like a stallion that was always inclined to rear up. The curate came later on his own and he had a long talk with the wife but no use. She locked the bedroom door and I could hear here praying all night. 'Twas like a monastery from that

till cockcrow. 'Tis no joke being yoked as I am. Yourself is a man I sets great store by. Maybe you'd know of some way of coming around her. I have heard of Coaxiorum but you know as well as me there is no such a thing. I'll be on the look-out for word from you. You're a man that knows the ins and outs of delicate matters.

Yours faithfully,
Thady Thade Biddy Mackessy.

★ ★ ★

Spiders' Well,
Ballybarra.

Dear Mr Glynne-Hunter,
Yours to hand on Monday last but it being a day I had a mechill of men engaged I postponed answering. I was took up most of the week cutting my year's supply of turf which I sells the week before Listowel Races so's I'll have a pound or two to play with. My fine honourable man I have some news for you. There is a handsome widow just gone the forty that has a desire to meet a respectable, well-away man with a view to matrimony. Her name is Mrs Lena Magee from Dead Man's Lane in the village of Ballylittle. Her precise age I cannot tell you as ladies are not hasty to release news of this nature but if appearances means anything she can't have all that mileage up. She is a most intellectual model of a female with a nice cottage and a fine collection of crockery and silverware and other costly items that she gathered one way or another from time to time. She is a famous cook and without wanting to bellows her coals too much I can guarantee that this is a lively bit of gear. You would be well advised to entrust me with the arrangements of a private meeting between the pair of you in some warm snug of a public house in Ballylittle or elsewhere where no one will be the wiser about the business in hand. Over a drink or two ye can be whispering and swopping soft talk. Ye can be humming and hinting and let there be a taste of a kiss and a bit of a hug thrown in if all goes well. A good honest house is

Morgan Shaughnessy's of Dead Man's Lane in Ballylittle village where there is no spitting on the floor or roaring or stamping. I'll have her there bar a fall at four o'clock on Sunday evening next. You'll have no trouble in finding the village. 'Tis well signposted after Abbeyfeale. Dead Man's Lane is on the left off the main street as you come from the east.

There is another tricky matter which you drew down in your last letter and that is concerning a nice boy who you say you would give a good home to and treat very nicely and all to that. I don't go in for no dealings in boys as I think a man should have more respect for his water-spout. However, every man's business is his own and I won't go no further on this subject. If the arrangements as regards Sunday don't suit you please let me know by return of post. Bring a bag of toffees with you. She likes toffees.

Courtesy and civility assured at all times.

Your obt servant,
Dicky Mick Dicky O'Connor.

★　★　★

Spiders' Well,
Ballybarra.

My dear Thady Thade Biddy,
Yours to hand. Holy God but you have a lot to endure. There can be no harder lot than yours. I know men would put the double barrel to her head if she was to cut off the supply. I never heard the bate of it in all my days and why Saint Brigid's Day of all the days of the year. I know next to nothing about Brigid bar alone that she's the Patron Saint but I'm sure saint or no saint, she wouldn't wish to support your wife's carry-on. You have two ways to dealing with this matter and I'll tell them to you now. You can lock her out at night till she comes to her senses from the cold but this is a hard thing to do to a woman even if it is well going to her itself. Your other alternative is this. I'm sure the two of you does sit down for a mug of

tea or cocoa before ye goes to bed at night. If this be the case you could start by doctoring the cocoa unknown to her. Better wait till some night she have a cold in the head when her sense of taste will be wanting and then when you get her back turned slip a small dollup of poitcheen or whiskey into the cocoa. After the first taste she won't notice when you lace the cocoa better. Bide your time and let the drink do the rest. You may be sure she won't be the same woman after dosing her. There's many a man Thady with your trouble but God nor man won't make them admit it. There's many a woman too but 'tis the fashion for generations to stifle all natural sorts of love notions and what do this lead to. It leads to too much thinking and no threading and where you have that sort of unnatural mortification you have a collapse of the brain. Mind now what I told you. I'll be most anxious to hear what way you got on.

Courtesy and civility assured at all times.

Your obt servant,
Richard Michael O'Connor.

★   ★   ★

Spiders' Well,
Ballybarra.

Dear Fionnuala,
I feel I have known you long enough to call you by the first name. Our man Carrolane is anxious to vet you and 'tis my way of thinking that you'd be anxious for a gander at him. He's a fine, big, hairy man and there is surely a space of two feet between his chest nipples. He's the last of his breed and need I say that he'd like to put his stamp on a few gearrcachs of his own. He was borned an American citizen but the father and the mother came to Ireland and died young. All the father's folk were swept away by ship fever and gonorrhoea and the mother's by galloping consumption so 'twas a miracle that the poor chap turned into the grand block of a man he is now. The forge is doing well and he is a man that's highly respected by his

neighbours. As you may know 'tis often the wont of small and middling-sized men to chance their arms against giants. They do this to make a name for themselves. One night after a wrendance he was provoked beyond endurance by a carload of craven cafflers from some distant town. The upshot was that he ran through the wretches like shite through a goose, leaving four stretched flat and two more holding their undercarriages like they'd be scalded. 'Tis many a long day now since Carrolane had any truck with women so you may say that he has catching up to do. He'll make for you the first night like a cow making for aftergrass. Hold steady for the present and compose yourself. There is good times coming soon. What would you say to a meeting in the snug of Ted O'Connor's pub in Killarney. 'Tis a cosy spot and many what went into it single came out doubled but I hope now in earnest that you won't be expecting too much from the man. Enough is enough. Be patient and kind and you'll get as good as you give. There is one thing about marriage that people should never forget and this is that one and one makes one and not two. Hoping to hear from you soon.

Courtesy and civility assured at all times.

Your obt servant,
Dicky Mick Dicky O'Connor.

★   ★   ★

Shamrock Inn,
Shillelagh Avenue,
Philadelphia.

Dear Dicky,
Guess what. The Cumangettum Love Parlour is closed and the guy that used to own it is doing one to ten in the state pen. It was all a racket. He was doing alright in Philly but the Feds busted him when he opened a branch in Baltimore. The guy was a crook. The computers were phony. Him and his operators were phony. He had a ball while it lasted. He had a fat blonde broad used to work

for him but she got away. No trace of her, holed up somewhere I guess waiting for him to be paroled. There's a helluva lotta dough stashed away somewhere maybe in safety deposit boxes or in the broad's name. Who knows. I liked the guy. Now I gotta favour to ask you. There's an ole guy belts it goodo here most nights name of Robert Emmet O'Bannion. The guy's mother was a narrowback. I guess his grandfather or grandmother musta been Irish cos he don't never let up yakkin about his mother and the Emerald Isle and Irish colleens and four leaved shamrocks and little bits o heaven and all that sorta crap. Man he's about the corniest, mushiest ole Yankee Irishman you ever did see. He's the original Irish Mick and then some but what matters is the ole guy's loaded. Some say he's a cousin to Dion O'Bannion but he don't never make no mention of Dion's name so who's to say. One thing is sure. He carries a rod and black-jack and he knows how to use 'em. If he's gonna be rolled he aint gonna roll alone. I guess he's seventy if he's a day. Sometimes he calls a taxi and I seen cabmen hand him call-girl cards but he don't pay no heed. He's got his eyes set on an Irish colleen. He believes the only pure girls on the face of this here shit-pile is Irish colleens. Sometimes the guy cries when he talks about his mother and some colleen he knew when he was a kid. This colleen married a cop and he never saw her no more so now he wants a real Irish colleen and he says he's gonna go back to the old country to get one. Maybe you can help him. You surely got some kinda colleen to suit the guy. He's old and his sight aint what it used to be and the way he drinks the colleen's sure gonna be a widow before the first wedding anniversary. Can you do something? He don't haggle when it comes to the pay off. I'll say that for the old guy. You see what you can do and I'll keep him on ice till you come up with something.

Marge is fine, just fine. You just wait. You're gonna see the two of us stepping out of a cab one day real soon. Write and gimme all the news when you get an hour to spare.

Your loving brother,
Jack.

★ ★ ★

Coolkera,
Coomasahara.

Dear Dicky,
The sooner the better. After the non-starter you fobbed
over on me that last time I would be well entitled to the
best you have. O'Connor's snug in Killarney would suit
me fine. There is buses back and forth the whole time
between Coomasahara and Killarney. Some of them bus
drivers are fine able men, well-fleshed and solid. 'Tis my
guess that they'd be lively at night over they being sitting
down all day. This Carrolane you have for me sounds like
a likely mark. I would be most anxious to leave no grass
grow so fix the meeting for soon. I have only one life and
the Catechism don't say nothing about courting or cou-
pling in the hereafter. I don't want to die without the
imprint of a man. Make the meeting for Sunday week or
for the Sunday after at the latest.

Fionnuala Crust (Miss).

★   ★   ★

Knockbrack,
Tubberdarrig West.

Dear Dicky,
My great friend. May the buds quicken for you and the
sap run. May all your sails be full of gales and all your
fields be green as the poet said and as I say to you now
and I looking out of the window into the face of a sickle
moon. May the stars shine for you and the rivers sing for
'tis you that has brought me from the black valley of
despair to the mountains of delight. Your advice was
sound. After getting your letter I bided my time and sure
enough didn't she complain this night soon after of having
a blocked nose and a cold in the head. Ha-ha says I to
myself and ho-ho and hey-hey we'll put Dicky Mick
Dicky's cure to the test. There she was in front of the fire
and the head bent by her and she sniffing and sneezing
like a badger rooting in a wood. I think I'll go to bed says

she. Don't says I till you have your mug of cocoa. Oh I couldn't bear cocoa tonight says she my nose is that stuffed. Try a drop of hot milk says I with a pinch of white pepper in it. I'll chance it so says she although I know for sure 'twill do me no good. I got my muller and poured in my milk. I sprinkled it with white pepper and while the head was still bent by her I took out a noggin of poitcheen from my breast pocket and laced the milk with a likely dart of it. Down goes the muller to boil and up comes the bubbles in no time. Here says I and I filled a mug for her. She took it and drank a small tint, then another tint and then a good swallow. I owe unto God says she but the white pepper is great stuff entirely. I find my nose loosening and my head clearing already. Finish the drop you have left says I and I'll make more for you or better still says I go up to your bed and I'll put a bit more pepper in it. She was said by me. As I was working in the kitchen I could hear her talking away to herself and humming and giggling and she getting ready for bed. 'Twas what you might call a contented sound. I doubled the dose of poitcheen and swallowed what was left in the bottle myself as a precaution against germs. When the milk came to the boil I filled up her mug again and made for the bedroom with the hope soaring in my bosom. I held it under her mouth and gave her sup after sup and by the hokey didn't she drain every last drop of it. First she cried and then she sighed and then she laughed. I got in beside her and I hadn't my head on the pillow when she wrapped her two hands around my neck and her two legs around my back. We must get more pepper tomorrow says she. I won't tell you no more except to say that no man be he black, white, brown or yellow ever spent a better night. I sold a yearling the day before yesterday at Bannabeen cattle-mart and invested in pepper. As you often says yourself there is good times coming. I'll be forever in your debt.

Your devoted friend,
Thady Thade Biddy Mackessy.

* * *

Spiders' Well,
Ballybarra.

Dear Jack,
Everything is fine at this side and going through my books
the other night I counted forty marriages in the past seven
years since I set up on my own. This client of yours what
wants the Irish colleen. Would he be suffering from bul-
locks' notions? If he's seventy that's the time of life for
them. Oul bucks of that age does be forever pinching
ladies behinds and tickling them and generally squeezing
them when they thinks no one is watching. 'Tis the final
kick before they let go life for good and no great notice
should be taken of them and full allowance made for their
last capers. Still you say in your letter that he does not
follow call-girls. What is call-girls? Is it women that
would call you in the morning for work or that would be
working for you and would call you if somebody wanted
to see you like secretaries or clerks and what not? I know
the kind of colleen he has in mind, a rosy-cheeked damsel,
all smiles with long red hair and a rose in it and she
sitting at a spinning wheel or knocking notes out of a harp
in the sunshine outside a thatched cottage with the wall-
flowers everywhere and the mountains in the distance and
the oul' mother sitting in the doorway with her hands
folded and she showing off an almighty amount of red
petticoat. You know as well as I do that there's no such
creatures in this country no more than there is lep-
rechauns or lorgadawns or banshees or Jack O' the
Lanterns. He might get one in New York or Chicago but
there was never the likes of those colleens seen in this
corner of the world barring at a fancy dress parade or a
concert. Find out more about him if you can. You say he's
well-heeled. Could you give me a rough idea of how much
he has altogether? What age exactly he is not that this will
be worth much because he'll hardly tell the truth anyway.
I had to stop sending out them circulars over the pack of
lies I was told. You'd get a one from a fellow saying he
had blue eyes and that he was tall, dark and handsome
whereas he might have a squint or be half blind and
instead of being tall, dark and handsome he'd be tall, grey

and dirty. The same with the women, ones fifty pretending to be thirty and ones seventy pretending to be forty and there was one with a wooden leg what said nothing about it. The match was nearly .nade but 'twas the luck of God I ran across a shoe clerk in a public house that told me about the leg being wooden. I hired a hackney car that minute and went to the house where she lived. What do you mean says I not telling me you had a wooden leg? What's wrong with a wooden leg says she so long as the other thing isn't wooden? Nothing says I but you didn't tell my client or myself. You never asked says she. What would make us ask says I? Ah look here says she and she caught me by the hand. A wooden leg is like an adopted child. With all the ups and downs of life it could be better to you than one of your own in the end. Kate is in bed with a dose of the flu this past week but she expects to be up any day now. Give our regards to Marge and send the reverent information.

> Your dear brother,
> Richard.

★   ★   ★

> The Tailrace,
> Feale River Cross.

Dear Mr O'Connor,
I am the Murphy girl from the Tailrace that got married lately to Tom Cuddy of Been Hill. I am enclosing the money that's due to you. All our thanks are due to you too. We are very happy although 'tis only a month since the knot was tied. Life was so lonely for the two of us especially and we so backward and tuathallach not knowing how to put one word on top of another in the company of strangers. You changed all that and I am sure that there is a happy future before us. What a shy man and what a grand man and what a loving man is my husband. Politer you wouldn't meet in a dreaper's shop. The night we got married he was slow about getting down to business but once he started he gave a good account of

himself. He's so mannerly. In the morning he gave me a little tap on the shoulder. 'I beg your pardon Miss Murphy', says he, 'but could I trouble you once more.'

Gratefully yours,
Catherine Morely nee Murphy.

★ ★ ★

Coolkera,
Coomasahara.

Dear Liar and Gallows fodder,
May Jesus and His Holy Mother and Blessed Martin and all the saints and martyrs come to my aid although 'tis me that's the real martyr. The clock is after striking twelve and down from the room like the mumbling of thunder in the McGillicuddys comes the snoring and grunting of my lover boy. We went to bed at nine and put out the lights. We lay side by side not stirring nor moving like two gamecocks each waiting for the other to make the first move. The next thing I heard was a yawn and after that a snore that would lift the roof from a hayshed. I thought of your words so I composed myself. I waited and waited till I heard the clock striking ten. Maybe said I to myself 'tis how he thinks the bed is only worked for sleep. I decided to wake him up. I shook him and pinched him high and low but you'd get better response from the pillow. I gave him a dag of a darning needle in the rump like my grandmother used to give the ass long ago and she driving him to the creamery but nothing from him saving a sigh. I dagged again and all he did was turn over in the bed. I dagged a third time till I met bone but I declare to God you'd get better results from dagging a statue. So here I am on my lonesome again. 'Twas an almighty fool that said lightning never strikes twice in the same place. What am I going to do at all. For sure you'll have to give my money back this time.

Mortified entirely,
Mrs Fionnuala Carrolane.

★ ★ ★

Hunter Hall,
Ballyninty.

Dear Mr O'Connor,
All's well that ends well. My first skirmish with your
nominee from Dead Man's Lane, namely the widow
Magee, has just ended. I won't say I'm entranced but I'm
bally well game to go into battle again if you can arrange a
meeting. Like all women she will probably give you an
outrageous account of what happened. Let us say I behaved like a man is supposed to behave and that I didn't
let the side down. I am available at all times for a second
brush.

Yours cordially,
Claude Glynne-Hunter.

★　★　★

Dead Man's Lane,
Ballylittle.

Dear Mr O'Connor,
If I was to give down in full what happened in the snug at
Morgan Shaughnessy's I would scandalise you surely or
leave you with the eyes popping out of your head. My
hayro landed with a big paper bag of toffees as you know.
He ordered a drink and we fell to eating the toffees and
supping our whiskies. The toffees were a good quality I
will say that. There is some good points to him he being
sweetly spoken and well shaved and a nice smell from him
likewise his shoes well shone and his trousers ironed with
an edgy crease on them. All things allowed he would pass
muster on first appearances. We were halfway through the
bag of toffees and well into the third whiskey when he
says out of the blue would you care to try another sort of
a toffee. I'm sure I don't know what you mean my good
man says I. Then like one of them circus quick-change
artists he had the trousers whipped off while you'd be
saying Jack Robinson. Sweet adorable Jesus man-alive
says I is the sense after deserting you. Then I gave a look

and I could see that the handle stood out straight from the belly by him and that he was dangerous. I rose and ran to the other side of the snug table. He rose too and came after me. Around and around the table we went and he chasing me. I couldn't call out in case the customers in the bar would think I was after inveigling him. All I could do was run and pray. I managed to stay in front of him. Steady girl, steady up there he would say softly now and again like he'd be talking to a mare and finally he stopped opposite me and he half-winded from the chasing. Leave me put it in a small little bit says he. I took to my heels while he was searching for breath. My one regret is that I left the toffees behind me. As I was going out the door he called after me. Steady the buffs he said. Steady the bally old buffs.

Could you remember what was the name of them toffees at all or how much a quarter are they? I left him anyway in the snug and he holding his halfpenny. What disgraceful behaviour opposite a lady. I never want to speak to him again not to mind seeing him. I don't know what came over him at all for you may be sure he got no encouragement from me. He's a quare buck to be sure. I hope you have something to say for yourself after landing me on my lonesome with that honourable ram from Bally-ninty.

Sincerely,
Lena Magee.

* * *

Spiders' Well,
Ballybarra.

My fine honourable boy,
I have you tagged at last. It took me a long time to get your markings. Like a dream it was at the back of my head. Wasn't it your ould mother that had the home for retired asses and ponies and didn't she give the law to Kateen Bruder of Ballyninty over she beating an ass with an ashplant and she trying to hurry home in a hailstorm

from Limerick city. Wasn't it that same oul' mother of
yours that saw the Black and Tans kick an innocent man
to death on the same day under the same sky on the same
road and not a word did she breathe. By Gor but she fed
them asses and ponies well when it would have been an
act of charity to put them down and while she was feeding
them weren't the children of her neighbours half starved
in the cottages round her demesne in Ballyninty, the same
demesne as you have now. 'Tis well you remember that
my honourable man for you would have been a big gorsoon in those woeful days. You asked for a nice boy in
your letters. You won't have long to wait, a few years at
most, and you'll have the nicest boy of all looking after
you, the oul' boy himself.

Courtesy and civility assured at all times.

Dicky Mick Dicky O'Connor.

   ★ ★ ★

 About this time when his new career was at its zenith
Dicky Mick Dicky received his first registered letter. At
the start he was loth to accept it but upon being repeatedly assured that it was common practice to send sums of
money in this fashion he decided to sign for it. When the
postman took his leave, after refusing the offer of a mug of
tea from Kate, Dicky held the letter up to the light in an
effort to render its contents visible to the naked eye. He
could discern nothing. Next he shook it but no sound
came from inside. From under the bed in their room Kate
took a noggin of Lourdes water which an itinerant clergy-
man had given her some years before. She thoroughly
sprinkled the letter before her husband decided to open it.

 Inside was a single sheet of foolscap filled with clear
characters written in red ink. At the top of the letter in
outsize capitals was written the terse message: 'A matter
of life or death'. Underneath this alarming introduction
the following appeared.

   ★ ★ ★

Ballyoodle,
Co. Clare.

Dear Mr O'Connor,
This is an emergency. If you have regard for human life
you will act at once. I am to be married next Saturday
fortnight to a small farmer in the next townland. My
fortune is given over to his mother and all I have to do is
walk in and take charge. All would be fine but for my
brother Mikey who will be left alone when I go. He is
fifty-five years of age with a nice place as I can verify.
The bother is that he is going to set fire to himself the day
before the marriage unless someone gets a woman for him.
He has gallons of lampoil and petrol hidden in every
corner of the farm and the Civic Guards say there is
nothing they can do unless alone I put him out of the way
by swearing him into a mental home. Sure if I do that
he'll never get a woman for nobody will want him when
he gets out. You are the only man in the world that can
save his life. If you turn your back on him you will be
guilty of murder so let you be landed here with a woman
for him before Friday week or you'll have the blood of an
innocent man on your hands.

Fair dues to him he's anything but choosy and any
sort of an old damsel in fair working order will suit him
nicely. Fail him and he'll be going to his funeral instead of
his wedding. Your wages will be waiting here for you
when you arrive with the woman. What he fancies is a
lady that would be middling fat but firm and having a
good bosom. He don't care whether she be grey, red or
black nor whether bollav or chatty. You may take from all
this that he is easy to please for isn't he thirty years on the
trail without rising a scent. If you don't want to be a
murderer and maybe swing for your crime you'll not renege on my brother.

Your sincere friend,
Agnes Tatty.

*   *   *

Guards' Barracks,
Ballyoodle,
Co Clare.

Dear Mr O'Connor,
I have given thirty years in the force. I am what you
might call a common or garden black guard of country
make. In the honour of God I beg and beseech you to find
some sort of woman for Mikey Tatty whose sister Agnes
wrote to you yesterday or the man will take his own life. I
remember when he was thirty he threatened to cut his
throat if his mother didn't give him the price of a motor
bike. Twenty-seven stitches. He means business again this
time. Do your utmost.

Sincerely,
Joe Doyle.

*   *   *

Spiders' Well,
Ballybarra.

Dear Miss Tatty,
At such short notice what you demand is impossible. I ask
you now to postpone your wedding until such time as I
can make out a longhair for your brother.

Your obt servant,
Dicky Mick Dicky O'Connor.

*   *   *

Ballyoodle,
Co. Clare.

Dear Mr O'Connor,
It's no good me postponing my wedding. Mikey is determined. Unless he has his own woman by the time laid
down you'll smell the burning over in Kerry and from
that day to the day you die people will point the finger at

you and they'll say there's the man that made a torch of poor Mikey Tatty the Lord be good to him. He has a hundred pounds put aside to bury himself and he has a grave taken in Ballyoodle graveyard. Other men will put the green scraws on top of him but 'twill be you that executed him.

Your sincere friend,
Agnes Tatty.

P.S. The reason he didn't marry up to now is that no one would have him not even the Hag Hanafin and she gone seventy-nine this Shrove and a whisker around her mouth like furze round a gap and the bare pinch of hair on her poll like the plume on a heron. You'll have a mortal hard job but you're the man that can do it if you put your mind to it. 'Tis that or put the black cap on your head and send him off to his doom.

Your sincere friend,
A. T.

★   ★   ★

Spiders' Well,
Ballybarra.

Dear Jack,
No one knows what I have gone through lately and I likely to be branded a black murderer without so much as drawing a stroke. There was this uncommonly ugly block of a man in Clare what promised to set fire to himself with lamp oil unless a woman was made out for him. I was badly caught for time only having the bare fortnight at my disposal and failing in my labours having a corpse on my hands. Hobson's Choice in dead earnest. This man's name was Mikey Tatty, clean out of his mind for a woman, as ugly a buck as ever drew on shoe leather.

Now posted in Limerick where she's in service with a doctor is a Turkish woman what weighs twenty-two stone, what drags the behind after like a fat heifer what would be going to the butcher. She came from her own country with the doctor and his wife and them what knows do maintain how she laid low her husband there with a lick of a skillet pot between the two eyes over he making out that the tapioca wasn't sweet enough for his supper. Whatever about that word came that she was anxious to marry and our man in Clare what looks like a monster in his own part of the world would be regarded as very handsome in Turkey over he having a drooping lip and yellow hide like to what they have in Turkey. Failing her there was another in Galway what had a wooden leg but was otherwise sound as a butcher's block. I threw up a penny between the two and it fell in favour of the Galway woman what was short of the leg. Off goes the pair, herself and Mikey Tatty in a hired car to view the country of Clare and to see know would they take a shine to each other. Didn't the wooden leg give under her and she facing for the Cliffs of Mohar. Out she fell on her face and eyes over the cliffs and into the salt water. Devil the sign of her since, only the half of her wooden leg washed ashore in the strand of Kilkee and her name and address written down on it in marking ink in case 'twould ever be lost by her. Please forward it said to Kate Gellico, Drumdoo, Co Galway and notify a Catholic Priest in case of an accident.

The Lord have mercy on her. The Turk landed to him next and they went the opposite way to the Cliffs of Mohar, to the city of Galway to take note of the sights there and so forth and so on as the man said what went about cutting the story short.

They got drunk in Galway and 'twas there in Cummerton's public house after the consumption of seventeen half ones of potstill whiskey that Mikey Tatty pronounced his love for the Turk. They went to the altar on the very day he threatened to burn himself. His sister was the bridesmaid and her husband-to-be the best man. The bride was given away by a black man what was working in the merry-go-rounds in Galway and we put it out about him that he was her father and that he was after coming all the way from the latter end of Turkey for the wedding and that he was very high up there with a fine farm of land what was black with olives and grapes.

It would be nice a thing to say now wouldn't it that they lived happy every after and that there was young Tattys all over the place but the opposite was to be the case. The wedding was held in Lisdoonvarna and there was lashings of drink, fiddlers from Feakle and concertina players from Kilrush. The Turkish lady threw the head sideways after she lowering the best part of a bottle of whiskey and she broke out into song. 'Twas long and high and lonesome like what you'd hear at a high mass and I declare to God there was several ullagoning like foster pups before 'twas over. It took five men for to lift her into the car and she taking off on the honeymoon to the Tatty home in Ballyoodle.

Now for the painful item. Mikey Tatty died the day he threatened but it wasn't fire that done away with him. He died accidental when the Turk turned over in her sleep, the whole twenty-two stone of her, and smothered him. God be good to him but he had little luck with the ladies. Still they say to die by fire is the worst way of all to go so that you might say he was lucky enough not to go that way. 'Tis an ill wind as the man said.

The trouble with me since he died is that I can't sleep. I done my best for him. I rose to the occasion when the sister asked me and I spread two fine bundles of daffodils on his grave what I swept out of a garden in front of a house and we coming to his funeral in the hired car. I handed over a mass card to the Turk and there's no night since we don't mention him in the Rosary. What man could do more.

Still and for all my conscience troubles me. Between them all they put me in a right pucker. If I didn't find him a woman he was faced with death and when I did find him one he died anyway. He was doomed I suppose from the start. Mad for women all his life only to be snuffed out by one in the finish. 'Tis a cruel world to be sure. Love to Marge.

Your loving brother,
Dick.

*   *   *

Drombeag,
Mullachmore.

Dear Mr O'Connor,
I have a favourite to beseech you. I would like a good firm
woman in the regions of thirty to forty. I have my own
place a bare mile from the village of Mullachmore. It's
there they have a new cinema and a parochial hall and all
sorts of amusements. I work steady with a big farmer that
breeds hunters and racehorses. I am age forty-two. I used
to be a jockey in the flat but I have to own up I never
won a race. My height is five feet feck-all and my weight
is seven stone but I'm as fit as a fiddler. Would you know
of anyone suitable. My cottage is in good repair and I
have no shortage of anything. You wouldn't notice me in a
crowd and you mightn't feel my weight but I'm a good
man to do a day's work and the woman that would marry
me would not want for much. There's my story long
enough. If you want anymore let me know and I'll answer
any question you might ask.

Yours fatefully,
Roger Speck.

★   ★   ★

Coolkera,
Coomasahara.

Dear Tricky Dicky,
No reply as yet in spite of my letters. I'm here at home
this dark night after leaving Carrolane the smith to his
horseshoes and his anvil. You may be sure he knocked
more sparks out of one shoe on that anvil than he ever
knocked out of me. I'm going to write to the bishop about
you. Ordinary law isn't half good enough for you and a
bishop don't charge nothing. You'll be quick to fork out
my money then. There's a round and a half of it coming
to me now not to mention the interest on the first lot. I
want no more to do with you only hand over my hard
earned money or you'll pay dear.

Fionnuala Crust.

P.S. I heard today from a tinker that Carrolane is after getting a stroke.

F.C.

★ ★ ★

Spider's Well,
Ballybarra.

Dear Mr Speck,

Got yours today. Don't despair. Every bush will nest its own bird sooner or later. You say you wouldn't be noticed in a crowd. I pays no heed to that. There's no crowds in my marriage beds only pairs. I have a woman in the back of my head for you but I'll disclose no name till I know more about the lie of the land. Being a jockey I'm sure you'll appreciate that a broken mare is better than an unbroken one. No bother to an unbroken filly to unsaddle you whereas your sound mare that's been around the course a good few times won't never dump you and you coming into the regulation if you follow. She'll get across it somehow whereas the filly might shy. I'll say no more for now Mr Speck as my missus is thrown down with a heavy dose of the flu and I'm faced with an almighty amount of work.

Courtesy and civility assured at all times.

Dicky Mick Dicky O'Connor.

★ ★ ★

Hunter Hall,
Ballyninty.

Dear O'Connor,

You're very hard on me. My late mother was, as you say, kinder to asses and ponies than she was to human beings. However, you must remember that the cottiers around the demesne were a shiftless lot, lying, evasive, dirty and thieving. Small wonder that she found asses more rewarding than people. It is very easy to condemn people like me but you should remember before you commence castigation that I am as God made me. I am not run of the mill alas. I have many parallels in nature. You might say I am one of the exceptions who proves the rule that only opposing sexes should complement each other. If this is so I have my rights and I also believe that there is room under the sun for men of my inclination. God would not have placed us here if the case were otherwise. Anyway why should I have to justify myself in a world which is full of misfits without my kind. If the truth were told every man is a misfit of one kind or another and that is basically why no two men are exactly alike in outlook. Take care then O'Connor for it could well be that you and your righteous contemporaries are far more flawed than I. You judge me by your standards yet I dare not judge you by mine. Is something not rotten then in the State of Denmark and all the other states that are conditioned against that which they cannot or will not comprehend. A fair hearing old boy, an open mind. In short, a modicum of tolerance for the other fellow.

In spite of your letter I am still in the market for a wife. Do you think you could induce our friend from Dead Man's Lane to agree to a second encounter. I promise to be on my best behaviour. I am trying hard to be what is often hopefully but erroneously labelled an ordinary man. This may help account for my seemingly extraordinary behaviour in the snug of Morgan Shaughnessy's highly respectable public house in Ballylittle. Do what you can and I shall not be unmindful of your efforts.

Do you know the name of the fair-haired boy with freckles and the buck teeth who stands regularly at the back of Ballybarra Parish Hall during the Sunday night dances. I would like to correspond with him. I haven't seen him about for some time and I am wondering if all is well with him. The last time we met there was a shortage of women (isn't there always). I asked him if he'd care for a dance but he declined with a shy smile and said that he felt too tired. I saw him no more after that.

I will be anxiously awaiting word from you, at your convenience of course.

Yours cordially,
Glynne-Hunter.

★   ★   ★

The Shamrock Inn,
Shillelagh Avenue,
Philadelphia.

Dear Dicky,
Sorry to hear of Kate's illness. You just wait. She'll be up and about any day now. Marge and me is jimdandy and nowheres, but nowheres seems as attractive as Spiders' Well country just now. We gotta freak storm here that nearly blew my goddam cobs off. You don't get no weather like this over there. This burg ain't gonna be the same for weeks. Our dear ole buddy Robert Emmet O'Bannion has been asking about you and wants to know what headway you're making on his account. I need some sorta progress report bad. It would be a crying shame if all that dough went to those bums in the Tax Department. I had a sidekick who used to be a private dick take a peek into O'Bannion's background and it seems the guy's legit. Now Dicky I want you should get a colleen for this guy and get one fast. The Dick uncovered quite a lot about O'Bannion's parents. His old man took a powder when the kid was only a year old. His old lady was no angel neither. She foisted him over on her mother and took to high-class hustling, then to middle-class hustling and finally to low-class hustling. All this time she visited the kid regularly and brought him expensive gifts. The kid had no idea his old lady was a hustler. Just about the time when she had one wrinkle too many she turned Jennie. Maybe you ain't never heard tell of a Judas Jennie. You know me Dickie. I was always a sucker for a good story and I never been mean with no man nor dame but one thing is sure. You won't never catch me going bail for no Judas Jennie. How they operate is this. You

get a fresh, pretty young dame from some hick town in the mid-west. She gets herself a job in the city. A lotta guys get fresh with her but this gal don't want none o that mush. She wants maybe a nice-looking guy with a job and then a decent apartment and a few kids, no more than that. Come to think of it that's what most dames want. Now some middle-aged guy comes in the picture. Maybe the guy's a crook. Maybe he's a businessman. Maybe he's a professional man but sure as shooting there's two things he ain't. He ain't broke and he ain't no gentleman. He sets his sights on this country chick and boy does he hanker after her. Like I say she ain't no cheap broad and she turns him down when he tries to date her. So he goes and gets hisself the services of a Judas Jennie, usually some hustler that's seen better days. No assin about now. He comes to the point. He wants the country kid and he wants her bad. He's prepared to cough up plenty provided the Jennie comes across with the goods. Here's what happens. The old broad makes friends with the kid which ain't too difficult when you figure the city's full of strangers mosta them wolves. The kid begins to trust the Jennie when she gets to know her better. Then the Jennie gets to work. First a little drink. Next time maybe two. It ain't no harm she says. Help you relax. Sleep better. Every body does it so what the hell. Then the little gal is introduced to night life. You got the glitter and you got the music and you got the champagne and it's all such good fun. Then the interested party is introduced casually, quite by accident. Then Jennie points out he's not such a bad ole guy. He spends plenty and he knows the best night spots. Then one night the kid gets drunk and she and the Jennie go to the guy's apartment or maybe some posh hotel. After that its all one-way sailing and soon, very soon the kid's a good-time girl. Gals like this don't never stay the distance. At thirty she's an old woman, worn out and unwanted. So you see Dick how it comes I don't cotton to this particular kinda doll they call a Judas Jennie. Ain't no job I can think of so Goddam despicable and I figure they ain't no God gonna forgive a dame does what a Jennie does. You ask me forgive a guy who maybe kills my wife I guess I'd just have to do it but a Judas Jennie never, not if she was depending on it to stay alive. Robert Emmet O'Bannion never knew how his old lady ended. He was told by his granny that she went down with the Titanic and he believes it cos it's what he wants to believe. He's a decent ole asshole. They ain't nobody can take that away from him. He keeps buzzin me about this Irish colleen every time he comes in to the Shamrock and I don't have nothing to say to him so git on your bike Dicky and do sumpin fast. Enclosed find a get-well card from me and Marge for Kate and a few dollars to get her a bottle of brandy or some sorta tonic wine to bust that flu. Take care man.

Your loving brother,
Jack.

* * *

Coolkera,
Coomasahara.

Dear Sir,
I'm going to the bishop this very day. You got your chance and you didn't take it. You'll be scandalised soon in the sight of the people. Since Carrolane died I didn't sleep a wink. He made no battle the poor man. What was he but a big soft heap. Still there was a nice turnout for his funeral. I put no wreath over this one. He cost me enough as it was. I'm going to put in for the widow's pension and resign myself to a life of celebrity and modesty but not before I put the bishop on your tail you ingrate you that was the father of all my misfortune.

A double widow,
Fionnnuala Crust.

* * *

Drombeag,
Mullachmore.

Dear Mr O'Connor,
I'm the jockey that wrote to you for the favourite which
was to know would you be able to locate a nice firm
woman for me in the regions of thirty to forty. In the last
letter I forgot to tell you I have five hundred pounds in
the post office. I'm not terrible choosy so long as she's
fairly firm. I have a new tarpaulin in the bedroom and if
the weather improves I'm going to plant a sit down toilet
beyond the back door so she won't have far to travel if she
get caught short. I'm surprised you never found anyone
for me and then again I'm not. I'm so miserable in size
and frail in appearance that people often mistakes me for a
corpse when I'd be lying down anywhere. Please don't
renege on me, I was told you once said that every man on
the face of this earth is entitled to a wife except them that
volunteers for the round collar.

Yours faithfully,
Roger Speck.

★   ★   ★

Knockbrack,
Tubberdarrig West.

Dear Dicky,
She's gone sex mad. I can't keep her contented. I swear to
God 'tis not in the power of one man to satisfy her since I
started dosing her. Fine if I could stay in bed all day but
I does have to be tending to the cows at cockcrow. The
quare thing is that she don't need no dosing now. I'm like
a lath from contending with her. There was one time I
thought I'd never get enough of it but now I'd sooner an
egg. Let me know soon if there is any way to control her.

Your devoted friend,
Thady Thade Biddy Mackessy.

★   ★   ★

Guards' Barracks,
Tullylore,
Co Cork.

Dear Mr O'Connor,

Yesterday I went through the effects of the late Cornelius J. McCarthy of Menafreghane, Tullylore. Among them was a letter from you from which I gather that you were endeavouring to find a wife for him. Mr McCarthy died in his bed a week ago tonight. It would seem that the bedclothes took fire from a cigarette which he had been holding when he fell asleep. We found his charred body a few days afterwards when his nearest neighbour raised the alarm. No smoke had come from his chimney in forty-eight hours and the neighbour went to investigate. The light of heaven to him he was a decent fellow for all his afflictions. A wife was all he wanted out of this life.

On the night of his death he had been drinking in the village of Tullylore. He hired a car to take him home. That was the last time anybody saw him alive. I hope he has better luck where he is now. No man deserves it more.

Sincerely,
Oliver Mowrey (Segt).

P.S. I'm fifty-two. I never married. My father and mother died young and my salary went to the upkeep of my younger brothers and sisters. They're all married now but here am I in my barracks with only a black cat for company.

O.M.

★ ★ ★

Following a strongly-worded letter from Fionnuala Crust of Coomasahara to the bishop of the diocese, the parish priest of Ballybarra, Father Andrew Dree, was summoned to the palace where he was handed the letter in question and told by his Lordship to digest its contents.

'In case', said the bishop, 'my presence imposes any constraint upon your digestion I will leave you to yourself for ten minutes after which time I will return when I will be most eager to hear your views.'

So saying the bishop withdrew and Father Andrew devoted his full attention to the letter.

'My dear Lord Bishop', it ran, ''Tis sorry I am to be driven to writing to you but I must reveal my tale to someone. There is a matchmaker operating in the north of the County by the name of Dicky Mick Dicky O'Connor, that pawned over two dead husbands on me and he knowing the creatures to be on their last legs. Twice I paid him the first time twenty pounds and the second time ten pounds. 'Tis an awful note in a Christian country that an honest woman can't marry legally in the Church of God without fear of ending up a widow before you'd know a man well enough to go calling him by his first name. He should be read from the altar the fifty-two Sundays of the year and faced with the bell, book and candle and at the end of that time transported to the farthest corner of Australia. If he gave me my money back itself 'twould give me some satisfaction. No indeed only going about his wicked business and splicing other poor devils that's wanting or demented or some way worse entirely. 'Tis a shame the church don't act against this monster and they content to give out wholesale agin ordinary poor sinners that knows no better. If there isn't satisfaction I'll write to Rome to the Holy Father complaining the whole lot of ye from top to bottom. Devil the world will oul' Dree the parish priest of Ballybarra let go and he coining out of the marriages. A pity he don't ask how they're made or do he care as long as he scores for tying the knot.

A badly-wronged martyr,
Fionnuala Crust.'

At the conclusion of the letter Father Dree thrust his right hand into his trousers pocket in search of matches with which he might consign the defamatory epistle to flames which was his wont with all letters of a spurious nature. He realised suddenly that the letter was addressed to the bishop and stayed his hand in the nick of time. With barely suppressed anger he slammed the offending pages on the gleaming mahogany table where stood the bishop's pipe-rack and writing paraphernalia. He paced the study in a rage, realising he must restore himself to a rational state before the bishop's return. As in all crises he blamed his curate Father Burk. It was Burk who had several times dissuaded him from attacking the loathsome matchmaker from the pulpit by pointing out the large number of marriages which had been arranged in the parish since O'Connor had begun operations. He realised now he had been misled by his curate. But, he told himself, if a curate is responsible for directing his parish priest into an impasse should not the curate be made to shoulder the blame. It was the apparent logic of this deduction that impelled Father Dree to address the bishop with the following opening remark:

'My curate,' said he, 'must take all the blame for this.'

'Your curate?' said the bishop.

'Yes my curate,' Father Dree affirmed.

'But,' said the bishop, 'I was under the impression that it was the parish priest and not the curate who ran the parish.'

'Granted,' Father Andrew answered most amiably, 'but one is forced to depend on the advice of his curate in certain matters.'

'In certain matters yes,' said the bishop. 'In serious matters no.'

'I was often on the point of paying this fellow O'Connor a visit but my curate always defended him and I must confess I heeded my curate. To whom else am I to go for information. It was often on the tip of my tongue to denounce this matchmaker from the pulpit but again on the advice of my curate I relented. Now I see that I was gravely mistaken to place so much credence in the recommendations of my assistant. I did so in good faith and in the belief that respect for his opinions would mature him in good time for the day when he would have a parish of his own.'

To this the bishop listened without comment. From his face it was obvious that he was not impressed. There followed a most arduous and probing succession of questions at the end of which he placed his hand on Father Dree's shoulder.

'My dear Andrew,' said he, 'a curate is but a curate. It is the parish priest who must shoulder the blame when things go wrong. Go now and never forget. I will trust you to deal with this matchmaker in your own way. I am not familiar with your part of the diocese and being a townsman the idea of matchmaking is anathema to me. In certain cases there may be some merit attached to it but the obvious pitfalls must far outweigh what little good might come from it.'

The interview ended on this note. On his arrival home Dree was greeted in the dining-room of the presbytery by Father Burk who was in the middle of a supper which consisted of two hard-boiled eggs and a plentiful supply of toast.

'Do you ever think of anything but your belly?' the parish priest shouted slamming the door behind him and at the same time calling to his housekeeper that he would be dining in his study. The curate was perplexed but not for the first time. After a moment or two of thought he resumed eating and halfway through the second egg he had forgotten altogether the castigating remark of his superior.

Bright and early the following morning, immediately after breakfast, Father Andrew summoned his curate to his study.

'We're going this morning', said Father Andrew, 'to the abode of Dicky Mick Dicky O'Connor. I am going to impress upon him the error of his ways and ask him to abandon this odious practice of matchmaking.'

'Odious', said the curate.

'Odious', said Father Andrew, angered at the pretended perplexity of his subordinate.

'You'll be exceeding your authority', said the curate.

'You're exceeding yours', said Father Dree.

'But the man is doing the world of good', Father Burk insisted. 'He's giving so much hope and the opportunity of love to so many.'

'And you're giving me a pain in the head', Dree retaliated. 'Now when we arrive I want you to hold your tongue. I want no comment of any kind from you or you'll find yourself facing your bishop. Understood?'

'Understood.' This in a mutinous undertone from the curate. When the pair arrived at Spiders' Well Dicky Mick Dicky was drying the breakfast ware with a faded cloth.

'How're the men', he said, 'and pray tell me what I can be doing for you this handsome day?'

'I won't mince words with you, O'Connor', Father Andrew started. 'I have just come from his Lordship the Bishop and I may say that he is most displeased with you. I wouldn't be at all surprised if you found yourself faced with excommunication unless, of course, you mend your ways.'

A look of horror and incredulity appeared on Father Burk's face. He turned abruptly and walked out of the house.

'What are you saying man?' Dicky Mick Dicky asked of Dree.

'I'm saying his lordship recently received a letter from a woman by the name of Crust from Coomasahara who quite rightly denounced you for the villain you are.'

'Lower your voice while you're under my roof', Dicky Mick Dicky cautioned.

'I will say what must be said', Father Andrew shouted. 'I came here to denounce you and denounce you I will and neither will I leave here till you recant and give over the evil practice of matchmaking.'

'Listen to me', said Dicky Mick Dicky, 'and listen good Father. My wife is ailing ever since she was struck down by the flu. For her sake I must ask you to lower your voice or else leave the house.'

'Don't you dare threaten me you heretic', Father Andrew shouted. 'How dare you join people in wedlock without authority from God or man.'

'It's you who does the joining Father and I never heard of you refusing money from them you joined. I never heard of you joining any couple without money neither.'

'How dare you talk to your priest like that. What does an ignorant clod like you know about these people you have the gall to match together.'

'I know more than you that marries them. I have known many of them all their lives and the others I know from confabbing and conversing with them. I know my people but you know nothing about them only what means they have in order to put a price on the ceremony.'

At this Father Andrew's face turned white with fury. His whole body trembled as he fought for control.

'You, you, you. . . .', he shouted with upraised hands as he sought to find a fitting form of denunciation. But nothing would come. In a rage he strode from the house announcing at the door that he would inveigh against Dicky Mick Dicky the following Sunday from the altar. Unmoving Dicky heard the hum of the car engine on the roadway. Then silence. It was then he noticed his wife's hand on his arm. She stood beside him in her bare feet, ghastly pale, dressed only in her nightdress.

'Excommunication', she whispered. 'Is that what he said?'

'Don't take any notice of him', Dicky told her. 'Come on back to your warm bed and I'll bring you a nice mug of tea.'

In her bed she clutched her beads and twined them about her blue-white fingers. Dicky noted the lacklustre look in her eyes, her ghastly pallor, in particular the awesome whiteness of her scalp under the greying hair. Then for the first time he knew she was dying.

'Rest yourself now', he said, 'and I'll get you the tea.'

On Sunday Father Andrew denounced the practice of matchmaking from the pulpit and advised his parishioners to have no truck with with a certain matchmaker since all such men were in league with the devil. His words served only to strengthen stands already well-established. Those who did not hold a brief for matching grew firmer in their resolve to denounce it at every hand's turn while those who held with it decided to ignore the pleas of their parish priest. On the following Tuesday Kate O'Connor died in her sleep. Earlier the curate administered the last rites while she still retained her senses. The likes of the funeral was never seen in Ballybarra. Men who had not come out of doors for years presented themselves at the graveside to sympathise with Dicky Mick Dicky. Others came out of curiosity. Most came because the matchmaker was a legendary figure and his wife was a respected woman. All were agreed that she made a poor battle in the finish. Some maintained that red-haired people were not renowned for their resistance to illness and in her hey-day wasn't every tress on Kate O'Connor's head like a tongue of flame. When the grave was thatched with the fresh green sods which had been put aside at the beginning Dicky Mick Dicky put on his cap and without a word to anyone went home to the empty house at Spiders' Well. For several weeks he was not seen by his neighbours but there was smoke at all times rising from his chimney so that there was no fear for his welfare. If there were no smoke it could well mean that he had taken the same road as Kate. Men were known to die of emptiness before this. Dicky Mick Dicky, however, had too much regard for the life that God had given him. After two months he threw off his sorrow and faced up to the living world around him. Inside him unknown to most was a void that could never be filled. No words could define the grief that lingered on but the world had to be met and life had to go on. We find him now writing to his brother in Philadelphia.

Spiders' Well,
Ballybarra.

Dear Jack,
The black times are back again. I was never so low in myself in all my days. She was the light of my life and the pulse of my heart. My heart breaks for her. Sometimes when I open a drawer I see a rib of her hair or a cake of fancy soap or a broach or a hairpin. At every hands turn there is something to remind me of her. What am I to do at all in God's name with every day blacker than the next and the endless nights like the inside of a tomb. You have no way Jack of knowing the meaning of grief until it lifts

the latch on your own door. I remember Kate and me was coming home one summer's evening from the meadow when the sky was blackened and the rain came down. We took shade under an old sycamore in the corner of the haggard. Drops of water trickled through the leaves and fell on the grass with whispers you could hardly hear. It was a slanted rain from the southwest and it didn't stay long. Soon the sun came out and lit up the water beads like diamonds on every blade of the green grass. The next thing was the birds started to sing in the heart of the sycamore over our heads and from every bush and bramble came one gay song on top of another. Kate took my hand and this is what she said:

'Isn't it grand for me and you Dicky', says she. 'Isn't it surely grand for you and me.'

Oh Holy Christ how am I going to endure it at all. She'll never call me again for my supper nor bring the tay to the meadows in the summer. I had great times entirely with her. I could come and go as I pleased the seven days of the week and if I was ever in a pucker she was the woman to sort it out. God knows the value of her. 'Twas He took her. To make my cross heavier the priest read me from the altar not long before she let go of life and a nate little man what was crippled and what was a client of mine was burnt in his bed after he taking a few scoops of porter on a Sunday night. Of all the men what ever sought my services he was the one I was most anxious to supply with a companion. 'Twas hard luck on the poor fellow because I had a woman almost engaged for him and she like himself with a wasted leg but a lovely girl whatever. Another month or two and I'd have the two of them tied. This is all I have to say for the moment. I takes a few drinks every night so's I'll harvest a few winks of sleep.

Good luck and success to the Council of Trent
What put fast upon mate but not upon drink.

'Tis a deal we have something in these woeful days. Write soon and give me the news.

Your dear brother,
Richard.

P.S. I might have news of an Irish colleen for your friend. Wait for the days to grow longer and for people to turn their backs to the hearth and take the air again.

Richard.

* * *

Coolkera,
Coomasahara.

Dear Sir,
I was sorry to hear that your wife was taken from you for as bad as you are that's a misfortune I'd wish on no one. I'm here again in my own corner at the heel of the hunt as lone and lonesome as a ewe lost on the mountain. There is two things I still have after all my suas-sios and them is my two fortunes. One is my five hundred pounds and the other is what God gave me. I do ask myself and I thrown down in front of the fire am I to be left with them forever or will I write once more to that thundering rogue that resides in Spiders' Well. Two times he harnessed me to cawbogues after landing out good money. What is your charge for a third attempt? If 'tis half price for widows surely 'tis quarter price for them that's double widows. What I'm saying is I'd be obliged to you if you was to be on the look-out once more for a suitable husband for me. Third time lucky as the saying goes. I'll be anxious to hear from you.

Fionnuala Crust (Miss).

P.S. And I pondering my problem by the fire it entered my head that the two men of mine that's underneath the sod were big, broad and weighty but still for all they could no more canoodle no more nor a carcase and 'twasn't for the want of incitement neither for no woman ever worked harder in that line of business. My grandmother God rest her used often say the bigger the tree the smaller the apple, the smaller the bush the bigger the berry. My grandmother was no daw and I'm thinking that

them you'd think you'd be made by is often the most
deceitful and them that has but the bare bones is mostly
the liveliest bucks of all. So don't let size be your guide
no more.

Fionnuala Crust (Miss).

★　★　★

Shamrock Inn,
Shillelagh Avenue.

Dear Jack,
Marge and me really feel for you and we're coming for
that holiday next month. We expect to be in Ireland for
Saint Patrick's Day. It's some day here but what the hell.
You and me was always close and I guess you need company pretty bad. We can't stay no longer than a fortnight
but I guess that oughta be long enough to lift you outa
the dumps and guess what! Robert Emmet O'Bannion is
gonna tag along with us, not just for kicks but in the hope
you'll come up with that Irish colleen. He's O.K. is
Robert Emmet. All he thinks about is the colleen. I'll send
a cable just so's you won't drop dead with the shock when
you see us.

Your loving brother,
Jack.

P.S. I wouldn't worry none about that padre. The way he
sees it you're muscling in on his territory and the way I
see it is you're maybe making more hay outa the marriages
than he is. Man he'd sure be cut down to size here in
Philly. See you boy.

Jack.

★　★　★

Spiders' Well,
Ballybarra.

Dear Lena,
What would you say to a Yank. His name is Robert
Emmet O'Bannion and he is most anxious for to settle
with an Irish colleen. He'll be here Saint Patrick's Day
with my brother Jack and Jack's wife and if I was you I'd
be investing in faldals like green ribbons and green dresses
with a bit of gold here and there. A good head of red hair
wouldn't do you no harm neither. It might suit you better
than the jet black head you have now and as I recall you
looked alright when you had brown hair. He's around the
seventy mark but he's not short of a shilling. You might
say that he has money to burn. Let me know soon. He
won't live forever.
    Courtesy and civility assured at all times.

Dicky Mick Dicky O'Connor.

★   ★   ★

Drombeag,
Mullachmore.

Dear Mr O'Connor,
I hope you haven't forgotten me. Unless the mercy of
God the race of life will be run out on me without an
engagement. Don't forget me.

Yours fatefully,
Roger Speck.

★   ★   ★

Spiders' Well,
Ballybarra.

Dear Fionnuala,
I have a jock for you. His name is Speck. He don't look
like much. He have his own place and five hundred

pounds in the post office. He's a horse breaker. By Gor says I when I read this I have a mare what will test you and that's Fionnuala Crust from Coomasahara for though the bit was in her mouth as a man said she was never rightly broke. He's only five feet tall but since he did most of his work on the flat this should be no encumbrance. There's no fear he'll drive you down through the bed because he's only seven stone. Still and for all I would say that he'll break from the starting gate like an onion fart when the white flag is raised. Remember what the oul' people say. The best of goods comes in small parcels. You had your nuff of weight and condition if ever any woman had. 'Tis time now to give a turn to the lightweights. As soon as I hear from you I'll set things in motion and as sure as there's cobs on a ram you'll be the first in the frame after your next outing.

Courtesy and civility assured at all times.

> Your obt Servant,
> Dicky Mick Dicky O'Connor.

★ ★ ★

> Dead Man's Lane,
> Ballylittle.

Dear Dicky,
'Tis my fond hope that you're coming around slow but sure after the loss of poor Kate. That the angels might sing for her till the two of you are joined once more. I enclose a mass card. Robert Emmet O'Bannion has the smack of a man that might suit. Of green dresses I have plenty. I'll wear tri-coloured ribbons for him if that's what he wants and since 'tis Saint Patrick's Day that's nearly down on my floor with us what's to stop me from having my bottom painted green and my nails painted yellow. If 'tis an Irish colleen he wants he needn't go no farther. By the way Dicky I'm sure there's a few pounds going to you after all the work you done on my account and if you didn't score itself it wasn't for the want of trying. Money is a commodity I never saw enough of

since the day I could first tell copper from silver so I can't offer you any at this present time. I could give you an antique pepper caster or a napkin ring but 'twould be a shame to spoil my fine collection especially over it having such sentimental value.

Instead of the money I could pay my account by way of work. With your brother and his wife coming not to mention Robert Emmet the house would want a thorough cleaning from top to bottom and the bed clothes would want airing and there's any number of other touches that a woman can give to a place. While you're whitewashing the outside I could be cleaning the inside. I have my bicycle and 'tis no more nor an hour to come and less than another to go.

Sincerely,
Lena Magee.

* * *

Spiders' Well,
Ballybarra.

Dear Roger,
I must apologise for not answering your letters sooner but my excuse is that I was making enquiries on your account and in the latter end of my investigations by pure luck I came across as fine a mare as ever whinnied a stallion. She is a woman what have a fine form-sheet having as you might say been well shod for the tar road as well as the bog if you follow. Her name is Fionnuala Crust and after untackling herself from a pair of fine husbands she is getting anxious for the harness again. I can recommend this grand woman to any perspective partner as the saying goes but I may as well warn you that she'll need a tight rein if she's not to run away with you. If you could present yourself at Morgan Shaughnessy's public house in Ballylittle I will land her there at seven o'clock any Sunday or if that don't suit you there is plenty other places that might be more contagious to you. As I often told you there is an end to every road of hardship and 'tis my honest opinion that you haven't far more to go. I'll await your directions.

Courtesy and civility assured at all times.

Your obt servant,
Dicky Mick Dicky O'Connor.

★   ★   ★

Spiders' Well,
Ballybarra.

Dear Thady Thade Biddy,
There's many an honest man would be glad if they had
your story. There's lone men making lamentation from one
end of the night to the other for the limbs of supple women
and there's you discontented in the middle of plenty as the
man said. I can offer no cure for what ails you beyond
advising you to fire back plenty raw eggs and not to draw
away from the table too soon especially if there is green
cabbage going. Fish is good too and there's them oysters
what does be took raw while some set great store by
ground-up nutmegs. The best cure of all, of course, is
to add to your present store of children. There is no
cure on the face of this earth better guaranteed to knock
the taspy out of a female than to place her in the family
way. I hope these few hints is of use to you. The brother
Jack is home from the States this past week and he
was enquiring for you. Why don't yourself and herself
knock over some night for a talk about oul' times. There
is drink galore, all bought by the Yanks. There is the
brother and his wife and there is a chap by the name
of Robert Emmet O'Bannion who is sparking hard with
Lena Magee. You should see her and she done up like
a Crolly doll. We goes to Killarney regular. Yanks does
have their dinner around the same time as we does have
our supper. There is great times in it entirely just now.
Jack bought a car for his stay and is giving me instructions in the use of the wheel as he says he won't carry it
back with him. Won't they have nice looking at me at the
creamery when I bowls in driving my car. They'll say
there's great money in matchmaking. We're off again to-
night. I remember the first time Robert Emmet O'Bannion

asked Lena Magee out to dinner. It was shoving on for seven o'clock in the evening.

'Who in the name of God', says Lena, 'would put down spuds for you this hour of the night?'

Business is good lately. You remember the Widow Snoss, Mickeen's wife that I matched with Carrolane the blacksmith. Well I have her all but soldered to a man from Mullachmore in Cork what used to be a jockey and what has a moderate enough way of living. They're for the rails in a month. There is others as well. There is a sergeant of the Guards what was the sole support of his family but what has been free with a while to get buckled. He is stationed in Tullylore and wonders of wonders isn't his landlady a widow the bare year older than him. When I put it to him that he would be well advised in making a case to her he commissioned me to do the same. I got a warm welcome. It was how the poor fellow couldn't see the wood for the trees. If you're standing too long next to a thing you'll set little store by it. They're for the rails too very soon and no doubt he'll be arresting her one of those nights for going astray in a bed.

So 'tis well you may say that times is good. If I could only latch up Lena Magee and the Yank before the end of the fortnight you might say as how all my prayers would be answered and that I could take a stretch from my labours for awhile. I'll miss this company when they're gone back although Robert Emmet has his sights set on settling in Dead Man's Lane. So we may see more of him.

Courtesy and civility assured at all times.

Your obt servant,
Dicky Mick Dicky O'Connor.

★ ★ ★

Hunter Hall,
Ballyninty.

Dear O'Connor,

May I take it that you have severed your connection with me. Please let me know by return post if this is so as my

immediate aim is to engage the services of another matchmaker.

Yours cordially,
Claude Glynne-Hunter.

★   ★   ★

The Presbytery,
Ballybarra.

Dear Dicky,
As you may have seen in the recently-published list of
Diocesan appointments we are to have a new parish priest.
Now that Father Dree has departed and while we are
awaiting the arrival of the new man why not start going to
Church again in the interim. As a personal favour I would
ask you to attend Mass next Sunday.

Yours in J. C.,
Father Burk, C.C.

★   ★   ★

Coolkera,
Coomasahara.

Dear Dicky,
May God increase your store and may you never see want
nor sickness for 'tis you that has presented me with the
liveliest man that was ever let loose in a house. The first
look at him nearly put me off him and didn't I stand to
the westward side of him for fear he'd be swept away by a
gale of wind before he had a chance to talk to me. He was
the iochtar of the litter if ever there was one. We are here
now the pair of us spending our honeymoon in beautiful
Coomasahara. I never knew such contentment. My grandmother was right. You might say I'm a happily married
woman at long last and my one great regret is that I
foolishly put quantity before quality in the past. Ah 'tis
me that knows better now and 'tis me that is looking

forward to a long life with my new husband. This time for sure you earned your fee. You'll hear no more out of me now.

Sincerely,
Mrs Roger Speck.

★ ★ ★

Spiders' Well,
Ballybarra.

Dear Mr Glynne-Hunter,
I never gives up on a client. Get another matchmaker if you want but I'm still prepared to work on your behalf if that's what you want. The bother with you is that you don't know what you want. As soon as you have sorted that out write to me again and I won't renege on you.
    Courtesy and civility assured at all times.

Your obt servant,
Dicky Mick Dicky O'Connor.

P.S. There's a one in Pulawadra between Tralee and Listowel that might suit. The reason I say she might suit you in particular is that I don't know what to make of her myself. Maybe you could make something out of her. She's an only daughter out of fifteen cows and a score of sheep. The father and mother is alive and they don't know what to make out of her neither. She's her own boss. That's for sure. She drives a Baby Ford. She went for a week working to Listowel when she was younger, about fifteen years ago. She came home to Pulawadra with a Yankee accent after three visits to the Astor cinema there. She would be shoving close to forty now. There's a bit of the lady in her put there by herself, of course, and so she might suit the kind of honourable you are.

As ever,
Dicky Mick Dicky O'Connor.

★ ★ ★

Shamrock Inn,
Shillelagh Avenue,
Philadelphia.

Dear Dicky,
We just got back. Boy am I droopy. Marge is pooped after
the trip but Robert Emmet takes the biscuit. He's got
black circles round his eyes and it don't look like he's
gonna be around for some time. That Magee dame sure
spun him a funny line. Imagine asking a guy on his last
legs like that to wait a year or two while she thought it
over. I figure if he lasts six months he'll be lucky.

I don't think she cottoned to him all that much, not
with the red eyes of his always bloodshot from shots.
Come to think of it he didn't smell so good neither. It
sure shows money ain't everything.

We sure had a good time over there Dicky and I
wanna thank you for being so all-fired nice to Marge and
me and forgetting about yourself. Maybe it was best that
way. I want you should go out and live and try not to
think about Kate. I reckon it wouldn't do you no harm if
you was to get hitched again. Kate would approve. Think
about it. One thing is sure. It sure as hell beats the ass
offa talking to yourself. Write soon. You hear now, real
soon.

Love,
Jack.

* * *

The Presbytery,
Ballybarra.

Dear Mr O'Connor,
I haven't had the honour of meeting you yet but as your
new P.P. I cannot tell you how pleased I am that you
have resumed your mass-going. Father Burk speaks highly
of you although I gather that you and Father Dree did not
hit it off too well. I daresay this is inevitable in small
parishes. There have to be differences of opinion between

men of different convictions so I'll say no more about it except all's well that ends well.

Now I have a favour to ask of you. You may or may not have heard that my poor mother went to her eternal reward about six months ago. My father is still alive and lives on the farm with my bachelor brother who would like to settle down if you would be kind enough to make out a suitable woman for him. Some farmer's daughter around thirty or thirty-five would be admirable. He's a shy man. He cannot make a case for himself and this is where you can help him. I'll be most anxious to hear from you.

Sincerely
Patrick Kimmerley, P.P.V.F.

★ ★ ★

Spiders' Well,
Ballybarra.

Dear Jack,
Glad ye all got back safe. A good rest now and ye won't know yeerselves again. By God Jack but 'tis powerful lonesome since. I didn't know what lonesome was till the full loss of Kate dawned on me. I could never marry again, not after Kate. God wouldn't make two like that in the same mould. She had no equal for holding her tongue. Thank God I never asked too much of her and to tell you the truth all I would ask of a woman in excess of normal duties is that she be not given to too much talk except alone for the breaking of awkward silences. I knew a man from Mullachmore that gave up talking to his wife. He worked by signs for ten years until they became known as the Dummy Gunnells. In the end she brought him into court on a charge of cruelty. When the judge asked him his reasons for not talking to his missus his answer was that he didn't like interrupting her. 'Tis talk and talk alone what has knocked the humour and the give and take out of marriage. 'Tis a great stroke of fortune to marry a woman what has a name for talking soft and seldom. 'Tis no joke to marry a gramophone. 'Tis fine in a marriage where you have a quiet man what won't fan the flames but

by the hokey where you have two with active tongues there can never be a minute's peace. I remember Kate and me went once to Ballylittle engaging a goose for the Christmas dinner. The house was to the west of the village and when we landed a small fat woman came to the door and got carried away at once by her own talk. We followed her into the kitchen where there was a thin man wearing a cap and he mending an ass's harness. To this day I don't know for sure who that man was, whether husband or lodger for the woman never let up spouting chatter at the top of her voice the whole time. When Kate and me thought she was tiring we would try to get a word in edgeways about the goose but the minute she saw us ready to talk off she'd go again. The man by the fire nodded his head in agreement with all she said. Fine for him said I to myself to know such contentment with a closed gob. She spoke about the geese and what she gave them to eat. She spoke about the hay and the cows and the cabbage. The likes of her cabbage was never seen.

'Of course the dung was druv on it', said she, 'double doses of it. High quality.'

Suddenly the man in the corner spoke. He took his chance nice and handy while she was drawing breath.

'Hard to beat horse's cowdung', said he, with a shake of the head.

'Hard indeed sir', said she and she went on gabbing like a blackbird you'd be after disturbing in a bush the same as if she never heard him. We drank tea and we eat bread but we left without engaging the goose. And we going out the front door she was still at it and your man in the corner nodding away like he'd be doting. The thing I'm trying to convey to you is that the pair were as happy as the day is long and that surely is what matters.

There is no meaning to the loneliness of the nights that's with us. They're hard to bear and 'tis no fun keeping a sane head on the shoulders waiting for the dawn of day to come round. Business is slacking somewhat these days. Since motor cars got common the demand is dropping but as I was saying lately to Father Kimmerley you'll always have men what cannot knot their ties or their laces proper. I made out a fine woman for a brother of his and he is most thankful. He is saying a special mass for Kate this coming Sunday. I could make no fist of that motor car you left. Everytime I sat into it it had like to run away with me. I'll stick to the ass what I was always used to. For the present I have it installed in the stable where the weather won't rust it. Tell Marge the widow Magee was asking for her.

Your fond brother,
Dicky.

★ ★ ★

Hunter Hall,
Ballyninty.

Dear O'Connor,
Good news at last. That woman from Pulawadra is a lady to her fingertips if I may say so. Prospects never looked brighter and when I explained to her about my outlook so to speak she broke out into a song:

> There's a balm for every woe, sang she
> And a cure for every pain.

Since I can find no trace of my former wife high or low there is every reason to believe that the Pride of Pulawadra as the locals call her will not reject me when I pop the question. She is a poetic soul and which is more important she has the art of infusing the spirit of poetry into others. I swear I have been gliding on wings of pure poesy since I met her. I am indeed most grateful to you and have composed the following song in your honour:

> From Toomevara to Ballybarra
> From Honolulu to the Cove of Cork
> From Bulawayo to County Mayo
> From Venezuala up to New York
> From West Virginia to Abyssinia
> From South Australia to Timbuctoo
> From Ballyseedy to Tourmakeady
> There's no matchmaker could match with you.

I shall be in touch. As soon as I know my exact position there will be a more material recognition of your services.

Cordially yours,
Claude Glynne-Hunter.

★   ★   ★

Spiders' Well,
Ballybarra.

Dear Jack,
I said I might as well write to you so that you would be the first to know about Lena and me. Looking out the window the other evening before I sat down to my supper I noticed the light failing in the sky and I saw the first mists of the winter thickening on the shoulders of the hills. As far as the eye could sweep there was nothing else to be seen save the smoke far away from Cud Muldoon's chimney and a straggle of pensioner crows flapping home to Parson Roberts Rookery God be good to him.

In no time at all it was dark and the strangest feeling came over me like as if I was the only creature in the whole wide world. My dog sat in his corner but he slept like a top and my cat took off hunting the minute the moon shone bright. There was no cold in the kitchen as I had the fire bright and well-banked but for all that a shiver ran through me that I can't explain to you. I never felt so alone. This was something I have never felt before and I guessed that it was the jostling between the tug of life and the tug of the grave. I was always a man that had a dread of nothing but the cold sweat came out through me and I made the sign of the cross.

'Twas fear Jack, a man's fear in his lonesome state. There is no lone man proof against that fear boy. I felt like going to my bed and pulling the clothes over my head when I heard a sound that was more welcome than the dews of the morning. 'Twas the voice of Lena Magee of Ballylittle and she cycling home after a day's visiting to Circes Muldoon. She was singing as she cycled but 'twas a forced song because women don't care too much for the dark. There is a bit of a rise outside the door so she dismounted and started to walk.

'Lena', I calls out, ''tis too dark to be travelling further.'

''Tis dark alright, Dicky', said she.

''Tis', says I, 'and the forecast is not good. To make matters worse', says I, 'the mist is after falling from the hills and in another ten minutes you won't see the back of your hand.'

She came in and sat by the fire. The cat came in behind her and he jumped on to her lap. The flames leaped in the hearth and the wind howled in the chimney.

''Tis fine for us', she said.

''Tis', said I, 'when you take all things into account.' Then that thing came between us that is beyond nature and beyond the flesh, a sorrow for each other that softens the heart and makes a bond of steel between one man and one woman.

The date is set for the Saturday before Christmas. A woman is a great thing in a house if 'twas only for wetting the tea you wanted her.

> Your fond brother,
> Dicky.

★　★　★

JOHN B. KEANE

Letters of an
Irish Minister of State

INTRODUCTION

I address this Introduction to readers who may not be familiar with the exploits of Tull MacAdoo, T.D. In the book *Letters of a Successful T.D.* we saw how Tull silenced his arch-rival, schoolmaster James Flannery by unorthodox means. Flannery would have the general public believe that the now-famous battle of Glenalee never took place. Flannery in fact claimed that the entire affair, in which Tull single-handedly killed one black and tan and wounded several others, was purely a figment of Tull MacAdoo's imagination. The following is a statement which Flannery had published in a local newspaper known as *The Demoglobe:*

Mr James Flannery, N.T. asserts that he has conclusive proof that there was never a battle of Glenalee. In an exclusive interview Mr Flannery told our reporter that there may have been a few scraps there between weasels and rabbits but there was no gun battle.

'There were battles,' he said, 'between weasels and rabbits and murder was perpetrated when a sparrow-hawk assaulted a wren.' He said, 'the battle was a figment of the imagination of Mr Tull MacAdoo, T.D.' He challenged Mr MacAdoo to refute his statement.

'I am convinced,' Mr Flannery concluded, 'that no battle was ever fought there and,' he added 'I have the evidence to prove it.'

Whether he had or not we shall never know for shortly afterwards Flannery went back on his statement. It appears that in his prime he sired a daughter through the good offices of one Jenny Jordan of Crabapple Hill. Tull MacAdoo informed the ultra respectable teacher that he would be obliged to reveal the existence of the illegitimate daughter who was called Maud after Maud Gonne unless Flannery performed a complete turn-around and published a retraction. This the schoolmaster was obliged to do in view of Tull's threat to expose him.

Almost immediately there was a general election in which Tull secured the largest personal vote ever recorded in the constituency. His surplus guaranteed the election of his running mate Din Stack, a feat which endeared him to his party boss and Taoiseach of the country Mr Lycos. Tull had more than one close friend in the cabinet but perhaps his most influential was the Minister for Continentals Relations, Mr James McFillen, who also happened to be god-father to Tull's daughter Kate.

One evening after a cabinet meeting McFillen called the Taoiseach aside and informed him that he was proposing Tull MacAdoo for the post of minister of state. At first the Taoiseach laughed but when there was no responding laugh he turned serious and said:

'I like poor old Tull. In fact there's nobody I like more and I happen to know that his loyalty is above question.'

McFillen seized his chance. The conversation was taking a direction which appealed to him. It was a time when the loyalty of some of the party's oldest members left a lot to be desired.

'Loyalty should be worth something,' McFillen said and waited lest any further utterance of his might compromise the gambit. The Taoiseach tweaked his upper lip as was his wont when he was giving his undivided attention to the question in hand.

'But what is there for him?' he asked. 'He lacks the eduction. He's not the most literate of men and he has yet to make his maiden speech after thirty years.'

McFillen waited. The Taoiseach, he sensed, was addressing these questions to himself. A long silence followed.

'Isn't there a danger,' the Taoiseach asked, 'that he might embarrass us?'

'In what way?' McFillen replied innocently.

'He is what certain academics on the opposition benches might call an ignorant man.'

'Forgive me my dear Lionel but they've called you worse.'

'Touche,' said the Taoiseach, 'but let's face it, poor old Tull is a born backbencher. He lacks the poise, the confidence and we both know he's anything but articulate.'

'That could be a blessing,' McFillen put in knowing the Taoiseach's abhorrence of effusiveness and longwindedness.

'You're scoring heavily Mac,' the leader said 'but there is the danger that he may make a show of himself and leave us down with a bang. Have you thought of that?'

'I've thought of everything. By the way the one thing he'll never do is let us down. He has intelligence and infinite cunning and he has a daughter who manages him most astutely from the wings.'

'I know all about the daughter.' The Taoiseach relapsed into silence. McFillen knew that Lycos had made up his mind.

'What would you say Mac,' said he, 'to Minister of State for Bogland Areas?'

'I would love it,' McFillen answered, 'although it seems a bit bare.'

'Alright,' said the Taoiseach tweaking his upper lip a second time, 'how about Minister for Bogland Areas with Special Responsibilities for Game and Wildlife?'

'Beautiful, absolutely beautiful,' McFillen's appreciation was genuine.

'The greater the number of words after his name the better,' he said. 'This will really impress his constituents. There will be bonfires in Kilnavarna when the announcement is made.'

So it was that Tull MacAdoo became a Minister of State. The Taoiseach need not have worried. Tull was a man of few words and if these were not always well chosen they were, at least, positively harmless. He opened every speech with a sentence in Gaelic: *Cuirim failte romhaimh go leir a chairde* and ended every speech with: May God bless ye all now and leave ye in good health! His daughter put the meat in the sandwich so to speak.

Tull MacAdoo, Minister for Bogland Areas, writes to his son Mick:

> McMell's Hotel,
> Dublin,
> Sunday night.

Dear Mick,

I have just finished reading your latest letter. Forty-five pounds for new books seems a bit farfetched. You're sure 'tisn't bookies you mean. You'll find it enclosed with your weekly allowance and I beg of you to make do from now on with what books you have. You must have a library at this stage.

For the want of something better to do and I driving up this evening I was adding up the years you've spent at the university so far. Nine all told and you haven't even a full stop after your name. Four years you gave at medicine and you wouldn't know a gumboil from a gallstone. Then there were the two years at commerce. What a shame there isn't some kind of a degree for drinking porter or backing horses. 'Tis you'd wind up with the high honours.

Ah but the best of all was the two years you gave at law. Oh 'tis you Mick was the dab hand at the law. You wouldn't know a statue from a statute. I should have guessed your form that evening at Micky Mac's pub in Tourmadeedy. When I asked you to say a bit of law for the lads you was like you'd be struck dumb. And now what is it? Business enterprises for the second time around. I'll indulge you for another year and if you don't pass at the end of that time you can say goodbye to the books. All I'm asking Mick is that you pass one more exam, one more to know would we be able to raise our heads and we going up the chapel of a Sunday, just one more to show Flannery the schoolmaster and all them others that you're not a complete fool.

If you fail this time there's only one career open to you and that's Dail Eireann. I'm long enough there now to draw the full pension. The MacAdoo name is good for a seat any time. I know you don't like politics but Mick, my friend, I'm afraid 'tis all you're fit for. I'll sign off now. See to your studies and don't forget to make your Easter duty.

> Affectionately,
> Dad.

P.S. Where's the skeleton I bought for you when you were at the medicine caper? He should be worth money now. I hope you're going to confession regular.

★ ★ ★

Tull MacAdoo writes to his wife Biddy:

Dublin,
Sunday night.

My dear Biddy,
Arrived safe. Am on the point of going to my bed. I'll say a rosary tonight that your pain will shift from where it is to some part that is better able to endure it. I wrote to Mick and cautioned him about his ways. I'm afraid he's taken after his uncle Tom. I hope the new pills do you some good. Doctor John told me in private that they were the very latest discovery in America. Please God we'll see you up and about now in no time at all. We might spend the Easter weekend somewhere if you feel up to it. I won't exhaust you now with anymore details. Look out for yourself and watch for drafts don't you get them cramps again.

Ever and always,
Your own Tull.

★ ★ ★

Joey Conners, Secretary of the Kilnavarna Land-For-all-League, writes to Tull MacAdoo:

Rocky Gap,
Kilnavarna.

Dear Tull,
I see your dirty hand in the division of Derrymore bog and demesne. We won't stand for it this time not when 'tis widely stated that yourself and your brother-in-law Tom Bluenose are earmarked for thirty acres apiece. The small farmers of Kilnavarna are united in their efforts to

prevent you and your party's supporters from hogging what is morally ours. We will spike every field in Kilnavarna if as much as one acre is handed over to the big farmers. Look out for pickets too. Look out for hell's fire.

> Your humble servant no longer,
> Joey Connors.

P.S. I always gave you the vote Tull and so did the boys. Don't forget that.

> Joey.

*   *   *

Gertie Fondee writes to Tull MacAdoo:

> Crabapple Hill,
> Tourmadeedy.

Dear Tull,
It has come to my attention that there is a vacancy for an auxiliary postman in the village of Tourmadeedy. Mick Morgan fell off his Toyota going up Crabapple Hill and done damage to his two shins and undercarriage. He's in the county hospitable undergoing surgery and will not be returning to work for some months according to reports. As you know I am a widow these four years with five young children all going to school. I have put in for the job and want you to do your best for me. It would be a great boast for the children to see their mother a postman. I always gave you the number one and so did himself God be good to him.

> Sincerely Yours,
> Gertie Fondee.

Tull writes to his daughter Kate:

McMell's Hotel,
Dublin.

My dear Kate,
No man was ever given my burdens nor no man my crosses. Your mother now has a moving pain. In other words it's a pain that could crop up anywhere. If it's cured or routed from one spot with pills or bottles there's nothing to stop it breaking out in another. From now on she will never be without some sort of pain. There's no one in Kilnavarna can boast the same. It's what she always longed for. You might say her prayers are answered at last. Then there's my brother-in-law your uncle Tom or Bluenose as they call him in Kilnavarna. Your mother says I wrong him, that he's a saint. You and me knows Kate that he'd drink Loch Erne if he got it free. He's the greatest unhung bum in the thirty-two counties with enough bastards in the constituency alone to make up a football team and a jury. Sixty-three years of age! Drunk every day and never known to stick his hands in his pockets to buy a drink. He says they won't let him buy he's so popular. If he wasn't my brother-in-law he'd be tarred and feathered and ran out of the country. 'That's the minister's brother-in-law,' they whisper. 'That's the man to see if you want Tull on your side'. He takes the full credit for all the favours I do and I wouldn't mind but he don't even listen when they tell him what they want done. In one ear and out the other but 'tis me has to answer the letters and pull the strings.

Then there's that depraved git, the Land-For-All latchiko, Joey Conners. A born bolshie that fellow, a low-down, pratey-snappin' perverted snipe, a republican moryah. Them are the republicans we have these days, misfits and drop-outs, retarded yo-yos that would steal the eye out of your head, refugees from a decent day's work not like my day when we fought the Tans and the free-staters.

Conners and his dolers will get no land while I'm around. What are they doing with the land they have already? Pool halls is all they want, pubs and pool halls. The land will go to the men that work it and I'll see to that. Gertie Fondee wants the job of temporary postman in Tourmadeedy. I rang the minister and fixed it but what did my hoor of a sub-postmaster say when I told him to take her on? What's her qualifications says he? Her qualifications says I is her number one. What about her Irish says he? She'll have to have some spattering. She can say the Our Father I told him and that's Irish enough for her. 'Tis more than many in the Dail has. It must be a great language to be still alive and kicking when you think of all them that's thriving out of it one way and another.

They'll start picketing one of these days about the division at Derrymore. Ignore and enjoy, especially if 'tis raining. Smile at them out through the window. Smile sad like you'd be sorry for them. You'd be amazed what comes into a man's mind and he facing his ballot paper. I'll sign off now. I'll be down at the weekend. I have to officially open a bogland walk in Offaly on Friday evening. But for that I'd be home Friday night.

> Affectionately,
> Your loving Daddy.

* * *

Mick MacAdoo writes to his Father:

> 20 Hangman's Close,
> Knacker's Well,
> Cork.

Dear Dad,
As you will see from the above address I have changed digs again. This is a tough area but considering the amount of money you send me I'm lucky I'm not in a doss-house. This place is world-famous for whores and sailors. White, black, yellow and brown are forever coming and going. Pimps abound as does V.D., stray dogs and cats and the smell of chips. I'm lucky I have a good constitution. That skeleton you ask about was ripped

asunder by uncle Tom's greyhounds and won't be seen in one place again till we all meet in the valley of Jehosaphat. Will you send fifty pounds at once for a new suit of clothes and a shirt? Every stitch belonging to me was stolen while I was at the college. Send the money quick or I'll have to go to confession naked. You don't have to worry about my passing this time. I'm working like a slave. You'll be the proud man in the fall of the year.

> Your loving son,
> Mick.

* * *

Biddy MacAdoo writes to her husband:

> Kilnavarna P.O.,
> Kilnavarna.

Dear Tull,
How quick you always are to blame Tom, Tom as was always the sweetest child ever reared and would be with the round collar today but for we being orphaned and we children, Tom as has the weak heart what turns his nose blue the misfortunate man, Tom as was crossed in love, as never rose his voice to me nor to no one and you begrudge him the drop of drink, the only comfort he has. Sweet adorable Jesus in His mansion forgive you. I'll pray for you.

Kathy Diggins is knocked up again. This is the fifth time in eight years. They have it down on a baldy traveller for zip fasteners and hooks and eyes. He has a squint and sad eyes and drives a white cortina. He's married in Wexford with twelve children. By all accounts 'tis not the first hit and run he's down for.

Kathy's eldest, Martina, is anxious to join the Ban Gardai. She has the height and the chest but the devil a much else. Do all in your power. I'll try a drop of beef tea now God help us. Not a thing am I able to keep down all day.

> Your wife,
> Biddy.

* * *

Kate MacAdoo writes to her Father:

Kilnavarna P.O.,
Kilnavarna.

Dear Dad,

The protest march is taking place. They have just vacated the post office where they squatted until the Gardai came and removed them. Most of the protesters are ne'er-do-wells, many are backward poor fellows too ignorant to know what it's all about except that it's better than working and this could be what attracts them. There are the pair who sell the I.R.A. papers outside the church on Sunday and two or three of the self-unemployed along for the crack. The ringleader is Joey Conners. They have placards. Here are some examples: 'Grabbers out or else', 'Land-for-all-now Tull', 'Free state farmers beware', 'Better treatment for prisoners'. God help the prisoners if they're depending on the likes of these.

Henry Lawless was in for some stamps today. He was civil, more than civil when you consider how I ditched him at the last moment. I was certain he'd turn catholic. We all were. Then on the week before the wedding when I tried to extract a definite promise from him he hedged. He wasn't even willing to give his consent to have the children baptised catholics. Every second one was what he would agree to. 'I'd sooner to see them black first', said the invalid upstairs. She's still in bed. She got up for a while yesterday, she didn't like it. She's had a visit from a sorely-swollen Kathy Diggins. It would do no harm if you got the job as auxiliary postman for Gertie Fondee. It would be a real feather in your hat, the first postwoman in this part of the world. Martina Diggins is a different proposition. She has all the physical qualifications for the Ban Gardai but from the neck up she's pure sawdust.

The protest is breaking up. The ranks swelled to twenty before it ended. At least ten are amadawns and national school drop-outs. Everybody knows that three of the poor fellows are somewhat retarded, everybody, alas, except themselves. They really don't know what it's all about except maybe that in some vague way they believe that the overthrow of law and order will bring them some recompense. I'll be looking forward to seeing you at the weekend. Take care of yourself.

Your loving daughter,
Kate.

*   *   *

Tull writes to Mick:

Dear Mick,
Find fifty pounds enclosed as requested. You're an amazing man. That's six pairs of pyjamas, seven overcoats, four suits of clothes, twenty books, five pairs of shoes, nine fountain pens and two suitcases you've had stolen from you since you started these new studies. I have no proof, of course, but I'd lay odds that your name is a household word with the pawnbrokers of Cork. Just one more request for money, one more and I'll cut you off entirely. You'll get your legitimate allowance but beyond that not a single copper and should you fail this time it's hard politics for you my boy, starting with the county council and ending, please God, with Dail Eireann. You're a sad case Mick but believe it or not there's worse nor you here.

Affectionately,
Dad.

*   *   *

Mick writes to his Father:

20 Hangman's Close,
Knacker's Well,
Cork.

Dear Dad,
To suggest that my name is a household word with the pawnbrokers of Cork is a slur and a lie. How can I be expected to concentrate on my studies when my own

father places so little trust in me? I am at least as honest as half the fellows here and there are a dozen publicans at least who would give me a reference in the morning for a position of trust not to mention the owners of three or four chip-shops and a respected bookie. Some of the students here are weak characters who would pick the eye out of your head. Many of them are half-starved most of the time and would stoop to anything for a good feed of steak and chips. One particular scoundrel sold my overcoat for the price of three pints and a hamburger to a drunken farmer he encountered by chance in a public house in the city centre. Another flogged my last pair of pyjamas and two shirts for a half one and a pint to a fresher. There is nothing I can do. Talk about a conspiracy of silence.

You just don't understand the student mind. Everyone here is chronically short of cash and anything left lying around is fair game. Basically most of the fellows are honest but it's the hardship and the everlasting shortage that turns some of them into hardened criminals. They don't seem to have any conscience. Some are like jackals. Turn aside for a second from your plate to speak to somebody and your dinner or supper is gone. Borrowing is a way of life.

I'm not certain that my pen won't be whipped before this letter is finished. In fact I'd better close before it disappears. Trust me. That's all I ask. Just trust me and give me the confidence I need to pass my exams. By confidence I mean money. Break your heart for once and send me a little extra so that I can hold my head high and walk into a hotel with an air of independence and not in my usual furtive shifty way with the eyes of porters and waiters watching me in case I'd walk out without paying or maybe lift an ashtray. Give me a chance to restore my confidence. Do the big thing and give your son the opportunity to win the respect he deserves. Let him have a jingle in his pocket like other human beings. Let him uphold the good name of himself and his family.

Your loving son,
Mick.

★   ★   ★

Tull writes to his wife :

Dear Biddy,

I'm sorry if what I said about Tom upset you and I'm sorry you were both orphaned so young although fair play it wasn't me orphaned ye. I agree he never spoke out loud but the truth my dear Biddy is that his vocal chords are that frayed from whiskey he couldn't raise his voice these days if it was to save his life. The man is a walking brewery. You must be colour blind if you haven't noticed his nose. 'Tis like the end of a purple black pudding if there is such a thing. The truth is bitter my love and the truth is that if Tom doesn't go away for a while he won't be alive for the division of Derrymore bog. He's entitled to his share. 'Twill be Mick's loss in the long run. Let him drink away to blazes till the land is given out. We'll have to talk serious when I'm down over the weekend. You must be happy to see Gertie with her postman's cap on the crown of her head, the first postman in Kilnavarna.

Kathy Diggins' daughter has no business applying for the Ban Gardai. She hasn't the education and the other things she has would not suit a job of this kind. The desire for men is sure to burst out sooner or later. She wouldn't be her mother's daughter if she was otherwise. I remember after Kathy's first mishap (the father of that one followed a threshing machine) her mother stripped the seat of a sugawn chair and manufactured a sugawn knickers for her with black knots at all points of entry. If 'twas rod iron itself it wouldn't preserve Kathy. She came to the mother a month after the Kilnavarna wren dance to announce that she had a powerful longing for doughnuts, a sure invoice for incoming goods. I'll say no more as I'm for the sop. I'm opening a seminar early tomorrow at Eagle Mountain for the preservation of snipe and grouse in bogland areas. Go easy on the pills and try to get exercise. Exercise is the best of all pills with fresh air to wash it down.

Your loving husband,
Tull.

★ ★ ★

Tull writes to his son Mick:

The Post Office,
Kilnavarna.

Dear Loudmouth,
I'm not off the train from Dublin when I hear of your outburst at Micky Macs of Tourmadeedy concerning the recent Belfast bombing by the provisional I.R.A. From now on keep your mouth shut about these people. Right or wrong it's not for you or me to say so. I live by votes and as long as the supporters of these people have votes I'll retain my link with them. They might be bastard republicans but every one of them has a number one. There's plenty there to condemn them without you butting in.

Some day I'll table a motion to Dail Eireann in the interests of peace and sanity that every man in this country be given the use of so many words and no more. Then when all the words are used we might see a bit of action from the gasbaggers. Now shut up and stay shut up.

Affectionately,
Dad.

P.S. Just remember where your bread and butter come from. I'll grant you the Belfast victims were innocent men and women but your lecture on bollixology in Micky Macs won't bring back the dead. Even if what you said only cost me one vote I'd regard it as too high a price. There used be a notice in Begley's the barbers one time saying when they lost a customer somebody had died. It's the same when I lose a vote. Someone has died because like Begley I give value for money and the public know they won't do any better.

There will be more bombings and shootings and there's nothing anyone can do about it. They killed John Kennedy and they could kill the Pope in the morning if they wanted. Remember Mick boy that in this world you're only a hare with every low hound as was ever slipped on your tail from the day you were born till the day you give over the ghost. You were put in this world to stay alive and not to stick your neck out. 'Tis hard enough to survive without you making it any harder for yourself or making it harder for me.

Any man with a vote is a man to be respected. I'll play with them, lie to them, sing dumb about them while I have a chance of a vote. That's my livelihood. Don't give me no more stink about the truth. Christ told the truth and they crucified Him. This does not mean that I condone murder or mutilation. I have no respect for cowards who kill innocent women and children. I have no iota of respect for them but I have respect for their votes. These perverts have voted for me in the past and they'll do so again if I play my cards right.

My mother gave me one worthwhile piece of advice after I was elected to Dail Eireann for the first time. 'Son,' said she, 'whatever you do don't forget the people that put you in because they're the very same people that'll put you out again.' Next time you meet Joey Conners retain the link. Buy him a drink. Put a different face upon what you said at Micky Macs. Build him up. Buy him a second drink. Listen to what he has to say. Be sympathetic. Let him talk. Talk is cheaper than piped water and there seems to be no end to it. The thing is to retain the connection even if 'tis only hair thin. When all the talk is over and all that once mattered no longer important a vote will still be a vote.

Your father,
Tull MacAdoo.

P.S. Enclosed find the price of a decent meal as requested. You should get a job with some charitable organisation. You're the best man I ever met to wheedle money.

Tull.

* * *

Kate MacAdoo writes to her father:

Post Office,
Kilnavarna.

Dear Daddy,
Any problem connected with the distribution of Derrymore bog and demesne has disappeared like the mist on that same bog when the southwest wind comes in from the sea. Gone like the snow that whitened Crabapple Hill when we walked up there last year with the Christmas box for Jenny Jordan. You'll wonder why I'm so elated. Your friend Joey Conners was whipped this morning together with two northerners and two locals whose names I don't know yet, in connection with the Tourmadeedy bank robbery. The Special Branch raided Joey's and found the aforementioned gentlemen together with a small portion of the money. By the time Joey comes out the Derrymore Division will be a thing of the past. Don't ask me who tipped off the Special Branch about Joey or the men hiding with him. Don't ever ask me.

The whole thing will be in tomorrow's papers I daresay. I hope you'll enjoy reading it as I will. I don't know whether you made any formal representation for the Ban Gardai on behalf of Martina Diggins. She has the same complaint as her mother and hard as it is to believe all the best informed sources maintain that it's the same baldheaded traveller with the sad eyes from the county Wexford. Take good care of yourself. Give McFillen my love. When is he coming for a weekend again?

Love,
Kate.

* * *

Mick MacAdoo writes to his Father:

> 20 Hangman's close,
> Knacker's Well,
> Cork.

Dear Dad,
So this is the menagerie you want me to join, a place where no man may speak his mind, where hypocrisy and villainy of every kind, known and unknown, flourishes. Where but to think is to be full of sorrow and leaden-eyed despairs. That was Keats not me. About my blabbing off re the bombing, how many more children must be maimed or annihilated before you consider it worth your while to speak? There was a man called Confucius you would have loved for his conciseness Tull. Shut mouth catch no fly. Confucius say. Big mouth catch no votes. You velly smart Chinese Tull. There will be no chance to talk to Joey Conners now. Poor bastard. I'm sorry for him. He knew no better.

Send on ten pounds to get a tooth filled and four to get my eyes tested by a quack down the road. I can't afford a specialist. The reading glasses, the very cheapest pair, will be about fifteen. Better send forty altogether to be on the safe side. I can't read the text books without glasses, 'tis a wonder I'm not blind long ago.

> Your mute son,
> Mick.

* * *

Biddy MacAdoo writes to Tull:

> Post Office,
> Kilnavarna.

Dear Tull,
So 'tis to be the mental for poor Tom. I'm going to Lourdes over you. Myself and Katty Stack and Mary

O'Dell we're off next Thursday with the diocesan pilgrimage. 'Tis you have me driven to this with your remarks about poor Tom and how can I exercise and my spine not straight and you know what fresh air does to my chest with my chronic catarrh or do you think of nothing but yourself. I'll pray to our Lady of Lourdes for you.

Biddy.

★   ★   ★

Tull writes to Kate:

McMell's Hotel,
Dublin.

Dearest Kate,
You are my oasis and my strength. Where would I be without you? I have a fair idea who put the tecs on to Joey. Thanks for the thousandth time. You are the real strength behind the throne. Don't forget to take a box of groceries to Joey's wife and tell her if there's anything she wants I'll be behind her. Those are the little things people remember. Joey would be too proud to take them but she knows the kids won't ask any questions when they sit down to their supper.

Poor Joey. There was no other way he could wind up, himself and his republicanism. Ten years while well-heeled armchair republicans enjoy the life of Reilly, fat, solemn and serious-faced with their fine homes and their respectability. 'Tis them should be where Joey is.

I remember his father. He was nothing but a bum and a layabout. He missed the War of Independence but he had some small involvement in the Civil War. I don't even remember what it was. He wasn't to be trusted but he managed to convince Joey that he was big time not only in the Civil War but in the real troubles. That was the legacy he gave poor backward, believing Joey, ignorant, blind hate of anything and everything connected with the authorities. Joey believed his father was a hero. What else could he afford to believe? What else could he hold on to? What else had an unfriendly world to offer him beyond a dole queue or a job as a menial? He was easy meat for the I.R.A. and now look at him, facing ten years away from his wife and family while his bosses with good jobs enjoy the fruits of the land. We were friends once Joey and me. There's a thing about me that makes me keep in touch with the Joeys of Ireland.

When I'm with my intellectual superiors I listen. When I'm with my own equals I argue but when I'm with those inferior to me I never, never, never talk down to them. That's why I have a seat in the Dail.

Joey's father may have been an idler and a bum but he had pride. He had nothing of value to pass on to his son so he invented a republican tradition and Joey clung to that tradition with his life. One day it might bring him up in the world, make a somebody out of him so that people would treat him with respect instead of contempt. His handlers know all this. The Joeys of Ireland are their ace cards. Rarely if ever do they imbue their own sons with their abortive republicanism. They don't have to while the likes of Joey Conners are tailormade for the job. God pity the cratur and others like him. God's curse on those who exploited him. The mills of God grind slowly but be sure that some day these people will pay the price. I'll see you at the weekend.

> Your loving daddy,
> Tull.

★ ★ ★

Mick writes to his Father:

> 20 Hangman's Close,
> Knacker's Well,
> Cork.

Dear Dad,
This is an emergency. Everything I possessed has been stolen, suit, shirt, underpants, pyjamas all gone while I slept like a log after a murdering day at my studies.

I would have sent a telegram but I recall you once told me you would shoot me if I sent you any more telegrams for money. I am wearing borrowed clothes which the landlord gave me out of the goodness of his heart.

The trousers is up to my shins and I can't even tie the coat in case the buttons burst. The shirt won't even cover my navel and people look at me in the street as if I were a nutcase. Send a hundred at once. Nothing less will do. I'll need it to buy socks, shoes, suit, overcoat, shirt, vest, underpants, pullover etc. Since I do not share your aversion to telegrams you can wire the money. Don't delay.

Your loving son,
Mick.

★   ★   ★

Jenny Jordan writes to Tull:

Crabapple Hill,
Kilnavarna.

Dear Tull,
Better not call again for a while. According as I think about it the more worried I become. The last time and you leaving there was two figures come out of the furze on the breast of the hill. One of them was like Flannery and the other was like the Canon. It can't be nothing good what had them there. Anyway with the election coming you will hardly have the time to call. They all say it will be close so take care.

Jenny

★   ★   ★

Tom Cably writes to Tull:

Drumriddle,
Tourmadeedy.

Dear Tull,
I hope this don't find you as it leaves me without a tooth
in my head. And I shaving in the open doorway three
weeks ago I took out my false teeth and left them on the
window sill outside the door. As I was barbering the butt
of the jaw a hoor of a magpie came down from the sky
and made off with the upper set. I flung the bottom set
after him thinking to make him release the upper set. The
bottom set landed in the glasha below the house and was
carried off by the high water. 'Tis how they're halfway to
New York by this time. I'm a pity these last weeks. I
can't chew nor grind only sucking up slops the same as a
bonham. In God's name Tull will you get after the Health
Board – don't I die for the want of meat.

Yours faithfully,
Tom Cably.

★ ★ ★

Tull writes to his son Mick:

McMell's Hotel,
Dublin.

Dear Mick,
Your last letter should be preserved. Everything you had
stolen! How can that be when I sent you five pounds for a
new lock last week and how could your pyjamas be stolen?
You had to be wearing something or is it how you sleep in
the nude like a horse. This is a nice cross I have to bear
and the constituency convention coming up next week.
Already there are undercurrents I don't like. There's ma-
licious talk and there are names being mentioned as co-
runners. All a co-runner wants is your seat whereas the
gossip mongers want your blood as well. In politics you

never know where the danger will come from. You'll never know the true mind of the grassroots and there's nothing to stop today's grassroot being tomorrow's councillor and any man who goes for the county council can be persuaded to go for the Dail. All he wants is enough persuasion. The Dail is in every man's head and why wouldn't it? Every man wants to be part of the power that governs him. Often when I look down from the rostrum during the annual general meeting of the constituency I know that my gaze has rested on at least one man with an innocent face who has an eye on my seat. He sits there silent and sober like a cow chewing the cud but underneath the machinery is working overtime on wrecking my foundations. It's generally too late when his identity is disclosed. By that time he has sown all his seeds, made all his contacts and sharpened his weapons waiting for his chance.

This is what's going to happen to me someday. I'm getting old and the constituency is bristling with young bucks looking for change. Not yet though. By God not yet!

My passage to my present position took some cutting out. I remember the first notion of politics to enter my head was put there by my dear, departed mother. 'Twas she moulded me for that first council election. My worldly possessions at that time were three acres of bog and four asses for drawing turf, one a blackcutjack, another a Spanish splithole and finally two fullballs. 'Twas the rail of turf that kept the hunger from the door. I was elected by men like myself, men of the fourth and fifth book or at most the sixth. My victory was theirs. I was one of them. Voting for me was the only way they could ever know the fine salty taste of triumph. Ignorant and illiterate, many of them were pauperised and hungry like my mother and myself. They put themselves in when they put me in. I was the poor man's candidate and I still am. But politics is like death itself. They can wipe you out overnight, a foolish word in haste or ignorance, a thoughtless act, one wrong move and it's all over. Then when the power goes the respect goes and it's the sidelines again. And you, you sonofabitch has me persecuted with lies. This time you can bloody well go naked and you can starve for all I care because you're doing nothing but codding me for the past nine years. Don't come the smart man with me no more. I have enough troubles of my own just now.

You'll find your normal weekly allowance enclosed. If you're still naked when you come home for the canvass Kate will see that you're outfitted from head to toe out of stock.

Affectionately,
Dad.

* * *

Biddy writes to Tull:

Dear Tull,
I'm here in agony after falling out of the bed in a nightmare where there was two black men chasing me without a stitch. The death sweat is on me as I write this with no one in the house and Kate gone off to some district party meeting. I must have twisted something in my back. I can't put one leg over the other. I'm a pure martyr God pity me. I have a novena started for Mick. I have the beads wore with prayers for all of ye and they made from Connemara marble. Are you seeing to Tom Cably's false teeth? The poor man was in the shop with the two grey cheeks caved in on him and his face like he'd be after sucking a gross of eggs and left that way. Puddings and sausages and bread dipped in tea or soup is all he can guzzle the creature with a fresh pig in the barrel by him and a deep freeze full of prime beef and mutton. He was in Kilnavarna drawing the dole. I promised him I'd get after you about the free teeth. All the small farmers on the dole here have coloured television now thanks be to God – the same as the best. I remember when they hadn't the radio but now they have cars better than the ram Flannery and they needn't do a stroke. I'll never know how this country keeps going and no one doing an honest day's work. Take it from me Tull it won't last. It can't last. My back is killing me. My bowels didn't move for

two days. My appetite is gone. I went for a walk yesterday but I had to turn back in case the breeze would knock me and anyway I thought I heard rumblings that turned out to be false alarms.

Tom collapsed in Kettleton's lounge last night and although Kate locked him in his room he got out through the window and down the drainpipe. Bad whiskey is the whole cause. Hell is filled with publicans and their families.

Your wife,
Biddy.

★   ★   ★

Tull writes to Kate:

McMell's Hotel,
Dublin.

My dear Kate,
What wouldn't I give for a bit of cheerful news. I'm after reading letters from Mick and your mother that would put a clown crying. I'm half drunk and I writing this. However, no one wants to hear cronawning but a cat. I was yesterday in Waterford for the releasing of three hundred pheasant and the official sanctioning of a grouse preservation area. I would have written for a few comments but the election is too near and all I'm prepared to announce between this and then is promises, true or false. All the electorate want is something for nothing and they want that something now this very minute in case there's no tomorrow. Aren't they right? What's the use in promising a rise in the old age pension in October to a man who knows he's only an even money chance to live till September? The best promise I ever made was at a party rally one wet night in Tourmadeedy.

'I'll make ye one promise', I said, 'and no more because the night is wet and I want to see no man or woman catching pneumonia.'

'What's that Tull?' they called, 'what's the promise?'

'If I gets in,' I called down to them from the top of Gertie Cronin's kitchen table, 'every man in Tourmadeedy will get more than the next.'

You should hear the screeching and roaring that followed. The following day I had a visit from a *Demoglobe* reporter who wanted to know what exactly I said the night before. Always a man to co-operate with the press I told him to have a raw egg. I have got away with murder for years in this respect as far as the press is concerned. They never seem to be around when I make my biggest bloomers. I'm all for freedom of speech but lately I find that political reporters are just smart-alecs on the make for juicy stories. All they want is a laugh at the politician's expense but they can't take no joke at all against themselves.

If I had said something sensible that night in Tourmadeedy *The Demoglobe* would have left me alone. As it is they're watching me like a hawk to know would I make a false move. They haven't caught me yet but there's always a first time. I'll close now. I'll be home the weekend to start the canvass in real earnest.

Love,
Daddy.

★　★　★

James McFillen was surprised when his secretary informed him that the Taoiseach was on the phone. Apprehensively he lifted the receiver. He sensed trouble. The Taoiseach never took up a Minister's time unless it was to rap or to praise. McFillen could think of no accomplishment in recent times worthy of his chief's approbation.

'Yes chief?'

'I want to see you Mac. Make it right away will you?'

'This instant,' McFillen promised. 'Nothing serious I hope?' The Taoiseach did not answer at once. McFillen waited uncertain as to whether he should hold on or hang up.

'I don't know Mac,' the voice came across ponderously. 'It has to do with your protege MacAdoo. Why don't you just come across right now and judge for yourself?'

The Taoiseach was not alone. Seated at one side of the outsize mahogany desk was Derek Freezer, the party P.R.O.

'Sit down Mac,' the Taoiseach's tone was pleasant. 'I called Derek in for an estimation of this new development.'

'What the hell?' McFillen spoke to himself. 'What sort of a mess has Tull gotten himself into?'

'How long have you known MacAdoo?' The Taoiseach's tone was now impersonal.

'From the very beginning.'

'Morally what sort is he?'

'What sort of morals do you mean?'

'Women.'

'Women?' McFillen echoed the word with absolute incredulity. 'In that respect,' he informed the Taoiseach coldly, 'the man is impeccable.'

'Good,' the Taoiseach sounded as if he needed the reassurance. 'The bother, Mac,' he continued coldly, 'is that I have been reliably informed that Tull is visiting a lady of easy virtue in his constituency.'

'I don't believe it!' McFillen's rejection was full of outrage. He had known Tull for thirty years and was familiar with his abstemious tastes. From a moral point of view his own behaviour had been nothing short of scandalous but luck had been on his side. He had never been found out. Tull on the other hand had always clung rigidly to his old-fashioned, homespun morality. The Taoiseach was speaking again.

'Would you believe it Mac if the parish priest of Kilnavarna told you?'

'Good God!' McFillen's answer registered amazement. He recovered quickly. 'The source of his information?' he asked.

'Absolutely reliable.'

'And the woman?'

Derek Freezer spoke for the first time. 'Jenny Jordan,

Crabapple Hill, Kilnavarna.' The words came out lazily, almost casually.

'But she's one of his oldest and closest friends,' Mc-Fillen exploded. Almost immediately he could have bitten his tongue off. The Taoiseach and the P.R.O. exchanged meaningful looks. Recovering quickly McFillen addressed himself to this chief.

'I don't accept it,' he said coldly.

'That's not the issue at stake,' the Taoiseach was getting annoyed. 'There's an election around the corner. Tull and Din Stack depend on a marginal vote. If Tull's stock drops we lose a seat. There's something else.' He tweaked his nose, sat back in his swivel and indicated to Freezer that he take over. The P.R.O. sat upright in his chair and looked directly at McFillen.

'In next Friday's issue of *The Demoglobe*, in the column known as constituency chit-chat, the following report will appear: "Tull MacAdoo, long serving Dail member, spends much of his time lately around sparsely populated Crabapple Hill. Votes or what?"'

'But that's speculation and besides it's almost libellous,' McFillen responded at once.

'It's neither,' Freezer, himself a distinguished journalist cut across with equal speed. 'It's factual reporting.'

'But it's damaging, it's nasty.'

'Of course it is. That's why it's included in the column although it's more of a local political miscellany thatn a column. It's the most avidly read part of the paper and with an election round the corner this hotchpotch of gossip and conjecture will be the centrepiece of the paper for the next few months. Most of the titbits will consist of dicey personal items and pure conjecture. There will be no in-depth coverage. That's a luxury *The Demoglobe* cannot afford. By aiming at the basest emotions they must perforce attract the highest readership.'

'What do you want me to do?' McFillen, resignation in his voice, turned to the Taoiseach. Inevitably that worthy man tweaked his upper lip.

'See Tull', he said. 'Make sure he cuts off all contact with this woman. He must ignore *The Demoglobe* report no matter what the provocation. Let him give the impression that the report is beneath his contempt. That's it except that we must face the possibility of Tull's not being ratified at his constituency convention next week.'

★ ★ ★

Mick writes to his Father:

20 Hangman's Close,
Knacker's Well,
Cork.

Dear Dad,
I never pass a beggar by. Let it be the last shilling in my pocket and I will part with it. You see I know how beggars feel. I know the humiliation. I too am a beggar. My parsimonious father, literally rotten with money, sees to that. Consequently I look upon each beggar I meet as the brother I never had. In God's name will you send me on money. That's all I want, money. I want enough to live, enough to survive until I can earn some of my own.

Your loving son,
Mick.

★ ★ ★

Tull MacAdoo writes to his son Mick:

The Post Office,
Kilnavarna.

Dear Mick,
You're the greatest scourge since the locusts descended on the Egyptians. A son is there to help and support his ageing father, not to suck him dry like you. I have prayed these past nine years that one day a letter would come from you enquiring about my health and welfare and looking to see that all was right with me and not looking for money. Just one letter Mick, that's all I ask, just one letter no matter how short or long so long as there's no

mention of money in it. I would die happy if you were to write such a letter Mick. I would say what God said: 'This is my beloved Son with whom I am well pleased.' I would go on my knees and cry Hallaloojey. I will light a bonfire on top of Crabapple Hill the day a letter comes from you that don't ask for money.

Have you any idea of the way I work to keep you at the university? If you worked one quarter as hard as I do you'd be qualified long ago. Here's a sample of a morning's work. Get the blind pension for Mickeen Morgan the man that won the Tourmadeedy open darts championship last Christmas. Get new false teeth for Tom Cably of Drumriddle and for three soupsuckers in upper Glenalee that never gave me a vote. Get the I.R.A. pension for the bummer MacLee. All he ever fired was snowballs and spits. Get contraceptives for a lady in Dry Valley. She's going with a small man from Tourmadeedy. Put him up on a butter box I told her and when you see the eyes rolling in his head kick away the butter box and you'll want no contraceptives. Get three graves in the old graveyard of Ballyfree for old natives of the place. Fix up nineteen cases of delayed unemployment assistance. Some of them like to give me a few pounds like they do to the dispensary doctors. Every single one of them is out to bankrupt the state. You think anyone of them worries about the next fellow or the future of the country? For them the future is now and the party that puts the most on the table is the party they'll vote for.

Did you ever try to imagine what it's like at times for me? There I am at a football match enjoying an hour away from it all when some bostoon comes up and addles me for the length of the game. Another time I might be sitting in a pub enjoying a quiet drink when a drunk sticks himself onto me swearing allegiance or the opposite. I might be taking a quiet stroll when I'm joined by a man who wants a disability pension or the old age pension. 'Tis no good saying to them come and see me at my office. Men that said that didn't hold their seats for long.

Then there are the constant callers. The addicts McFillen calls them. Women are the big offenders. One calls looking for repairs to the roof of her cottage. I take particulars and get the job done as fast as I can. Success goes to her head and she calls again and again looking for other favours. In the finish she asks if there's anything else going that she hasn't applied for. Whether she wants it or not if 'tis for nothing she'll take it.

There is one mystery I have never resolved. When I was in the county council and obliged to count my coppers to make ends meet two men came to my door one night wearing dark glasses. I was in bed when they knocked. I got the fright of my life when I opened the door. I was about to bang it out in their faces when one of them produced an envelope instead of the gun I expected. He handed me the envelope but came no nearer so that I had no way of knowing who he was. When I had the envelope in my hand he spoke:

'Don't forget Dousey,' he said. With that the pair made a bolt down the bohareen to a waiting car. In the envelope I found the sum of one hundred pounds in cash, twenty of those big, white English fivers. At the time there was a vacancy for a rent-collector in the county. Sure enough Dousey was one of the candidates. You might ask did I vote for Dousey. Well I did and I make no apologies. He got the job. The contest was hung until the two boys came to my door. They knew what psychology was. There was ten opposition votes for Dousey and thirteen for our man. This meant that they would have to buy two of ours to swing it in favour of Dousey. I don't know who got the other hundred pounds but there was holy war in our ranks for many a long day after. I was the one man who was never suspected. You may be sure that the pair who gave me the envelope knew that I would never be accused. That's why they chose me. To this day I don't know who these men were. I don't want to know. I know too much as it is. Then in the latter end of all who is to say but the money might be from God. The main thing my son is to stay ahead of the posse and be openly against no man. Your weekly allowance is enclosed.

Affectionately,
Dad.

P.S. We have decided, Kate and I, that you are not to
come home for the canvass until your exams are over. You
see now that I put your exam before myself although Kate
says we'll get more votes without you. Ne need then to
come till the day before voting. We'll want you for carting
the old ones and cripples and for standing behind illiter-
ates in case they do the wrong thing.

Tull.

★ ★ ★

James Flannery, N.T. writes to Tull:

The Elms,
Kilnavarna.

Dear Tull,
I have just finished reading the political medley in *The
Demoglobe*. Who would believe that Tull MacAdoo ever
sought anything but votes on Crabapple Hill? The thing
in *The Demoglobe* is but the tip of the iceberg Tull. For
instance only a fortnight ago Canon Cosly and myself
were fowling in the area when I saw you parking your car
behind Johnny Mac's spruce plantation. At the time we
were hidden in a spinney hoping for a shot at a hare or a
fox when who should emerge from his car but the canniest
old fox of all, Tull MacAdoo, Minister of State for Bogland Areas with special responsibility for Game and
Wildlife. We noted with interest how furtively you
glanced all around. You passed within feet of us. Then
you panted off towards Jenny Jordan's. You were admitted immediately as though you were expected. You didn't
even have to knock. How respectfully she relieved you of
your overcoat and shortcoat before drawing the blind. Our
last glimpse of you was fascinating. The canon's mouth
was open wide in total incomprehension. You threw your
tie to one side. Quite properly Jenny drew the blinds at
that stage. I passed no remark. There was no need. The
Canon, as you probably know, prays regularly to Patrick
Pearse believing him to be a saint. All the way back to the

presbytery he kept repeating one remark: 'This shall not pass. This shall not pass.'

Other people know about your visits. I have known for some time but not until the most recent one did I succeed in manipulating the Canon into a position where he would have an unrestricted view. So Tull the wheel turns and the hero of Glenalee finds himself in the corner where he once had me. This is but the start oh mighty minister. The imagination of the electorate will do the rest. *Fama nihil est celerius.*

James Flannery, N.T.

* * *

Tom Bluenose writes to Tull:

Kettleton's Lounge,
Kilnavarna.

Dear Tull,
What a jockey we have in you and what a mare you picked, as grey as the badger, as drawn as a drum. My poor sister. I hope no one tells her. If I had my hands on you now I'd tear out your heart. You have me driven to drink so you have. By gor I often stooped low and did many the terrible thing but I drew the line at the old grey mare. Do me a favour. Cross to the other side of the street the next time you see me or I won't answer for my doings. My poor misfortunate sister. I hope they break it gently to her.

What odds now for you to be ratified at the convention? They're talking about young Scard from Tourmadeedy. He's an economist whatever that is. Don't look now Tull but your lace is ripped and you're heading for a fall.

Your brother in-law,
Tom.

* * *

Mick MacAdoo writes to his Father:

> 11 Horseshoe Heights,
> Amparn Avenue,
> Cork.

Dear Dad,
I never thought you had it in you. It's like as if I was smitten by a thunderbolt. My acquaintances here have begun to shun me since that report appeared in *The Demoglobe*. They must be badly caught for news. A true friend of mine here said it would be the death of my mother. He doesn't know my mother. The only way to kill my mother is to put her down. What in God's name got into you Tull? Have you any sense of discretion? Will they ask you to resign or what? It's a terrible bloody mix-up. I'll never get used to it.

> Mick.

* * *

Tull writes to Kate:

> McMell's Hotel,
> Dublin.

Dear Kate,
How can I ever explain to you? How can I ever justify my weekly visits to Jenny Jordan? All I'll ask you is to believe what I tell you. I visited Jenny regularly whenever I failed to establish any line of communication with my lawful wife but I didn't visit Jenny for anything other than talk. When I would arrive it was like entering a different world, a world of peace and sympathy and understanding. A turf fire was always burning in the hearth. There was the grand old smell of turf smoke and the light was low. If she drew the blind down as Flannery said she did I never noticed. I would take my overcoat off, my shortcoat and tie and sit on the back of a chair. She would

massage my shoulders until the tension left me and I was normal and pliable and relaxed. All the time I would be talking about this, that and the other thing and in between she would say, 'I see faith,' and 'Is that so?' Remember dearest Kate that we are lifelong friends long past our primes with a gentle and serene relationship that only long years can mould, that only the deepest trust can bring about. Only the old fully understand old friendships. Often there's no other comfort available to them and it's too late in the day for the shaping of new friends. I know that others will not believe this and I don't care. All that matters to me is that you believe it. I'm here at McMell's with McFillen. He sends his love and will be bringing you a gift when he arrives down there for the constituency convention on Friday. I have been with the Taoiseach and told him what I have just now told you. I thought he'd take his lip from his face with the twigging he gave it.

'Fair enough Tull,' said he, 'if the convention endorses you I'll be down to back you up.' But Lycos is deep Kate and I have the feeling he knows something I don't know. We can only wait and see.

I had a letter from your mother. See you on Friday morning around noon God willing. Only the convention will tell what damage has been done.

Your loving father,
Tull.

★ ★ ★

Biddy writes to Tull:

Kilnavarna P.O.
Kilnavarna.

Dear Minister,
I'm under sedation and even the rising of my hand is an agony. Still this letter must be wrote. God in His mansion and His crucified Son and our divine Mother knows that no man saving yourself ever laid hands on me. Four stitches in the head after I firing the skillet at him Cormac

the drover got the night he tried to put his hand under my skirt in my father's kitchen and didn't I fling Mailer the shoemaker out of Piper's swinging boats because he tried to look under my clothes when my end of the boat was above him. Three ribs he broke and one collarbone and hasn't he one leg lower than the other to this day. Even after the slow foxtrot landing in Kilnavarna in nineteen thirty-four was a man's belly near mine and we dancing and didn't I draw a kick at Nuley the undertaker over he trying to dance cheek to cheek with me. You were the first and last man to lay hands on me Tull MacAdoo and what was it all for, all my years in the Children of Mary, my nine Fridays, my novenas, my pounds for masses and my martyrdom to what pains is to be found in the doctor's volumes of this country. What is my reward but to have my Casanova gallivanting like a puck on the slopes of Crabapple Hill, my grey oul' galloper with his tail cocked high like a boar as should be on his knees before the altar of God atoning for his sins past and present and preparing his black soul for the grave that's facing him sooner nor he thinks. What a ram we have in him and he down on the door of seventy and what a nice ewe he flushed out of the crags of Crabapple, a ewe that if you was boiling her and stewing her from Xmas day to Whit you wouldn't find a scrap of mutton that could be chewed by a man with iron teeth and jaws like a bulldozer, my rawney oul' devil with the eyes pulled back into her head from late night carousing and the A.B.C. like the map of Europe on her shanks and shins from dossing in front of the fire. I ask the good God in His heaven if this is to be the payment for my chastity and virginity, is this the mouldy harvest I'm to reap for keeping my two legs together through thick and thin, through hail, rain and storm, in sickness and in health in the name of the Father, the Son and the Holy Ghost?

Biddy.

★ ★ ★

Tull writes to Mick:

Kilnavarna P.O.
Kilnavarna.

Dear Mick,

At last you have done it. You have achieved the impossible. You have written, without knowing, a letter that hasn't a single mention of money. Everywhere around the tidings are as black as the ace of spades but at least I have the satisfaction of knowing that my only son can indeed write me a letter without a request for money.

Kate tells me you told her on the phone that Judge O'Cargivaun's daughter Gertrude snubbed you the last time you met in Cork. A bad right for one of her breed to ignore a MacAdoo for my dear Mick only for me her oul' father would still be a famished hoor of a barrister and not a district justice like he is today. What harm but the oul' reprobate has an appetite for young women that would put a navy to shame. I remember the time that Micky Moocher's son Patten went amok after flooring two bottles of home-made whiskey in Kettleton's lounge. He crashed into nine different cars, did seven thousand pounds worth of damage, knocked down two people, broke the two legs in one of them and smashed to smithereens the hip of another. Then he tried to drive the tractor in the front door of a house in Tourmadeedy where one of the daughters had jilted him the night before. Already he had been convicted twice of drunken driving not to mention several convictions for assault and battery on innocent members of the public. He had nothing at all in his favour except the one mitigating circumstance that he voted for me, that his father and mother voted for me and that every Moocher from Tourmadeedy to Kilnavarna male, female and neuter voted for me from the first day I threw my hat into the ring of politics.

Beyond question there was jail staring Patten Moocher in the face. They came to me, his father and mother and his uncles and aunts and himself the craven curmudgeon with a face like an altar boy and they all talking at the one time, ullagoning and pillalloing like seven litters of greyhound pups and they lamenting that poor Patcheen would serve ten years and leave the bloom and blossom of his manhood behind him in Limerick Jail. It looked bad. There was nothing I could do to save him from jail but then I thought of two things. I thought first of O'Cargivaun's heat for women and the next thing I thought of was Patten's Auntie Maggie, a fine plump lump of a girl with the promise dancing and rippling in her handsome flesh and a gamey eye to boot.

Between the jigs and the reels I made an appointment with O'Cargivaun. He was staying at the time in the Sandhills Hotel in the seaside resort of Ballyee. I landed with Maggie in tow and introduced them. Then I skedaddled and left them at it.

Time passed and the court came to Kilnavarna. Patten was called. He had his story like his name, Pat. A blackout he suffered. Nothing could he remember. He would never again put a drink to his lips. Compensation would be paid in full. He got off. What his Auntie handed over to O'Cargivaun in the Sandhills Hotel will never be known but by herself and O'Cargivaun. A week later Patten was roaring drunk and without provocation broke every window in the main street of Tourmadeedy. He got eighteen months from another judge.

I will now conclude. I hope you're in your health and that you didn't get a knock in the head or anything bad that put the thoughts of money from your mind.

Affectionately,
Your father.

★   ★   ★

Flannery writes to Tull:

The Elms,
Kilnavarna.

Dear Tull,
I have just heard the constituency noninations. I have, as a result, discovered that I am not as charitable as I should

be, the reason being that you have failed to get the nomination and I am overjoyed. Your successor, young Monty Scard is a good fellow, already a distinguished economist with a string of degrees after his name that have to be seen to be believed. In fact he could give one or two to your son Mick and not miss them. His has the kind of mind which this country desperately needs in this day and age. He is making the supreme sacrifice, abandoning a brilliant academic career to serve his country. The people of this constituency will show their appreciation of his great gesture when the ballot boxes are opened this day month.

It took a long time Tull but it was inevitable. Your kind of politician is a dead duck. You've been an anachronism for some years now. I very much fear that you don't even comprehend the full implications of what it means to be European. Scard will go far. I have never supported your party as you know but in view of the fact that they have kicked you out and replaced you with a scholar and a gentleman I will vote that way for the first time.

Remember what I told you about scandal-spreading. Your affair with Jenny Jordan is the main topic of discussion in every public house for miles around. It's being told in twenty different ways and may I say Tull that you are not being spared. I wish you a pleasant retirement.

James Flannery, N.T.

★ ★ ★

Mick writes to his Father:

> 11 Horseshoe Heights,
> Amparn Avenue,
> Cork.

Dear Dad,
To hell with you and Kate. I'm coming down. You were right to go independent. You may not get in but by the Lord God we'll go down fighting. I'll get Bluenose off the drink and I'll organise most of the local graduates of this

place. There's no sanctimonious horsefeathers growing on these fellows. Expect me tomorrow and have five hundred pounds cash ready for me, I'll want it to buy drinks. Bluenose never bought one in his life.

Mick.

★   ★   ★

McFillen writes to Tull:

Romple Avenue,
Dublin.

Dear Tull,
The boss man is livid. 'Why,' said he, 'couldn't he take his defeat like a man? Why couldn't he retire and live on his money not to mention his pension?'

All the time he paced up and down the room like a tiger. Then came the tweaking of the upper lip.

'Mac,' he said, 'plead with him. Tell him I'll nominate him to the Senate if he withdraws his name. Tell him that this way nobody's going to gain except the opposition. If he withdraws Scard and Stack are certainties. If not Stack will go and so will Tull. There can be no other outcome.'

You'd enjoy the Senate Tull. You need never open your mouth and there's only a fraction of the work. It sounds good. Senator MacAdoo, Senator Tull MacAdoo. Say it to yourself a few times and see what you think of the sound of it. You needn't do a damn thing only sit there. Just don't fall asleep. I personally think you would be well advised to settle for it. *The Demoglobe* is out for your guts. The clergy and the nuns, once your stalwart supporters, have all gone over to Scard. Be sensible, old friend. For old times' sake accept the Senate and make your peace with himself. There is no room for a loner in politics today.

What a terrible pity that report appeared in *The Demoglobe*. Until that moment you were heading straight for the cabinet. He mentioned your name more than once in connection with agriculture. Don't blame him Tull, say you'll accept the Senate. I'll be waiting eagerly and praying that you'll see it my way. Whatever happens it must not affect our personal friendship. Give my love to Kate.

Your old friend,
James McFillen.

★   ★   ★

Tom Cably writes to Tull:

Drumriddle,
Tourmadeedy.

Dear Tull,
Them are great teeth. Yesterday I ground a lamb cutlet into powder and today downed a pound of prime bacon direct from the barrel. Man dear the juice ran down the sides of my jaw like syrup. I had lately a longing for meat that would drive an ordinary man mental. You done me proud Tull and them that does Tom Cably proud gets Tom Cably's vote and Tom Cably's wife's vote and all the other Cably's that can be counted from here to Kilnavarna. My brother Jack is dead but his name is on the register and he'll be voted for.

I see the latest report in *The Demoglobe* says you refuse to comment on your relationship with Jenny Jordan. I hope it don't do you no harm Tull all this publicity. As for me I was never a man to comment but as little when I was threading. Who would want to capsize a girl's good name? In my heyday I used to ramboozle them as fast as you'd pull them out from under me. Men that makes no comment before or after are never short of women. Them that blew and boasted weren't long being left high and dry. That's the way with women. Don't mind the carpers Tull. A longing for ramboozling is many a good man's cross and them that say otherwise is not right in the head by no manner nor means.

These teeth are powerful. 'Tis great to have a grip of the pipe again, to be able to hack the lean meat from bones and to grind gristle. Long life to you Tull.

Tom Cably.

★ ★ ★

Bluenose writes to Tull:

The Half-Moon Hotel,
Tourmadeedy.

Dear Tull,
Mick and myself is here constant. 'Tis our headquarters you might say. He's a great gosoon, full of my fire and temper. He knocked down two fellows in a row here the other night and gave a guard as had no uniform and as tried to stop it a left hook that landed under the butt of his ear and laid him out handsome for five minutes. Men now looks at Mick like he'd be Jack Dempsey. He's a great comfort to me. Not a drink did I put to my lips since the canvass.

Now here's a strange thing. Since word went out that you were ramboozling Jenny Jordan, true or false, there is a great interest being taken by the common workmen, small farmers and out-of-the-way mountainy men of these parts as regards your ramblings and rovings on Crabapple Hill. They takes a certain pride out of the fact that an old buck of your years is still belling for fallows. They boasts about you and they does be speculating among themselves as to the manner and means you applies for the threading of the old grey doe of Crabapple. That's what she's called. At first myself and Mick was inclined to get annoyed but the allusions was well-meaning and it was plain to see these peasants, that's what Flannery calls them, regards you as a man after their own heart. They would love to be like you and when you does your caper on Crabapple Hill you're doing it for every man Jack of them. You're carrying their colours to the post and their hearts goes out to you. Mick used to get narked when some poor blighted labourer without chick, child nor hearth would ask us quiet and out of earshot if you are an uncommon man as regards the love accoutrements. This happens all the time and in the beginning Mick was inclined to haul out with that deadly left hand of his but we came to see the advantage of it in time.

Now whenever the question is asked we nods our heads and winks and all that and if some gets more nosey nor more we stretches out our hands like a fisherman describing the one what got away and letting on that you were likewise designed south of the navel.

'Tis an ill wind that don't blow some good and if there's a vote in the balance we need every persuader we can get. They does be genuinely delighted to hear that you are so well outfitted under the surface. They shakes their heads with pride and claps their hands with delight. They slaps one another on the back and says: 'Isn't Tull the hardest bloody man at all!' There was one fellow. He came down a bohreen from a bohawn and he wearing only a long black coat over the pair of turned-down wellingtons. There was a smile the size of a manhole on his face. When we asked him for the vote he turned serious.

'Tell us boys,' said he, 'is it that Tull is hung like a Whitehead Bull?'

'True,' says I not wanting to disillusion the poor chap.

'Ah,' says he, ''tis no wonder they made a minister out of him.'

On the bad side there is doors closed against us here and there. They're inside alright, the holy josies and crawthumpers but they don't want to be seen talking to us. There's many you done a turn for peeping out through curtains they hadn't one time. A few nights ago while we were canvassing upper Drumriddle we met Doctor John coming from a sick call.

'How's Tull?' he asked us.

'Never better,' we told him.

'A great man,' said the doctor, 'a man who'll get my number one like always.'

'Thank you doctor,' we said.

'There are no thanks due,' says he. ''Tis my way of

saluting the first politician to open the flop on the trousers of holy Ireland.'

'Will Scard beat him?' we asked.

'I'm afraid so,' says he, 'although he's not a politician. He's a bookman, an academic. He should stick to his books and leave the politics to Tull.' With that he drove off but what he said put an idea into my head. Says I to Mick isn't there something funny and odd about these jokers as hangs around books all the time, as does be always reading and writing and letting go with big rockers of words, pale faced tricky looking latchikoes that's not natural like ourselves. I mean I says to him you'd never see them behaving like other christians only always done up to kill, regular Fancy Dans with never a rib of beard to be seen no more nor a lady. I knew I had Mick thinking so I said no more. I decided to wait and see what he might come up with. When we came to upper Drumriddle there was a platform awaiting and upwards of fifty people waiting to hear Mick talk. He made a great speech but it was near the end that he stripped away the cow-leaves and came to the white of the cabbage. What I said about Fancy Dans had put him thinking. Give Mick the cards and he'll score the tricks. He stood on the platform and handed me his overcoat.

'My father,' said he, 'is what the good God made him, a man. If he made a mistake itself and I deny he did it was a man's mistake and I'll make no apology for that.' There was a weak clap from the crowd. He had scored his first point. 'My father,' says he, 'is a man's man and not a prettyboy. If you want a prettyboy or a nancy boy don't vote for my father because you'll be voting for the wrong man.'

Mick let the words sink in. There was fierce whispering in the crowd. Who was he referring to? Why had he brought up the subject of prettyboys?

'Make your choice,' he told them, 'but don't ever forget what I tell you this night. Tull MacAdoo is no queer. He's a man.'

That was the shouting and roaring in the crowd, some for, some against. There were a few opposition diehards breaking their sides laughing to see us fighting amongst ourselves. Mick stepped in and stopped the row with a few neat lefts that no one saw coming. When we returned to the car there was a reporter from *The Demoglobe* waiting for us.

'Would you like to confirm what you said a moment ago?' the reporter asked and he started to read from his shorthand. When he finished reading Mick nodded agreement.

'Now,' said the reporter, 'would you like to add anything to what you have just said?'

'No I would not,' says Mick.

'Were you referring to anybody in particular when you spoke just now?'

Mick didn't answer at once. A crowd was gathering and he wanted to make the most of his chance. When everybody was listening he answered.

'If the cap fits,' said he, 'let them wear it.' This drew a cheer from the MacAdoo supporters.

'Are you suggesting,' the reporter asked, 'that there are queers running against your father?'

'If the cap fits,' Mick threw back at him and the crowd roared. Better diversion they couldn't ask for.

'Have you any person or persons in mind?'

'I have more natural things nor that on my mind,' Mick shouted and he went behind the wheel of the car while the crowd cheered him. What he said will appear in *The Demoglobe* tomorrow in that cesspool known as Constituency Chit-Chat. You know what people are like. Monty Scard is no homo but then you're no whoresmaster. Let the hare sit now for the while and then see what way will he break. The public is a quare one Tull, quarer nor a snipe.

Your brother-in-law,
Tom.

* * *

Tull writes to McFillen:

The Post Office,
Kilnavarna.

Dear James,
Your letter came as a great relief. I value our personal friendship and would hate to see it go. I have read it with great care. How can you ask me to take a seat in the Senate, me that escaped from the third year of my national schooling for to complete my studies in Derrymore bog where I graduated with first class honours in turf-cutting, turf-futting and turf-clamping – nice qualifications for the Senate. Anyway I sets little store by promises.

I'll see to my guns now Mac and I'll go down fighting. One thing is sure, either Din Stack or Monty Scard will lose the seat. I'm not saying I'll be elected myself but the vote I get will not transfer. The party has seen to it that I am on my own so by all the laws my vote should also stay on its own. It could be costly for the government if the seat goes and remember Mac it's not outside the bounds of possibility that oul' Tull would hold on and if Tull holds on the Taoiseach, if 'tis still Lycos, might want to have a few words with me. Beggars can't be choosers you know, especially when majorities are narrow. I'll convey your regards to Kate. My beloved wife has gone to Lisdoonvarna. She says her nerves are frayed, her headaches are growing worse, her bowels won't move, all her old pains and aches have come back to stay and she's suffering also from a new disease which she's just only after contracting. When someone goes against her she puts her fingers into her ears until the person goes away. She won't be coming home till the actual voting. I'm sure you have your own troubles so I'll say no more. Win or lose you and me will never fall out Mac. Till another day, so long.

Tull

★　★　★

Biddy writes to Tull:

The Purewater Guesthouse,
Lisdoonvarna.

Dear Tull,
We'll be down to vote but that's as long as I can stay as
one of my knees is after giving out on me and my nerves
is terrible. I do have awful dreams at night with monsters
chasing me up and down the stairs without a stitch of
clothes. We'll hire a car. That's the best way. We'll be
beholden to nobody. We'll leave at first light and be home
in time for our lunch. I couldn't bear the thought of being
in Kilnavarna during the voting. Mutton they mostly
serve. I takes a bit boiled with white sauce and half a
potato. I hope your antics on Crabapple Hill is done
forever. 'Twas the talk before I left that your seat would
go, a nice reward for the virgin that married you, as there
was never a leg thrown across. May God and His holy
mother forgive you. I'm saying novenas for all of you and
receiving every morning. We goes to the baths twice in
the day. I hope good will come of it and at night we have
a game of cards with a Christian Brother and his sister.
He's as consoling to me as any priest and he pale like a
ghost and saintly without a copper except what few
pounds myself and the sister gives him so he can have a
whiskey or two at night to keep the life in him and the
odd thing is he'd eat frostnails. God knows where he puts
it. He says the government will go. He's praying for you.
Little do he know of the rutter we have and he facing the
pension. Rams and jackasses is innocent compared to you.
Jack Hanlon's puck that served forty goats on his lonesome is only trotting after you. 'Tis a wonder I didn't
leave you entirely. Blessed Martin my source and my
strength in my agony come to my aid. Send a po. 'Tis a
thing they never has here. Put it in a strong hatbox so's
they'll think 'tis for my head and give them no fodder for
gossip. Maggie Fritters from Tourmadeedy is here with
her sister Jane, a lovely salute she gave me yesterday the
bitch and she on her knees from first light till last praying
you'll be at the tail of the poll. I gave her back just as nice

my whipster that wouldn't know mutton from goat and her false teeth fit to burst her mouth and she nodding like a trotting horse, moryah she was royalty at every Tom, Dick and Harry. Dripping on the bread they had when even the paupers of the land was spreading butter and to see her now like a doctor's wife or a surgeon and she urbing and orbying left, right and centre like she'd be the Pope. My hoor that wouldn't know the inside of a confessional from a horsebox and I had a letter from Mick for a hundred pounds. I sent it on to the poor boy. He mightn't have me long more. Any child has only one mother. Why are ye all down on Mick and never a word about her ladyship. Is it because he's taken after my father? There's a bell ringing here. It's a signal for the supper. I must go.

Your wife,
Biddy.

★   ★   ★

When Lycos, McFillen and their entourage arrived at Tourmadeedy they were greeted by a pipe band, twenty mounted torch-bearing horsemen, forty I.R.A. pensioners marching in double file, a fairly large crowd and the usual complement of idiots and mischief-makers. From a timber platform in the village square Lycos addressed the gathering. Before he did an unprecedented occurrence took place. Alone and unaided Tull MacAdoo mounted the platform and grasped the Taoiseach's hand in his, shaking it warmly and, before leaving, swiftly embraced his former boss wiping a tear from his eye as he turned his face to the crowd. Need it be said that not even the ranks of Tuscany could scarce forbear a cheer. It was a well calculated move. It put the pressure on the Taoiseach. Would he, the man on the street was saying, do the big thing too and call to Tull MacAdoo when passing through Kilnavarna on his way back to Dublin? Against McFillen's advice Lycos bypassed the Kilnavarna P.O. without as much as a glance. Word spread like wildfire through the public houses and homes of the countryside. Tull knew the Taoiseach would not call in case it might be interpreted as weakness on his part.

'Who was the bigger man?' The question was being asked by Tull MacAdoo's agents in town and country. Tull should never have mounted the Tourmadeedy platform, his enemies said. It was the Taoiseach's night.

'Of course it was,' Tom Bluenose announced in a short speech at Dreemnagopple but would Tull MacAdoo be Tull MacAdoo if he did not greet his old friend and leader with the warmth and affection for which Tull and the entire people of the constituency were renowned. It was a point for Tull in a game which was always swinging against him. In an opinion poll, fairly conducted by *The Demoglobe* although not comprehensively, it was estimated that Tull would not be elected unless there was a sudden upsurge in support for him. Neither Tull nor Bluenose took this report seriously. They both firmly believed that the electorate was made up mainly of pathological liars. It worried Mick who was impressed by the detached manner in which the survey was conducted.

★   ★   ★

Mick writes to his Father:

The Half-Moon Hotel,
Tourmadeedy.

Dear Dad,
I need money. Bring it with you for the big rally here on Monday night, a hundred and fifty at least. I intend to have an open house after the meeting. They'll be half drunk by that time and it won't cost all that much. I have the snatch squads ready for lightning raids on every hospital, nursing home, old folks home, private home and every other resort of invalids and cripples in the constituency. These will move in at exactly one hour before the booths open. We'll lodge them in sympathetic houses till the time is ripe. My informants tell me that the other

candidates are calling at different hours during the day. There won't be much left for them when I'm finished. A good start is half the battle and this should give us a flying one of over a hundred votes. I can capture half the inmates, the half that voted for yourself and Din Stack the last time and, of course, the usual quota of softheads who'll think they are voting for their own man. It's easy to turn a one into four with the help of a minor distraction. I have experts on the ready for this chore. I have voting cards for two hundred of the absent and the dead. I could have laid my hands on as many more but these would be challenged by watchful and conscientious personating agents. We don't want to overdo it but don't worry. This cow will also be milked for what she's worth.

My own feeling at the present time is that we're running behind Stack and Scard, not very far behind but we definitely need something dramatic to catch up and pass them out. We need sympathy desperately. At the present rate of going we are going to be pipped at the post. Stack is working hard and looks good. Scard is finding it hard to shake off the prettyboy image but people are more liberal these days especially in the towns and it's not doing the damage we expected. We'll keep playing it for what it's worth however. I'm drawing up plans for the final rally at home on Tuesday night. I have two bands and horsemen galore not to mention torchbearers and banner-carriers. I have seen to everything but I need extra trappings and touches of finesse if we are to knock maximum value out of the business. By maximum value I mean votes. I'll close for now. I'm on my way to the convent where our stock is none too high over the Crabapple affair. I know how to handle nuns, plenty gossip and grapes. There are fourteen not counting the Reverend Mother who is on our side and is doing all in her power by way of prayer, fasting and persuasion. I'm bringing a box of grapes. I've always believed in them. They have a profound effect on women be they nuns or the opposite not that I know much about the latter. Bluenose is working like a Trojan. He'll break out shortly. I know the symptoms, brushing imaginary specks of dust from his sleeves and lapels and stamping the ground like a horse. He lasted a long time considering all the free drink that was going.

> Your affectionate son,
> Mick.

* * *

Tull writes to Biddy:

> The Post Office,
> Kilnavarna.

Dearest Biddy,
I think about you all the time and I'm praying for your recovery. Don't forget what I've always said. Keep away from doors and windows and reduce the chances of getting involved with draughts. We are up to our neck in it here. I've sent what you asked for by bus. I couldn't find a hatbox. They don't seem to be as plentiful as before. I put it instead in an old timber butter box and stuffed it with newspapers. It's a good quality one made from aluminium. I wouldn't insult your behind with plastic. I'll have to leave you now. I'll be looking forward to seeing you on polling day. There will be no face more welcome in this house.

> Your loving husband,
> Tull.

* * *

Kate writes her Father:

> Neery's Guesthouse,
> Ballyee.

Dear Daddy,
Mission accomplished. We have had a reasonably good canvass in this windswept and most westerly corner of the

constituency. The way I see it it's going to be neck and
neck. The old guard in this place have stayed with us.
They look upon Scard as a Red. Not so the younger set.
Scard is their man. They wear his photo encased in a
circular green and gold frame on their lapels. Now for the
details of the visit to Alexander Muffy, the grandfather of
the party as Lycos once called him. I laid my cards on the
table and he laid his. His practice has dwindled to such a
degree that he now finds himself in debt. His two sons,
although qualified solicitors, are totally incompetent. They
are his chief worry. If they would be placed in positions
from which they could not be shifted all his worries would
be over. We went to Sandhills Hotel for a drink and there
he revealed the terrible disappointment his sons had been
to him. In their student days they promised so much that
he over-indulged them. Passing exams was no bother to
them unlike more we could name. The elder son is apparently addicted to the dog track while the younger prefers
horse-racing.

Alexander Muffy is a shrewd and able man. He gives
you an even money chance, with him and his sons and
friends on your side. He reckons that if the government
get back into power it will be with a majority of one or
two. Muffy says that if it works out this way Lycos will
begin to make overtures immediately. Muffy wants little,
just that his sons be appointed district justices within a
year. Not one mark you but two. I thought about it while
at the counter buying a drink. He wanted an immediate
answer. I never before heard such an outrageous demand.
I returned to our table with the drinks and excused myself. I hastened to the ladies where I gave the matter
further thought. Beggars cannot be choosers I told myself.
Besides that it's Alexander Muffy who's taking a real
gamble. We have nothing to lose but politically he'll be
out on a limb if you lose your seat. Still it was a bit much,
two judges from the same untalented family. I remembered you had given me full plenipotentiary powers. For
the first time I knew how Michael Collins must have felt
when Dev sent him to England.

I came back and extended my hand to Alexander
Muffy. All the odds were against him. There were too

many ifs to contend with as far as the sons were concerned. We finished the drink and he accompanied us on the canvass. People were surprised to see him with us and I have the feeling that I invested wisely. In my opinion his support is worth a cool fifty number ones that might not otherwise be ours. In addition he volunteered to appear on your platform in Kilnavarna on Tuesday night and will speak on your behalf if necessary.

I must say you engineered all this with great skill. The Muffy vote could be the deciding factor in your favour. I still sense, however, that at best we have a fifty-fifty chance, no more than that at this present time. I rely on your natural political genius to come up with a few big trumps before we go to the polls on Wednesday. We definitely need something.

> Love as always,
> Kate.

★　★　★

Mick writes to his Father:

> The Half-Moon Hotel,
> Tourmadeedy.

Dear Dad,

Money received. It will be well spent I assure you. Every chronic drunkard in this part of the constituency will be putting a number one in front of Tull MacAdoo or if not someone else will be doing it for him. In the beginning in this area a few of the stalwarts were inclined to waver. Bluenose convinced them that when the votes were being counted we would know who voted for who and we would remember. It put them thinking. Now for the bad news. He has broken out. It happened out of the blue. Late last night we returned from a canvass of Tobarnanuv. I was exhausted as were the rest of the party. The bar was closed so I bought a case of stout and two bottles of whiskey. We adjourned to the double room which we share and settled down to serious drinking. We discussed the campaign and while all are agreed that we are making a promising canvass we will be fighting on our backs for that last seat unless something miraculous happens. We clattered the first bottle of whiskey in jig time and settled into the stout. The more we drank the more votes we collected. All this time Bluenose was nursing a small bottle of soda. He sat as if in a coma with his head bent, showing no interest in the proceedings. I sensed something was wrong but decided to play it by ear. One of the boys opened the second bottle of whiskey and wiped the neck with his sleeve.

'Here,' said Bluenose, 'I'll do that for you.' Lovingly he caressed the bottle, polishing it with the front of his cardigan and holding it up to the light to admire the surface bubbles which disappeared as quickly as they came. All eyes were upon him. Suddenly he sat bolt upright in his chair and put the bottle to his lips. There followed a gurgling and a grunting as he consumed a glass or so. He swallowed hard a few times and then from his stomach there came a succession of skirls, drones and assorted rumblings. I thought he was about to explode but no. Silently he elevated his left buttock and breezily broke wind. All this time there was no word out of the onlookers. I must concede that the natural colour was returning slowly to his face. He lofted the bottle again and this time did not stop till it contained equal parts of light and whiskey.

In a matter of moments he was his old self, reeling off variations of outrageous profanities and stringing together character assassinations of Din Stack and Monty Scard that left us with our mouths open in admiration and wonder. What a transformation there was inside of a five minute period. He placed the bottle on the ground between his feet and growled like a bulldog when somebody tried to remove it. We offered him stout but this he scorned. In a half hour the whiskey bottle was empty and my beloved uncle Tom Bluenose was at the peak of his form.

In the morning for breakfast he had two glasses of hot whiskey after which we resumed the canvass. When we arrived back that night he made straight for the lounge although we estimated that he had two bottles of whiskey consumed already. He refused to sit with the rest of us for the good reason that he knew he would be unable to rise again if he did. He bumped into people and made a general nuisance of himself. The barmaids refused to serve him with more whiskey not because he was drunk but because he neglected to pay for several previous rounds. At this stage he started to polish off any unguarded drinks which caught his eye. In the end we got him to bed where he now lies in a drunken stupor, the worst in which I have ever seen him. I write so that you will be forewarned. See you Monday night. We will need all the luck that's going and anything else you can think of.

Your affectionate son,
Mick.

★　★　★

Tull writes to Mick:

The Post Office,
Kilnavarna.

Dear Mick,
The chips are down in earnest. The crucial time is from here until the booths close on Wednesday night. What is said and done now cannot be taken back so what's said and done must be done right as there will be no second chances. I wrote to Kate this morning. I told her to make her way up the main aisle at Ballyee church for Holy Communion on Sunday morning. It's no good being first to the rails. The time to go is when most has received and there's only a handful left. That way all eyes will be upon her. You my son will do the same, if not for the love of God for the love of the father, your own father. You'll get Confession and Absolution tomorrow night at Tourmadeedy Church if you go to Father Tobler's box. He's as deaf as a stone. Then on Sunday morning up that aisle with you at the proper moment. You have a good face

Mick and no matter what else and when you come back down that aisle with the host in your mouth let that face be the cause of turning a vote or two in our direction. Put on that pained look you're so good at whenever I ask are you backing horses. Take careful stock of what I have to say now because an awful lot will depend on how my instructions is carried out. Mind you I admire your arrangements for the final rally and do not propose to tamper in any way with the ones you have already made. You said in your letter that we needed something dramatic. I agree, so follow carefully.

On the night of the rally you will organise a half dozen of the biggest blackguards in the Tull MacAdoo Youth Club and instruct them to smash every window in the Kilnavarna Church of Ireland. Have them then spread word that they saw supporters of Din Stack and Monty Scard in the vicinity of the church with stones in their hands. You might go as far as to get one of the youth club to say he was paid by a man he once saw on Stack's platform. This is purely your department. I must be kept out of all this. If all the windows are broken and the doors smeared with dung or the like we could gain a few Protestant votes. While the rally is in progress, preferably while I am speaking, have the same young bucks smash the windows of the post office. Before the meeting closes it will give me a chance to accuse Stack and Scard of low tactics, tactics to which I would never stoop. I will then appeal to my supporters not to retaliate but to observe the democratic system which I have always stood for. By the time the story of these atrocities are published in the daily and evening papers the following day, it will be too late for our opponents to do anything about it. They can say or do what they like after the election because by then nobody will care a rattling damn. That is only phase number one for the winning of sympathy. The next item on the programme is the letting out of the air from the car wheels of our leading citizens, my most solid supporters but likewise men who are respected in Kilnavarna and beyond. This will not go down well. The blame will fall on Stack and Scard and their supporters. Now here is the move to cap them all. I have given this the most careful thought and if it doesn't win us a substantial number of votes I honestly don't know what will. You are well aware of the existence of an old man by the name of Barney Malone who resides at the other side of Crabapple Hill in a place called Glounclooney. He is eighty years of age and he is without doubt the best-loved man in this part of the world. He has over forty grandchildren with votes to make no mention of his sons and daughters. I got the I.R.A. pension for him but it was no trouble as he was a genuine member of the Flying Column and spent a number of years in jail for his country. He is a man without bitterness and in all the years I have known him I have never heard him to say a bad word about any one.

He was in a ferocious pucker when I decided to go independent. There was, you see, never a more faithful party man. It was only the other night he finally decided what way he would vote. I called to see him late and we sat in front of the dying fire in his kitchen reminiscing about the old days and remembering our companions who had fallen in the struggle for freedom. Barney is now without a rib of hair on his head or without a tooth in his mouth although many's the time I volunteered to get him false teeth free of charge. We cannot do enough for those who fought or died for Ireland. What a fine wholesome face Barney Malone has. Children in particular love him with his ever-steady smile and warm nature. When he decided to come my way not all his children and grandchildren could be persuaded to go with him. Roughly half will vote for Din Stack and Scard. The other half will vote for me. In order to get the other half I have devised a good plan.

Barney will be attending my final rally the same as always. He will wear the light blue American suit which he has worn for the past twenty years. This suit is a gift from his brother Martin R.I.P. who used to live in America. Barney always walks bareheaded on the final night and he will lead the parade this time in the absence of our friend Mr Lycos. He will march about twenty yards ahead of all the others. I could not have a better man leading my followers. With that infected smile, with his military record and his love of humanity every man's heart will go out to this well-beloved, gentle soul on the final night. Here is what you must do. Line up three or four of your closest and most trusted pals and have them arrive here in Kilnavarna at a quarter to nine just before the parade starts. They can park at the entrance to my yard at the rear of the post office. It's a restricted area and nobody will dare park there beforehand. When they hear the music of the bands they must ready themselves at once and pull masks over their faces. They must then proceed through the yard till they reach the vans' exit near the corner on the main street. They will have with them a bucket of mud or any kind of soft dirty muck or filth. They will not lock the gate behind them having entered the street. This gate will be their only means of a getaway.

Here is what comes next. They will wait for the parade to approach the corner. It is unlikely that anyone will be standing around. Everybody will be in the parade except maybe a few elderly folk and these will not come in the way. Split second timing will now be called for. Cool heads and movements according to plan will be essential if the mission is to succeed. The parade draws near. First man to come around the corner is Barney Malone. He is well ahead of the horsemen who come next in the procession before the pipe band. The moment he appears your friends will rush him. Two will hold him firmly by the hands and I must warn you here that it will have to be firm for he is still a strong and dangerous man. When he is firmly held the third man will give him a good pucking and ram the bucket of muck on top of his head, not too hard. He will then lay on two or three good kicks to his rear and send him staggering towards the oncoming horsemen. All is not over yet. Next act is to drop two badges, one of Stack and one of Scard at the scene of the crime by the way that they were lost in the tussle. As the horsemen are about to dismount, horrified by the treatment of Barney, your gang will shout out, 'To hell with MacAdoo' and 'Glory Monty Scard, Glory Din Stack.' Then as fast as their legs can flake they retreat through the open gate which they will lock behind them, cutting off any chance of pursuit. Back the way they came then, into their cars and escape. The sight of Barney Malone covered in mud and blood and badly battered will bring tears from the hardest hearts in Kilnavarna and if I don't get the other half of the Barney Malone votes itself 'tis sure and certain that neither Stack nor Scard will get them. We will clean up poor Barney, not too clean. We will want him for the platform where every man, woman and child can clearly see the state of him. The badges will have been found by this time or if not you'll see to it that they are located quickly. I will then address the meeting counselling restraint and begging my friends and supporters not to demean themselves by stooping to such cowardly tactics. I will then bring forward Barney Malone and ask the crowd never to forget this terrible treatment of a national hero.

If this ruse comes off successfully I should just about scrape home but no more than that. After the whole business of parade and speechmaking is over all the talk will be of the vandalism and brutality which will have just taken place. The pubs will be open. The sergeant allowed unlimited extensions when Scard and Stack had their rally. He has no choice but to do the same for me. The sergeant is a Stack man. It might do no harm if the barracks was rung about quarter to nine to say there has been a fatal crash on the main road about three miles from Kilnavarna. Traditionally he is always the last man to vote. He likes to supervise the closing proceedings at the booths and more or less set the seal on things by casting his vote so late. If the phone call is convincing he will miss the chance to vote.

I'll say no more for now except that no stone is to be left unturned from now on. Buy votes if you have to. A fiver or a tenner in the hand of a bum on his way to vote never did no harm. Let us now put our trust in God and ask Him to aid us in every way possible and maybe reveal Himself in some way so that it can be seen He is on our side. One last thing. Don't forget to vote yourself. I wouldn't put it past you to disremember.

Affectionately,
Your Father.

* * *

Biddy writes to Tull:

The Purewater Guesthouse,
Lisdoonvarna.

Dear Tull,
Aluminium would pierce the hide of a mule. My underneath is so sore I can hardly sit. What possessed you to
purchase it? God be with the fine earthenware pots they
used to make when I was a girl. You caused a right
commotion with that butterbox. The manageress thought
it was a bomb and called the guards. I was rightly mortified. I got out of it by saying it was how someone was
playing a joke. I told them I got poes the whole time. It's
in the river now and you needn't bother sending another.
I bought a plastic bucket and that does nicely. There's no
cars to be had here on the day of the polling so send a car
or you'll be short two number ones. We'll want it for
going back again that night. I don't know how I'll ever
stick three hundred miles in the round of a day.

Biddy.

P.S. Send by return the jelly Doctor John prescribed the
time I had the bedsores. Send the brown capsules in the
black bottle. You'll find them in my old white purse I
bought for Kate Nugent's wedding. Send on the cough
mixture Johnny O'Dell made specially for me. Just tell
him to repeat Biddy MacAdoo's bottle and ask him for
something to rub to my right shoulder, it's stiff. Send on
my nerve pills in the small tin. They are under the mat-
tress of my bed and ask Nance McGinn to send a cake of
griddle bread.

Biddy.

The outcome of every General Election since nineteen
twenty-two has been the cause of considerable surprise
among people and pundits alike. Change is never more

than marginal, often less than three or four votes to the
booth but it is nevertheless sufficient to kick successive,
well-entrenched governments unceremoniously out on
their ears.

Kate MacAdoo was an exceptional woman in that
nothing ever surprised her on the political front, not even
a summons from her godfather James McFillen who was
on the phone from the capital. Before leaving the counting
area for the office of a sympathiser in the bowels of the
rambling county courthouse she summoned her chief of
tallymen and made a copy of his latest reckoning. Of
course one could never be sure till the votes were pigeon-
holed in neat sheafs of fifty. Hurriedly she left the room
ignoring well-wishers and others who clamoured for her
inside knowledge of the outcome. It would never do, she
felt, to keep Mac waiting. Near the exit where two stout
civic guards restrained a mob of unaccredited partisans
she brushed past Stack and Scard, the latter grim-faced,
Stack the more experienced showing no emotion whatsoever. Kate nodded politely to both men and left the count.

Lycos whistled joylessly upon beholding the figures
presented to him by McFillen.

'How in Christ's name did he bring it off?' he asked.

'By using every trick in the book and some not in the
book. He's going to be elected in the first count with a
substantial surplus.'

'That surplus,' Lycos announced triumphantly, 'and
Scard's distribution after elimination should put Stack in.'

'Tull's surplus will not transfer,' McFillen spoke with
conviction.

'Oh come,' Lycos admonished, 'and if they don't
transfer to Stack to whom will they transfer?'

'You're not listening.' There was a shade of impatience in the tone, not for the first time that day. 'I've told
you the surplus will not transfer and what that means
exactly is that it will not transfer anywhere.'

'Before I believe that,' Lycos cut across sharply, 'I'll
have to see the official figures.' By nine o'clock that night
the official returns were in from all over the country. The
government was back but by the slenderest possible
majority. It had one seat to spare over the combined

opposition which for divisional purposes included Tull MacAdoo.

In Kilnavarna there were unprecedented celebrations. Tull had surpassed his own best expectations with a poll-topping return of nine thousand, nine hundred and four votes. This meant a surplus of two thousand and ten votes. If but one quarter of these were to transfer to Din Stack he would be elected. The transfer, however, as predicted by McFillen, was negligible. Only ten percent of the surplus went to Stack. Another ten percent went to Scard and died there. After a dog fight which was never less than bitter and after a full recount which had everybody on edge before it ended Din Stack was narrowly beaten for the third seat in the constituency. Really, however, it had been a foregone conclusion after the distribution of Tull's surplus.

There comes in every count a crucial period which decides the eventual outcome. It is a time when an uneasy hush dominates the counting chamber and when speculative whispers are few if any because the moment of truth is in the immediate offing. It is a time when pubs in the neighbourhood of the count are deserted, when the corridors leading to the counting chamber are thronged, a time when absolute confirmation of a candidate's worst fears or best hopes is realised. Generally it happens fairly late in the count but in the case of Scard and Stack it happened after the first count with the distribution of Tull's surplus. Suddenly there was complete silence. The council clerks had finished their calculations. The council auditor had carefully checked and re-checked the figures. They were now in the hands of the county registrar. A tall handsome woman, she cleared her throat and adjusted the microphone. This was the psychological moment. Much would happen afterwards but it would be irrelevant as far as the pundits were concerned. Her announcements brought gasps of despair from the Scard and Stack supporters who were sure that their candidates would score heavily. It brought cheers from the supporters of the two opposition candidates. Thereafter the large following which had accompanied Scard and Stack during their comings and goings from the chamber were greatly reduced. Tull was the man to be seen with, the man to be courted for surely now no power on earth could deprive him of the seat he had held for so long.

That evening having studied the results on a national scale he wrote a short note to his old friend James McFillen who, incidentally, had also been returned with a handsome surplus.

* * *

Kilnavarna P.O.
Kilnavarna.

Dear James,
Congratulations on being returned so overwhelmingly. I won't beat about the bush. The purpose of this letter is pure and simple. It is to tell you that my door is open and that I would be deeply interested in anything Mr Lycos might want to say to me. I didn't think I'd poll so well. It must have been the persecution we received on the final rally here in Kilnavarna. The people wanted to show their disgust with the conduct of our two friends although it is possible that Stack might see the Dail again if he had the right running mate. I'll sign off now as the celebrations are in full swing. Kate wishes to be remembered. See you soon I hope.

As ever,
Your old pal,
Tull.

* * *

Biddy writes to Tull:

Purewater Hotel,
Lisdoonvarna.

Dear Tull,
'Twas my prayers and novenas as did it. I want a Senator made out of my brother Tom. I wants no excuses. Lycos can nominate him.

Biddy.

* * *

McFillen writes to Tull:

McMell's Hotel,
Dublin.

Dear Tull,
My heartiest congratulations. At the back of my mind I
knew you'd get there but I ventured no opinion here,
having to play my cards close to my chest so to speak. He
gasped when I recited your terms. Then he settled back in
his chair tweaking his upper lip. Your coming back will
mean a majority of three. He feels this would be safe
enough. Quite frankly he is relieved, we all are, that he
doesn't have to go to the country again. Here is what he is
prepared to concede. Alexander Muffy's sons to be made
district justices before the end of the year. You retain the
Ministry for Bogland Areas with special Responsibility for
Game and Wildlife and Mick to be made a Health Inspector. Under no circumstances will he nominate your
brother-in-law to the Senate. I think it's a good deal. If I
were you I'd take it. Our man will not be pushed beyond
a certain point.

In haste,
James McFillen.

★   ★   ★

Tull writes to McFillen:

Kilnavarna P.O.
Kilnavarna.

Dear James,
No Senate for Bluenose, no Tull for party. It won't be for
long. He won't survive another whiskey coma. That's my
final words.

Tull.

★   ★   ★

Biddy writes to Tull:

Purewater Guesthouse,
Lisdoonvarna.

Dear Tull,
I had a note from the Senator this morning. What a credit
he'll be to us all. I'm in bed laid up with a wrenched back
after the bucket gave under me last night. You'll find my
old whalebone corset in the big chest in the attic. Send it
at once don't I die with the pain and send the black skillet
that had the flowers in it at the back of the house. Throw
out the flowers.

Signed,
Biddy, the senator's sister.

★   ★   ★

A HIGH MEADOW

JOHN B. KEANE

Mollie's face clouded as it always did whenever she thought of the Ram of God. She was careful not to show her annoyance. The more she considered their relationship the more her fury mounted. She was fond of saying that there was a fly in every ointment no matter how settled the scene. There was always one hitch and the Ram of God was hers. Somehow, in the course of time, she would bring him down. There was no doubt whatsoever about that in her mind. She would use the man by her side and his powerful connections, unknown to either, but use them she would in pursuance of her steely determination to ruin the one man who had so far proved to be invincible as far as Mollie was concerned. She would find a way. She tried in vain to subjugate the intense annoyance which the mention of his name always seemed to stimulate ... 'I'll even the score with the Ram of God and he'll rue the day he crossed swords with Mollie Cronane'.

THE CONTRACTORS

JOHN B. KEANE

Tom Reicey was the labourers' father figure and their fixer. He knew the high-ups in the police force. He went on holidays with chief superintendents and even a member of parliament! He was sometimes nicknamed the Cement God because every day of the week aeroplanes were landing on concrete strips laid down by his Rangers. Children played on his playgrounds. Trucks, buses and cars trundled and sped over his concrete roads.

Dan Murray's idea of maintaining a labour pool in Ireland was unprecedented in the English building world – finishing ahead of time was the difference between giant profits and small. With any luck Dan hoped to clear a quarter of a million pounds on his first major contract.

The Contractors is a stirring story of people who were forced to emigrate and work in England in the early 1950s. Before leaving Ireland they were warned about the likely evils that they would confront in that pagan place. John B. Keane, with his wonderful skill and humour, brings them to life in these unforgettable pages as he gives us the fascinating details of their daily existence, their exhilarations and their sorrows.